S0-AAZ-642

SIDEWAYS IN CRIME

Also by Lou Anders

As Editor

Outside the Box: The Best Short Fiction
from Bookface.Com

Live without a Net

Projections: Science Fiction in Literature & Film

Futureshocks

Fast Forward 1: Future Fiction from the Cutting Edge

As Author

The Making Of Star Trek: First Contact

SIDEWAYS IN CRIME

An Alternate Mystery Anthology
Edited by Lou Anders

Kage Baker
John Meaney
Stephen Baxter
Paul Park
Jack McDevitt
Kristine Kathryn Rusch
Mary Rosenblum
Paul Di Filippo
Jon Courtenay Grimwood
Theodore Judson
Pat Cadigan
S.M. Stirling
Mike Resnick & Eric Flint
Tobias S. Buckell
Chris Roberson

SOLARIS

Flagstaff Public Library
Flagstaff, Arizona

First published 2008 by Solaris
an imprint of BL Publishing
Games Workshop Ltd,
Willow Road,
Nottingham.
NG7 2WS
UK

www.solarisbooks.com

Trade Paperback
ISBN-13: 978-1-84416-566-7
ISBN-10: 1-84416-566-3

Sideways in Crime: An Alternate Mystery Anthology © 2008 Lou Anders
"Introduction" © 2008 by Lou Anders
"Running the Snake" © 2008 by Kage Baker
"Via Vortex" © 2008 by John Meaney
"Fate and the Fire-lance" © 2008 by Stephen Baxter
"The Blood of Peter Francisco" © 2008 by Paul Park
"The Adventure of the Southsea Trunk" © 2008 by Cryptic Inc.
"G-Men" © 2008 by Kristine Kathryn Rusch
"Sacrifice" © 2008 by Mary Rosenblum
"Murder in Geektopia" © 2008 by Paul Di Filippo
"Chicago" © 2008 by JonCG Ltd.
"The Sultan's Emissary" © 2008 by Theodore Judson
"Worlds of Possibilities" © 2008 by Pat Cadigan
"A Murder in Eddsford" © 2008 by S.M. Stirling
"Conspiracies: A Very Condensed 937-Page Novel" © 2008 by
Mike Resnick & 1632, Inc.
"The People's Machine" © 2008 by Tobias S. Buckell
"Death on the Crosstime Express" © 2008 by MonkeyBrain Inc.

The right of the individual authors to be identified as the authors of this work
have been asserted in accordance with the Copyright, Designs and
Patents Act 1988.

All rights reserved. No part of this publication may be reproduced, stored in a
retrieval system, or transmitted, in any form or by any means, electronic,
mechanical, photocopying, recording or otherwise, without the prior permission
of the copyright owners.

10 9 8 7 6 5 4 3 2 1

A CIP catalogue record for this book is available from the British Library.

Designed & typeset by BL Publishing

Printed and bound in Great Britain by
Mackays of Chatham Ltd, Chatham, Kent, UK.

3-F
SIDEWAYS

With love.
For Marsha Adams Anders,
Who has forgotten more about the mystery genre
than I will ever learn.
This one's for you, Mom.

Acknowledgments

First and foremost, thanks are due to George Mann and Christian Dunn, and the rest of the crew at Solaris Books, who were good enough to believe in this project. I'd also like to thank Robert J. Sawyer and Norman Spinrad, for the use of their words in my introduction and for being such stellar guys. A universe or two of thanks to Michael Moorcock, whose inspiration and influence cannot be discounted. Then there's Bob Eggleton and Darius Hinks for a great cover. I am thrilled to have "my first Eggleton," and I hope it isn't my last. I'm grateful also to S.M. Stirling, for sending me two great stories before anyone else sent one. When you read the one I chose, I'm sure you'll want to hunt down the other as well. Finally, infinite thanks are due to my wife and child, for their enduring love, patience, and support. I'm grateful to be in the universe where they are in my life. Without them, the mystery of existence wouldn't be nearly so compelling or pleasant as it is.

Contents

Introduction: Worlds of If

Lou Anders

Every good story begins with a question, but not every question is the same. In mystery, that question is traditionally rendered as "Who dunnit?" A crime has been committed, and the journey of our narrative will be to discover who did what to who, where and why. Certainly, there are a thousand variations on this theme, but unraveling the mystery is at the heart of the story's promise and thrill. In the sister genre of science fiction, the question is a somewhat broader "What if?" An alteration in our contemporary reality is postulated—What if aliens invade? What if teleportation becomes a viable means of travel? What if a new drug made it impossible to lie?—and the story that follows explores the ramifications for humanity of this new development. The mystery here is in figuring out what makes the world of the story different from the world we know and then examining the light that those differences cast on our everyday notions of society and self.

Who and what. Mystery and science fiction. The two genres actually share a lot in common, beyond loyal readers and their own dedicated section of the bookstore. Hugo- and Nebula-winning science fiction author Robert J. Sawyer, who, incidentally also won the prestigious Arthur Ellis Award from the Crime Writers of Canada, put it best in an interview with John Scalzi (posted on *Ficlets.com*,

June 27, 2007): "Science fiction and mystery are not an unnatural pairing—indeed, I've always thought that science fiction has way more in common with mystery than it does with fantasy. SF and mystery, after all, both prize rational thinking and both require the reader to pick up artfully salted clues about what is really going on—although in SF that's mostly because of the narrative conceit we use."

"SF is, as I like to say, the mainstream literature of an alternate reality—it's written as if for an audience of people already familiar with the milieu of the story. Of course, you can't really do that—a tour de force like *A Clockwork Orange* requires a glossary, because the book is gibberish without it, since no one really is familiar with its milieu, and so the dropping of clues and hints is crucial, and, just as in a mystery, they have to be inserted so transparently, without drawing attention to themselves, that the reader doesn't even consciously notice them."

Which is why every science fiction author is a natural born mystery writer, whether they know it or not. There's another genre that has close parallels with science fiction—and often overlapping readerships—and that's the genre of historical fiction. The skills necessary to invoke another time and place in the minds of the reader are the same, whether one is trying to conjure the details of life in the Twenty-Fourth Century or the Fourteenth. In both situations, the writer must take nothing for granted and must "artfully salt" all those everyday realities—from the trivial to the monumental—that the writer of contemporary fiction may take for granted. This takes a certain skill to do, and affords a particular joy to read, which may explain both why time travel stories to the past are a popular conceit of science fiction scribes and why there is some degree of crossover in the readership of science fiction and historical novels.

This brings us to the most obvious intersection of science fiction and historical fiction, the alternate history. Certainly the alternate history was not invented by Philip K. Dick, but it was his landmark *The Man in the High Castle,* which postulated a San Francisco in an America overrun by Nazis, which brought such attention to the form. As Norman Spinrad writes in "The Multiverse," in the April/May 2008 issue of his On Books columns for *Asimov's Science Fiction Magazine,* "Indeed, despite all the alternate world stories that have been written afterward and the few that were written before, it is Dick's classic novel of a world in which the Nazis and the Japanese won World War II, and the alternate reality within it in which they didn't, *The Man in the High Castle,* which really opened the door for the alternate history story as a subset of 'science fiction,' as well, in a way, at least in literary terms, for a certain kind of 'fantasy' as a subset of 'SF.'

"In literary terms, science fiction, or speculative fiction if you will, is by definition the literature of the could-be-but-isn't, and fantasy by definition is the literature of the demonstrably impossible, and the alternate history story takes place in a region between, a fictional reality in which the laws of mass and energy may be the same as in our own, but which never 'happened.'"

Spinrad goes on to point out that Dick did not just craft the definitive counterfactual tale. In his novel, the character of Mr. Tagomi has a vision of our reality, a world in which Germany lost World War II. In showing that both worlds could exist simultaneously, Spinrad credits Dick with introducing the "multiverse" as science fiction rather than fantasy.

The term "multiverse" was created by pioneering American psychologist and philosopher William James (1842–1910), who also gave us the term "stream of consciousness," though he intended it to describe different psychological states. It was science fiction and fantasy master Michael Moorcock who, independently of James, conceived the term to describe a universe of near-infinite parallel worlds for a story called "The Sundered Worlds" (published in *Science Fiction Adventures,* December 1962). Moorcock's use became the prevailing definition of the term, and has entered the popular consciousness to such a degree that it is now on the lip of every quantum physicist. In fact, this notion that our universe may be only one of a transfinite number of such realities, all stacked up against each other, each only a few quantum decisions distance from its neighbor, is rapidly gaining credence as the most likely explanation for the mysteries of quantum mechanics. As mind-boggling a concept as the multiverse is, Occam's razor increasingly comes down in its favor. This means that the "alternate history" may be graduating to the front of the line in cutting edge, relevant science fiction. Far from being simply a fanciful conceit in the service of a good story (as many see notions like teleportation and the faster-than-light drive, seeming implausibilities that simplify some of the problems of space opera), tales of histories that diverged from our own are now explorations of the vanguard of contemporary scientific thinking. So it shouldn't come as any surprise to learn that the counterfactual narrative has recently become the subject of widespread mainstream attention. In 2004, Philip Roth published his acclaimed/winning *The Plot Against America,* and more recently, Michael Chabon has given us *The Yiddish Policeman's Union.* Predictably, the Roth was published without any recognition that he was writing within an established tradition, though Chabon is much more generous and knowledgeable in the acknowledgment of his genre roots. Furthermore, Philip K. Dick's *The Man in the High Castle* was one of four novellas chosen for a prestigious Library of America collection of his works, assembled and with a preface from literary darling Jonathan Lethem.

Meanwhile the Chabon novel is a bona fide, dyed-in-the-wool "Who dunnit?"—a novel with the double-barreled pleasure for the reader of unraveling both the mystery of the narrative and the mystery of the history. This intriguing combination of historical, mystery, and science fiction is the impetus for the anthology you now hold in your hands, an entire book's worth of "alternate mystery" stories that might one day constitute a sub-subgenre of their own. But, as Charles Fort (1874–1932), the American champion of the unexplained and no stranger to uchronia himself, once wrote, "It steam engines when it comes steam engine time." Certainly, we are in the midst of steam engine time for the alternate history novel. Presented here, then, are fifteen stories by sixteen wonderful authors, set in universes just around the corner from our own, where steam engine time came early, came late, or came not at all. And in each of them, our two questions—"What if?" and on top of that, "Who dunnit?"

Running the Snake

Kage Baker

Famous for her "Company" time-travel stories, a sequence which spans eight novels, two short story collections, and several related tales, Kage writes that twenty years immersed in Elizabethan history "has paid off handsomely" in affording her a working knowledge of period speech and details she mines for her fiction. Her fans, amongst whose number I most definitely count myself, would agree. The story that follows is not a "Company" tale, but it might be my favorite of her short works to date.

Will Shaxpur stood before the queen, trying not to look at her breasts. This was difficult, as they were bare, painted bright blue and court custom dictated he raise his eyes no higher than her knees, where (she being a lady of advanced years) they happened to be resting, like a pair of elderly robins.

He twisted his hat in his hands. "I can't imagine how it happened, Ma'am."

"Can't you?" The Living Boudicca, Andraste Twdwr, high queen of Greater Brithan, leaned back. "We find that hard to believe. You were defrocked for *imagining*, as we have heard." She nodded at her chief druid, Volsinghome.

Volsinghome smiled balefully. "Expelled, Madam. For having the temerity to *imagine* he could improve the sacred texts."

"It was only the hymns," said Will. "I made them scan. And, er, adjusted the imagery a little."

"And, having blasphemed, you were sent from the sacred island in disgrace, and now you damn your soul by persuading weak-minded fools to abandon our ancient gods—" Volsinghome's tirade was cut short as the queen raised her hand.

"We will thank you to remember, little druid, that it has pleased us to welcome strangers *and* their faiths. And if it pleases us, it pleases our gods." She fixed her gimlet stare on Will once more. "Now, boy. Tell me how it was my son-in-law was found dead in the temple of Glycon."

He had been working Temple Street, minding the horses of wealthy worshippers. Will found that a smile and a bow as he handed back the reins might earn him a thrown copper. However, a smile, a bow, and an apt quotation from Homer—or Catullus, or the *Mahabharata*, or the *Avesta*, depending on the place from which the patron had emigrated—got him silver at least, and the patrons remembered him. Now and again patrons gathered around and challenged him to other tricks of memory, and of course he could recite as much as they wanted of anything he knew.

Busker economies being precarious at best, his fellows on the street had suffered from the competition. One afternoon, after holding a crowd spellbound with the *Thebaid*, Will was gleefully scooping coins from the pavement into his hat when he encountered four pairs of feet planted across the remainder of his earnings. He looked up, and his heart sank.

There stood Wat the fire-eater, and Bran the juggler, and Empidocles who did sleight-of-hand tricks, and most notably there stood Soumaoro the African balladeer, who was seven feet tall and wore a model of Cleopatra's barge in his wild hair. When singing, he would sway his head in such a manner that the barge rocked to and fro, exactly as though it sailed black foaming seas, to such striking effect that until lately he had been the top earner in the street.

"You. Shaxpur," he said. "We hear there are lots of people who appreciate poetry on the other side of the river. We think you should go there." He jerked a thumb in the direction of Southwark. Will blinked up at him.

"Why, certainly, gentlemen," he said, knowing better than to argue. "If you'll just step to one side so I can collect the rest of the take, I'll be on my way."

"Take what you have and go," said Bran, smacking one of his juggling clubs against his thigh with a meaningful look. He picked up a silver drachma with his toes, flipped it into the air, and caught it with his free hand. "We'll collect the rest."

"Look, I earned that—" said Will, and broke off as he saw the dagger in Wat's hand.

"You know, I don't think you've ever paid dues to the Guild of Street Entertainers," said Soumaoro. "Druid. How many weeks has he been peddling his act on our street, boys?"

Will was calculating his chances of escape when the Fates threw him a crust. A pair of arms encircled him from behind and a voice, heavily accented, screamed next to his ear: "Beware! This man is touched by all the gods! He has been chosen for a momentous destiny!"

Will turned his head and looked into the shawl-draped face of a fat man. He had wild bulging eyes and an immense mustache. The man screamed again. "Momentous destiny, I said! Leave the money, my friend!"

"Fortunate mortal!" chimed in a second voice. Will swiveled his eyes and saw another man to his left: young, tall, and handsome, with a mane of fair hair. "Beloved of the gods!"

"And who might you be?" said Soumaoro, scowling.

"Why, friend, this is Scorilo, the famed Dacian soothsayer," said the tall youth. Will meanwhile felt himself being dragged backward by the fat man, and the youth stepped in front of them. "Look! Riches!" He held up a fistful of coins and opened his hand. As the members of the Guild of Street Entertainers scrambled for the money, Will's rescuers hurried him away.

In a sad-looking Roman taverna, over bowls of wine, they had made him their offer.

"We are victims of religious persecution," explained Alazon, the youth.

"We fled the crushing grip of Caesarion-imposed Mithraic monotheism to the pantheistic sanctuary of your green and pleasant land, so graciously offered by your beautiful Queen of Queens," said Scorilo.

"We've been watching you for days now," said Alazon. "Look, we said to each other, here's an educated Brithon! Knows the classics by heart, speaks eight languages fluently, lovely speaking voice."

"Yet, incredibly, he seems to be down on his luck!" said Scorilo. "How, we asked ourselves, can this possibly be?"

Briefly, Will related the series of misunderstandings that had gotten him booted out of the druid seminary at Mona, which did, in fact, amount to more than a few rewritten hymns. When he had finished, his new friends looked at each other and smiled.

"Mocking the bards, faking divine possession, and poaching! Can it be you haven't a great deal of respect for the gods?" said Scorilo.

"That might be the case," said Will sourly. "Yet see, gentlemen, the wages of impiety. I'm as talented a man as you'll find in a long summer's day; I can pull your tooth, cure your fever, paint your likeness, sit in judgment on your small claims, sing you all the lays of old Rome, foretell the hour of your death, and recite a solemn prayer over your ashy bones. And, thanks to that unwise moment of levity at High Bard Amaethon's expense, I now scramble to earn my bread in the gutter."

"What if impiety could be made to pay?" inquired Scorilo, with a coy leer.

"What if, indeed? I'm listening."

"Well then!" Scorilo leaned across the table. "My colleague and I operated a profitable concern in Pergamum, before Caesarion XXIII sent in his priests. Given the nature of our business, it seemed like a good time to relocate."

"And the nature of your business was—?"

"Soothsaying, what else?" said Alazon. "Divinations, relaying messages from the dead, that sort of thing. Scorilo's a true prophet! Runs in the family. His great-great-several-times-great grandfather was the one who persuaded Julius Caesar to stay home the day Mark Antony was assassinated."

"We like to think of ourselves as purveyors of consolation," said Scorilo. "Now, your cosmopolitan London seems a perfect place to set up shop. Unfortunately, we are strangers. We would benefit by having a native-born partner in our enterprise to advise us concerning local laws, customs, and so forth. *You* might be that partner."

"Could you be a little more explicit about the enterprise?"

"A time-honored dodge known in the trade as *running the snake*," said Scorilo. "Introducing to an unenlightened populace the profitable worship of the great god Glycon."

"And who would Glycon be?" inquired Will.

Alazon smiled. From under his cloak he drew a small basket with a lid, and opening it he drew forth a tiny snake. He set it on the table. "Say hello, Glycon."

"Hello," said Glycon.

Will gaped at it, until he remembered Enoch the Ventriloquist, who used to ply Temple Street with his talking dog. He grinned. "Tell me more," he said.

There were a few former residences of Roman gods down at the eastern end of Temple Street. Of late years, with the increasing turmoil on the continent, the Roman immigrant population had increased; but they tended to worship at a pantheon over in Knightsbridge nowadays. Therefore the owner of the old shrine to Apollo was happy to sell it at any price, given that the roof leaked and the foundation had cracked. He pocketed the money Will paid him and went his way chuckling. Will and his associates moved in and made their preparations.

The busy hour of the morning had just come to Watling Street when, seemingly from midair, a naked youth appeared in the middle of the street. He frothed at the mouth, he pranced and tossed his wild hair, he cried out in an unknown language. Ordinarily no Londoner would have looked twice at him—there were plenty of naked madmen in Brithan—but this madman was so extraordinarily well endowed, and his wild hair so abundant, that not a few matrons forgot about shopping and stared, rapt. Tradesmen and idlers followed suit, and soon there was a crowd.

As crowds will, they followed him down Watling to Temple Street, where he mounted the steps of the old shrine to Apollo and stood straight. Raising his arms above his head, he began to speak coherently. Will, who had discreetly joined the crowd, prepared to translate for him; but a Greek oil merchant beat him to it.

"He's telling us a new god is born!" he said. "He says, uh, we're three-times-blessed. He says the great god... Glycon, son of

Asklepios, grandson of Apollo, has come to live among us. In this very temple. And... he himself is the god's priest."

"He *does* look like Apollo," said an elderly wine merchant.

Alazon, for it was he, sprang down from the steps and scrabbled in the mud at the base of the temple's foundation. With a triumphant cry, he held aloft a goose egg. Running back up the steps with it, he broke it open and stared a moment into the shell; then held up the little snake that had been hidden inside, coiling and twisting on his fingers as the morning sunlight warmed it.

The crowd murmured. Will shouted, "It's a miracle!"

"Yes!" cried Scorilo, from the other side of the crowd. "A miracle!"

The crowd took up the cry and repeated it. Scorilo began to froth at the mouth and shriek, babbling; Will slipped a piece of soapwort root into his mouth and, chewing briskly, produced a fine lather; then he ran to the steps, where he proceeded to fall as in a frenzy and deliver the same message in eight languages, one after another:

"The god speaks! He bids you return here tomorrow at the same hour! He will have an important message for you then, but now he is weary from his journey into this world and would rest!"

This impressed the crowd no end, for Will was clearly a native-born Brithon. Alazon turned and, with a graceful flash of his buttocks, bore the snake godling into the depths of the old shrine.

It was a much bigger crowd the next day, and accordingly a much bigger snake was produced for them—a python purchased from a Bharati sailor, so docile and well-trained it would submit to wearing a false head made of painted canvas, with a human face and flowing wig. Alazon, whose body had been colored gold with a liberal application of turmeric rubbed into his skin, sat on the high dais in the shadowed rear of the temple, with the snake twined about his body.

Will and Scorilo, divinely chosen acolytes, admitted the curious throng. When the temple was full they closed the street doors, which threw the place into stygian gloom; one dim oil lamp flickered above the dais, so it was almost impossible to see the snake clearly. Yet it was plain he was a living creature, as the flamelight winked now and then on a slowly moving coil.

"Good people!" Will raised his hands. "Behold how great Glycon has grown, in one day! Soon he will be able to speak to you directly. Until that time he has appointed us to make his intentions known. True son of Asklepios, he comes to heal and to advise you with gifts of prophecy. Pleasing to him are votive offerings of gold and silver. Great Glycon accepts all currencies in any denomination."

"And I, his prophet, carry messages!" Scorilo sprang up beside the dais. He had circled his eyes with soot, so as to make their stare even more startling, and he swept the crowd with his wide gaze. His voice echoed like rolling thunder. "Hear me! Great Glycon says there is a man here who has committed infidelities! If he is to avoid detection he must purify himself in the sacred waters of Glycon's pool and make an offering of gold! Yes! You! Great Glycon knows your name!

"Great Glycon says further that there is a woman here who wishes to conceive a child! If she will come in private to the sanctuary at nightfall, with an offering of silver, great Glycon will ease her sorrows. Yes! You, dear lady! And the man who has received a troublesome letter recently... and the man whose son is not sufficiently respectful... and you, the woman whose daughter loves an unsuitable young man!

"Great Glycon has counsel for each of you. Do not wait, but come soon to make offerings!"

The golden stream began to flow that very night, and in a matter of six months Will was richer than he'd ever been in his life.

Scorilo had improvised suitably general prophecies to keep people coming in until they had enough cash to remodel the temple. The back wall had been knocked out and a sanctum sanctorum built beyond, even more dimly lit. There great Glycon was installed, or rather the articulated puppet-head Will built for him, wonderfully realistic if seen in the dim light of the temple and from a respectful distance. There were besides yards and yards of snake body, painted canvas stuffed out with bombast, which could be made to move by various means.

Several steam-operated devices were installed, old stage tricks to miraculously open the inner sanctum's doors or provide a battery of awe-inspiring sound effects. The scummed-over reflecting pool at the rear of the temple precinct was cleaned out and stocked with water lilies and Cathay carp.

"And we ought to build a dormitory back there," said Will, one night as they sat around a table, opening sealed prayers to Glycon.

"Dormitory? What for?" Alazon held the blade of his knife in the lamp flame, then slid it under the wax seal and popped it off intact. Will looked at him in surprise.

"So that supplicants can sleep back there and have their dreams interpreted next morning," he said. "That's how it was done in the temples of Asklepios. You're a Greek! Surely you knew that."

Alazon shrugged. "He was obliged to leave his native land at an early age, to escape the tyranny of the One True Faith," Scorilo explained. "So his knowledge of the old Olympians is necessarily imperfect. It's not a bad idea, though, my learned colleague. 'Dream interpretation available with a slightly higher donation! Enjoy a spiritually refreshing night as Glycon's guest!'"

Alazon, reading the prayer he had opened, snickered. "Listen to this one. 'Oh Great Glycon, I am subjected to ridicule by my wife and business associates because of my baldness. Please grant that my hair grows again and I will offer you a golden ring set with a perfect amethyst.'"

"Poor bastard," said Will ruefully. He took the scroll without reading it—indeed he could not read, but had memorized its request—and re-affixed the seal. "What's the name on this one?"

"Geoffrix Thorkettle."

"We're getting a lot of Brithons as converts now," said Scorilo. "Your druids aren't going to be happy about that, eh? Do we need to offer them a bribe?"

Will shrugged. "We might. They'll hate us anyway, but there's nothing they can do. Not as long as Andraste's on the throne."

"Gods save the queen!" said Scorilo.

Will, standing before Glycon's sanctuary, swayed slightly and put his hand to his forehead.

"The god speaks to me... he has a message for... for Geoffrix Thorkettle!"

"Oi!" A man wearing a hood raised his head and pushed his way to the front of the crowd. Will put out his hand and Scorilo gave him the appropriate scroll.

"Here is your still-sealed petition, its contents known only to yourself and Divine Glycon," Will intoned. He gave the scroll to Master Thorkettle. "Divine Glycon says: 'Mortal, bear patiently what the gods have seen fit to inflict. Caesar himself suffered your state without complaint, and him the gods favored to father pharaohs.' Praise Glycon!"

"Thanks be to great Glycon," said the man, looking dejected.

"And now..." Will summoned the next name from his memory. "The Divine One informs me—" He broke off, hearing the shouts and seeing the crowd surge to avoid the oncoming chariot. Four milk-white mares drew it, led by a man in the royal livery who shouted:

"Way there! Way for the most puissant Princess Arnemetia Dudasmede! Her consort, Anextiomarus, earl of Gloucester! Her son, Vellocatus!"

"What the hell?" said Scorilo out of the side of his mouth, and in Greek.

"It's the Queen's second daughter," replied Will in the same wise. "Quick! Go tell Alazon. She'll want to talk to the god himself."

The chariot pulled up before the temple steps. Glycon's supplicants cleared a path for the princess, falling to their knees as she ascended; Will himself dropped to his knees, fists clenched until he heard the faint *thump* that meant that Alazon had scrambled into the compartment under Glycon's sanctuary and thrust his arm up the god's neck.

"Welcome, gracious princess! Welcome, noble princes to the sanctuary of Divine Glycon!" Will prostrated himself.

"You may rise," said Princess Arnemetia, with a wave of her hand. Being only a princess, she was not obliged to go naked nor paint herself blue, nor had she her mother's flaming hair; she was a sallow brunette. Her son, a sullen-looking teenager, had inherited her looks and a clubfoot besides. The prince consort was a florid man in early middle age, puffing slightly from climbing the stairs. *Heart disease*, Will thought, studying him with a druidic eye. Aloud he said:

"How may we priests of Glycon serve, madam?"

"We would consult the god on the matter of our husband's health," said the princess. "And some few matters concerning our own interest."

"Please step within," said Will, bowing them into the temple. He shut the doors behind them and presented them to Scorilo. "This humble servant of the god will lead you in prayers first. Complimentary holy water, Brother Scorilo, of course."

"Of course," said Scorilo, rummaging in his purse for coins to feed the vending machines. Will backed out of the royal presences and then ran like a hare behind the drapes concealing the inner sanctum. He paused long enough to make certain Alazon had lit the boilers under the mechanisms, and then scrambled under Glycon's lair. Spotting Alazon's feet, he crawled close enough to whisper:

"It's Princess Arnemetia. The husband's the Earl of Gloucester. He's got progressive heart failure, or I miss my guess. Tell him to drink willow-bark tea for breakfast, hawthorn-leaf tea before bed. Got it? And the son's with them, and he's got a clubfoot and is known to have seizures, so—"

"Tell them it's a gift of the gods because Caesar and Alexander had them," said Alazon, ducking his head to wink at Will. "Got it. Do I tell her she's going to inherit the throne?"

"No! We could hang for that. Stay away from anything to do with the succession. Just, you know, imply great things will happen and her name will live forever and so on."

"And she's..."

"Arnemetia!"

"Right."

Will backed out of the crawlspace, got to his feet and ran back just as the unearthly note sounded that signified the show was about to start. He stepped from behind the curtain into the outer sanctum, where Scorilo was praying with his hands raised and the royal family lip-syncing in an attempt to follow. The sanctuary curtains parted, as if drawn by unseen hands.

"Our prayers have been heard!" yelled Scorilo, falling to his knees.

The great doors swung open of themselves, and there, within a sort of booth, rose great Glycon. He blinked his startlingly lifelike eyes. He opened his mouth.

"WELCOME, ROYAL ARNEMETIA, BELOVED OF THE GODS!"

"We are *made*," said Alazon smugly, counting out the day's take. "A royal patron. It's all nectar from here."

"I wouldn't say that," said Will. "It all depends on whether or not the princess outlives her sister. Berecyntia, the older one."

"Which one's going to get the throne when the old lady dies, eh?" said Scorilo.

"The older one, of course," said Alazon, but Will shook his head.

"We don't always follow primogeniture here. The princesses may engage in single combat to decide who gets the throne. More likely they'll make their consorts fight."

"But the throne will pass to the nasty boy in any case, eh?" said Scorilo.

"No," said Will. "There's Damara, the third sister. She's still at school. And anyway the boy's damaged goods; he can't sit on the throne. It's our law."

"Groups of threes!" Scorilo drew his shawl over his head. "That's bad, women in threes. Three Fates. Three Hecates. I feel a foreboding in the cosmic ether."

"That's the fish you had for lunch," said Alazon, and bit a gold piece.

With royal favor, Glycon had become more than just another new god; he became *fashionable*. Courtiers, at least those of Princess Arnemetia's party, had flocked to the temple in droves. Alazon had found himself with a dozen or so very young admirers of both genders, who were eager to jump into bed with Glycon's high priest. His attention to their needs spiritual and temporal had left Will and Scorilo to see to running the temple, and unfortunately Scorilo had developed a taste for Brithish cider.

So it was primarily Will who had overseen the miracle cures, sitting up at night as supplicants slept in the rear of the temple around the new statue of the god. It was Will who had bowed in the Earl of Gloucester, arriving for a private slumber session with the god; it was Will who had made up a sumptuous pallet for Anextiomarus, and dimmed the sanctuary lights, and bid him pleasant dreams. It was Will who sat in the rear chamber, going over the earl's symptoms (indigestion, toothache, generalized joint pain) in his mind, composing a prescription that could be plausibly worked into the interpretation of whatever dreams the earl would have reported in the morning.

Though of course he hadn't reported any, because when Will had crept out into the sanctuary at first light, the earl had been lying there stone dead, grinning, with a stonily erect penis and two immense fang marks in his arm.

"Were you aware," said Volsinghome, "that when we autopsied him, we found the distance between the wounds was exactly the distance between the canine teeth of a man? And has not your god a man's head?"

"But great Glycon is a *nice* god," said Will desperately. "Why would he kill one of his worshippers? Especially a royal one?"

"Fool! How can you pretend to know what foreign gods will do? They cannot be trusted! They have overrun this island with their filthy foreign ways—"

Volsinghome's spittle began to fly. The Living Boudicca looked sidelong at him, and sighed.

"Volsinghome, you may retire. We would speak with this man alone."

Glaring, the high druid stalked from the room. The queen turned back to Will. "Listen carefully, priest. We know well our son-in-law was murdered, and by no gods. But *you* must prove it. You say you were awake in the anteroom by the sanctuary the night long. Did you hear nothing suspicious? Did you leave the antechamber at any time?"

Will drew on every memory trick the druids had beaten into him on Mona. The night replayed itself for him, at high speed and in perfect detail. "Only once, Ma'am. And that was only to see that all was well with the earl."

"Why?"

"Because I heard..." Will's eyes widened. "Because he cried out. And there was a splash; I thought he might have gone sleepwalking and stepped in the fish pool."

"Had he?"

"No. He was sitting up in his bed, rubbing his arm. He lay down again without speaking to me. Then he began to laugh. I thought he'd had a funny dream. I went back into the antechamber. A little later I heard him coughing. I would have gone out again, but it stopped."

"Which arm was he rubbing?"

"The right one," said Will.

"Which was the arm that was wounded, my druids tell me."

"Yes, Ma'am." Will hung his head, imagining the noose already around his neck. "That must have been when he was bitten. But I saw nothing when I looked out, I swear."

"He laughed, you say." The queen looked opaque, unsmiling. Her hand clenched a moment on her spear. "And you use the word *bitten*. Do you truly think something bit him?"

"Well—no, Ma'am." Will dared to look up. "At least, not Glycon, because—"

"Because Glycon is a clever puppet," said the Living Boudicca. "Tush, man, did you think we hadn't already found out as much?"

Will fell to his knees. "Oh, great queen, be merciful. We never meant to mock the gods! Only to make money."

She waved him to rise, impatiently. "Which is an honest desire, compared to what some men lust after. Little man, you have our protection, as far as we may give it. Volsinghome and his party will make political capital of this death, if they can; they will incite the people to fear foreign gods. They cannot see that it is in our interest to shelter fellow polytheists."

"Your majesty is indeed a loving and merciful great mother," said Will, heart pounding.

"No; Volsinghome is a fool," said the queen. "Caesarion converts with the sword, and his one-god priests are ruthless in suppressing any thought they do not approve. What happens then? The best minds of the east flee his empire in droves. Because we offer them refuge, they bring us their skills, their inventions. If rogues like your accomplices come with them, it makes no odds; our nation grows rich all the same.

"Perhaps Volsinghome fears that foreign gods are stronger than our own, in which case we don't think much of his faith," she added, with a fearsome sneer. "Perhaps he simply dislikes seeing brown faces in the marketplace, or smelling strange spices in the air. Ha! We will not shape our state to suit his delicate nerves. We absorbed his Saxon race and remained Brithan; these hordes too we shall gather in.

"And therefore we have made our decision. We shall announce that it was a man, and no god, who killed the earl." She pointed her spear at Will. "But you must furnish us with some plausible proof of murder. What made the splash you heard, little Master Shaxpur?"

Scorilo and Alazon were packing frantically when he returned.

"Where do you think you're going?"

"Down to the river at midnight," said Alazon. "We steal a boat, we go over to Gaul. Coming with us?"

"No," said Will. "I had an audience with the queen." He looked around the sanctuary, thinking hard. "Has anybody been out to feed the fish this morning?"

"What?" Alazon turned to stare at him.

"It's all this rain," said Scorilo, with a groan. "Makes their brains mildew. Where are you going?" For Will had turned and run out to the pool in the rear of the temple precinct. They followed him.

"Oh! Look at that!" cried Scorilo, falling to his knees in dismay. "It's an omen! A terrible omen!"

"Damn!" said Alazon. "Those fish cost a fortune!"

For all the red carp in the pool were now floating belly up, quite dead. Will was pacing along the edge of the pool, peering down into the water. He went into the antechamber long enough to fetch a pair of tongs from its fireplace; coming back he knelt on the pool's coping and, using the tongs, carefully pushed aside the lily pads to look beneath. "Ah," he said.

"What have you found?" Alazon ran to his side.

"The murder weapon, I think," said Will. Using the tongs, he drew out a long slender object. It was a tin novelty backscratcher in the shape of an arm and flexed hand, the sort that tourists brought back in hundreds from Cornwall every summer. This one had a twist of thick wire wrapped around the hand, the two sharp ends bent downward. Will pulled his sleeve down to cover his hand and picked it up, swinging it experimentally. It punched two neat holes in the surface of a lily pad, just like fang marks.

Will peered at the wire points again. They were discolored.

The murderer had clearly scaled the rear precinct wall, which was not especially high, and left in the same manner. The following day a body was found floating in the Thames, a thin and ragged man with a cut throat. Oddly, he had not been robbed; he had a golden guinea in his purse.

The verdict on both the beggar and the earl was *murder by persons unknown.*

Standing at the late earl's pyre, as Scorilo chanted hastily improvised funeral rites, Will watched the royal family and wondered just how much was known. Princess Arnemetia and her son looked daggers across the flames at Princess Berecyntia and her husband, the Earl of Kent, where they stood by Volsinghome. All three were smirking, making no effort to conceal their glee. The queen looked on, impassive, her eyes hooded.

Oddly enough, the temple of Glycon grew more crowded than before. Princess Arnemetia was loud in her unshaken faith. Young Vellocatus let it be known he had spent all his pocket money on most puissant curses, and such a touching act of filial piety was sure to bring his father's murderers to justice. Before a packed audience of courtiers and celebrity chasers, they knelt together without Glycon's sanctum and prayed for justice. The great god, stammering a little, was heard to promise that death would swiftly find the wretched sinners who had dared to defame him.

"You have an awful lot of murderers in this country, do you know that?" complained Scorilo. Will, who had been composing a new prayer to Glycon as Guardian of Innocent Lambs, looked up, startled.

"What?"

"And your cider gives a man a damnable headache too," said Scorilo, dropping down on the bench beside him and fanning himself. It was two days to Lammas, hot sticky weather. "All I wanted were some anodyne powders for this hangover. Hermes the

Egyptian had a nice little apothecary shop in Silver Street. *Had*, notice I said. Somebody laid him out beside his mummies last night. The place is all closed off and the street wardens won't let anybody in. What am I to do about my headache, eh?"

"Willow-bark tea," said Will, leaning back again. "You can get it anywhere." He was about to close his eyes so he could concentrate on composition when his attention was drawn by the royal messenger, ascending the steps of the temple. "Oh, shite—"

"Priests of Glycon!" The royal messenger brandished his spear. "The Living Boudicca commands the presence of Master Shaxpur!"

Volsinghome was just emerging from the audience chamber as Will was ushered in. He wasn't smiling now; in fact he looked at Will with something like fear as he hurried past him.

Nor was the queen smiling as she received Will. Andraste Twdwr seemed to have aged twenty years in the month since he'd seen her. She looked at him bleakly and said: "You are a clever little man. I wonder if you are clever enough to solve another murder?"

The royal messenger and a brace of royal guards escorted him to the mansion of Princess Berecyntia. Grim-faced street wardens blocked the door, but as they stood aside to let Will enter there was fear in their eyes too. He was marched in through the house and out to the back garden, which sloped down to the Thames. There was a big pavilion there, its screened windows standing open. In the pavilion was a bed, lately slept in but empty now.

"The princess and her lord took their rest here last night, as was their custom in summer's heat," said the royal messenger. "The servants slept in the house. None of them heard anything untoward. At daybreak the earl's valet came out to wake his master, and found him gone, nor was the princess to be seen."

Will was opening his mouth to suggest they had simply gone swimming when he saw the track on the floor of the pavilion, clear in a layer of summer dust. It circled the bed, a strange looping sprawl of a print full of smaller marks... scales? It looked something like the track a snake would leave, but a snake of monstrous size.

"Was it your god devoured them, priest of Glycon?" demanded the valet, who had followed the guards out to the garden.

"No," said Will steadily. "But we were meant to think so." He squatted to look more closely at the curious print. Here and there beside its length was a little parallel track, not continuous, a thin dragging mark such as might be made by a twig. In some places it paralleled the left side of the main print; in some places it was on the right. Will tugged at his beard, studying the print a moment longer.

He rose and looked at the bed itself. Not a drop of blood, but the bedclothes were in wild disarray: sheets flung aside, pillows here and there, the blanket wadded up on one side of the bed. But nothing on the floor. Nothing to obscure the scuffed print. Will bent down and looked again at the print's pattern. It reminded him of something... he crouched further and peered under the bed. Gingerly he reached under and pulled close what he saw there, and stared at it a moment.

It was a scaled and stubby thing, like a mummified hand with black claws. A brown bone protruded from one end.

Will stood up abruptly. "You have been charged to help me solve this murder, haven't you?" he said to the royal messenger.

"I have. You agree it's murder, then?"

"Most foul," said Will. "Take me to Silver Street, if you please."

It was early afternoon when he was once again admitted to the presence of the Living Boudicca. He bowed low. She regarded him with a flinty stare.

"We see we were not mistaken in our judgment of you," she said, in a hoarse voice.

"You have been told, then, Ma'am."

"We have. Both of them in a fresh-dug grave in Hampstead. Not a mark on the bodies to show how they died, but the strangest thing: they shared their grave with a stuffed crocodile. A three-legged one, no less."

Will nodded. "And now I must grieve you further."

She shrugged. "We may sorrow, but we doubt we will be surprised. What have you to tell us?"

Will wondered how best to break the news. "You may have heard, Ma'am, that the crocodile was stolen from an apothecary's in Silver Street."

"We had. They murdered the poor devil for it, it seems."

"So it seems. He did not die quietly; there would appear to have been a fight. His jars of mummy-dust and his curative powders were knocked over and broken. His murderers left tracks in the dust. There were three of them: two men, both barefoot, and a boy, shod. And the boy's shoes—"

"Showed that he had a clubbed foot," said the queen.

"Yes," said Will. "And the crocodile was taken to drag along the floor of the pavilion, to make it look as though a great snake had been there."

A long silence followed. "We expect his mother put him up to it," said the queen at last. "Though he's poisonous enough to have had the idea on his own."

Will cleared his throat. "There was also evidence, in the shop, that one of the men cut his foot on a broken jar. If the servants' feet are examined—"

"Yes. We take your meaning. You have done well, Master Shaxpur."

"I am sorry, Ma'am."

"We don't know that we are," said the Living Boudicca, tapping her fingers on the haft of her spear. "Berecyntia was a murderess. Just as well she was stopped before she made a habit of it."

"Ma'am?"

"Shall we tell you how we became queen, little man?" Andraste Twdwr looked him in the eye. The unaccustomed familiarity unnerved Will, for her gaze was like a spear, but he met it steadily. "I was young, and in those days fair; my sister Genupa was much older, and not so fair. As the years drew on and she bore no children to her husband, she came to envy me my state. Our Aunt Magaidh was queen then, growing old.

"Genupa's husband lusted after me. The gods know I didn't want the man; but Genupa caught him trying to kiss me, at a drunken banquet, and she went mad. She challenged me.

"Aunt Magaidh gave us weapons and bid us fight it out. Poor Genupa was no fighter; she rushed at me, screaming, and fending her off I wounded her in the shoulder with my spear's point. She came at me and I blocked again, and again, and so we circled each other, as Aunt Magaidh looked on in silence.

"Genupa began to laugh. She laughed, and staggered as though she was drunk. She shouted at me, hateful things, but happily, as though I were crawling in the dust at her feet. At last she tripped on the haft of her own spear and fell sprawling. I stood back and waited for her to rise, but she never rose. I heard her choking and ran to turn her over. She was past rising; she died then and there, grinning like a skull.

"I stood, weeping. I looked at the point of my spear and saw the poison smeared there, and my aunt said: 'She was old and barren, and not so clever as you. This granted her an honorable death. And now there will be no dispute over the succession.'

"My aunt died not long after. I inherited her throne and the secret of the poison. It's rare potent stuff, brewed in the east, reserved for kings. It kills quickly and painlessly. The victim experiences euphoria. You will remember how Arnemetia's husband laughed, that night, after he'd been wounded. To say nothing of his other symptoms." The queen smiled bitterly. "I have never kept it; I detest poisoners. But Berecyntia obtained some easily enough, from Caesarion's ambassador. I made her confess as much.

"Well, well. What to do now, Master Shaxpur? We have no doubt it will be proved that Arnemetia had her sister killed. And there is the matter of the poor little Egyptian apothecary. Who answers for his blood?"

"That is not for me to say, majesty," said Will, bowing his head.

"Quite so." The queen stared into space. "We must bear it alone. It's one thing to kill off a mere consort; another thing entirely to kill your own sister. We will hand her over to the druids, she and the boy. It is good for the people to see that no one is above our justice." She looked down at Will. "But we fear Great Glycon has been the cause of too much trouble. We think it were best your friends pack up their puppet and seek their fortunes over in Gaul. You, however, must remain here."

"I, majesty?" Will began to sweat.

"Even you." The queen looked at him critically. "You are not a fool; your wit pleases us. You must not end your days telling fortunes in Gaul. We have another fate in mind for you."

A veiled girl entered the room then, and drew back when she saw Will.

"Come in, girl," said the Living Boudicca. "We sent for you an hour since."

"I was reading," said the girl, a little sullenly. "And may speak to no man."

"The case is altered, child," said the queen. "Holy Modron can do with one less nun in Her service. You will be queen after us, now, and this man will be your consort. Look upon him."

Affronted, the girl raised her veil and glared at Will. He was already breathless from shock, and now he gasped. Princess Damara was young and fair as her mother had been once, with the same coppery hair. Her eyes, however, were green as the sea. She regarded him steadily a moment, before shrugging.

"He's handsome enough. I don't mind about his hair. Still, you can't mean to marry me to a commoner?"

"Of course not," said her mother. "That's easily fixed. What say you, Master Shaxpur, to an earldom? Oxford, we think. Yes. Ought to suit you nicely."

Via Vortex

John Meaney

John Meaney's Nulapeiron Sequence, which comprises the novels Paradox, Context *and* Resolution, *is, in my humble opinion, the most exciting and important space opera written since Frank Herbert's* Dune. *I was a tremendous fan of his work years before it was my privilege to edit him. Lately, he's been fishing in the darker pools of his imagination, without losing any of the brilliant SF extrapolations for which I love his work, as his new duology* Bone Song *and* Dark Blood *attest. The story that follows comes from a similar place as his novels of "Tristopolis," if from another universe entirely.*

They call it courtroom chaos, that reactive moment when the judge pronounces sentence, when the defendant learns that he—nearly always a man—has lost everything because of a moment's impulse or a lifetime traveling some inevitable path of violence and suffering. But I was calm as Judge Zimmer told Morton the worst, because for me this was vindication, a moment of clarity. It ended a story that began when I started working the case, a sequence played out against a backdrop of grieving families, unable to comprehend the hellish foreshortening of their daughters' lives.

Morton screamed: "No!"

He launched himself from the dock, arcing his manacled fists toward the guards. But they were big men, well trained, who were almost gentle as they smothered his lashing limbs with superior mass, becoming a living cell. They kept in motion, moving toward the exit as a flexible unit, with Morton a wriggling, trapped nucleus who had no choice but to leave with them.

Judge Zimmer raised the gavel, then gently lowered it. He had kept order throughout the trial; now he could allow the spectators a few moments of excited commentary. For a second, his steel eyes focused on me—I fancied I could hear the servomotors' tiny whine—and I nodded. Then the journalists in the row in front of me stood up, blocking my view.

"Sir?"

The voice came from the aisle. Klaus Schröder, fit, tanned, and too fresh-looking to be on my team, was waving.

"One moment," I called.

As I worked my way along the row, with polite apologies, I decided to order Klaus to take a vacation. His wife and two-month-old son needed him.

We moved away from the benches, and stood beneath a federal black-eagle insignia.

"In England," said Klaus, "they reckon only Amerikans and Deutschlanders enjoy *Schadenfreude*."

I glanced at the journalists. Some of them *were* smiling. And most of the spectators had been fascinated throughout the trial. I wasn't sure that was the same thing.

"Come on, Klaus. What the hell do you know about England?"

"Less than you, Herr Leutnant. Obviously. So she's here to see you, not me."

I raised my eyebrow, and gave him my cut-the-shit-right-now look. "Who? What? Where?" My first questions, at the start of every new case.

Klaus's mouth twitched. "A chief constable from New Scotland Yard, which I believe is in London, not so? I drove her here from HQ. She's outside in the foyer."

"Wonderful."

Because I could do with time off, too. Alone in a tent in the Catskills, hiking during daylight, shooting deer with my digital camera rather than a rifle, staring up at the infinite stars every night. Or I could fall straight into the next case without a rest.

A bailiff said: "The court will stand to order."

Everyone got to their feet. Judge Zimmer's steel eyes glinted as he rose, straightening his scarlet robe.

"Judgment has been served," he said. "God bless Amerika."

"God bless Amerika," murmured the crowd.

I tugged Klaus's sleeve, but we were only half way to the exit before the rest of the spectators spilled in to the aisle, forming a slow, viscous tide of people. Klaus kept close to me.

"Her name is Chief Constable Brown. That's B-r-o-w-n, not B-r-a-u-n."

"All right." A woman's shoulder bumped against my chest. "Is there anything else I should know?"

"I would think so."

"So what is it?"

"I don't know either, herr leutnant, or I'd have told you."

When we started working together, I'd said that I hated yes-sir-no-sir subordinates without any sense of humor. So that'll teach me.

The swirling crowd flowed through the choke point that was the exit, and opened out into the marble foyer. A large woman got up from a polished wooden bench. She was wearing a light-gray skirt suit, no frills. Her pale hair (I figured it for gray-white, lightly bleached) was cut in a stylish, functional bob. I'd guess her age at late fifties, twenty years older than me.

Her handshake was a good one, and when she spoke, her Deutsch was flawless.

"I'm very pleased to meet you, Herr Leutnant Weber."

"It's my pleasure, Frau Chief Constable Brown." I used the English rank. "And I'm curious as to how I might help you."

"Can I begin with mentioning my authorization? Not just your bosses' approval, but my Interpol credentials, in addition to my own as a Metropolitan Police officer."

"That's the London regional force," said Klaus. "Am I correct?"

"Absolutely correct." Brown smiled at him. "And I hope we get to work together, you and I. It's just that I have to talk to the herr leutnant privately first."

"Of course."

"But I can tell you both that we need to take a suspect into custody some time tonight, probably quite late. Are you well rested, herr leutnant?"

"Always," I said, as Klaus smirked. "So who is the suspect?"

"That's the thing I can't tell you yet."

Who? What? Where? She'd fallen down on the first question.

Klaus said: "And the crime?"

"Multiple homicide. In half a dozen different countries."

Without specifics, it sounded like she'd come to the right people. As we exited the courthouse and descended the steps, the sky was already dark over Manhattan. This was November, the evening air was cold, and none of us was wearing an overcoat. A patrol car was waiting at the curb with its engine running. This would be the vehicle Brown and Klaus had arrived in, hopefully with the heater on.

"We should get back to Headquarters," I said.

"If you say so." Brown looked at the car. "But do you know, I've never seen the Empire State Tower."

Just as I started to insist, Klaus shook his head. He probably did know more about the English than I did, so I paused and mentally replayed Brown's words. *Ah. Obvious.* She wanted to talk alone, away from official surroundings.

"You take the car," I told Klaus. "We'll take a cab."

"Um, sure, chief."

"And go home to the family. That's an order."

"Yes, sir." He smiled, and saluted.

Winds twisted across the outdoor observation balcony of the Empire State. As Chief Constable Lisa Brown (she'd shown me her badge) and I walked around the circumference, the only other visitors, a group of well-bundled-up Japanese tourists, went back inside. The souvenir store was warm and well lighted. Out here it was freezing.

"It's so beautiful." Brown gestured toward the Chrysler Building. "Iconic."

I could see the orange-and-yellow sphere two hundred feet above the once-Christian cathedral on Fifth, now known as Flare Abbey, Manhattan's premier place of worship for the Church of the Holy

Solar. The plastic sphere was lighted from within, mounted on top of a black steel needle hidden in the night.

Call that iconic too, if you like. I think of it as one more monument to stupidity.

"So," I asked, "is this your first trip to Neu München?"

Most Englanders would call it New Munich, but Brown was comfortable with the language.

"Oh, no, herr leutnant. But always for work. I've never had time to come up here before."

I looked eastward to Brooklyn and Blauwald, where I grew up.

"There's more to the city than Manhattan."

"I've seen some of the other neighborhoods. So can we take a walk around? Just the balcony here, I mean."

We walked along the north and west sides, then stopped at the corner. Brown pointed out to the dark waters of the bay, where the great ovoid glistened white, with non-linear patterns of gold and scarlet drifting across its surface.

"Ellis Vortex," she said. "I was wondering how you feel about that."

She's vetting me, for God's sake.

"It was necessary." My voice tightened, against my wishes. "Otherwise the Nazis would never have stopped, never surrendered."

"But two days earlier, the Allies had already shown what they could do. With the Hanover Vortex lighting up the night, did the Axis really need to face a second demonstration? And with the Amerikan vice-chancellor on the island?"

"Ancient history, frau chief constable. Before either of us was born."

"So you've no objection to working with an Englander?"

I crossed my arms, more against the wind than as a defensive gesture.

"On your previous trips," I said, "did you get a chance to visit Brooklyn?"

"In point of fact, I did."

"And perhaps you noticed small discs about so big"—I made a semi-circle with thumb and forefinger—"set into the sidewalk, in front of some houses?"

"Yes." Brown focused on me. "I was astonished, when my companion explained their meaning."

Each brass disc bears the name of a Jewish individual or family, pulled from their home by ASA brownshirts during the late 1930s. Mostly, the Amerikanische Sturmabteilung dragged their prisoners to Grand Zentral, to put them aboard the death trains.

"You'll find my grandparents' names," I said, "on one of those discs."

"Ah."

"And it was a very long time ago. So are you happy to work with me now, frau chief constable?"

"I think you might be good enough." She was smiling. "Perhaps we can go to your place?"

"You mean the office."

"Well, of course, herr leutnant."

"I'd be honored, ma'am."

The Eavesdropping Suite is much as you'd expect: dark ceiling, bright-lit consoles, each with a shining steel-and-glass resonator some twenty centimeters long. The officers are plainclothes, in shirtsleeves with loosened ties, and their job is to listen in on encrypted traffic, the comms that make the underworld go round.

A mix of languages came softly through the speakers. Brown listened, then said: "I heard, on my last trip, that Deutsch became the country's official language by exactly one vote, in 1776. You nearly ended up speaking English."

"Something of an urban myth." I waved to Andre, who sat at a console across the room, and he waved back. "Partly, it grew from the vote that made Deutsch the *second* language on all legislation, in 1795. And there was the influx of Lutherans from Europe, after the Vatican's Revenge."

"I thought it was Benjamin Franklin's doing."

"He pushed for Deutsch, all right. But there wasn't a *legally* official Amerikan language until the 1950s, and Senator Hayakawa."

The history was familiar because, as a sophomore studying psychophysics, I'd read Hayakawa's classic texts on semantics. I'd been interested enough to learn about the background.

"Hey, herr leutnant," one of the guys, Karl, called out. We've known each other a long time; in a bar he'd address me as Peter, but not here. "We got the Red Hot Doktors smooching on the vortex flow again."

"Give them my love."

"Right."

There were smiles around the room.

"You surely can't transmit on the flow," murmured Brown. "That was a joke, right?"

"That's right," I told her.

It's hard enough to establish a listen-only resonance on an encrypted flow, without perturbation sending the link into non-linear chaos. Transmitting is impossible, and when we're eavesdropping on genuine criminals, we wouldn't want them to hear a thing.

"Red Hot Doktors." said Brown. "Using hospital crypto kit for private conversations?"

"You've guessed it." Karl flicked a fingernail against his console. "They're married, just not to each other. And they like describing things in, um—"

"In clinical detail?"

"Uh, right, ma'am."

"Well"—Brown gave a tiny smile as she scanned the room— "that's not exactly what I thought you'd be eavesdropping on."

"Um..." Karl stopped.

I said, "We're not supposed to target minorities, not even the Church of the Holy Solar."

Tiny muscles tightened in Brown's face.

A connection to the case you've still not explained?

"Right." Karl pointed at his monitor screen, with its list of eaves-dropping subjects. "There's your ordinary criminal activity, but Solar fundamentalists are dangerous. And they think vortex encryp-tion is an unholy use of the flow, except when they're using it themselves."

Brown looked at her watch. It was plain but elegant, therefore expensive.

"You must be hungry," I said, guessing she wanted to change the subject.

"Well, my body clock thinks it's two pm and I've missed lunch. But I'm waiting for a crypto signal first, from London or Berlin."

"And then you'll be able to tell me what's happening tonight?"

"I hope so," said Brown.

Across the room, Andre was busy at his console. If there were an incoming signal for a ranking visitor, I'd expect him to field it. Meanwhile, beside me, Brown started yawning.

"Sorry."

"Flying takes it out of you," said Karl. "Going eastward is even worse."

"I didn't leave my home until four hours ago. Just weeks of putting in long hours, is all."

Four hours?

But we'd spent the last two hours here in Manhattan, which meant—

"You resonated from London," I said. "You didn't fly."

Karl stared at Brown.

"Yes." She looked from Karl to me. "Is that a problem?"

"Um..."

"Obviously I got through the Intention Scan."

"Sorry, ma'am," said Karl.

"Accepted. And you, herr leutnant? Do you have a problem with my mode of transport?"

"I didn't say—"

And then Andre, from across the room, called out: "Ma'am? Incoming signal, highest priority."

Call it a lucky rescue.

Though Brown was a big woman, she was across the room very fast. Andre had scarcely popped an unformatted silicon/gallium sliver into his data resonator by the time she reached him. I got there as Andre clicked the glass cover shut.

"Tell me when," said Brown.

"Done."

I hadn't caught the flicker. To me, the sliver was unchanged.

Andre opened the resonance cavity, removed the sliver with tweezers, inserted it into a thumbnail-sized data plug, and sealed the thing up. He handed it to Brown.

"There you are, ma'am."

"Many thanks."

She pulled a PDA from her pocket, and clicked the data plug into a USB port. Then she turned away as the small screen swirled into life. She continued walking, intent on the message, ignoring us.

Andre shrugged.

"If it wasn't confidential," he said, "they could've just made a phone call."

"True."

But it might have been nice if she'd demonstrated some trust.

"Do you think she was impressed with my books?" Andre nodded toward his small desktop bookcase.

"Definitely," I said, touching the original English edition of Hawking and Penrose's *Vortex Field Theory*. "She noticed, for sure."

I was lying. What I really thought was, Brown was so intent on her job that everything else was secondary, including ethical considerations. Because with a little forethought and planning, she surely could have left London yesterday, and simply flown.

When she came back, she gave another yawn.

"Early to bed and to depart," said Andre, "makes one healthy, rich and wise. Ben Franklin said that."

Brown looked at me. "And he might have said it in English, if history had been different."

"In English," I said, "it wouldn't have rhymed."

"So he'd have worded it differently."

"All right. Is there any chance of your telling us what's going on now?"

Andre pulled his head back, withdrawing from the hostility.

"Herr leutnant," said Brown. "You might not approve of my priorities, but I have eight high profile victims already in the morgue. Still, the urgency has nothing to do with them, it's the *next* victim, the one who hasn't died yet."

"Shit."

"So if you could get us to Grand Zentral right this minute, it would be a big help."

"The station?"

"Exactly right."

But before we could get going, Karl called something, then Andre's phone rang. He picked up. "What? Oh, right. Thanks, Karl." He held the phone out to me. "Sorry, Chief."

"No problem."

It was Klaus on the line.

"Herr leutnant, you said go home, so I did, but I have a telephone here. I made a few calls to London. One of my pals just rang back."

"That's... interesting," I said.

"Oh, she's there, is she? The frau chief constable?"

I smiled. "You're a smart guy."

"Tell that to my mother-in-law. So you want to hear some Interpol gossip? There's allegedly a series of resonance deaths across Europe. Not a whisper on TV or any newspaper."

"My God, I'm not surprised." If anything was covered by the European versions of the Restriction of Information Act, it would be fatalities caused by vortex technology. "Is there anything else?"

"No, but Sabine says hi. And when are you coming to dinner?"

"Hi back. Soon. And take it easy."

I gave the handset back to Andre.

"Anything interesting?" asked Brown.

"Wrong number," I said. "So, Grand Zentral. You want to get something to eat there?"

As we walked through the building's exit, three armored vans squealed out of the side street, and went tearing off. I stopped, as did Brown. Then I headed back inside. Ignoring a clump of civilians in front of the duty desk, I said to the sergeant: "Any idea what's going on?"

Brown came in, and walked close enough to hear.

"Officers down." He rubbed his moustache. "Herakles team, on a bust. Wearing vests."

"Damn it."

"Exactly. You take care, herr leutnant."

I went back out. Beside me, Brown asked: "What's a Herakles team?"

"A police commando unit. We wear armored vests, so the other side have started using armor-piercing rounds. It's what biologists call co-evolution, meaning—"

"I know what it means," said Brown. "If you don't want to call me chief constable, you can call me Doktor Brown, all right?"

"My apologies."

"That's all right, herr leutnant."

On the sidewalk, I stopped. "Or you can call me Doktor Weber, if you prefer."

"Oh, really? In what discipline?"

"Psychophysics, from MTI in Boston."

We work in vortex tech. What did you expect?

After a moment, she held out her hand.

"Pleased to meet you, Herr Doktor Weber."

"Likewise, Frau Doktor Brown."

We shook, as we had several hours earlier, not quite smiling.

"You're all right," she said. "Why don't you call me Lisa."

"I'm Peter."

"And are you buying, Peter? Dinner in Grand Zentral, I mean."

"Absolutely. And claiming it on expenses."

"I should hope so."

I flagged down a yellow cab, and told him our destination.

"Aw, man," the driver began. "That's too short a drive for—"

When I unbuttoned my jacket, it fell open. My Luger was under my left armpit.

"I mean, hop right inside, officer."

"Twenty Marks if you're fast."

Opening the door for Lisa Brown, I added: "Welcome to Neu München."

Twenty minutes later, we were dining on the balcony overlooking the Grand Zentral concourse. The pale, polished stone was clean and ornate: the architecture of more leisurely times. Orange characters scrolled down electronic boards, naming destinations: Stamford, Poughkeepsie, Neu Hafen.

But I liked to watch the travelers, read their body language, modeling them in my mind with neuroflow equations. Call it keeping in practice, or a hankering for the purity of science, away from law enforcement.

Brown—I mean Lisa—was dividing her attention between cutting her steak and staring over the balustrade. "I love these old stations."

"Yes. I guess."

I heard the overtones in my voice, too late to soften them. Lisa nodded. I guessed she'd seen my gaze flicker. But then, the setup is obvious, though most commuters wander around the thing without paying attention.

In the center of the concourse, fashioned in stone that matches the surroundings—as if they've been here since the station's inception—stands an oval arrangement of twelve resonator booths. Each is massive, double the size of a phone booth. From above, a discreet awning hides the glass door on each booth, facing the center of the oval.

And always a squad of marines stands guard, Heckler & Koch carbines held across their chests.

"Welcome to modernity," I said. "When I was a kid, you'd never see military in the city."

"Progress brings change."

"That's one way of putting it." I raised a forkful of vegetable curry half way, then lowered it to the plate. "Does progress bring information sharing?"

"When I get authorization. I follow orders, like the guys down there."

I'd been in the Rangers for four years. I'd learned initiative as well as obedience.

"You're predicting a suspect will come through here, is that it?"

"Maybe. So"—Lisa put down her knife and fork—"Ben Franklin, as we discussed earlier. If he hadn't spoken Deutsch, those things"—nodding to the resonance booths down below—"wouldn't exist. By the way, this is me changing the subject."

"Uh-huh. So how do you figure that, Lisa? And this is me playing along, for a time."

"Well, Herr Doktor Weber. Peter. My subject was the history of science—"

"Ah."

"—and I was thinking about Albert Einstein. You know, his first half dozen breakthroughs, from the photoelectric effect and Brownian motion to restricted relativity, were all developments that would eventually have been made by other people. It was astounding that one man came up with all of them, but without Einstein, science as a whole would have discovered the same things."

I felt myself smiling, not because this was new to me—it wasn't—but because of the animation in Lisa's voice, the shining of her eyes (remarkably clear, given her age), and the obvious love of history. Perhaps I wasn't the only one who regretted not taking a different path.

"But when the Nazis rose to power, and Einstein fled to France, that was when he met up with de Broglie. Between the younger man's energy and odd ideas, and Einstein's own genius, they came up with a new framework that could never have arisen otherwise."

"If they hadn't come up with vortex mechanics," I said, "no one would have."

Nearly every scientist with occasional interest in history knew this much.

"So we agree," said Lisa. "But here's my real point. If Amerika hadn't spoken Deutsch, the Nazis would not have risen to power here as well."

"Have you *been* to Alabama?"

"But the whole country's not like that. There would have been places for Jews to flee other than France. Countries farther from the Nazis."

"And no psychophysics." I ate some curry, finding my appetite again. "But without vortex mechanics, you'd have those other old theories. Um..."

"Wave mechanics and matrix mechanics," said Lisa. "Same thing, really. What they used to call *quantum*, which was accurate in its limited way, but implied—"

"But it gave a special place to human consciousness." As a psychophysicist, I knew how ridiculous this was. "It was nonsense."

"Like placing the Earth at the center of the universe, in pre-Copernican times. I know. But Peter, without vortex mechanics there would have been no alternative but to adopt the quantum formulations."

"With no idea how complexities arise from layered vortex patterns," I said. "No theory of consciousness, of cultural mechanics."

"And no Church of the Holy Solar."

Perhaps Lisa's words had carried. I noticed several diners turn around. So I gave them *that* stare, the one that broadcasts on subliminal levels—a capacity beyond primate anger, to access the reptilian brain we all have, which is fast and cold and can process violent action without emotion. I could recite the vortex flow equations that describe how it works.

And I could use it to effect, as the civilians blinked and turned back to their food.

"I hope you're not blaming psychophysics for Solarian fundamentalism."

"Come off it, Peter. You know how misinformation moves through a culture. You can probably write a mathematical description of the—"

Her PDA buzzed.

Within minutes, we were down on the concourse, presenting our IDs to the marines' officer-in-charge. Lisa explained that a suspected killer, almost certainly a Solarian fundamentalist, was likely to pass through the booths.

"We don't have his name." She held up her PDA, currently displaying a complex graph. "Just a predicted travel pattern."

"So how can you confirm—?"

"It's as likely to be the victim we identify. Herr Leutnant Weber has the authorization and expertise to open a cache."

"On the resonance booth? Both the killer *and* the victim are likely to pass through here?"

"Exactly."

The officer looked confused, which was a good sign: he understood that the Intention Scan should rule out someone traveling in order to kill. My instinct had been to shut down the booths, but it would take an hour to decouple them, and Lisa had pointed out the real result: the killer would shift to compensate, and take down his victim elsewhere.

"Goddam Solarians," muttered the officer, heading back toward his men.

It was vortex mechanics that had predicted the layers upon layers of complexity that swirled inside our Sun, and every star. And it was vortex-based psychophysics that had revealed what those patterns meant: a form of self-aware cognition that lay so far beyond human thought that it was nonsense to describe it with the same word.

Call the Sun god-like if you want, but to assume it cares about our worship is like expecting a bacterium to adore a human being, and the human to be pleased. Why can't people get that?

"We think," Lisa said to me now, "that the bastard uses something like your eavesdropping tech, passing through the booth, leaving a perturbation behind him."

"That's not easily done."

"I know."

Because in the Eavesdropping Suite, we have guys with big brains—I'm not talking about me—and a massive hardware budget, in order to set up resonances that are subtle enough to listen in without destroying the link they're overhearing. That's the trick. And if this killer was able to perturb a booth's resonance while leaving its vortex link intact, he knew more than I did.

"Your job is to track the bastard," said Lisa. "But I've a question I need to ask. It's important."

"Uh-huh."

"Would you travel through a booth to catch him?"

I stared at her.

"You eat steak," I said. "Have you ever been inside a slaughterhouse?"

"What relevance does that have?"

"I'm a vegetarian." As I spoke, I was aware of the booths' presence beyond the marines. "So I'll let you work that out."

"That's an interesting attitude"—Lisa's accent became very crisp, very Hochdeutsch—"for a policeman to have. Especially one responsible for convicting killers."

"Live with the paradox. That's what I do."

But perhaps Lisa had seen deeper than I had, for when we walked through the ring of marines, what I saw jolted me, even though I knew what to expect.

"Fuck," I muttered.

Each of the twelve booths, as we could see when we entered the oval configuration, was fronted by thick armored glass. The remaining three walls of each booth were of pale stone, matching the concourse floor. But inside the booths—

"Morton. My God."

The booths alternated: six empty, six occupied, for inside every second booth was a manacled naked man. And the booth in front of me contained someone I'd last seen struggling in the courtroom, yelling when the judge pronounced sentence, thrashing while the guards maneuvered him away.

"Who is he?"

"His name," I told Lisa, "is Elwyn Morton. Child molester. Killer."

Morton was staring at us through the glass. Not screaming, just watching.

"And you caught him? So this is justice."

"Call it what you like," I said, "but I do *not* want to watch."

"Stand easy, Peter. There are civilians here."

"What—? Oh, shit."

A well-dressed businessman, escorted by two travel assistants wearing white coats, was passing through the ring of marines. One assistant placed a silver cap on the businessman's head, while her colleague checked a monitor screen set next to a booth.

"All clear," she said. "Have a fine journey, sir."

The businessman gave a small, emotionless nod.

Heartless bastard.

But even from here I could see the resonance interpretation on the screen. According to the parameters of the Intention Scan, the businessman was a well-intentioned traveler, with a justifiably urgent reason for using resonance.

"Wait a minute." I focused on the businessman, who was beginning to undress. "If the killer travels through, then he passes the Intention Scan."

"Exactly. See how consistent that is?"

I rubbed dry saliva from the corner of my mouth. My stomach felt sour, though I'd eaten little of my curry. But Lisa was right: anyone who could perturb a booth's resonance could also subvert the Intention Scan. This took things to another level.

I breathed consciously, a time-honored way of telling the unconscious to relax. You don't need flow equations to understand it works.

Exhale.

The businessman, now naked, looked fleshy and soft, nothing like a terrorist. He walked toward an empty booth. The naked men chained in the booths on either side watched him without moving. Resigned or horrified, I could not tell which.

And I did *not* want to watch this.

Inhale.

Exhale.

An assistant opened the booth, and the nude man stepped inside. Then—it was excruciating, the care they took—the assistant closed the booth, while her colleague pressed the—

Breathe.

—button, and red meat exploded against the glass, spattering the booth. Gobbets of flesh smacked, stuck to the glass, then began to slide down through viscous layers of blood.

"Oh, very nice," said the first assistant, checking the screen.

"He got through okay?" asked the other.

"All the way to San Francisco, safe and sound."

"Good. Initiating clean-up."

Inside the booth, nozzles began to spray water and detergent, and rotating brushes started to clean away the unstructured flesh that only moments earlier had been a living, conscious, sentient human being.

But the businessman had taken exactly zero time to reach San Francisco.

Call it progress.

After I checked the cache, mostly to reassure myself that I could operate the system, I told Lisa that everything appeared to check out fine. As I spoke, the vortex flux within the cache swirled, went non-linear, and spun away. The cache was now clear, and unreadable.

"So we wait for the next one." Lisa held up her PDA, pointing at the graph on the screen. "We're only tracking probabilities here."

"Wonderful."

"You're doing fine, Peter."

It wasn't any kind of praise I needed.

It was another half hour before a small violet light began to wink above one of the occupied booths. Not the one containing Morton. I wondered how they chose.

The assistants, in their laundered white coats, were coming back. "Incoming," one of them said to me.

In one of the booths, the naked, manacled prisoner turned toward the rear, his shoulders bobbing. The armored glass and thick glass walls kept the sound inside.

But the prisoner whose booth was flashing, expecting someone to arrive—

"I can't watch." My voice.

—knew he was next. One of the assistants had put on glasses, and the flashing light reflected in her lenses like a violet strobe. The man shook his head, lips drawn back as he fought against his chains, as though he could rip them free from the concrete—impossible—then he threw his head back and howled, so loud I could almost hear a distant attenuated sound, a ghost's agony, before he—

"I can," said Lisa.

—just *swirled*, red and pink and gray, a tornado of color and movement—

"Oh, sweet God."

—and then a narrow-bodied Afrikan American woman was standing there.

"Here you are." One of the attendants held up a fluffy robe, as the glass door clicked open. "Welcome to Neu München, ma'am."

"Thank you." The arrival stepped into the robe. "Thank you very much."

She glanced at me. I tried not to remember the flash of chocolate-brown nipple, of firm breast.

"Peter." Lisa touched my shoulder.

"Sorry. Yes."

I went to the booth, trying not to look at the gobbets of flesh inside. A faint pink mist, a pastel vapor, billowed from the still-open booth, like steam from a shower.

The prisoner had weighed perhaps forty pounds more than the woman whose flesh he'd reconstituted. That was forty pounds of waste organic matter, left over from the transport process, untargeted by the resonance effect.

While I opened the brass hatch set into the outside of the booth, one of the attendants closed the door and set the cleaning cycle going. Detergents washed, while I tried to concentrate on pattern traces in the resonator's cache.

"No perturbations remaining." I ran through the phase space displays once more, and then the information was gone, dissipated into random flux. "An ordinary resonance."

Ordinary, except to the man whose sentence had just been carried out.

"All right." Lisa checked her PDA, and put it away. "We were playing the odds, but if we go home without a crime happening, I'll be happy for it." •

"But you—"

"What?"

"Never mind," I said.

Lisa nodded toward the booth, where the cleaning cycle continued. "You mean, I'll have had a wasted journey? A wasted *resonance* journey?"

I closed the hatch. The newly arrived Afrikan American woman was gone, escorted to the shower room by the assistants. Other staff would already have laid out a full wardrobe for the woman to choose from. All part of the very expensive service that is resonator travel.

"Oh, God," I said. "Another one."

"Get ready."

Again, a violet light flashed. Again, it wasn't Morton in the receiving booth. I supposed they worked through the men in chronological sequence, except when body mass was insufficient to receive the incomer. Did the staff wait until all six men had been reconstituted as incoming travelers before replacing them with six new prisoners? Or did they wait for a certain time of day, when they brought in just the right number of prisoners, like refills for the vacant booths? And if a really heavy person was due to come in, would they chain two prisoners into a single booth?

I didn't want to ask.

Then it happened, as before.

This time, when the maelstrom of red gore had ceased swirling, it was a pale, doughy young man in his early twenties who stood there. His dirty-blond hair was untidy. He stepped over the mass of misshapen metal that had been the prisoner's manacles.

"Thank you," he told his attendants, as they wrapped a robe around him.

Unlike the previous arrival, he looked back into the booth. There was less excess mass this time. Still, some remains lay like scattered mincemeat on the floor.

"Bloody hell," muttered Lisa in English. "It's getting busy."

Another violet light was flashing.

"What's that?" said an attendant.

The other looked puzzled.

"We're not supposed to have another incoming for—"

Inside the booth, the waiting prisoner exploded into gouts of meat.

"Jesus Christ," said Lisa. "Open this, now."

An arrival?

No.

Because whatever had arrived wasn't what you'd expect to—

"Peter."

"Sorry."

I helped her pull the booth open. It was partly reconstituted, the body of the incomer: a torn-apart corpse with two faces on the deformed skull. One face was that of the original prisoner, distorted into a final scream. The other surely was the features of the failed arrival, also dead.

This was the traveler.

And this was the murder, the kind of murder that Lisa had been talking about. I wanted to throw up, but I was supposed to be able to think logically in a crisis, to integrate the cortex when amygdala-led vortices of neural flow were not enough, when the neural cliques that represented my reaction of horror were simply not useful. There's psychophysical jargon but we call it getting a grip, and that's what I did now, finally.

The scheduled traveler.

And the attendants had been expecting only one traveler at this time, so if that was the dead person, then who—?

I ripped the Luger from under my jacket as I spun around. But the doughy-skinned young man had already leaped inside a vacant booth. The attendants looked shocked as the booth began its transmission cycle.

"Fire!" said Lisa.

"I..."

But red flesh exploded, and my opportunity was gone.

"Shit. Shit."

Reholstering the gun, I ran to the booth, popped the brass hatch, then worked the tracing tools fast, before the cache could clear.

"He's in Berlin." I looked at Lisa. "Phone Berlin Tiergarten, quick. Because if he goes on to Beijing or Mumbai, we've lost the bastard."

"I know."

Lisa didn't move.

"Then why are you—?"

I stopped.

"Lisa. What's that in your hand?"

"It's fast acting." The small device was of polished metal. It might have been a lipstick holder. "I'm so sorry."

"That's not—"

The world snapped out of being.

And back into focus, except that I was naked, inside a booth the size of a large shower cubicle. Outside, through the glass, I could see Lisa, standing with a marine to either side of her. One of them sketched a salute.

"No!" I yelled. "I don't want to—"

Shit.

"—do this."

There was a pavilion outside the booth, with glimpses of night-covered parkland beyond. I was in the Tiergarten terminal.

Lisa. No.

Little blood or meat stained the floor. I guess the prisoner hadn't been much heavier than me.

"Oh, God."

My hand trembled as I pushed open the door.

I'm a police officer.

Had I been offered the choice, I would have refused this resonance. But the doughy young man, the killer, was on the other side of the pavilion, eyes widening as I stepped out of the booth.

Don't let him get away.

"Halt," I croaked. "Do not move."

There were attendants, three men in pale blue tunics, but they looked confused. The booths were widely spaced, unlike Grand Zentral, standing around the pavilion's outer circumference.

"Stop him," I added.

But the killer was running now, heading for the nearest vacant booth, and I didn't think I could get there in time. And if I didn't, was I willing to travel onward once more, maybe following him across the globe on a lengthening chase with a prisoner dying every time I or the man I was hunting stepped out at a new destination?

No.

I could run, but not that fast.

Yet Solar fundamentalists are everywhere, so there were armed Border Police here, just as in Amerikan resonance sites. The killer was on the far side of the pavilion, almost at a booth, but the nearest uniformed officer was just feet away from me.

I felt my lips draw back from my teeth as I leaped forward.

You can still...

A part of my mind popped up the suggestion that I could identify myself, but there are times when even a psychophysicist must let the reptile brain take over, moving fast.

...stop this.

And I was on the officer, immobilizing his arm with my left hand as I ripped his sidearm free with my right. It was a Luger, and I had the safety off as I spun away, sinking my body weight, stabilizing, seeing the killer inside the booth and smiling at me, but I was—

Exhale.

—steadying as I squeezed the trigger. On the armored glass, a bullet hole spider-webbed into existence.

Air, wavering.

The killer was frozen but so was the bullet, suspended in mid-air just inches from the killer's face as the resonance took hold. There was stasis for a second before the red tornado of exploding flesh, and he was gone.

I threw the Luger aside and raised my hands.

"Police officer!" I shouted. "Police officer!"

I learned afterward it was a good job I spoke Deutsch, like the armed officers, because they nearly shot me.

* * *

They offered me a choice of travel methods. I flew home on a Messerschmidt 787. Klaus met me at the airport at ten am, and drove me in an unmarked car to Headquarters. In the Eavesdropping Suite, I got a round of applause, from the members of my own unit as well as from Lisa Brown. I'd thought she might have already left.

"I'll be returning to London"—her smile shone with vindication—"the way you got here from Berlin. No resonance."

"That's nice," I said.

"It's been great to—"

"No. We're not friends. You betrayed me."

"Enabled you to do your duty. Would you have gone of your own volition?"

I didn't answer. We both knew I wouldn't have, which was exactly the point.

There's no talking to some people.

Not exactly profound psychophysics.

"Hey, herr leutnant," called Andre. "How did you figure about the manacles?"

"Pure genius," said someone else.

"That's why he's a leutnant, and you're a pleb." In Klaus's face, the grin was innocent triumph. "Right, Chief?"

"If you say so."

Did I know? Did I work it out?

I wasn't sure of my own actions. Perhaps it had been ordinary anger, firing an armor-piercing round through the glass, or perhaps it *was* scientific intuition. I'm not convinced I'll ever know.

But if the prisoner's flesh provided enough materials to reconstitute a breathing human body, then the manacles that held him in place were more than enough to reassemble a moving bullet, with all the momentum it had originally acquired.

"Goodbye, Lisa."

"Where are you going, Peter?"

"To pray."

Puzzled looks followed me as I left the Eavesdropping Suite, and took an elevator down to the first floor. I walked through the foyer, ignoring the duty sergeant who called my name, and out onto the street.

Squinting, I stared up at the sun, wondering what was going on inside that complexity of vortices that so surpassed human cognition. I could write down the equations, but I could never grasp the solutions. No person could. No tiny, planet-bound primate could dream of it.

"What does it mean?" I asked the sky.

Passers-by stared at me.

Had I expected an answer?

Fate and the Fire-lance

Stephen Baxter

Years ago, I read an amazing story about the discovery of a final Beatles record that had slipped through from another universe where the Fab Four stayed together an extra year before dissolving the band. It was called "The Twelfth Album," it was published in the April 1998 issue of the distinguished UK magazine Interzone, *and it was my introduction to Stephen Baxter. A multiple award-winning author, and one of the acknowledged kings of big concept hard SF, Stephen Baxter is no stranger to alternate history. His "NASA trilogy" of* Voyager, Titan, *and* Moonseed *depicts an alternate timeline where John F. Kennedy survived his attempted assassination and the American space program did not lag as it has done in our reality. The tale that follows is part of his Time's Tapestry series, which includes the books* Emperor, Conqueror, Navigator, *and* Weaver.

"Imogen. Oh, Imogen, you must wake up. He's dead, Imogen. Gavrilo, the son of a Roman emperor, killed in London! It's such a frightful mess, and I don't know what I'm going to do..."

The thin, tremulous voice dragged Imogen Brodsworth out of a too-short sleep. Her eyelids heavy, she had trouble focusing on the face before her: young, oval-shaped, with big eyes but a small nose and mouth, not pretty despite all the efforts of the cosmeticians. And Imogen, just for a moment, couldn't remember where she was. The bed was big, too soft, and there was a scent of old wood, a whiff of incense—and, oddly, cigarette smoke.

Incense. This was Lambeth Palace, residence of archbishops.

The day was bright, the light streaming through the big sash window where a servant had pulled back dusty curtains. She glanced at the small clock on her bedside table. At least that was her own, an ingenious French-Louisianan contraption that told you the time and date on little dials. It was June 29, 1914, fifteen minutes past six on this summer morning.

The girl before her, her face swollen with crying, was Alice, daughter of the English king Charles VII, a princess babbling of killing. She had a maidservant with her, who flapped and fluttered as Alice's mood shifted.

Imogen struggled to sit up. "Ma'am? What did you say of Gavrilo?"

"That he's been murdered, Miss Brodsworth." That was a male voice, grave, and Imogen reflexively ducked back down under the covers.

A soldier stepped forward, crisply uniformed, immaculately shaved, walrus moustache trimmed despite the earliness of the hour. He was perhaps forty. He held a small cigarette in his right hand. He kept his eyes politely averted. "My intrusion is unforgivable, but it is a bit urgent. We met yesterday at the reception at St. James's Palace—"

"I remember. Major Armstrong."

Imogen was a teacher of Latin and Greek, employed by a small private girls' school in Wales. She had been attached as an interpreter with special responsibilities to support the Princess Royal at the reception for her fiancé, the second son of Caesar Nedjelko XXVI Princip. Major Archibald Armstrong was charged with the security of the party, working with a splendidly dressed Roman prefect called Marcus Helvidius.

Imogen had little interest in politics, but she could imagine the implications of the murder of an imperial scion on British soil. "My word."

Alice's tears were turning to temper. "What about *me*? Gavrilo was my fiancé, if you've forgotten! I'm a widow before I was even married—I'm not even eighteen—everybody will look at me and laugh!"

Imogen glanced at Armstrong. "Major, please..."

Armstrong coughed, and turned his back.

Imogen got out of bed. Her nightdress was thick and heavy, too hot but quite suitable for spending the night in the residence of the Archbishop of Canterbury. She faced Alice and took her hands; they were weak and clutched a soggy handkerchief. "My lady. You must be strong. Dignified. This is bound to be difficult, and your father will be relying on you today."

Admonished, Alice did calm a little. "Yes. I know. It's just—is my whole life to be defined by this moment? I hardly knew the man, Imogen. I spent more time with him yesterday on his quireme than we've ever spent before. Even when I visited his palace in Moscow he was always off hunting. Marie Lloyd sang for us on the ship, you know. 'Everything in the Garden's Lovely'..."

And you did not love him, Imogen thought. Of course not; how could you? "I'm sure the future will take care of itself. For now, I know you will do your duty."

"Yes..." Alice let her maid lead her away.

"You're good with her," Armstrong said, back turned, puffing calmly on his cigarette.

"I have pupils older than her. I think you'd better let me perform my toilet, major."

"Thirty minutes," Armstrong said briskly. He nodded and walked out.

On the bedside table, her little clock chimed the half-hour.

In the event she took only twenty minutes.

She checked her appearance in the mirror behind the door: her hair tied up in a neat, practical bun, high-necked blouse and long black skirt, her sensible schoolmistress's shoes for a day she expected to spend on her feet. She was twenty-five years old, and prettier than at least one princess, she told herself defiantly. But she knew she had a sensible air about her, and tended not to attract the eye of any but the most sensible of men. For sensible, she meant *dull*, she conceded wryly. Certainly none of the exotic grandees from across the globe present at the sessions yesterday had noticed her, not like that. None, perhaps, save Marcus Helvidius, who had, she thought back now, smiled at her once or twice...

She was woolgathering, and blushing like a girl. She glared at her own pink cheeks, ordering herself to calm down; she would not have Major Armstrong think she was a ninny. She picked up her handbag and left the room.

Armstrong was waiting outside, puffing on another skinny American cigarette. Without a word he hurried her down a broad staircase and out of the palace.

An automobile was waiting for them on the embankment. They clambered aboard. An armed soldier sat up beside the driver, and two more climbed in behind them. The driver worked the ignition bulb, the engine started up with a smoky roar, and they pulled away into the road. More automobiles joined them, so it was quite a convoy that headed up along the embankment toward Lambeth Bridge. They all sported Union flags, but like most of the automobiles on London's roads they were Roman designs powered by Roman petrol; innovation in the automotive industry was driven by the demands of the empire's huge battlefields in central Asia.

The sun was still low but the sky was a bright cloudless blue, and the air was already warm. London's buildings and bridges were adorned with wreaths, flags and streamers, marks of celebration for the coming of a Roman prince to the city. But there was no air of celebration this morning. Soldiers lined the route, alternating with police, rifles at their shoulders. Aside from them there was nobody to be seen, and only Navy boats moved on the Thames.

Armstrong said, "I do apologize for hoiking you out of your bed like that. Had to force my way in to make sure the summons got through to you. And I know you were up to the small hours with those ecclesiastical types."

"Well, it's true," she admitted. "And coping with all that theological language does make the brain spin..."

The Romans were in London for the formal announcement of the engagement of Princess Alice to Gavrilo. The marriage was essentially political, a way to unite the British Bourbon dynasty to the house of Caesar Nedjelko XXVI Princip, a Serbian line of emperors who had ruled in Constantinople for more than a century. The British government, ever eager to maintain a balance of power on the continent, had used the occasion to host a summit conference of the great powers, notably the French and the Ottomans, territorial rivals of the Romans in central Europe and Mesopotamia, and the Americans, locked in their own perpetual rivalry with the French over their long border with the Louisiana Territory. The churches had been communing too, and while the temporal leaders had been gathered at St. James's, the Archbishop of Canterbury had used Lambeth Palace to host delegations from the Vatican and the Patriarchate of Constantinople to discuss theological issues and ecumenical ventures.

Imogen murmured, "It was a long evening. Compared to the princes at St. James's, the prelates might be long-winded, but they enjoy their wine just as much." *And* a good few of them had roving eyes and wandering hands, she and the other girls had found.

Armstrong laughed. "Well, I'm afraid you have another long day ahead of you today, Miss Brodsworth. Only a few of us are being summoned back to Saint James's. He asked for you specifically."

"Who did?"

"The prefect, Marcus Helvidius. He was impressed by your language skills, and your sobriety. I think he believes you will be an asset today."

Thinking of the prefect, she blushed again.

They were crossing Lambeth Bridge now, and they both turned to see the centerpiece of the Roman presence in London. Drawn up at a quay not far from the shimmering sandstone cliff that was the Palace of Westminster, the Roman ship that had brought Gavrilo here was a quireme. With her rows of oars she might not have looked out of place in the imperial fleets of two millennia before. But smokestacks thrust out of a forest of masts, and rows of gun ports were like little dark windows in the hull.

Having crossed the bridge the convoy turned right and sped up Millbank toward Westminster Abbey and Parliament Square.

"That ship's a remarkable sight, isn't she?" Imogen breathed.

"Oh, yes. But she's more than a floating hotel, you know. And this morning, after the fuss yesterday—well, look what she's disgorged."

The convoy drove up Horse Guards Parade, past the government buildings, and turned into the Mall. And Imogen saw that a row of massive vehicles had been drawn up here, great blocks of steel that towered over the automobiles speeding past. Mounted on caterpillar tracks, with gun nozzles peering from every crevice, these were the vehicles of war the Romans called *testudos*, and the standards of the 314th Legion Siberian fluttered over their ugly flanks.

"A statement of strength," Armstrong muttered. "Given we let their prince be assassinated, we could hardly refuse, though nobody's happy about it. And besides it's hardly *our* fault; this unfortunate incident just happened to have occurred on our territory, that's all."

Of course there was an implicit assumption in what he said that the assassin had not been British. She wondered what basis he had for believing that. But she did not question him, knowing nothing of the case.

More soldiers had set up a perimeter of sandbags and barbed wire around St. James's Palace. Imogen and Armstrong were made to wait while a sergeant checked papers and telephoned his headquarters, and photographers wearing Roman insignia took their pictures. Armstrong accepted this delay laconically; he lit up another cigarette.

Inside the palace, Marcus Helvidius was waiting for them. He was conferring with a Roman senator, representatives of the French and Ottomans, British commanders—and a stout, bristling man dressed in a drab black morning suit who Imogen, feeling faintly bewildered, recognized as the British Foreign Secretary, David Lloyd George. They were speaking in broken Latin, their only common tongue.

When Imogen entered with Armstrong, Marcus turned to her. "Miss Brodsworth. Thank you for coming." He spoke Greek. He was a prefect of the 314th Legion, which, supplementing the Praetorian Guard, had been given responsibility for the security of Gavrilo during this expedition. Yesterday he had worn an archaic ceremonial costume of plumed helmet, cloak, breastplate, short tunic, and laced-up boots; this morning he was dressed more functionally in an olive-green coverall, though the number and standard of his legion had been sewn into the breast. Aged perhaps thirty, he was a heavy-set, powerful man with thick dark hair; his look was more Slavic than Latin, she thought. But his blue eyes were clear, his jaw strong.

She glanced around, and replied in Greek, "Am I the only interpreter you've called?"

"My decision," Marcus said firmly. "It's not seven hours since Gavrilo was murdered. I think it's best if we involve as few people as possible until we know what we're dealing with. Don't you agree?"

"It seems sensible. But why me?" The party yesterday had included senior academics from the great universities, experts in all the languages of the empire: Greek, Latin, Serbian, Georgian, Russian, German. "I'm just a schoolteacher, you know. I was only attached because it was thought best that Princess Alice should be accompanied by somebody closer to her own age."

"You are too modest," said the Roman. "I saw how you handled that most difficult of charges, a princess royal! You are evidently able, and sensible, Miss Brodsworth. I think you will be a great help today."

He smiled at her, and she thought she would melt. But he wanted her only for her sobriety, she reminded herself. "I'll do my best, I'm sure."

Armstrong coughed. "Now, the only Greek I have is what they managed to beat into me at Harrow, Miss Brodsworth, and I think I can follow, but you'd better start earning your corn."

Imogen glanced at the party. The Foreign Secretary was waiting for her with a face like thunder. As she hastened over and slipped into her role, she seemed to become invisible to them—all save Marcus, who smiled at her again.

Marcus led the party through a part of the palace Imogen hadn't seen before. One particularly grand chamber must have been the Hall of the Ambassadors, with its famous ceiling depicting a vision of an austere Protestant heaven, painted by Michelangelo under the patronage of Henry VIII, who had built the palace in the first place. Imogen wondered how many other commoners had ever got to see it.

Marcus said, "As it happens Gavrilo received only a few visitors yesterday evening, in a small reception room at the back of the palace. Exchanging gifts and so forth. In fact he spent much of the day aboard the ship. He did receive Princess Alice during the day, but in the evening was rather unwell."

They all took this with straight faces. The rumors circulating among the interpreters was that Gavrilo, who had served on the Chinese front, had come back with an unhealthy liking for opium. He had spent the evening indulging with his companions and a few guests, including Jack Dempsey, the well-known American-born gladiator, who had put on a show of mock combat against the empire's finest.

"Of course that makes our task easier," Marcus went on. "Since only a small number of people had access to the prince, we have a small number of suspects to consider." Imogen, attuned by now to diplomatic niceties, chose to translate "suspects" as "personages." Armstrong caught her eye and gave her an approving nod.

They came at last to the reception room where Gavrilo had, from eleven in the evening onwards, grudgingly greeted his handful of visitors. More Romans took their pictures, the flashes dazzling, and British soldiers and police stood by uncomfortably among the legionaries.

Imogen was shocked by the state of the room. The portraits on the walls were scorched and blistered, the heavy wallpaper blackened; the molded plaster of the ceiling was cracked and scorched, and at the very center of the room a thick pile carpet was as black as if it had been used as a hearth. Many of the fittings had been soaked, by the water that must have been used to put out the fire that had blazed here. Over that scorched patch of carpet a chair had evidently been blown to bits; Imogen recognized fragments, an arm, a seat cushion, a carved leg. The cushion was stained with a brown pigment—blood, perhaps.

The party poked around the mess. The Foreign Secretary pressed a handkerchief to his face. There was a prevailing smell of smoke and soot, and a heavy underlying iron smell that reminded Imogen of a butcher's shop.

Marcus was at her side. "Are you all right?"

"I'm fine," she said.

"Then you're stronger than me," he murmured. "I've seen war— I've fought in the east. One never gets used to the smell of dried blood."

"This is where Gavrilo died?"

He pointed. "He sat in that chair. He was blown apart in the explosion; he probably died instantly. His body was scorched in the resulting fire. It has been taken away—returned to his ship."

"Was he alone in here?"

"Alone save for his own companions, and one of our legionaries. Their injuries were minor. They reacted well, actually; they raised the alarm, got rid of the fires."

"But what caused all this? Was it a bomb?"

"You can see it here, Miss Brodsworth," Armstrong said in his Harrovian Greek. He pointed to a metal tube on the floor. "Don't touch it—Scotland Yard, you know."

It seemed to be a primitive weapon, an iron lance, perhaps. At its tip, bound with cord, were the remains of a rolled-up tube of paper, perhaps two feet long. The paper tube was blackened, blown apart, like a failed firework. And scattered around the lance were bits of joinery, the remnants of a smashed wooden box.

"Ironically," Marcus said, "the force of the explosion preserved the remnants of the fire-lance itself, even the paper tube; the fire was blown toward the walls. But poor Gavrilo was not spared, of course."

Imogen inspected the weapon. "A 'fire-lance?'"

"A very early gunpowder weapon," Armstrong said. "Actually of Roman design. In battle you would carry a small iron box of glowing tinder, to light the tube. Flames would shoot out, perhaps covering ten, twelve, fifteen feet."

"It's a flamethrower, then."

Marcus said, "This particular specimen was captured during our war with the Seljuk Turks, over eight hundred years ago. It was a gift, presented in a display case—you can see the remnants of the case, reduced to matchwood. It appears Gavrilo was pleased with the gift, and was cradling it, box and all, when it detonated."

"But how could it have exploded?"

"Well, it was rigged," said Marcus. "Aside from the gunpowder in the lance itself, there was a simple fuse, and a trigger mechanism like a flintlock attached to a clockwork timer, all concealed in the body of the wooden box." He pointed, and she could just make out an intricate mechanism amid the wreckage.

She nodded. "So that's how he died. But who's responsible? Who gave him this gift?"

"Ah," Armstrong said. "That's where it gets tricky... It was a gift from Vizier Osman Pasa." Who was, Imogen knew, a senior official of the Ottoman government. "So this appears to be the murder of a Roman prince, by an Ottoman assassin, carried out right here on British soil." He shook his head. "Shocking business."

Imogen frowned. "The Ottomans I've met haven't been fools, major. Would Vizier Pasa really implicate himself so obviously? And do the Ottomans actually want conflict with the Romans right now? I've read that on the contrary—"

Armstrong snorted. "I doubt very much that whatever racy stuff you read in the penny papers has much relation to a complicated diplomatic reality, Miss Brodsworth."

Offended, she withdrew. "Yes, major."

But Marcus would have none of it. "No, no. You have a good point, Miss Brodsworth. We must not jump to conclusions. Gavrilo was a scion of an imperial house two thousand years old, and here we are at the meeting point of empires. It's hardly likely that anything about his death would be simple, is it? What would *you* suggest we do, Miss Brodsworth?"

Armstrong was starting to get agitated. He stubbed out his latest cigarette and protested, "Now look here, prefect, Miss Brodsworth is an able translator, but a mere slip of a girl who..."

Marcus wasn't listening. He kept his eyes on Imogen while the major ran down.

Imogen smiled at Marcus, flattered. "Well, you need to find out who had access to the prince. One of them was the murderer—or more than one—that seems clear. When you know who the suspects are, you can begin to eliminate them, one by one."

"Eminent common sense," said Marcus. "But I disagree on one point."

"Yes?"

"You said 'you.' You meant 'we.' I want you to work with me on this, Miss Brodsworth."

Armstrong seemed outraged. "Oh, now look here, this is all—"

"Just for a period of grace. The police can continue their work in parallel. Miss Brodsworth is surely right, major. We need to establish the truth of this incident before we start murdering each other's populations over it. And fresh eyes, untainted by diplomatic calculation, British eyes at that, might help a great deal. We do need an interpreter, too, of course." He turned back to Imogen. "You spoke of who had access to Gavrilo. That at least is easy to establish." He glanced at the photographers. "A thorough lot, we Romans. We keep a record of everything..."

It wasn't yet nine o'clock. As the relevant photographs were assembled, hastily developed overnight, Imogen took the opportunity to have a breakfast of pastries and Brazilian coffee.

Aside from the prince's companions and guards, only four men had been admitted to the reception room last night, while Gavrilo held his bleary court. "The prince was in such a delicate temper," Marcus said carefully, "that it was decided to restrict the interview to representatives of the three great powers, other than the Romans: the British, the French, and the Ottomans."

So the Americans, the Spanish, and the German and Italian princelings had all been left kicking their heels. "That must have pleased the others."

"But at least they are not under suspicion. Well, the photographs match the testimonies," Marcus said.

Imogen stared at the grainy plates. There was a fresh chemical smell about them. She studied the Romans first: legionaries in traditional costumes, though armed with automatic weapons, a handful of the prince's companions in stylish American-fashion modern dress, and senators and other ministers in togas. Gavrilo had himself worn a toga, and a wreath of laurels on his head.

"I know none of these people," Imogen said.

"I think we can rule them out as suspects," Marcus said rather grimly. "They're all now in the hands of the Praetorian Guard." This traditional bodyguard of the Caesars had evolved into a secret police. "After several hours I think we can be sure they've nothing to reveal. Why, the very threat of being handed over to the Praetorians is enough to keep any Roman in line, believe me." If he harbored any fear of what might be done to *him* as punishment for his failure to protect Gavrilo, he showed no sign of it.

Imogen studied the photographs of the visitors. Here was Vizier Osman Pasa carrying the fateful wooden case containing the fire-lance, and Prince Philippe, second son of the French king come to greet the second son of Caesar, and the Foreign Secretary representing the British government—and Lloyd George had Armstrong at his side. Even as he had been admitted to the Roman's presence, Imogen saw, Armstrong was smoking his customary cigarette.

"I'm surprised you were there, major," Imogen said.

"I do have a responsibility for security," Armstrong said. "In this case it was actually the Foreign Secretary's welfare I was concerned with, for you'll notice we had no British soldiers in the chamber at that time."

Marcus studied another photograph, which showed the visitors submitting to searches by helmet-clad legionaries. "You're still smoking. They left you your cigarette! Few Romans smoke, you know."

"Well, I know that. In fact I only lit up to annoy the Frenchies, if you must know." His schoolboy Greek was studded with English: "Frenchies."

This was a rivalry that dated back to Napoleonic times, when the French emperor, confronting the Romans in Europe and locked in war with the British, had refused to sell the Louisiana Territory to the new United States. A century later, as if in spite, the French refused any imports of tobacco products from the former English colonies, and very few Europeans smoked.

"Well." Marcus lined up four photographs: of the Foreign Secretary, the major, the vizier, and the French prince. "Our suspects."

"I do find it hard to suspect the Foreign Secretary," Imogen admitted.

Marcus referred to a sheaf of documents. "I have testimony from the prince's companions and the legionaries. It was after all these men left the prince's presence that the explosion went off. It was indeed the fire-lance that killed Gavrilo, and all the witnesses confirm that it was the vizier who brought it in personally."

The major sat back, hands behind his head. "It all seems clear enough to me."

Marcus ignored him. "What now, Miss Brodsworth?"

"We should interview our suspects. I would start with the man who brought in the fire-lance in the first place."

Marcus summoned a runner. Then he set about finding an office suitable for interviews.

Armstrong raised his eyebrows, but did not object.

It took forty minutes for Osman Pasa to be brought to the palace from his suite at the Savoy.

Pasa's title was vizier, but Imogen understood this was something of a formality; power under the Ottoman sultan Mehmed V lay with parliament, and the vizier had little influence outside the court. Pasa was an elegant man, perhaps fifty, his dark complexion set off by the sharp, silver-gray suit he wore. He spoke fluent Latin, the nearest thing to a common international language, and Imogen translated for the major.

"The fire-lance was of course a Roman artifact," Pasa said languidly. "Captured during the Seljuk war of 1071, as the Christian calendar has it. It has languished on palace walls or in museums ever since. This seemed an appropriate occasion to hand it back. After all, that conflict, so little known to western historians, was a turning point in the fortunes of the Romans..."

The East Roman empire, with its capital at Constantinople, had survived the collapse of its western counterpart. But the explosive advance of Islam in the Seventh Century had seen it lose Syria, Palestine, Mesopotamia, and Egypt to the Arabs. And in the new millennium the Seljuk Turks assaulted Asia Minor, the very heart of the empire.

"I've always been convinced that if not for the fire-lances, Asia Minor would have been lost," the vizier said. "And the decline of the empire would have been assured. But the fire-lances, just like this one, and other gadgets like crude bombs, turned the tide. The Seljuk armies had nothing like it, and were driven back.

"It's said that gunpowder was brought to Constantinople by a single man, a Chinese dissident who fled the Sung emperors and came wandering down the Silk Road. And he carried a new idea out of China, as many ideas had traveled to the west before—silk, paper... In China, as you may know, gunpowder was an accidental discovery of Taoist chemists who sought an elixir of life." Pasa grunted. "What they discovered was a recipe for death. Of course the East Romans had always used Greek fire against the Islamic armies; they knew how to develop super-weapons, and how to keep them secret. As a result they had a monopoly on gunpowder weapons in Europe for two hundred years. Remarkable, isn't it, the difference one man can make?"

Imogen pressed the vizier, "But as to the fire-lance itself—you did not hand over a live weapon to the prince, did you?"

"Of course not." He glanced at Marcus, quite relaxed. "There should have been no gunpowder in it at all—only black pepper—certainly not such a potent modern mix. To place such a weapon in the hands of a young man so liable to, ahem, confusion? It would have been asking for trouble."

Imogen said, "And did the lance leave your possession at any time before you handed it over to the prince?"

"Yes." Both Roman and British soldiers, and British police, had checked over the weapon and its box. He glanced meaningfully at Armstrong.

"I oversaw some of this myself," the major said. "We were looking for poison—doped needles, that sort of thing; we thought *that* was the most likely way one might get at the prince. We missed the gunpowder, I admit."

"A bit of an oversight," Marcus said in English, mocking the major's tone.

Armstrong eyed him stonily. "We're not as experienced with assassinations and palace coups as you are in your ancient empire, prefect."

"Really?" Osman Pasa asked, glaring at Armstrong. "I wonder if these questions of yours are directed at the right party, prefect."

Armstrong just laughed at him.

They asked further questions of the Ottoman diplomat, but learned nothing new.

Prince Philippe was fat, fifty, his face red and puffy, his hair elaborately coiffed. He smelled of perfume, pomade, and Roman vodka.

As he tried to squeeze his ample frame into a hard, upright English chair, Armstrong murmured to Imogen, "Always the same, the Frenchies. Every diplomatic occasion they send over a prince of the blood—if not Fat Phil here, one of his equally unappealing brothers. They know these Orleanist princes get up the noses of our Bourbon royal family."

Philippe's own gift to Gavrilo had been a remarkable jeweled cane, still in the possession of the Romans, beautiful and quite harmless. What Philippe chose to talk about, however, was the gift Gavrilo had handed to him. It was a bit of cloth mounted in a glass case, very old, coarsely woven. It bore a red cross, faded with time, and was stained with rust-brown splashes.

"It is a relic of my own ancestor," Philippe said, speaking defiant French. "George of Boulogne took the cross of Christ in 1203; this was stitched to his tunic when he died before the walls of Constantinople..."

The East Romans had always had a prickly relationship with the crusades. These great military missions, aimed at recovering the Holy Land from the Muslims, were seen from Constantinople as grabs for power by the popes in Rome, who hoped to rule the squabbling statelets of Western Christendom. At last resentment had boiled over, and Western Christians assaulted the capital of the East Christian power. But by now the East Romans had advanced weapons, bombs and mines, cannon, rockets, even handguns, at a time when gunpowder was still entirely unknown west of Constantinople. The crusaders were scattered; the city was saved.

"The cross was ripped from the chest of my fallen ancestor, and stored in some vault in Constantinople for eight hundred years. And now here it is," Philippe said. "Hurled back in my face!"

Imogen frowned. "Perhaps the Romans meant to honor you, and the memory of George."

Philippe said dismissively, "Perhaps there is honor in defeat for you British; not for us. Remember we have kept the Romans at bay for centuries, while you sit behind *la Manche* building ships..."

Even before the East Romans had acquired their fire-lances, Orthodox Christendom had spread far from Constantinople, with the conversion of Bulgaria, Georgia, Russia, Serbia. When in the Thirteenth Century the Mongols had erupted from central Asia to assault Georgia and Russia, the East Romans struck back, using their firearms to drive off the ferocious nomads: the Battle of Kiev in 1240 was remembered as the day the Mongols were repelled and a dream reborn. After this smashing victory a new geographically contiguous empire was born, absorbing the Orthodox countries, sweeping from the Balkans to the Baltic.

By now the secret of gunpowder was out; the Mongols acquired it from the Chinese, and through them the technology was adopted by Islam and Western Christendom. But the East Romans were the first to reorganize their society as a gunpowder empire, with an expansion of mining and manufacture, government control of resources, the raising of vast armies, and a centralizing of the state. To do this they reached back consciously to the forms of the old Roman Empire. By 1300 the Caesars once more wore the imperial purple, and legions armed with muskets and field artillery marched in the field.

The empire expanded cautiously, east across Asia, south into Mesopotamia and Persia, and west into Europe. By 1500 Europe had been partitioned between Roman and French spheres, with a hinterland of petty German and Italian statelets between the two— ironically Rome itself was an independent city-state, governed by the Pope.

"We stood against them," the French prince said bitterly. "If not for France the eagle standard would fly in London as it does in Baghdad and Vladivostok—"

"I'm sure we're all jolly grateful to you Frenchies," Armstrong said dryly. 'But getting back to the matter in hand—"

Marcus said, "You regarded the gift of your ancestor's cross as an insult. Was it grievous enough to kill for?"

Philippe sneered. "I would not trouble myself to spit upon a dissolute boy like Gavrilo. The Caesar will feel France's wrath at the next round of trade negotiations..."

"His motive is flimsy," Marcus said after the prince had gone.

Armstrong said, "Flimsy unless he, or the Ottoman, or both, wanted to start a war. You heard what he said about trade negotiations. There are always factions in such courts spoiling for a fight..."

As they argued about motives, Imogen felt impatient, convinced they were on the wrong track. She begged leave to take some lunch, and left them to it.

* * *

She walked back to the Hall of Ambassadors. A butler on the palace staff brought her lunch: a sandwich and a glass of fresh milk.

Eating slowly, she peered up at Michelangelo's marvelous ceiling. She knew that historians thought it an irony that King Henry, who had enriched himself by plundering the wealth of the Church through the English Reformation, had used those funds to hire great artists like Michelangelo who could not find suitably wealthy sponsors in the impoverished city-states of Catholic Italy, trapped as they were between the flaring ambitions of the French and Roman empires. She was grateful the work had not been harmed by last night's fire.

The others kept talking of motives. Certainly you could say both Ottoman and French had a motive to murder Gavrilo, if you really believed that one of them wanted to start a war. Conceivably Philippe also had a personal motive, if he felt insulted by the crusader rag. But Philippe certainly did not have the means, as far as she could see, however strong his motive, for there was absolutely no evidence he ever came into physical contact with the fire-lance.

Perhaps Osman Pasa could have done it. But he wasn't alone in handling the murder weapon; the British and Roman authorities had both had a hold of it, and could perhaps have tampered with it. She supposed some of the Romans might have a motive to do down Caesar's son, if they despised his reign sufficiently—even if it meant their own death. What she couldn't work out was what possible motive the British could have for killing Gavrilo. After all he was here to be betrothed to a British princess. And yet the means existed.

Means, not motive, had to be the key to this murder. That was what she kept telling Marcus, and here she was forgetting it herself.

On impulse she made her way back to Gavrilo's reception room, alone. The police stationed here recognized her and allowed her in.

She looked again at the bloodstained carpet, the fire-damaged walls. Aware of the stern warnings not to disturb anything, she bent down and kneeled, peering at the weapon and the damage it had caused: the smashed chair, the remains of the lance itself, the trigger, the traces of the fuse. The timer was a mass of components, like the innards of a watch. They gleamed, finely worked. The trigger was simpler, but was just as well made. It looked remarkably *clean*, she thought. Too clean perhaps. She leaned closer yet, holding her hair back from her forehead.

And she saw something. A trace she longed to take away. She left it in place.

She sat back on her heels, thinking hard. A British peeler, standing alongside a Roman centurion, watched her cautiously.

Then she walked slowly back to the office Marcus had requisitioned.

Marcus and Armstrong were still arguing about motives.

Marcus said, "Perhaps we should suspect the Pope, then, major! After all Martin Luther nailed his Ninety-Five Theses to a church door in Wittenberg, a Roman city. Was it all a Roman plot to destabilize the Vatican? Or what of the natives of the Americas? If the Romans had not blocked off trade routes to the east, Columbus would never have sailed..."

"Now you're being absurd."

'Of course I am. But my point is... Oh! Never mind.'

As Imogen sat down, Armstrong folded his arms. "I think we've spent enough time on this. It seems perfectly obvious that the culprit is our Ottoman friend, for his was the gift that turned out to be the murder weapon. He had the motive; he had the means. I think the best thing we can do now is announce our conclusions to our superiors."

"And risk a war?" Imogen asked softly. "Without being *sure*, major?"

They both looked at her. Marcus said, "Miss Brodsworth? Do you have something?"

She considered the conclusion she had been forced to come to, hoping to find holes in it. Unfortunately it seemed to her as complete and perfect as the jeweled cane Philippe had given to Gavrilo.

"Means and motive," she said to Armstrong and Marcus. "We kept talking about motive. But the means was the key to this crime. *How* was it committed? That would tell us *who*. That was what I was thinking after my lunch. I went back to Gavrilo's reception room. I suppose I hoped I would find some bit of evidence, something clinching, that would establish the means beyond doubt, no matter what the motive. Perhaps I was being absurd..."

"Yes," said Armstrong heavily. "What did you imagine you would spot that evaded the Criminal Investigation Department?"

Marcus hushed him. "What have you found, Miss Brodsworth? Tell us plainly."

She took a breath, avoiding Armstrong's eye. "A shred of tobacco."

"What?"

Armstrong said with a dangerous calm, "This sounds like nonsense to me, Miss Brodsworth, and dangerous nonsense at that." He made to stand up, pushing back his chair. "I think it's time you were removed from this comical investigating—"

"Sit down," said Marcus. And for the first time Imogen thought she could hear the authority of the Caesars in his voice.

Armstrong complied.

Marcus asked, "A shred of tobacco?"

"There was something odd about that trigger mechanism," she said. "I don't pretend to understand the clockwork of the timer. But the trigger itself was such a simple thing. And perhaps it's because it is so simple, there is something about it nobody seems to have noticed."

"Yes?"

"*It was never fired.* Even though the bomb detonated, the trigger never fired. You can see it quite clearly from the cleanness of the hammer. And so, I wondered, what was it that could have lit the fuse?"

"Ah. And when you looked closer—"

"I found a shred of tobacco, stuck in the trigger mechanism of the bomb. I left it in place for the detectives to find—I'll show you later, prefect."

"Well, well." Marcus turned to the major.

For long seconds Armstrong stared at them stonily. Then he relaxed, subtly. "Miss Brodsworth, I now rather regret getting you out of your bed this morning."

Marcus faced him. "You were the only smoker, major. The legionaries would have removed any weapon from you—even your matches, a lighter. But you walked into the presence of Gavrilo with a lit cigarette in your mouth."

Armstrong shrugged. "I suppose you may as well know the rest. It was simple enough to rig the fire-lance and the box; we worked on it through the night after purloining it from the Ottoman's room on his first arrival at the palace.

"I always had it in the back of my mind that I might need a back-up, though. And I was quite right. Bloody cheap bit of American clockwork—I could *hear* the timer fail even while I stood beside the prince, smelling his wine-sodden breath. I knew the lance wasn't going to go off of its own accord. So, just as I was leaving..." He mimed reaching down with a lit cigarette, to light the fuse.

"As simple as that," Marcus said, marveling.

"It was always a cock-eyed sort of plot," Armstrong admitted. "But I thought we'd get away with it. I never had much faith that the earnest peelers of Scotland Yard would work out what had happened. Besides, I thought that the incident itself would soon be overwhelmed by a storm of diplomatic notes and ultimatums. The balance of power is after all precarious." He mimed a series of topplings. "And so the empires would fall into war, one after the other."

Imogen shook her head. "But why would you want that?"

"National interest," he said simply. "The guiding light of all British policy, Miss Brodsworth. The Ottomans and French have a pact, you see, of mutual protection against the Romans. They both rightly fear the rather awesome arsenal of weapons the Romans have developed in their Chinese wars. If war came it would be the pair of them against the Romans, a war of two fronts, and a right mess it would be."

Marcus listened, stone-faced. "And the British?"

"We would come in on whichever side was winning. The Romans, even, if necessary, though I would expect that antique empire to implode. For what we want is not victory for one side or the other."

"What, then?"

"Oil," Armstrong said simply. "Those oceans of oil, locked up under Baghdad, and in the Caucasus—all under the sway of the Romans. Oil that will drive our industries, and our own *testudos*, and especially our ships—we are a maritime nation, and you may know we recently converted most of our ships from coal. It's oil we need, prefect, oil to fight the wars of the Twentieth Century, and it's oil we mean to take."

Imogen said, "If war comes from this, the slaughter will be immense."

"Miss Brodsworth, you will never grasp the solemn contemplation of empires."

"No," she said, "and listening to you I'm jolly glad of it."

Marcus said coldly, "By cable, the Emperor will hear of this within the hour."

Armstrong was relaxed. "Fine. Everything I've told you is for your benefit only—I've come to feel rather fond of you two idiots. Tell Caesar what you like. No evidence will be found; my boys will make sure of that. The death of Gavrilo will no doubt be put down to an accident, muddy and unresolved. And even if some link were proven between the death and myself, the British government would deny all knowledge of it. I would be seen as a rogue, a maverick acting without instruction."

Imogen stared at him. "And is that the truth? That you acted alone, that His Majesty's government knows nothing about this dreadful plot?"

He looked at her steadily. "If that's what you want to believe, then it's the truth. I'll tell you this, Miss Brodsworth. You have done your country a disservice today. A great disservice."

Marcus and Imogen walked to the embankment, breathing in air that was fresh with barely a hint of soot. The security cordon had not yet been relaxed, but it was a relief to Imogen not to be surrounded by the usual crush of Londoners.

They stared at the powerful lines of the quireme on the Thames. "I feel giddy," Imogen said. "It's been such a long day."

The Roman glanced at Big Ben. "It isn't yet three o'clock. Yet so much has happened. A shred of tobacco has unraveled a plot that might have toppled empires!"

"I can't believe we allowed him simply to walk away."

Marcus shrugged. "What else could we have done? He's right; he and his conspirators will only refute everything, having destroyed the evidence. Let him go. With the British government's fervent denials, I have at least a fighting chance of convincing Caesar that the death of his son was the action of a rogue element, and not worth going to war over."

"But there are surely other men like him in Britain, and the other powers. Men who long for war, for what they imagine is their country's interests."

"Yes. And he was right, you know, that the world is a precarious place. In Europe you have four empires, counting Britain, all jealous of their interests, all armed to the teeth. If this incident does not drive us to war, it seems more than likely that *something* will trigger it all."

Imogen tried to imagine an all-out European war fought out with modern weapons, with immense guns and steel-hulled ships, and *testudos* crawling over the broken bodies of men. "That Chinaman who came wandering down the Silk Road has a lot to answer for."

He laughed. "But perhaps we would all have ended up in this situation even if he had stayed home. Fate is stronger than the will of any of us."

On impulse she grabbed his hand. "But if war is to come in the autumn, or in the winter, or the spring of next year, at least we have this summer's day. Spend it with me, Marcus Helvidius."

"Are you serious?"

"Never more."

"I have duties," he said. "I will be missed—"

"I know the city well enough. There are places they'll never find us. Come on. I've had enough of being sensible!"

Laughing, he let her pull him away. They hurried down the embankment, not quite running, until they had slipped through the cordon of British and Roman troops, and they lost themselves in the bustle of London.

The Blood of Peter Francisco

Paul Park

Paul Park's "The Last Homosexual," which appeared in the June 1996 issue of Asimov's Science Fiction, *is one of my favorite short stories for some time. I've been looking for an excuse to work with him for years, and I had a feeling he might be a good fit for an alternate history mystery anthology. The basis for my suspicions? His recent work includes the brilliant and critically acclaimed alternate-history quartet,* A Princess of Roumania, The Tourmaline, The White Tyger, *and* The Hidden World.

That winter, near midnight on the second of February, I stood in the rain outside the old Regent's Theatre, hands in my pockets, cap pulled over my face. This was hardly twenty-four hours after the murder. Seventh Avenue was full of constables in their wet oilskins, or in the shelter of the porch. As usual, I was invisible to them. They were looking at the ladies and gentlemen in their high hats and fur collars, while I stood with the others on the curb, against the line of carriages and motor-cars on Fifty-seventh Street.

The doors opened and the crowd spilled out. Disgusted, I listened to their talk, their clipped, happy voices as they praised the soloists. A beautiful young woman had been shot twice in the face during the previous performance, but they didn't care. The rich have no memory, so they can live without fear. I turned my back to them and to the ugly pile of bricks that is their temple. I followed the surge of umbrellas across the avenue but then continued west, hands in my pockets, whistling a little song. It was from the movement, from our friends in Russia and Germany. No one would recognize it here.

I had gone to the theater to see if I could learn something from the cabbies in the street. This night at least, I shared a mission with the cops I'd left behind me on the corner. The chief of police had made a public promise to track down Madame Rothschild's killer. He spoke of the city's reputation and its shame. But I was more ashamed than anyone because of my involvement. Our society does not carry the people's fight against women, even the wives of parasitic Jewish financiers.

This was a claim I had made twice that day in secret meetings. And I made it without any kind of heat or sympathy, because I myself am a rabbi's son. We are soldiers, not monsters, and the difference must be clear in everything we do. Because the newspapers serve the interests of the warmongers and capitalists, they will twist and disfigure everything. So I had to find the murderer before the police found him. I had to break any link between him and us. Already there was a story in the *Daily Mail*, and the governor-general had made a statement. He was no fool. He knew how close he'd come to death. It was just like him to crouch behind a woman.

I went west beyond Eighth Avenue, where the cobblestones gave out to unpaved streets. Close to the railway tracks (I won't give you the address!) I turned in under the archway and climbed the worn stairs to my rooms. Yes, I had made my argument to the platoon leader without any kind of anger, but to tell the truth I was shivering with rage as I made my ascent (I will not tell you how far!), and hardly noticed my freezing clothes or saturated cap. How could the man have made such a mistake? How could he have turned such an opportunity into another measly debacle? For three months I had been thinking about this, ever since the dauphin had announced his travel plans.

There in the box above the stage, the fellow had a French prince, an English general, a Jewish industrialist, and Sir Rudolph Hicks himself, all at the end of his revolver, as well as several other officers. Instead he had shot the most beautiful woman in Europe in the face, and stood over her and shot her again. Then he had leapt over the rail and down into the dark hall. He had run across the stage roaring, "*Sic semper tyrannis,*"—absurdly, as if Brutus had killed Portia or Calpurnia! And you couldn't even say he'd lost his nerve. He'd overcome a dozen men on his way out to the street, broken down the doors they tried to shut against him, smashed a lot of noses, all for nothing. He had clean escaped.

Now he'd disappeared. For all my bold talk, I didn't know where to find him. Out of breath, I paused on the landing, listening at the door. Then I unlocked it as quietly as I could, not wanting to disturb my sister. But as usual she'd waited up for me and fallen asleep at the card-table, her cheek against the back of her hand. At the sound of my key she raised her head, then sat up straight against the brown wallpaper. The chimney lamp was on the table, and in its light I watched her turn her face to me, her hair dishevelled, her cheeks wan and colourless. But even so I thought she was a match for the famous Katarina Rothschild, as I had seen her in the photographs. I thought there was a resemblance. At twenty-six, my sister had the same pale skin, dark eyes, dark brow, dark hair. I even imagined the same beseeching look as I burst on her unaware in a small space. She was always frightened when I came home late. I'd told her I was working in a restaurant.

The lenses of my spectacles were streaked with rain. It wasn't warm enough in the kitchen to fog them up. Even so, I took them off and polished them, while at the same time I thought about the bullet that would kill her one day. Maybe it would be news of my arrest.

"Ah," she said, "I algo tengo a desirte. Mira—I was so worried. Where have you been? Look at you—you're soaked through." Then she continued in the language of the old country, the Ladino language we had spoken in Cuba and Mexico when we were children. She got up to take my coat and cap. She hung them up over the mat, and lit the kettle for a cup of tea. Overcome with some kind of emotion, I allowed her to fuss over me, while at the same time I watched her face. What had I seen when I opened the door?

Maybe in that moment I understood my pity for the murdered woman in the governor's box, a pity that had nagged at me all day, and not because she deserved it! She was nothing to me, a whore and worse, a Jewish whore, a "confidante" (as she had been described in the society papers) of the late King Edward, the biggest and the fattest whoremaster on either side of the Atlantic Ocean. Rothschild hadn't been too proud to pick through his leavings.

"There's no milk, but I'll get you sugar," Marta said. Shivering, I sat down at the table. I could hardly listen, because there was some other section of the puzzle. The pity I felt was part of it—the dead woman was also someone's sister, maybe. And so I wondered if the assassin had known her, recognized her suddenly in the dark box. Maybe he'd seen something in her eyes, her beautiful dark eyes under her dark brows—I was looking at my sister as she fussed and tried to smile. But when I first opened the door, startled her out of sleep, I had seen a frightened flash of something in her face. The lamp, after all, was by her hand. She would not have been able to see me clearly as I stood beside the stove.

Who else could I have been? Who else was she expecting? The situation was different. Madame Rothschild would have turned to see a man in evening clothes slip into the box. There was nothing unusual about that. There'd been no struggle at the door. Fooled by his self-confidence, the soldier in the vestibule hadn't even challenged him.

"Please tell me where you've been," my sister asked me. "Es el uniko favor ke rekalmo de ti. I get so lonely in the nights. So worried, so frightened. Please."

I didn't explain. I was too tired to invent some made-up story. Instead I reached to touch her hand. She pulled away from me. "Ke notche fria—you're so cold," she said.

There was a connection between the assassin and his victim, I thought. Did he think he had no choice except to shoot her first, because she knew him? Or had he gulled us from the beginning, pretending to work with us, when all along he had a different plan? He was not one of us, that much was sure. It was because he was not one of us that he had managed to get so close.

Could I have swaggered up the stairs of the Regent's Theatre, a cigarette in my gloved hand? Not with my big nose and steel-rimmed spectacles, my foreign face and foreign voice. I was a stranger everywhere but here in this kitchen, these two rooms, and even here I could not be myself. Marta poured me out another cup of tea. I muttered a few things while my mind was somewhere else. I asked her how her shift was at the Triangle factory. She shook her head and shrugged her shoulders, and I thought that everything I did was for her sake, so she wouldn't have to work so hard and joylessly, sewing shirt-waist dresses for pennies apiece. Maybe she'd get married to a man who'd treat her well, a simple man who would confide in her as I could not. I could not tell her anything. When the day came and the police asked her what she knew, ignorance would save her.

She turned to look at me. What was the connection between Madame Rothschild and her killer? Maybe the police had already discovered it. Maybe they were already on the way to follow up some clue. What was obvious to me might just be obvious to them. But I still had an advantage.

"Anton," said my sister. (There, I've told you!) "Te rogo ke me eskutches. I went by the address you gave me, the Café Salonika. They said they never heard from you, it has been months. What should I think? Then I came home—look what I found."

She stood in her slippers on the cold floor. She reached down into one of the pockets of her flannel robe, and brought out the snub-nosed Colt. "My God, Marta," I said. "It's loaded." She held it up like a snake or a spider. She couldn't even look at it. It hung from her fingers and I thought she'd drop it. But she laid it on the table by my teacup and I put my hand on it. She was in tears.

"Oh, Anton, ke es esto?" I couldn't tell her. Relieved, I felt like hitting her. She had something else that she had stolen from my things. Now she drew it out of the same pocket, a gold chain with a round locket and a gold crucifix about an inch and a half long. Catholic women wear them. You've seen them.

Marta had opened the locket to show the tiny portrait inside, an old woman in a hat. Again she let it dangle from her finger. But she dropped it into my palm when I held it out.

"Anton, mi hermano, what's become of you?" she said.

"You are a stranger now," she said, and she held out her hand. But what would be better, a stranger or a thief? I couldn't tell her anything. I took the gun, the little chain.

"Va te, va te. Ya me etcho in la kama," she said, waving her fingers. So I got to my feet. I put on my wet coat again and went out into the cold, promising myself I'd find Katarina Rothschild's killer and shoot him down.

I was so angry, I thought it would be easy to kill a man. This was when I was still young to the movement, too impressionable, too green, my beard still soft, as my people say. I had not yet shot that gun or any gun. That winter I was nineteen years old. I did not know how to control myself. When I came out into the street, I was close to tears. The rain had turned to snow when I was inside. Clean flakes drifted down out of the dark as I walked past the abandoned lots. I was glad the rain had stopped. It seemed like some luck. I told myself that maybe I could be successful. Maybe I'd be able to track down Mr. Spotswood, Mr. Dandridge Spotswood, Esquire, of Petersburg, Virginia.

This was my advantage over the police. I knew the man. I'd first met him at a hotel bar in Chelsea Gardens. (Never mind which one!) But it was a small, smoky room, made smokier by his incessant cigarettes.

I don't drink alcohol. He spoke about it like a connoisseur, about a brand of Scottish whiskey he couldn't find since the start of the European war. These subjects made me angry, his bourgeois grumbling. He was reduced to drinking some other kind of whiskey from Kentucky, something named for the French monarchy. He complained about it after every shot. He said there was water in it, and he was probably right, because it had no effect on him that I could see. He was very tall, clean-shaven, with massive hands. He wore his hair in long black ringlets, an old-fashioned style. His dark wrists contrasted with his white cuffs.

I found reasons to distrust him. I was suspicious from the beginning. He boasted he was the grandson of Colonel Robert Spotswood, hero of the second rebellion, which he called "the cause." And I was sure he told the truth, because Spotswood also had been a gigantic man, almost seven feet tall. He had fought with Wellington in Texas after General Bonaparte surrendered at New Orleans. Later, he had fought for the Virginia militia against the redcoats. He'd won a name for cruelty, burning the loyalists out of the Shenandoah Valley. He'd been with Lee when he surrendered to Lord Cardigan at Appomattox courthouse. I had to listen to all that.

You couldn't have guessed the truth from anything Dandridge Spotswood said, that the second rebellion had ended with a terrible defeat just like the first.

These southerners, I thought, could not be anything but partners of convenience, no matter how much we hated the same enemy. These Virginians had not fought their war for freedom but for slavery, after it had been outlawed by an act of Parliament. And for fifty years since Appomattox, the grievance of these people never went away. I could see it in Spotswood's high-handed contempt, the way he treated the Negro waiter at the bar. "The hypocrite," I thought. "His own skin is just as dark."

Then I thought that was the point. In his arrogance there was some self-hatred. Robert Spotswood had been the grandson of an even greater hero, a man whose strength was famous in the Continental Army. He could carry a twelve-hundred pound cannon over his shoulder. By himself he had cut down a company of Tarleton's Horse. General Washington had given him a sabre with a five-foot blade. And he had died at Yorktown with the others, when Lafayette and Rochambeau turned tail.

At the bar I asked Spotswood about him. "Peter Francisco," he said. It was like something from a children's story, a child brought to Jamestown by a Spanish ship, dropped on the pier without a letter or a note or any kind of explanation. He was dressed in silk and leather, with silver buckles on his shoes—a five-year-old boy, and all he knew was his own name. "People said he was from Portugal."

My people also were from Portugal. "But didn't he have African blood?" I almost said. What would have been the point? Peter Francisco had married into a rich family, after all. Dandridge Spotswood could boast of his black ancestor, but no one thought of him as black, because he was a gentleman. He disgusted me—there was a bar-maid who had caught his eye. She had soft yellow hair and a face covered in freckles. "What would you do with that?" he asked me, smiling. "Tell me what you'd like to do with that."

I couldn't tell him anything. Later, we found a quiet table. He looked around the room, hardly listening as I spoke. The desperation of our plan did not impress him. He didn't seem to understand or care he might be caught or killed. I thought this was bravado or stupidity. There were several things about him I misjudged.

I met him twice before the night of the attack. Now, walking toward Seventh Avenue in the fresh snow, I tried to remember the details. I tried to think of some things I'd missed. I'd arrived the previous evening at eight o'clock. I had waited with the others in the cold. I had not seen Spotswood at our rendez-vous that afternoon. Nor had he entered with the crowd, so for an hour I wondered if he'd come at all. I thought it was just like him to desert us. I thought I'd never trusted him. I remembered the blonde-haired waitress and thought it was disgusting how a black man could talk about her in that way. I walked back and forth knocking my fists together. Then I heard the shots, heard the screams, and went to take up my position at the doors. And when I saw him from the portico, bare-headed, pointing with his gun, towering above the men who tried to drag him down, kicking them aside like dogs, I saw in him the savage strength of Robert Spotswood or Peter Francisco—this was before I understood what he had done. I ran to the big doors as he came through, and he pushed me over as we'd planned. He pressed the snub-nosed Colt into my chest and I grabbed hold of it, hiding it under my coat as I floundered on the sidewalk. When I got to my feet, he was already gone, disappeared into the dark night, and I took to my heels soon afterward.

This was the gun I still had in my pocket, the weapon that had killed Madame Rothschild. She had been murdered by a "Levantine assailant," as an out-of-town newspaper had described him. Mistakes like that were all to the good. Maybe I had a head start, but I didn't know where to go. I had always met Spotswood in public places. And he had already disappeared from his rooming house, where I'd tried to visit him the previous day.

Now someone came up to me as I stood in the dark street by the dark theater. "Hey," he muttered, "comrade." I realized I was whistling the same tune as before, a Russian song called "Winter Sun."

Snow swirled around us. Fifty-seventh Street was deserted, though there was traffic on the avenue. "I saw you last night," he said. "When the lady was shot. The Jewess, there."

I didn't say anything. "Hey, come on," said the man. "I saw you tonight, too. I thought you'd be back again, so I waited."

He was maybe sixty, with a nose like an electric bulb, gray hair, leather cap. He wore woolen gloves, and a woolen vest under his coat. He had a horse-whip in his hand. His hansom was across the street. "I saw the other fellow, too—I followed him. Six blocks from here. Tall fellow. Regular toff—gave him a ride. Looked like an Italian or a Greek."

He himself was Irish like most of his trade, most of the West Side. I turned to face him. "What do you mean?"

"Last night. Almost he pulled Dido down. Stopped her. Hand on the traces—never saw the like. Then he was in before I could say anything."

"Where did you take him?"

He squinted. "Oh, sir, I think you know."

I weighed this. He could be some kind of stool-pigeon, it was true. But they're not usually so devious. So I told him the address of the rooming house. (But I won't tell you!)

I was going to walk there anyway, not for a good reason. It was the only address I had. Spotswood had been staying there when he approached us. And the previous afternoon, when I hadn't found him at the bar, I'd gone to look for him.

The woman was already cleaning the place out. She wanted to know where to find him, because he'd left without paying to the end of the week. I didn't know anything about that, but I pretended I knew him so she'd let me into the room. He'd taken everything, so I guessed it wasn't a trap.

The place stank of cigarettes, and there were empty bottles on the carpet. But I didn't think there'd been a struggle, even though one of the chairs had lost its leg. The pillows were on the floor. As I stood next to the bed, I felt something under my boot. The landlady was complaining about some filth in the basin, and when she turned away I bent down to pick up the little golden chain with the locket and the cross at the end of it. "He owes me money, too," I said. There was nothing else under the bed, except for balls of dust.

"Airs and graces," she said. "Look at this pig-sty."

I couldn't help her. I was concerned for our success. If I had only known!

Now I mentioned the same address, and the cabbie squinted. "Close," he said. "West of there." Then he shrugged. "I'll take you."

"I can't afford it," I said.

He scuffed his feet in the snow, a quarter-inch deep. "Well, aren't you just like all the others? The other fellow, now, he paid triple fare."

"Then you won't mind taking me."

That made him angry. "Well, I reckon you're a Jew as well. And here's me wanting to help you. You know, fight the bloody bastards when you can. But it's nothing to me."

Past one o'clock, the air was getting colder. There was traffic on the avenue. Sometimes people stumbled past us down the street, mufflers around their mouths. The cabbie touched his cap. "Take you home, sir?" he said to one of them.

It was obvious, I thought. Spotswood had meant to trick us all along. That's why I didn't know where to find him now. Only... why had he approached us in the first place? What did he need from us? Surely there was someplace else to find a gun?

But maybe you can't tell yourself you're going to shoot a woman in cold blood. Even a murderer needs a cause to fight for. "Comrade," I said, "I don't have any money. But you know something that could help us."

"Oh, so it's 'comrade' now, is it? I reckon I know something, too. What about that pistol, do you think?"

So the fellow had seen everything. "Don't think I'm afraid of you," he said. "Anarchist—bloody hell!"

"You win," I said. Then I followed him across the street to where his cab was by the post. I got into the compartment while he climbed up behind. "Your kind always has a few bits," he said. He made a clicking noise with his tongue, touched up the horse—Dido, I supposed—and wheeled out onto Seventh Avenue. We headed down-town, then west toward the river. On the green banquette, I unfastened the chain from the locket and the cross. "Anarchist," I thought. "Bloody hell."

He pulled up after ten minutes. "It's Number 429," he said as I stepped down. "I left him at the corner, like he asked. Then I watched where he went in. What's this?"

He was angry. But I had a gun, and the chain was something he could pawn, at least. He threw it up in the air, caught it in his gloved palm, then turned his back on me without a word. The hansom wheeled away, and I found myself in a dirty neighborhood of brick-front houses, each divided into ten or twelve bed-sitting rooms, with a pump and a water-closet in the yard. We weren't far from the rooming house or the hotel in Chelsea Gardens.

I stood for a long while on the stoop of Number 429. There were names on the mail-boxes inside the door. The snow had dwindled down and stopped. The night was cold. The sky was clear, and there were stars.

I was half-frozen by the time I saw the blonde-haired waitress. I had crossed the street to Number 442 during the night, and that's where she came out. At first dawn she stood on the steps behind me, fixing her hat and scarf. Startled, I walked off down the street.

But after a minute I turned back. I followed her a few blocks up the avenue and onto Twenty-third Street. She was walking east toward the hotel. We passed a line of new conscription posters for the war.

Spotswood must have seen the cabbie waiting when he stepped down. He must have gone in the wrong door. "Miss," I said, "miss," and she turned around. She was tall for a woman, taller than me. Shivering, half-frozen, I pulled out the little locket and the cross, and I watched her face light up. "Oh, sir," she said, "thank you. Did I drop them?"

She didn't even know. She shook my hand and gave her name, Helen Mullody. She didn't ask how I had found her, found her things. She didn't ask about the gold chain. I wondered if she knew she was part of a crime—probably not. Why would the fellow tell her what he'd done?

I smiled and stammered, but inside I was cursing Spotswood and his black heart, which had come down through his ancestors. I looked into Helen Mullody's face. I wondered if I should warn her. But then I thought Dandridge Spotswood had already put his mark on her, and I could see the lines around her eyes and mouth—I let her go. I watched her getting smaller down the block. Then I turned and retraced my steps, the revolver heavy in my pocket. I moved slowly, because I was so cold.

My joints were frozen, my fingers clumsy from my long night. I had what I wanted. Could I see myself pounding on Helen Mullody's door, pistol in my hand? But why else was I there? After a few minutes I was standing at the second floor back, Number 442.

I rapped with my knuckles. I didn't make much noise. "Hey," I whispered. "Spotswood. Hey."

He opened the door, he himself, unshaven, with his collar undone and his suspenders down. I gripped the revolver in my pocket and looked up at him. Maybe he also had not been to sleep, I thought, hating him. There was something in his face I had not noticed the other times we'd met, a tiredness. Even so, he smiled. "So, it's you. The bill collector."

Maybe he thought I wasn't up to it. He stepped aside and let me enter. I kept my hand in the pocket of my coat, counting the seconds under my breath—he gestured toward himself. "You can see I wasn't expecting visitors. Let me take your things. No? I guess it's cold outside."

There was a Franklin stove. There was a tea-kettle on the hob, and the remains of breakfast on the little table. "You must excuse me," he said. "Please sit down—no?"

My spectacles had fogged, and I could hardly see. "You must think I am a terrible host," he said, mocking me. "But there's fresh water. I can toast some bread. Have you eaten? I don't think so, at this hour."

I stood with my back to the window. I was grateful for the warmth from the stove, and I could feel my anger coming back. This little room—with its singed wallpaper, its oval photographs of Mum and Pa over the mantel, its stained curtains and tablecloth, its pictures cut from magazines—was as familiar to me as my own self. Everything was dismal and discoloured and scrubbed clean—Spotswood didn't belong here. He stood with his head near the ceiling in the center of the room, and he opened his big hands. "God," he murmured. "What am I supposed to say to you?"

I told myself a man might act this way, with this kind of cheek, out of nervousness or fear. He turned away from me, busy with the kettle and the toasting fork. After a while, I took off my cap. I stood by the cushioned armchair, hand in my pocket, waiting for my opportunity.

"One lump or two?" I shook my head. I knew he was laughing at me. But that wasn't all of it. Maybe also he wanted to persuade me, or part of him did. "Her father kept a store in Dinwiddie County," he said, finally. "Her name was Kitty Wolff, Katharine Wolff."

He spoke as if this wasn't so important. At first I didn't understand him. But then I realized he was offering an explanation for what he'd done. "If you could have seen her," he said. "My God! If you could have seen her in a crowded room."

He stood in the center of the rug, a piece of bread on the end of his fork. And maybe he just wanted to say these things aloud. I didn't think he could have mentioned them to Helen Mullody. "Was it nothing?" he asked. "Was it nothing to be Mrs. Dandridge Spotswood, of Petersburg? Nothing for a Jewish grocer's daughter?"

He loomed above me, his head near the dark ceiling. Warmer now, I stared at him. He was a handsome man, I saw—sharp features, thin lips, heavy eyes. I could feel the heat from the fire, and it was easier for me to play his games. "Katarina Rothschild was from Bohemia," I said. "I read it in the magazine."

He was a black-hearted scoundrel. What were these lies he told? I had my hand in my pocket, finger cramped around the trigger of the Colt. We stood looking at each other. Seconds passed. "Now is the time," I thought.

But then he smiled at me and turned his back, fussing with the stove. "No trace of her," he said. "She stole away in the middle of the night. My son was one year old. 'Bohemian'—that's what she called herself."

"No," I persisted. "I read about it in the magazine."

For the first time I saw a flash of temper, a grimace as he turned his head. "Then I saw the photograph of her," he said. "She was stepping into a Rolls-Royce. There was a series at a hospital in France." He grimaced, smiled. "Once she told me she wanted to live in France."

It was obvious we'd read the same article. "I had to know for sure," he said.

I thought he was pleading with me. Seconds passed. I couldn't help myself. "And was it her?"

He shrugged. "She had her hand on the rail, and she turned as I came in. There were some other men—I didn't notice. You should have seen her!"

In my mind I saw my sister by the card table, a mixed expression on her face. "And...?"

He shrugged his shoulders. "She didn't say one word to me. I meant to shoot her pig of a husband. All of them, but her. I swear I didn't mean her any harm."

He held the toasting fork in one hand. He reached out toward me with the other, his palm open, his fingers spread. "Now is the time," I thought. "Exactly now."

He said, "I would have spared her if she'd made a sound. Said my name. No, anything—if I'd seen something in her face. One mark of recognition. Anything at all."

I thought he was pleading for forgiveness or else trying to fool me. "So it wasn't her," I said.

He stared at me. The smile faded from his face, and I saw his hand close to a fist. At the same time there was a noise in the street, and I knew what it was. Maybe I'd been waiting.

I fumbled with the gun, tried to pull it from my pocket. But it caught on a seam of the cloth. He didn't pay attention. With one long step he crossed the room, threw me aside so he could look out the window.

I thought the constables must be across the street at Number 429. Unsatisfied with the gold chain, the cabbie must have gone to the police.

I heard a whistle. They would cordon the entire block, I thought. They would take no chances. They'd go from house to house. They wouldn't make mistakes.

But why did I have so much faith in my enemies? Dandridge Spotswood stood at the window with his back to me, the fork in his hand. I had the gun out now, had it in my trembling hands. I had it pointed toward him when he turned to look. He smiled.

"A little young for this work," he murmured. "Comrade. Couldn't do it yourself, I wager?"

Why did I care if he thought I had betrayed him? I felt a stupid urge to tell him about the cabbie and the chain. But then I imagined the toasting fork at my throat. I imagined Spotswood choking me and breaking my arm, imagined his snarling, dark face as he leapt at me like a savage animal, and I pulled the trigger, fired.

I heard the noise of the gunshot. It filled the little room. I watched the man stagger forward, collapse to his knee, clutch at his chest, while I stepped back. I watched the window break behind him as he curled onto the rug, his white shirt black with blood.

No, but that's what I imagined in my other history, my other memory of that first winter of the war. I imagined it, but then I kept the story to myself—the world can split apart at any moment, what we've done, what we might have done. I told my friends I hadn't found him, that he left the city, which was probably half-right. But I stood with the revolver clasped in front of me and watched him raise his hands, drop his fork, then turn away from me, turn to the door, step toward it, open it, look back at me, close it behind him. I heard him on the landing, heard him climb the stair. He must have escaped over the rooftops. After half an hour I climbed the fence in the back yard and walked up-town toward home.

The Adventure of the Southsea Trunk

Jack McDevitt

Jack McDevitt is a former English teacher, naval officer, Philadelphia taxi driver, customs officer, and motivational trainer. Since adding "writer" to that string of vocations, he has won the Nebula Award, the Philip K. Dick Special Award, the Phoenix Award, and the John W. Campbell Award, and been short-listed for the Hugo, Arthur C. Clarke, Campbell, and many more Nebulas. But I first met Jack through a dinner with my friend Robert J. Sawyer, when we were seated together at the end of a long table and didn't know each other from Adam. Now I'm a friend and a fan and delighted to add him to the list of wonderful writers in this (and future!) anthologies.

Henry Cable was, if anything, true to his word. When he told people he was going to do something, they could, as the saying goes, put it in the bank. So alarm bells went off when he failed to show up for the Victorian Club luncheon, at which he'd been the featured speaker. He not only failed to show up, he didn't warn anyone. The liaison, Mrs. Agatha Brantley, was left to make apologies as best she could.

For Cable, it was unheard of.

He didn't answer his phone. And when, after the luncheon had staggered to a desultory end and a worried Mrs. Brantley went to his house, she got no answer. At that point she called us. *"Something's terribly wrong,"* she told the watch officer. There was of course nothing we could do. So she took charge. She got on the phone, located Cable's maid service, and persuaded them to come early and open up.

The place had been ransacked. And there was no sign of Cable. She called us again.

When I got there, she was visibly upset. *"The luncheon was at the Lion's Inn,"* she said in a shaky voice. *"We kept waiting for him, and waiting for him, and he never showed up. I* knew *something was wrong."*

Cable was a literature professor at the University of Edinburgh. He'd written some books and did guest columns occasionally for the *Edinburgh Evening News.* He lived in Morningside, in an upmarket mansion with broad lawns and a fountain and a long arcing driveway. A statue of a Greek goddess, or maybe just a naked female, stood in front.

The senior officer present was Jack Gifford, probably the tallest man in Edinburgh. "Can't find where they broke in, sir," he said. "He must have *let* them in."

"How about his car?"

"There's no car here."

We put out a look-out request for the car and went inside. Drawers had been torn out and cabinets opened, their contents dumped on the floor. With Agatha in tow, I climbed the stairs and looked at the bedrooms. The beds were made. Whatever had happened had apparently occurred the previous day.

The living room was spacious, with a high ceiling. Packed bookshelves lined the walls, but a lot of the books had been pulled out and thrown on the floor.

A long leather sofa and matching armchairs were arranged around a coffee table. The table had been pushed onto its side and its two drawers removed.

There was no sign of Professor Cable. But the good news was there was no blood anywhere. Gifford poked his head out of a side room and motioned me over. The room must have served as Cable's office. There was a desk and a side table, piled high with books and magazines and note cards. A second table held a keyboard and a display screen.

"But no computer," I said.

Harry nodded. "My thought exactly, Inspector."

"It's not possible." Mrs. Brantley looked helplessly around at the floor, littered with the contents of desks and drawers. "Things like this just don't happen."

Unfortunately they do.

We checked his calls. There'd been three early the previous evening: one to Levinson Books in Old Town; one to Madeleine Harper; and one to Christopher McBride. "Madeleine is an old friend," said Agatha. "He was her mentor." And McBride, as the whole world knows, was the creator of Sherlock Holmes.

We found Ms. Harper at her home in a Bruntsfield town house. She was an attractive woman, about forty, with blonde hair, moody blue eyes, and a worried smile. "I do hope nothing's happened to him," she said.

"As do I." I would have liked to be reassuring, but the circumstances didn't look promising.

Her living room could have been right out of Cable's place, but on a smaller scale. Two bookcases were filled to overflowing. Books and magazines were on every flat surface. She had to move a few to make room for us to sit. "Tell me what you can about him," I said.

"Henry's a good man." Her voice trembled. "He spent thirty years at the university. He's published half-a-dozen major biographies. He's—" Her voice broke and she fought back tears. "Inspector, please do what you can for him. If anything's happened to him—"

"I understand. Is he still teaching?"

"He retired three years ago." She closed her eyes for a moment. "No, I think it's more like five."

"Very good."

"Time goes by so quickly."

"I know. So now he just writes books?"

"And does speaking engagements. Lately he's been working on a biography of Robert Louis Stevenson."

That sounded rousing. I wondered briefly how many Stevenson biographies were already in existence. "Ms. Harper, do you have any idea what might have happened to him today? Have you ever known him to disappear like this before?"

"No." She shook her head and tears rolled down her cheeks. "Never. I don't believe it yet."

"Does he have any enemies?"

"There's no way he could avoid it, Inspector."

"How do you mean?"

"He's a literary critic. Sometimes he says things that upset people. But I can't believe any of them would resort to something like this."

"Did he ever write about the Holmes stories?"

"*Sherlock* Holmes?"

"Yes."

"Not that I know of."

"Very good. Ms. Harper, I'm going to ask you to provide me with a list of people who might have harbored resentment against him. Will you do that for me?"

"I can try."

"Good." Outside, a child ran by with a kite. "He called you Friday evening."

"Yes."

"May I ask what you talked about?"

"We're going to the Royal Lyceum next weekend. To see *King Lear.*"

"I see. Anything else?"

"Not really. He asked me to try to be ready when he got here. He always claims I'm slow getting out the door. It's sort of a running joke."

"And that's all you talked about?"

She started to say *yes,* but stopped. "As a matter of fact, there *was* something more. He mentioned a surprise."

"A surprise?"

"Yes. He said he had a surprise for me. Big news of some kind."

"Have you any idea what he was referring to?"

"None whatever."

"Had you been planning anything?"

"Other than *King Lear?* No."

"Did it sound as if he was talking about *good* news? Something personal between you, perhaps? If you'll forgive me."

"It's quite all right, Inspector. But no, I didn't get the impression it was about *us*. It was something else." She sat for a long moment, gazing wistfully through the window at the cluster of trees in her front garden. "He sounded, not angry..."

"But..."

"He gets on a horse sometimes. A crusade, if you understand what I mean. Henry Cable off to right the wrongs of the world."

It was as far as we got. I asked her to call me if she thought of anything further.

There was a picture of Cable on a side table. He looked amiable, with white hair and spectacles and an easy smile. He almost resembled Eliot Korman, who was playing Dr. Watson in the Holmes film that had just arrived in theatres.

I got up to leave and gave her my card. "If he contacts you, I'd be grateful if you'd inform me. And let him know we're looking for him."

"Of course."

I stopped at the front door. "One more thing: Do you know Christopher McBride?"

"Christopher McBride?" Her eyes widened. "I met him once. At a party. But that was long before Sherlock Holmes."

"Do you know of a connection between him and Professor Cable?"

"No," she said. "Why do you ask?"

"He called McBride Friday night. Just before he called *you*."

"Really?" She looked surprised. "I can't imagine he'd have been talking to Christopher McBride and then not mention it to *me*."

"Maybe it had something to do with the surprise?"

She shook her head. "Amazing," she said.

I wandered over to Levinson's Books, in Old Town. The store manager, Sandra Hopkins, was there when I walked in the door. Sandra and I went back a long way. "I wasn't here when he called, Jerry," she said, consulting the computer. "But I've got the order right here."

"Okay. What did he want?"

"*Catastrophe Well in Hand: The Collected Letters of James Payn*, edited by Gabriel Truett."

"James Payn? Who's he?"

"Victorian era novelist and editor." She looked inside. "It's just been released."

"Any idea why Cable would have been interested in it?"

"Cable was interested in anything having to do with the Victorians."

I was leaving Levinson's when a call came through: Cable was dead. A patrol vehicle had located his body in a patch of woodland off the car park at the Newbury Shopping Center outside Portobello.

I drove over. His Prius was on the edge of the car park near the trees where his body had been found. He'd been beaten and robbed. There was no wallet or watch. Nor any car keys.

A lab team was on the scene when I got there. "He's been dead between eighteen and twenty-four hours," the medic said. "Skull fractured. Multiple blows."

A path cut through the area from the car park to the street. The body lay off to one side of the path, and wouldn't have been visible to anyone walking casually through. It had been found by one of the attendants doing a cleanup. He was lying face down. The back of his skull had been caved in, and the murder weapon, a broken branch, lay beside him.

It looked as if he'd been ambushed and forced off the lot. Then they'd killed him, taken his keys, driven to his house, and robbed the place.

"Pretty cold-blooded," said one of the officers. I'd seen it before.

A book lay on the front seat. It was *A Study in Scarlet*. The lab team had already dusted the interior for fingerprints. And the book.

I picked it up and opened it. The title page had been signed:
For Henry, with best wishes,
Christopher McBride
It was dated Friday night.

They'd found two sets of prints. One was Cable's. The other, on the book, would turn out to be McBride's.

But there *was* a surprise. "There's blood in the boot, Inspector," said one of the techs.

"The victim's?"

"Still checking. There's just a trace. But it's there."

It *was* Cable's.

So he was murdered somewhere else. I was looking at *A Study in Scarlet*. At the inscription. It was easy to guess why Cable had called McBride.

I went by Agatha Brantley's house to deliver the news. She knew as soon as she saw me, and she crumpled. Tears leaked out of her eyes and she fought back her emotions as I explained what we'd found. Then she seemed to get hold of herself. I've been through this kind of thing before. It's the suspense that kills. Once you know for sure, whatever the facts are, it seems to be easier to calm down.

"He mentioned to Madeleine Harper that he had big news of some kind," I said. "Have you any idea what that might have been about?"

"No. He never said anything to me."

"Is there anyone you can think of who wanted him dead?"

"Henry? No, he didn't have an enemy in the world." That brought on a round of sobbing. When she'd got through it I asked if she wanted me to call someone.

She said no, that it was okay. "We were very close, Henry and I. But I'll be all right." She wiped her nose, began beating her fist against the arm of the chair. "He never hurt a soul." And finally, when she had gotten control of her voice: "Hoodlums. They don't deserve to live."

The creator of Sherlock Holmes lived in a quiet two-story house on a tree-lined street in Gullane. He'd been a high school English teacher before hitting the big time with his detective hero. He'd retired six years earlier, and apparently had put his time to good use by starting on *A Study in Scarlet*.

The houses were modest structures, surrounded by hedges. Swings hung from several of the trees. And a few kids were playing with a jump rope in the early dusk.

I pulled into McBride's concrete driveway and eased up behind a late model white Honda, which was parked in a carport. Lights came on, and I followed a walkway to the house. I rang the bell and, moments later, McBride opened up and peered at me through thick bifocals. I identified myself and he nodded.

"Inspector Page," he said. "I've been expecting you. I was so sorry to hear about Professor Cable." He stood aside and opened the door wider. "Please come in. Have you caught them yet?"

A fire crackled pleasantly in the living room. There were a couple of oil paintings, two young women gazing soulfully at the sky in one, and at the sea in the other. A plaque was centered between them, announcing that Cable had won the Amateur Division of the annual Edinburgh Golf Festival. As had been the case at Madeleine's and at Cable's, books and magazines were stacked everywhere. The windows were framed by dark satin drapes. He pulled them shut and showed me to a worn fabric armchair.

"No," I said. "But we will."

"Yes. I'd be surprised if you didn't, Inspector. Not that it will do Cable any good." He was tall and lean, with dark hair, a long nose, and dark laser eyes. I couldn't help thinking that he resembled his fictional detective. All he needed was a pipe and a deerstalker cap.

"One of your former students asked me to say hello," I told him.

"And who would that be?"

"Mark Hudson. He's one of us now. A detective."

"Good old Mark. Yes, he was an excellent student. I'd hoped he'd become a teacher. But he wanted something more exciting, I guess."

"He speaks very highly of you." And he had. I'd talked to him before leaving the station. Hudson had nothing but good words for Christopher McBride. "He tells me he's especially happy to see your success with Mr. Holmes."

"Well, thank you. Please pass my best wishes to him."

"He'll appreciate that." He offered me a drink. When I explained how it would not be a good idea, he said he hoped I wouldn't mind if he got one for himself.

"Mark says you're related to Arthur Conan Doyle."

"Yes." He smiled. "It's a distant relationship, but I used it in school. It was a back door I could use to get the kids interested in historical novels."

"They liked his work?"

"Oh, yes." His eyes lit up. "They loved *The White Company*. And they liked the Professor Challenger novels as well." He was looking at something I couldn't see. "There's no profession like teaching, Inspector. Introducing kids to people like Doyle and Wodehouse. Makes life worth living." He sat back. "Time to get serious, though. What can I do for you?"

"Mr. McBride, you had a phone call from Henry Cable on Friday evening."

"Yes. That's correct."

"Did you know him previously?"

"No. I'd never met him. Until Friday. He wanted me to sign a copy of *A Study in Scarlet* for him."

"I see. Isn't that a bit unusual? Do people often call you about autographs?"

"It happens more often than you might think, Inspector. Usually, I let them know where the next local signing is. And invite them to go there."

"But in this case you invited him over."

"Yes," he said. "I did. When he told me what he wanted, I explained that I was not engaged, and if he wished to come to the house, I'd be glad to do it for him." He lifted his glass—it was bourbon—from a side table, stared at it, and let his eyes slide shut. "What an ugly world we live in."

"Tell me, are you always so obliging?"

"With teachers and police officers, yes. Absolutely. Teachers give us our civilization and policemen hold it together." He smiled. "And especially with teachers who, in their spare time, write reviews that are read all over the country."

"We know you signed a book for him."

"That's correct."

"Did you by any chance sign a second book? For anyone else?"

"Why, no, Inspector. It was just the one."

So I still didn't know what the surprise for Madeleine was to be. "When did he get here, Mr. McBride?"

"About eight."

"And how long did he stay?"

"Not long. Five minutes or so." His eyes fixed on me. "When did it happen?"

"Sometime Friday evening or early Saturday morning."

"Shortly after he left here."

"Yes, sir. Did he say where he was going?"

He thought about it. "No. He just said nice things about *A Study in Scarlet*. We talked a few minutes about the rise of illiteracy in the country. Then he left." He shook his head. "Pity. He seemed like a decent man. Who'd want to kill him? Do you have any idea?"

"That's what we're trying to find out, sir. At the moment I must confess that we could probably use the assistance of your Mr. Holmes."

I could see why Mark liked the guy. He was friendly, energetic, and when we talked about his golfing accomplishments—he'd won several local tournaments—and his extraordinary success with Sherlock Holmes, he shrugged it off. "I was in the right place at the right time," he said. "I got lucky." He told me he'd been trying his entire life to sell a piece of fiction. He showed me a drawer full of rejections. "Don't ask me what happened," he said. "It's not as if I suddenly got smarter. It's just that one day lightning struck."

"Just like that?"

"Inspector, it was as big a surprise for me as for everybody else."

But still it seemed odd that he'd invite a stranger to his house on a Friday night for a signing. Why not lunch on Sunday? I called George Duffy in the morning. George was the only other published author I knew. He wrote science fiction, but otherwise he seemed rational. "Would you do it?" I asked him.

"*Invite somebody into my home? At night? To sign a book? I'd say no if it weren't Henry Cable. For Cable, I might make an exception.*"

We put together a list of persons Cable had criticized in his column over the past few months. It was pretty long. I spent the next few days talking with them. Some seemed angry. Even bitter. But nobody struck me as being a likely psychopath.

In the evenings, I took to reading *A Study in Scarlet,* which turned out to be a historical narrative about Brigham Young, as well as a murder mystery. And I read the others. *The Sign of the Four* and the stories. Ordinarily I don't read much. Don't have time, and I never cared for fiction. But I enjoyed McBride's stuff.

I was bothered, though, that he'd dragged in the historical business in the first book. And why, especially, was he writing about a detective living in the Nineteenth Century? I knew I was being picky, but it felt wrong. On the other hand, you're not supposed to argue with success.

"It was as big a surprise for me as for everybody else."

I stopped by the university and caught Madeleine between classes. "You haven't had any ideas about Cable's surprise, I suppose?"

"No," she said. "Sorry, Inspector. I haven't the faintest idea what he was referring to."

We settled into a corner of the faculty lounge, where she poured two cups of tea for us. "You said Cable had been working on a biography of Robert Louis Stevenson."

"Yes. Stevenson grew up in this area, you know. Edinburgh has been home to quite a few literary figures."

I knew that, of course. You could hardly miss it if you'd gone through the Edinburgh schools. I grew up hearing from all sides how we were the literary center of the world. Robert Burns. Walter Scott. James Boswell. Thomas Carlyle. Edinburgh was where the action was. "When was the last time you saw him?"

"Thursday. We went to dinner."

"The day before he died."

"Yes."

"And he didn't mention anything about a surprise then?"

"No."

"You said he was working on the Stevenson book."

"That's correct."

"What does that mean exactly? Is he at home on the computer? Is he conducting interviews? Is he—?"

"At this stage, Inspector, he was going over the primary sources."

"The primary sources. What would they be?"

"Stevenson's diaries. Letters. Whatever original material of his that's survived."

"Where would that be?"

"At the National Library of Scotland."

The National Library, of course, is located in Edinburgh on the George IV Bridge. The staff assistant who controlled access to the archives wished me a good morning, told me I needed a reader's ticket, and showed me how to get one. I showed a driver's license at the main desk, and minutes later I had my official approval. The staff produced the archival register. I checked to see what Cable had been looking at, and ordered the same package. It was a collection of letters from Robert Louis Stevenson written in 1890–91. She led me into a reading room, occupied by an older man bent over a folder.

I consulted a reference, and learned that Stevenson was at that time in the Samoan Islands. He'd been in poor health for years, and was getting ready to settle there. The letters were in a ringed binder, each encased in plastic. A log listed the contents by date and addressee. Most of the addressees were unfamiliar names. But I knew Henry James, Oscar Wilde, and Herman Melville. And of course Doyle.

I sat for hours, reading through them, but saw nothing that could have led to Cable's murder. Of course, my literary knowledge was limited. Something that might be a surprise to him, or to Madeleine, would probably mean nothing to me.

Then I discovered that two letters listed in the register were missing. Both were dated April 16, 1890. One to Doyle. And one to James Payn.

"That shouldn't be," said the young woman who'd signed me in.

Who else had had access to the letters? Since Saturday? The register showed one name: Michael Y. Naismith.

"This is terrible," said the assistant. She'd begun checking the wastepaper bins.

"Do you remember this Naismith?" I asked.

"Not really," she said. "We have a lot of people who come in here."

There was no Michael Y. Naismith listed anywhere in the area. While I was looking, Sandra called from the bookshop. *Catastrophe Well in Hand* of course hadn't come in yet, she explained, but she'd discovered a copy at the library. In case I was interested.

I read through it that evening. Payn had been the editor of *Chambers's Journal* for fifteen years, and *The Cornhill Magazine* for fourteen more, ending his run in 1896. He wrote essays, poetry, and approximately one hundred novels. I wondered what he'd done with his spare time.

I was looking for connections with Stevenson or Doyle. They all seemed to know one another, and letters had been exchanged. Payn was an admirer especially of the Professor Challenger novels. But there was one item that caught my eye: Payn comments in a letter to Oscar Wilde that he'd rejected a short novel from Doyle. "An excellent mystery," he says, "that unfortunately takes a sharp turn into the American West."

A sharp turn into the American West.

I began looking into McBride's background.

He'd been head of the English Department at his high school. The administration there couldn't say enough kind words about him. The students had loved his classes. Test scores had risen dramatically during his tenure. He'd taught drama for fifteen years, had edited the yearbook for a decade. He'd helped found a support group for handicapped kids.

He'd invited student groups to his home for discussions during which his wife Mary had prepared lunches and served soft drinks. (Mary had died seven years earlier of complications from heart surgery.)

To date, he'd published eight Holmes adventures: two short novels, *A Study in Scarlet* and *The Sign of the Four,* and six stories. All had appeared in the *Chesbro Magazine,* headquartered in London, although the novels had proven so popular they'd later been published separately in hard cover editions. The stories had appeared at intervals of approximately three months, but there'd been no new one for a year. The most recent one, "The Man with the Twisted Lip," had been published last winter.

I took the train to London and, accompanied by a local officer, called on *Chesbro's* editor, Marianne Cummings. She was a diminutive woman, barely five feet tall, well into her sixties. But she showed a no-nonsense attitude as she ushered us into her office. "I don't often receive visits from the police," she said. "I hope we haven't done anything to attract your attention. How may I help you?"

I couldn't help smiling because I knew how my question would affect her. "Ms. Cummings," I said, "have you scheduled a new Sherlock Holmes story?"

She peered at me over her glasses. "I beg your pardon?"

"Sherlock Holmes? Is there another one in the pipeline?"

She broke into a wide skeptical smile. "Is Scotland Yard using Mr. Holmes for training purposes?"

"I've a good reason for asking, Ms. Cummings."

That produced a standoff of almost a minute. "No," she said finally. "We've not scheduled any."

"Will there be any more?"

"I certainly hope so."

"Why the delay?"

She sat down behind a desk and turned to stare out a window. A pigeon looked back at us. "Will my answer go any farther?"

"I can't promise that, but I'll be as discrete as I can."

"Mr. McBride has submitted several stories since 'The Twisted Lip.'"

"And—?"

"I think he's hired someone else to do the writing. That he's just putting his name on the work."

"They're not as good as the ones you've published?"

"Not remotely."

"You've told him that?"

"Of course."

"What's his explanation?"

"He says he's been tired. Promises that he'll get something to me shortly."

Christopher McBride's connection with the Doyles was through his cousin Emma Hasting, who'd married Doyle's grandson, three generations removed. Emma Hasting lived in Southsea, just a few blocks from the site where Doyle had lived during the 1880s.

She was widowed now. Her husband had been a software developer, and Emma had taught music.

She lived in a villa with a magnificent view of the sea. I arrived there on a cold, gray, rainswept morning. "I've been here all my life," she said, as we settled onto a divan in the living room. There was a piano and a desk. And a photo of a young Conan Doyle. "It's from his years here," she said. "According to family tradition, it was taken while he was working on 'The Man from Archangel.' It was also the period during which he was trying to save Jack Hawkins."

She turned bright blue eyes on me. The gaze, somehow, of a young woman. "He was also a physician, you know."

I knew. I had no idea who Jack Hawkins was, though, and I didn't really care. But I wanted to keep her talking about Doyle. So I asked.

"Jack Hawkins was a patient," she explained. "He had cerebral meningitis. But Conan refused to give up on him. He took him into his home and did everything he could. But that was 1885, and medicine had no way to deal with that sort of problem." She used the first name casually, as if Doyle were an old friend. "In the end they lost him."

"I see."

"During the course of the struggle, Conan fell in love with his sister, Louise Hawkins, and married her that same year."

I called her attention to the photo. "Has anything else of his survived and come down to you?"

She considered it. "A lamp," she said. "Would you like to see it?"

It was an oil lamp, and she kept it, polished and sparkling, atop a shelf in the dining room. "He wrote *The Exploits of Brigadier Gerard* by its light," she said. "And several of his medical stories. According to family tradition." She gave me a sly wink. There was really no way to be certain of the facts.

"And is there anything else of Doyle's that you have? Or that Christopher might have received?"

"Oh. Do you know Christopher?"

"Somewhat," I said. "It's he who first got me interested in Doyle."

"There's a trunk that once belonged to the doctor," she said. "It's upstairs."

"A trunk."

"Yes. James had it. My husband."

"May I ask what's in it?"

"I use it for general storage. Mostly I pack off-season clothes in it."

"Is there anything connected with Doyle?"

"Not anymore."

"I see. But there was something at one time?"

"Oh, yes," she said. "My husband never bothered with it. When I first looked into it, it was packed with old clothes and a few books.

And several folders filled with manuscript pages. The books were not in good condition. I got rid of them, got rid of everything, except the manuscripts. I thought someone might be interested in them. A scholar, perhaps."

"Where are they now?"

"The manuscripts? I gave them to Chris. He was an English teacher. I knew he'd find a use for them. He used to show them to his students."

"You gave them away?"

"I wasn't giving them away, Inspector. I knew they might be valuable. But Chris was a member of the family."

"And he showed them to his students?"

"Oh, yes. He has all kinds of stories about their reactions."

I was sure he did. "But you never read them?"

"Have you ever seen Conan's handwriting?"

When I got to McBride's place, he was waiting. "I expected you earlier," he said.

"Emma called you."

"Yes."

We stood facing each other. "You didn't write the Holmes stories, did you?"

"Doyle wrote them."

"Why didn't he publish them?"

He retreated inside and left the door open for me. "He considered them beneath him. Stevenson quotes him as saying he didn't want to have his name associated with cheapjack thrillers. That was the way he thought of them."

"But he wrote eight stories."

McBride nodded. "As far as he was concerned, they were entertainments for him. What we would call guilty pleasures. Something he did in his spare time. God knows where he found spare time. Stevenson suggested he publish them under a pseudonym, but Doyle believed the truth would leak out. It always does, you know."

"Yes, I suppose it does." Finally, we sat. "That was what was in the two letters you removed from the library."

"Stevenson had read two of the stories. 'A Scandal in Bohemia.' And 'A Case of Identity.' He pleaded with Doyle to publish. But

Doyle's career as a historical novelist was just taking off. And that was the way he wanted to be remembered."

"The other letter? The one to Payn?"

"Payn had a chance to publish *A Study in Scarlet*. In 1886, I believe. He was editor of the *Cornhill* magazine then." McBride shook his head slowly at the blindness of the world. "He rejected it. Rejected *A Study in Scarlet*. Imagine. So Stevenson wrote to him. He mentioned Holmes and Watson in his letter and told Payn he'd missed a golden opportunity. He suggested he reconsider his decision."

"Did Payn ever respond?"

"Not that I know of."

"Where did you get the false driver's license? Michael Y. Naismith?"

"I'm sure you know of places where that can be done. When you spend years with adolescents, finding an establishment that sells IDs is not really difficult."

"Of course." Suddenly he had another glass of bourbon in his hand. I didn't know where it had come from. "And Cable knew."

"Yes." His eyes grew dark. "He'd seen the letters that very day. And he couldn't wait to come over here and confront me."

"Didn't you think, before you stole the stories, that you'd be found out eventually?"

"The stories were *mine*," he said. "*I* found them."

"Why did you not move Holmes into modern times?"

"It would have lost the atmosphere." He finished his drink and stared at the glass. "No. I thought it best to leave Mr. Holmes where he was."

"So Doyle's characters became world famous, and you with them."

"Yes. That is what happened. Although they were *my* characters, not Doyle's. He had no faith in them. I was the one who recognized them for what they were. The world would not have Holmes and Watson, had I not intervened."

"And you'd expected to continue the series yourself."

"Yes. I thought it would be easy to imitate Doyle's style. I'd established my name as a major writer. I thought the rest would come easily enough."

"But it hasn't."

He managed a smile. "I've had some difficulty. But given time, I would be all right."

"So, last Friday evening, Cable walked in and challenged you. What happened? Did you decide you couldn't trust a blackmailer?"

"Oh, no. He wasn't here to blackmail me, Inspector. He was hell-bent on *exposing* me."

"So you killed him."

"I never intended to. I really didn't. Even now, I can hardly believe it happened. But he was enjoying himself. He was laughing at me. I offered money. He told me that he wasn't for sale. That I would get exactly what was coming to me. That I deserved to be held up to public scorn. And he walked out."

"You did it in the driveway."

"I didn't mean to. I really didn't. But I was outraged."

"Then you hosed it down."

"If you say so, Inspector."

"What was the weapon?"

"My driver."

"Ah, yes. You're an accomplished golfer. I'd forgotten. So you put him in the boot and drove him over to the shopping center and, when you got a chance, you dumped the body in the woods."

He looked away. Into the dining room, where it was dark. "You took his keys, went to his house, and stole his computer. In case there was anything on it about the Stevenson letters. And you made it look like a burglary."

He remained silent.

"I thought signing a book for him, after the fact, was a nice touch. You knew we'd tie you into it, that we'd come here, so you had your story ready."

"Inspector, you've no proof of any of this. And you can do nothing more than ruin my reputation. I suspect you can't be bribed, but I *would* be extremely grateful if you looked the other way. You owe me that much. And you owe it to the world. I can make Holmes and Watson immortal."

"It's over, McBride. I have some people outside. And a warrant. I can't bring myself to believe you would have destroyed the Doyle manuscripts. They're here somewhere."

"Yes, they are," he said. "But that will only show that I allowed my name to be used on someone else's work. That's serious enough, but it isn't murder."

"You're right," I said. "But I'll be surprised if we don't also find the Stevenson letters. Not that it would matter at this point. We can probably match your handwriting on the register at the library. Combined with everything else, I think it will be more than enough to persuade a jury."

On the way into town, he asked whether I'd read the Holmes stories. I told him I had.

"I wish he'd listened to Stevenson," he said. "Can you imagine what might have been had he gone on to create a series with Holmes and Watson? What a pity." Tears appeared in his eyes. "What a loss."

G-Men

Kristine Kathryn Rusch

In addition to science fiction and fantasy, Kristine Kathryn Rusch is also a prolific writer of mystery and romance. She has won multiple awards in all three genres, including the Hugo Award, the John W. Campbell Award, the Ellery Queen Reader's Choice Award, and the Romantic Times Reviewers' Choice Award for Best Paranormal Romance. She's made several bestseller lists and been translated into thirteen languages. It's hard to make me feel lazy, but she succeeds. She also succeeds admirably in the story that follows, with a Sixties' era tale of murder and the FBI that could easily be a novel in its own right.

> "There's something addicting about a secret."
> —J. Edgar Hoover

The squalid little alley smelled of piss. Detective Seamus O'Reilly tugged his overcoat closed and wished he'd worn boots. He could feel the chill of his metal flashlight through the worn glove on his right hand.

Two beat cops stood in front of the bodies, and the coroner crouched over them. His assistant was already setting up the gurneys, body bags draped over his arm. The coroner's van had blocked the alley's entrance, only a few yards away.

O'Reilly's partner, Joseph McKinnon, followed him. McKinnon had trained his own flashlight on the fire escapes above, unintentionally alerting any residents to the police presence.

But they probably already knew. Shootings in this part of the city were common. The neighborhood teetered between swank and corrupt. Far enough from Central Park for degenerates and muggers to use the alleys as corridors, and, conversely, close enough for new money to want to live with a peek of the city's most famous expanse of green.

The coroner, Thomas Brunner, had set up two expensive, battery-operated lights on garbage can lids placed on top of the dirty ice, one at the top of the bodies, the other near the feet. O'Reilly crouched so he wouldn't create any more shadows.

"What've we got?" he asked.

"Dunno yet." Brunner was using his gloved hands to part the hair on the back of the nearest corpse's skull. "It could be one of those nights."

O'Reilly had worked with Brunner for eighteen years now, since they both got back from the war, and he hated it when Brunner said it could be one of those nights. That meant the corpses would stack up, which was usually a summer thing, but almost never happened in the middle of winter.

"Why?" O'Reilly asked. "What else we got?"

"Some colored limo driver shot two blocks from here." Brunner was still parting the hair. It took O'Reilly a minute to realize it was matted with blood. "And two white guys pulled out of their cars and shot about four blocks from that."

O'Reilly felt a shiver run through him that had nothing to do with the cold. "You think the shootings are related?"

"Dunno," Brunner said. "But I think it's odd, don't you? Five dead in the space of an hour, all in a six-block radius."

O'Reilly closed his eyes for a moment. Two white guys pulled out of their cars, one Negro driver of a limo, and now two white guys in an alley. Maybe they were related, maybe they weren't.

He opened his eyes, then wished he hadn't. Brunner had his finger inside a bullet hole, a quick way to judge caliber.

"Same type of bullet," Brunner said.

"You handled the other shootings?"

"I was on scene with the driver when some fag called this one in."

O'Reilly looked at Brunner. Eighteen years, and he still wasn't used to the man's casual bigotry.

"How did you know the guy was queer?" O'Reilly asked. "You talk to him?"

"Didn't have to." Brunner nodded toward the building in front of them. "Weekly party for degenerates in the penthouse apartment every Thursday night. Thought you knew."

O'Reilly looked up. Now he understood why McKinnon had been shining his flashlight at the upper story windows. McKinnon had worked Vice before he got promoted to Homicide.

"Why would I know?" O'Reilly said.

McKinnon was the one who answered. "Because of the standing orders."

"I'm not playing twenty questions," O'Reilly said. "I don't know about a party in this building and I don't know about standing orders."

"The standing orders are," McKinnon said as if he were an elementary school teacher, "not to bust it, no matter what kind of lead you got. You see someone go in, you forget about it. You see someone come out, you avert your eyes. You complain, you get moved to a different shift, maybe a different precinct."

"Jesus." O'Reilly was too far below to see if there was any movement against the glass in the penthouse suite. But whoever lived there—whoever partied there—had learned to shut off the lights before the cops arrived.

"Shot in the back of the head," Brunner said before O'Reilly could process all of the information. "That's just damn strange."

O'Reilly looked at the corpses—really looked at them—for the first time. Two men, both rather heavy set. Their faces were gone, probably splattered all over the walls. Gloved hands, nice shoes, one of them wearing a white scarf that caught the light.

Brunner had to search for the wound in the back of the head which made that the entry point. The exit wounds had destroyed the faces.

O'Reilly looked behind him. No door on that building, but there was one on the building where the party was held. If they'd been exiting the building and were surprised by a queer basher or a mugger, they'd've been shot in the front, not the back.

"How many times were they shot?" O'Reilly asked.

"Looks like just the once. Large caliber, close range. I'd say it was a purposeful headshot, designed to do maximum damage." Brunner felt the back of the closest corpse. "There doesn't seem to be anything on the torso."

"They still got their wallets?" McKinnon asked.

"Haven't checked yet." Brunner reached into the back pants pocket of the corpse he'd been searching and clearly found nothing. So he grabbed the front of the overcoat and reached inside.

He removed a long thin wallet—old fashioned, the kind made for the larger bills of forty years before. Hand-tailored, beautifully made.

These men weren't hurting for money.

Brunner handed the wallet to O'Reilly, who opened it. And stopped when he saw the badge inside. His mouth went dry.

"We got a feebee," he said, his voice sounding strangled.

"What?" McKinnon asked.

"FBI," Brunner said dryly. McKinnon had only moved to homicide the year before. Vice rarely had to deal with FBI. Homicide did only on sensational cases. O'Reilly could count on one hand the number of times he'd spoken to agents in the New York Bureau.

"Not just any feebee either," O'Reilly said. "The Associate Director. Clyde A. Tolson."

McKinnon whistled. "Who's the other guy?"

This time, O'Reilly did the search. The other corpse, the heavier of the two, also smelled faintly of perfume. This man had kept his wallet in the inner pocket of his suit coat, just like his companion had.

O'Reilly opened the wallet. Another badge, just like he expected. But he didn't expect the bulldog face glaring at him from the wallet's interior.

Nor had he expected the name.

"Jesus, Mary, and Joseph," he said.

"What've we got?" McKinnon asked.

O'Reilly handed him the wallet, opened to the slim paper identification.

"The Director of the FBI," he said, his voice shaking. "Public Hero Number One. J. Edgar Hoover."

* * *

Francis Xavier Bryce—Frank to his friends, what few of them he still had left—had just dropped off to sleep when the phone rang. He cursed, caught himself, apologized to Mary, and then remembered she wasn't there.

The phone rang again and he fumbled for the light, knocking over the highball glass he'd used to mix his mom's recipe for sleepless nights: hot milk, butter, and honey. It turned out that, at the tender age of thirty-six, hot milk and butter laced with honey wasn't a recipe for sleep; it was a recipe for heartburn.

And for a smelly carpet if he didn't clean the mess up.

He found the phone before he found the light.

"What?" he snapped.

"You live near Central Park, right?" A voice he didn't recognize, but one that was clearly official, asked the question without a hello or an introduction.

"More or less." Bryce rarely talked about his apartment. His parents had left it to him and, as his wife was fond of sniping, it was too fancy for a junior G-Man.

The voice rattled off an address. "How far is that from you?"

"About five minutes." If he didn't clean up the mess on the floor. If he spent thirty seconds pulling on the clothes he'd piled onto the chair beside the bed.

"Get there. Now. We got a situation."

"What about my partner?" Bryce's partner lived in Queens.

"You'll have back-up. You just have to get to the scene. The moment you get there, you shut it down."

"Um." Bryce hated sounding uncertain, but he had no choice. "First, sir, I need to know who I'm talking to. Then I need to know what I'll find."

"You'll find a double homicide. And you're talking to Eugene Hart, the Special Agent in Charge. I shouldn't have to identify myself to you."

Now that he had, Bryce recognized Hart's voice. "Sorry, sir. It's just procedure."

"Fuck procedure. Take over that scene. *Now.*"

"Yes, sir," Bryce said, but he was talking into an empty phone line. He hung up, hands shaking, wishing he had some BromoSeltzer.

He'd just come off a long, messy investigation of another agent. Walter Cain had been about to get married when he remembered he had to inform the Bureau of that fact and, as per regulation, get his bride vetted before walking down the aisle.

Bryce had been the one to investigate the future Mrs. Cain, and had been the one to find out about her rather seamy past—two Vice convictions under a different name, and one hospitalization after a rather messy backstreet abortion. Turned out Cain knew about his future wife's past, but the Bureau hadn't liked it.

And two nights ago, Bryce had to be the one to tell Cain that he couldn't marry his now-reformed, somewhat religious, beloved. The soon-to-be Mrs. Cain had taken the news hard. She had gone to Bellevue this afternoon after slashing her wrists.

And Bryce had been the one to tell Cain what his former fiancée had done. Just a few hours ago.

Sometimes Bryce hated this job.

Despite his orders, he went into the bathroom, soaked one of Mary's precious company towels in water, and dropped the thing on the spilled milk. Then he pulled on his clothes, and finger-combed his hair.

He was a mess—certainly not the perfect representative of the Bureau. His white shirt was stained with marinade from that night's takeout, and his tie wouldn't keep a crisp knot. The crease had long since left his trousers and his shoes hadn't been shined in weeks. Still, he grabbed his black overcoat, hoping it would hide everything.

He let himself out of the apartment before he remembered the required and much hated hat, went back inside, grabbed the hat as well as his gun and his identification. Jesus, he was tired. He hadn't slept since Mary walked out. Mary, who had been vetted by the FBI and who had passed with flying colors. Mary, who had turned out to be more of a liability than any former hooker ever could have been.

And now, because of her, he was heading toward something big, and he was one-tenth as sharp as usual.

All he could hope for was that the SAC had overreacted. And he had a hunch—a two-in-the-morning, get-your-ass-over-there-now hunch—that the SAC hadn't overreacted at all.

* * *

Attorney General Robert F. Kennedy sat in his favorite chair near the fire in his library. The house was quiet even though his wife and eight children were asleep upstairs. Outside, the rolling landscape was covered in a light dusting of snow—rare for McLean, Virginia even at this time of year.

He held a book in his left hand, his finger marking the spot. The Greeks had comforted him in the few months since Jack died, but lately Kennedy had discovered Camus.

He had been about to copy a passage into his notebook when the phone rang. At first he sighed, feeling all of the exhaustion that had weighed on him since the assassination. He didn't want to answer the phone. He didn't want to be bothered—not now, not ever again.

But this was the direct line from the White House and if he didn't answer it, someone else in the house would.

He set the Camus book face down on his chair and crossed to the desk before the third ring. He answered with a curt, "Yes?"

"Attorney General Kennedy, sir?" The voice on the other end sounded urgent. The voice sounded familiar to him even though he couldn't place it.

"Yes?"

"This is Special Agent John Haskell. You asked me to contact you, sir, if I heard anything important about Director Hoover, no matter what the time."

Kennedy leaned against the desk. He had made that request back when his brother had been president, back when Kennedy had been the first attorney general since the 1920s who actually demanded accountability from Hoover.

Since Lyndon Johnson had taken over the presidency, accountability had gone by the wayside. These days Hoover rarely returned Kennedy's phone calls.

"Yes, I did tell you that," Kennedy said, resisting the urge to add, but *I don't care about that old man any longer.*

"Sir, there are rumors—credible ones—that Director Hoover has died in New York."

Kennedy froze. For a moment, he flashed back to that unseasonably warm afternoon when he'd sat just outside with the federal attorney for New York City, Robert Morganthau and the chief of

Morganthau's criminal division, Silvio Mollo, talking about prosecuting various organized crime figures.

Kennedy could still remember the glint of the sunlight on the swimming pool, the taste of the tuna fish sandwich Ethel had brought him, the way the men—despite their topic—had seemed lighthearted.

Then the phone rang, and J. Edgar Hoover was on the line. Kennedy almost didn't take the call, but he did and Hoover's cold voice said, *I have news for you. The President's been shot.*

Kennedy had always disliked Hoover, but since that day, that awful day in the bright sunshine, he hated that fat bastard. Not once—not in that call, not in the subsequent calls—did Hoover express condolences or show a shred of human concern.

"Credible rumors?" Kennedy repeated, knowing he probably sounded as cold as Hoover had three months ago, and not caring. He'd chosen Haskell as his liaison precisely because the man didn't like Hoover either. Kennedy had needed someone inside Hoover's hierarchy, unbeknownst to Hoover, which was difficult since Hoover kept his hand in everything. Haskell was one of the few who fit the bill.

"Yes, sir, quite credible."

"Then why haven't I received official contact?"

"I'm not even sure the President knows, sir."

Kennedy leaned against the desk. "Why not, if the rumors are credible?"

"Um, because, sir, um, it seems Associate Director Tolson was also shot, and um, they were, um, in a rather suspect area."

Kennedy closed his eyes. All of Washington knew that Tolson was the closest thing Hoover had to a wife. The two old men had been life-long companions. Even though they didn't live together, they had every meal together. Tolson had been Hoover's hatchet man until the last year or so, when Tolson's health hadn't permitted it.

Then a word Haskell used sank in. "You said shot."

"Yes, sir."

"Is Tolson dead too then?"

"And three other people in the neighborhood," Haskell said.

"My God." Kennedy ran a hand over his face. "But they think this is personal?"

"Yes, sir."

"Because of the location of the shooting?"

"Yes, sir. It seems there was an exclusive gathering in a nearby building. You know the type, sir."

Kennedy didn't know the type—at least not through personal experience. But he'd heard of places like that, where the rich, famous, and deviant could spend time with each other, and do whatever it was they liked to do in something approaching privacy.

"So," he said, "the Bureau's trying to figure out how to cover this up."

"Or at least contain it, sir."

Without Hoover or Tolson. No one in the Bureau was going to know what to do.

Kennedy's hand started to shake. "What about the files?"

"Files, sir?"

"Hoover's confidential files. Has anyone secured them?"

"Not yet, sir. But I'm sure someone has called Miss Gandy."

Helen Gandy was Hoover's long-time secretary. She had been his right hand as long as Tolson had operated that hatchet.

"So procedure's being followed," Kennedy said, then frowned. If procedure were being followed, shouldn't the acting head of the Bureau be calling him?

"No, sir. But the Director put some private instructions in place should he be killed or incapacitated. Private emergency instructions. And those involve letting Miss Gandy know before anyone else."

Even me, Kennedy thought. *Hoover's nominal boss.* "She's not there yet, right?"

"No, sir."

"Do you know where those files are?" Kennedy asked, trying not to let desperation into his voice.

"I've made it my business to know, sir." There was a pause and then Haskell lowered his voice. "They're in Miss Gandy's office, sir."

Not Hoover's like everyone thought. For the first time in months, Kennedy felt a glimmer of hope. "Secure those files."

"Sir?"

"Do whatever it takes. I want them out of there, and I want someone to secure Hoover's house too. I'm acting on the orders of the President. If anyone tells you that they are doing the same, they're mistaken. The President made his wishes clear on this point. He often said if anything happens to that old queer—" And here Kennedy deliberately used LBJ's favorite phrase for Hoover "—then we need those files before they can get into the wrong hands."

"I'm on it, sir."

"I can't stress to you the importance of this," Kennedy said. In fact, he couldn't talk about the importance at all. Those files could ruin his brother's legacy. The secrets in there could bring down Kennedy too, and his entire family.

"And if the rumors about the Director's death are wrong, sir?"

Kennedy felt a shiver of fear. "Are they?"

"I seriously doubt it."

"Then let me worry about that."

And about what LBJ would do when he found out. Because the President upon whose orders Kennedy acted wasn't the current one. Kennedy was following the orders of the only man he believed should be President at the moment.

His brother, Jack.

The scene wasn't hard to find: a coroner's van blocked the entrance to the alley. Bryce walked quickly, already cold, his heartburn worse than it had been when he had gone to bed.

The neighborhood was in transition. An urban renewal project had knocked down some wonderful turn of the century buildings that had become eyesores. But so far, the buildings that had replaced them were the worst kind of modern—all planes and angles and white with few windows.

In the buildings closest to the park, the lights worked and the streets looked safe. But here, on a side street not far from the construction, the city's shady side showed. The dirty snow was piled against the curb, the streets were dark, and nothing seemed inhabited except that alley with the coroner's van blocking the entrance.

The coroner's van and at least one unmarked car. No press, which surprised him. He shoved his gloved hands in the pockets of his overcoat even though it was against FBI dress code, and slipped between the van and the wall of a grimy brick building.

The alley smelled of old urine and fresh blood. Two beat cops blocked his way until he showed identification. Then, like people usually did, they parted as if he could burn them.

The bodies had fallen side-by-side in the center of the alley. They looked posed, with their arms up, their legs in classic P position—one leg bent, the other straight. They looked like they could fit perfectly on the dead body diagrams the FBI used to put out in the 1930s. He wondered if they had fallen like this or if this had been the result of the coroner's tampering.

The coroner had messed with other parts of the crime scene—if, indeed, he had been the one who put the garbage can lids on the ice and set battery-powered lamps on them. The warmth of the lamps was melting the ice and sending runnels of water into a nearby grate.

"I hope to hell someone thought to photograph the scene before you melted it," he said.

The coroner and the two cops who had been crouching beside the bodies stood up guiltily. The coroner looked at the garbage can lids and closed his eyes. Then he took a deep breath, opened them, and snapped his fingers at the assistant who was waiting beside a gurney.

"Camera," he said.

"That's Crime Scene's—" the assistant began, then saw everyone looking at him. He glanced at the van. "Never mind."

He walked behind the bodies, further disturbing the scene. Bryce's mouth thinned in irritation. The cops who stood were in plain clothes.

"Detectives," Bryce said, holding his identification, "Special Agent Frank Bryce of the FBI. I've been told to secure this scene. More of my people will be here shortly."

He hoped that last statement was true. He had no idea who was coming or when they would arrive.

"Good," said the younger detective, a tall man with broad shoulders and an all-American jaw. "The sooner we get out of here the better."

Bryce had never gotten that reaction from a detective before. Usually the detectives were territorial, always reminding him that this was New York City and that the scene belonged to them.

The other detective, older, face grizzled by time and work, held out his gloved hand. "Forgive my partner's rudeness. I'm Seamus O'Reilly. He's Joseph McKinnon and we'll help you in any way we can."

"I appreciate it," Bryce said, taking O'Reilly's hand and shaking it. "I guess the first thing you can do is tell me what we've got."

"A hell of a mess, that's for sure," said McKinnon. "You'll understand when…"

His voice trailed off as his partner took out two long, old-fashioned wallets and handed them to Bryce.

Bryce took them, feeling confused. Then he opened the first, saw the familiar badge, and felt his breath catch. Two FBI agents, in this alley? Shot side-by-side? He looked up, saw the darkened windows.

There used to be rumors about this neighborhood. Some exclusive private sex parties used to be held here, and his old partner had always wanted to visit one just to see if it was a hotbed of communists like some of the agents had claimed. Bryce had begged off. He was an investigator, not a voyeur.

The two detectives were staring at him, as if they expected more from him. He still had the wallet open in his hand. If the dead men were New York agents, he would know them. He hated solving the deaths of people he knew.

But he steeled himself, looked at the identification, and felt the blood leave his face. His skin grew cold and for a moment he felt lightheaded.

"No," he said.

The detectives still stared at him.

He swallowed. "Have you done a visual i.d.?"

Hoover was recognizable. His picture was on everything. Sometimes Bryce thought Hoover was more famous than the President—any President. He'd certainly been in power longer.

"Faces are gone," O'Reilly said.

"Exit wounds," the coroner added from beside the bodies. His assistant had returned and was taking pictures, the flash showing just how much melt had happened since the coroner arrived.

"Shot in the back of the head?" Bryce blinked. He was tired and his brain was working slowly, but something about the shots didn't match with the body positions.

"If they came out that door," O'Reilly said as he indicated a dark metal door almost hidden in the side of the brick building, "then the shooters had to be waiting beside it."

"Your crime scene people haven't arrived yet, I take it?" Bryce asked.

"No," the coroner said. "They think it's a fag kill. They'll get here when they get here."

Bryce clenched his left fist and had to remind himself to let the fingers loose.

O'Reilly saw the reaction. "Sorry about that," he said, shooting a glare at the coroner. "I'm sure the Director was here on business."

Funny business. But Bryce didn't say that. The rumors about Hoover had been around since Bryce joined the FBI just after the war. Hoover quashed them, like he quashed any criticism, but it seemed like the criticism got made, no matter what.

Bryce opened the other wallet, but he already had a guess as to who was beside Hoover, and his guess turned out to be right.

"You want to tell me why your crime scene people believe this is a homosexual killing?" Bryce asked, trying not to let what Mary called his FBI tone into his voice. If Hoover was still alive and this was some kind of plant, Hoover would want to crush the source of this assumption. Bryce would make sure that the source was worth pursuing before going any farther.

"Neighborhood, mostly," McKinnon said. "There're a couple of bars, mostly high-end. You have to know someone to get in. Then there's the party, held every week upstairs. Some of the most important men in the city show up at it, or so they used to say in Vice when they told us to stay away."

Bryce nodded, letting it go at that.

"We need your crime scene people here ASAP, and a lot more cops so that we can protect what's left of this scene, in case these men turn out to be who their identification says they are. You search the bodies to see if this was the only identification on them?"

O'Reilly started. He clearly hadn't thought of that. Probably had been too shocked by the first wallets that he found.

The younger detective had already gone back to the bodies. The coroner put out a hand, and did the searching himself.

"You think this was a plant?" O'Reilly asked.

"I don't know what to think," Bryce said. "I'm not here to think. I'm here to make sure everything goes smoothly."

And to make sure the case goes to the FBI. Those words hung unspoken between the two of them. Not that O'Reilly objected, and now Bryce could understand why. This case would be a political nightmare, and no good detective wanted to be in the middle of it.

"How come there's no press?" Bryce asked O'Reilly. "You manage to get rid of them somehow?"

"Fag kill," the coroner said.

Bryce was getting tired of those words. His fist had clenched again, and he had to work at unclenching it.

"Ignore him," O'Reilly said softly. "He's an asshole and the best coroner in the city."

"I heard that," the coroner said affably. "There's no other identification on either of them."

O'Reilly's shoulders slumped, as if he'd been hoping for a different outcome. Bryce should have been hoping as well, but he hadn't been. He had known that Hoover was in town. The entire New York Bureau knew, since Hoover always took it over when he arrived—breezing in, giving instructions, making sure everything was just the way he wanted it.

"Before this gets too complicated," O'Reilly said, "you want to see the other bodies?"

"Other bodies?" Bryce felt numb. He could use some caffeine now, but Hoover had ordered agents not to drink coffee on the job. Getting coffee now felt almost disrespectful.

"We got three more." O'Reilly took a deep breath. "And just before you arrived, I got word that they're agents too."

Special Agent John Haskell had just installed six of his best agents outside the Director's suite of offices when a small woman showed up, key clutched in her gloved right hand. Helen Gandy, the Director's secretary, looked up at Haskell with the coldest stare he'd ever seen outside of the Director's.

"May I go into my office, Agent Haskell?" Her voice was just as cold. She didn't look upset, and if he hadn't known that she never stayed past five unless directed by Hoover himself, Haskell would have thought she was coming back from a prolonged work break.

"I'm sorry, ma'am," he said. "No one is allowed inside. President's orders."

"Really?" God, that voice was chilling. He remembered the first time he'd heard it, when he'd been brought to this suite of offices as a brand-new agent, after getting his "Meet the Boss" training before his introduction to the Director. She'd frightened him more than Hoover had.

"Yes, ma'am. The President says no one can enter."

"Surely he didn't mean me."

Surely he did. But Haskell bit the comment back. "I'm sorry, ma'am."

"I have a few personal items that I'd like to get, if you don't mind. And the Director instructed me that in the case of..." and for the first time she paused. Her voice didn't break nor did she clear her throat. But she seemed to need a moment to gather herself. "In case of emergency, I was to remove some of his personal items as well."

"If you could tell me what they are, ma'am, I'll get them."

Her eyes narrowed. "The Director doesn't like others to touch his possessions."

"I'm sorry, ma'am," he said gently. "But I don't think that matters any longer."

Any other woman would have broken down. After all, she had worked for the old man for forty-five years, side-by-side, every day. Never marrying, not because they had a relationship—Helen Gandy, more than anyone, probably knew the truth behind the Director's relationship with the Associate Director—but because for Helen Gandy, just like for the Director himself, the FBI was her entire life.

"It matters," she said. "Now if you'll excuse me..."

She tried to wriggle past him. She was wiry and stronger than he expected. He had to put out an arm to block her.

"Ma'am," he said in the gentlest tone he could summon, "the President's orders supercede the Director's."

How often had he wanted to say that over the years? How often had he wanted to remind everyone in the Bureau that the President led the Free World, not J. Edgar Hoover.

"In this instance," she snapped, "they do not."

"Ma'am, I'd hate to have some agents restrain you." Although he wasn't sure about that. She had never been nice to him or to anyone he knew. She'd always been sharp or rude. "You're distraught."

"I am not." She clipped each word.

"You are because I say you are, ma'am."

She raised her chin. For a moment, he thought she hadn't understood. But she finally did.

The balance of power had shifted. At the moment, it was on his side.

"Do I have to call the President then to get my personal effects?" she asked.

But they both knew she wasn't talking about her personal things. And the President was smart enough to know that as well. As hungry to get those files as the attorney general had seemed despite his Eastern reserve, the President would be utterly ravenous. He wouldn't let some old skirt, as he'd been known to call Miss Gandy, get in his way.

"Go ahead," Haskell said. "Feel free to use the phone in the office across the hall."

She glared at him, then turned on one foot and marched down the corridor. But she didn't head toward a phone—at least not one he could see.

He wondered who she would call. The President wouldn't listen. The attorney general had issued the order in the President's name. Maybe she would contact one of Hoover's assistant directors, the four or five men that Hoover had in his pocket.

Haskell had been waiting for them. But word still hadn't spread through the Bureau. The only reason he knew was because he'd received a call from the SAC of the New York office. New York hated the Director, mostly because the old man went there so often and harassed them.

Someone had probably figured out that there was a crisis from the moment that Haskell had brought his people in to secure the Director's suite. But no one would know that the Director was dead until Miss Gandy made the calls or until someone in the Bureau started along the chain of command—the one designated in the book Hoover had written all those years ago.

Haskell crossed his arms. Sometimes he wished he hadn't let the A.G. know how he felt about the Director. Sometimes he wished he were still a humble assistant, the man who had joined the FBI because he wanted to be a top cop like his hero J. Edgar Hoover.

A man who, it turned out, never made a real arrest or fired a gun or even understood investigation.

There was a lot to admire about the Director—no matter what you said, he'd built a hell of an agency almost from scratch—but he wasn't the man his press made him out to be.

And that was the source of Haskell's disillusionment. He'd wanted to be a top cop. Instead, he snooped into homes and businesses and sometimes even investigated fairly blameless people, looking for a mistake in their past.

Since he'd been transferred to FBIHQ, he hadn't done any real investigating at all. His arrests had slowed, his cases dwindled.

And he'd found himself investigating his boss, trying to find out where the legend ended and the man began. Once he realized that the old man was just a bureaucrat who had learned where all the bodies were buried and used that to make everyone bow to his bidding, Haskell was ripe for the undercover work the A.G. had asked him to do.

Only now he wasn't undercover any more. Now he was standing in the open before the Director's cache of secrets, on the President's orders, hoping that no one would call his bluff.

As O'Reilly led him to the limousine, Bryce surreptitiously checked his watch. He'd already been on scene for half an hour, and no back-up had arrived. If he was supposed to secure everything and chase off the NYPD, he'd need some manpower.

But for now, he wanted to see the extent of the problem. The night had gotten colder, and this street was even darker than the street he'd walked down. All of the streetlights were out. The only light came from some porch bulbs above a few entrances. He could barely make out the limousine at the end of the block, and then only because he could see the shadowy forms of the two beat cops standing at the scene, their squad cars parking the limo in.

As he got closer, he recognized the shape of the limo. It was thicker than most limos and rode lower to the ground because it was encased in an extra frame, making it bulletproof. Supposedly, the glass would all be bulletproof as well.

"You said the driver was shot inside the limo?" Bryce asked.

"That's what they told me," O'Reilly said. "I wasn't called to this scene. We were brought in because of the two men in the alley. Even then we were called late."

Bryce nodded. He remembered the coroner's bigotry. "Is that standard procedure for cases involving minorities?"

O'Reilly gave him a sideways glance. Bryce couldn't read O'Reilly's expression in the dark.

"We're overtaxed," O'Reilly said after a moment. "Some cases don't get the kind of treatment they deserve."

"Limo drivers," Bryce said.

"If he'd been killed in the parking garage under the Plaza maybe," O'Reilly said. "But not because of who he was. But because of where he was."

Bryce nodded. He knew how the world worked. He didn't like it. He spoke up against it too many times, which was why he was on shaky ground at the Bureau.

Then his already upset stomach clenched. Maybe he wasn't going to get back-up. Maybe they'd put him on his own here to claim he'd botched the investigation, so that they would be able to cover it up.

He couldn't concentrate on that now. What he had to do was take good notes, make the best case he could, and keep a copy of every damn thing—maybe in more than one place.

"You were called in because of the possibility that the men in the alley could be important," Bryce said.

"That's my guess," O'Reilly said.

"What about the others down the block? Has anyone taken those cases?"

"Probably not," O'Reilly said. "Those bars, you know. It's department policy. The coroner checks bodies in the suspect area, and decides, based on... um... evidence of... um... activity... whether or not to bring in detectives."

Bryce frowned. He almost asked what the coroner was checking for when he figured out that it was evidence on the body itself, evidence not of the crime, but of certain kinds of sex acts. If that evidence was present, apparently no one thought it worthwhile to investigate the crime.

"You'd think the city would revise that," Bryce said. "A lot of people live dual lives—productive and interesting people."

"Yeah," O'Reilly said. "You'd think. Especially after tonight."

Bryce grinned. He was liking this grizzled cop more and more.

O'Reilly spoke to the beat cops, then motioned Bryce to the limo. As Bryce approached, O'Reilly trained his flashlight on the driver's side.

The window wasn't broken like Bryce had expected. It had been rolled down.

"You got here one James Crawford," said one of the beat cops. "He got identification says he's a feebee, but I ain't never heard of no colored feebee."

"There's only four," Bryce said dryly. And they all worked for Hoover as his personal housekeepers or drivers. "Can I see that identification?"

The beat cop handed him a wallet that matched the ones on Tolson and Hoover. Inside was a badge and identification for James Crawford as well as family photographs. Neither Tolson nor Hoover had had any photographs in their wallets.

Bryce motioned O'Reilly to move a little closer to the body. The head was tilted toward the window. The right side of the skull was gone, the hair glistening with drying blood. With one gloved finger, Bryce pushed the head upright. A single entrance wound above the left ear had caused the damage.

"Brunner says the shots are the same caliber," O'Reilly said.

It took Bryce a moment to realize that Brunner was the coroner.

Bryce carefully searched Crawford but didn't find the man's weapon. Nor could he found a holster or any way to carry a weapon.

"It looks like he wasn't carrying a weapon," Bryce said.

"Neither were the two in the alley," O'Reilly said, and Bryce appreciated his caution in not identifying the other two corpses. "You'd think they would have been."

Bryce shook his head. "They were known for not carrying weapons. But you'd think their driver would have one."

"Maybe they had protection," O'Reilly said.

And Bryce's mouth went dry. Of course they did. The office always joked about who would get HooverWatch on each trip. He'd had to do it a few times.

Agents on HooverWatch followed strict rules, like everything else with Hoover. Remain close enough to see the men entering and exiting an area, stop any suspicious characters, and yet somehow remain inconspicuous.

"You said there were two others shot?"

"Yeah. A block or so from here." O'Reilly waved a hand vaguely down the street.

"Pulled out of one car or two?"

"Not my case," O'Reilly said.

"Two," said the beat cop. "Black sedans. Could barely see them on this cruddy street."

HooverWatch. Bryce swallowed hard, kept that bile back. Of course. He probably knew the men who were shot.

"Let's look," he said. "You two, make sure the coroner's man photographs this scene before he leaves."

"Yessir," said the second beat cop. He hadn't spoken before.

"And don't let anyone near this scene unless I give the okay," Bryce said.

"How come this guy's in charge?" the talkative beat cop asked O'Reilly.

O'Reilly grinned. "Because he's a feebee."

"I'm sorry," the beat cop said automatically turning to Bryce. "I didn't know, sir."

Feebee was an insult—or at least some in the Bureau thought so. Bryce didn't mind it. Any more than he minded when some rookie said "Sack" when he meant "Ess-Ay-Cee." Shorthand worked, sometimes better than people wanted it to.

"Point me in the right direction," he said to the talkative cop.

The cop nodded south. "One block down, sir. You can't miss it. We got guys on those scenes too, but we weren't so sure it was important. You know. We coulda missed stuff."

In other words, they hadn't buttoned up the scene immediately. They'd waited for the coroner to make his verdict, and he probably hadn't, not with the three new corpses nearby.

Bryce took one last look at James Crawford. The man had rolled down his window, despite the cold, and in a bad section of town.

He leaned forward. Underneath the faint scent of cordite and mingled with the thicker smell of blood was the smell of a cigar.

He took the flashlight from O'Reilly and trained it on the dirty snow against the curb. It had been trampled by everyone coming to this crime scene.

He crouched, and poked just a little, finding three fairly fresh cigarette butts.

As he stood, he said to the beat cops, "When the scene of the crime guys get here, make sure they take everything from the curb." O'Reilly was watching him. The beat cops were frowning, but they nodded.

Bryce handed O'Reilly back his flashlight and headed down the street.

"You think he was smoking and tossing the butts out the window?" O'Reilly asked.

"Either that," Bryce said, "or he rolled his window down to talk to someone. And if someone was pointing a gun at him, he wouldn't have done it. This vehicle was armored. He had a better chance starting it up and driving away than he did cooperating."

"If he wasn't smoking," O'Reilly said, "he knew his killer."

"Yeah," Bryce said. And he was pretty sure that was going to make his job a whole hell of a lot harder.

Kennedy took the elevator up to the fifth floor of the Justice Department. He probably should have stayed home, but he simply couldn't. He needed to get into those files and he needed to do so before anyone else.

As he strode into the corridor he shared with the Director of the FBI, he saw Helen Gandy hurry in the other direction. She looked like she had just come from the beauty salon. He had never seen her look anything less than completely put together but he was surprised by her perfect appearance on this night, after the news that her long-time boss was dead.

Kennedy tugged at the overcoat he'd put on over his favorite sweater. He hadn't taken the time to change or even comb his hair. He probably looked as tousled as he had in the days after Jack died.

Although, for the first time in three months, he felt like he had a purpose. He didn't know how long this feeling would last, or how long he wanted it to. But this death had given him an odd kind of hope that control was coming back into his world.

Haskell stood in front of the Director's office suite, arms crossed. The Director's suite was just down the corridor from the attorney general's offices. It felt odd to go toward Hoover's domain instead of his own.

Haskell looked relieved when he saw Kennedy.

"Was that the dragon lady I just saw?" Kennedy asked.

"She wanted to get some personal effects from her office," Haskell said.

"Did you let her?"

"You said the orders were to secure it, so I have."

"Excellent." Kennedy glanced in both directions and saw no one. "Make sure your staff continues to protect the doors. I'm going inside."

"Sir?" Haskell raised his eyebrows.

"This may not be the right place," Kennedy said. "I'm worried that he moved everything to his house."

The lie came easily. Kennedy would have heard if Hoover had moved files to his own home. But Haskell didn't know that.

Haskell moved away from the door. It was unlocked. Two more agents stood inside, guarding the interior doors.

"Give me a minute, please, gentlemen," Kennedy said.

The men nodded and went outside.

Kennedy stopped and took a deep breath. He had been in Miss Gandy's office countless times, but he had never really looked at it. He'd always been staring at the door to Hoover's inner sanctum, waiting for it to open and the old man to come out.

That office was interesting. In the antechamber, Hoover had memorabilia and photographs from his major cases. He even had the plaster-of-paris death mask of John Dellinger on display. It was a ghastly thing, which made Kennedy think of the way that English kings used to keep severed heads on the entrance to London Bridge to warn traitors of their potential fate.

But this office had always looked like a waiting room to him. Nothing very special. The woman behind the desk was the focal point. Jack had been the one who nicknamed her the dragon lady and had even called her that to her face once, only with his trademark grin, so infectious that she hadn't made a sound or a grimace in protest.

Of course, she hadn't smiled back either.

Her desk was clear except for a blotter, a telephone, and a jar of pens. A typewriter sat on a credenza with paper stacked beside it.

But it wasn't the desk that interested him the most. It was the floor-to-ceiling filing cabinets and storage bins. He walked to them.

Instead of the typical system—marked by letters of the alphabet—this one had numbers that were clearly part of a code.

He pulled open the nearest drawer, and found row after row of accordion files, each with its own number, and manila folders with the first number set followed by another. He cursed softly under his breath.

Of course the old dog wouldn't file his confidentials by name. He'd use a secret code. The old man liked nothing more than his secrets.

Still, Kennedy opened half a dozen drawers just to see if the system continued throughout. And it wasn't until he got to a bin near the corner of the desk that he found a file labeled "Obscene."

His hand shook as he pulled it out. Jack, for all his brilliance, had been sexually insatiable. Back when their brother Joe was still alive and no one ever thought Jack would be running for President, Jack had had an affair with a Danish émigrée named Inga Arvad. Inga Binga, as Jack used to call her, was married to a man with ties to Hitler. She'd even met and liked der Führer, and had said so in print.

She'd been the target of FBI surveillance as a possible spy, and during that surveillance who should turn up in her bed but a young naval lieutenant whose father had once been Ambassador to England. The Ambassador, as he preferred to be called even by his sons, found out about the affair, told Jack in no uncertain terms to end it, and then to make sure he did by getting him assigned to a PT boat in the Pacific, as far from Inga Binga as possible.

Kennedy had always suspected that Hoover had leaked the information to the Ambassador, but he hadn't known for certain until Jack became President when Hoover told them. Hoover had been surveilling all of the Kennedy children at the Ambassador's request. He'd given Kennedy a list of scandalous items as a sample, and hoped that would control the President and his brother.

It might have controlled Jack, but Hoover hadn't known Kennedy very well. Kennedy had told Hoover that if any of this information made it into the press, then other things would appear in print as well, things like the strange FBI budget items for payments covering Hoover's visits to the track or the fact that Hoover made some interesting friends, mobster friends, when he was vacationing in Palm Beach.

It wasn't quite a Mexican standoff—Jack really was afraid of the old man—but it gave Kennedy more power than any attorney general had had over Hoover since the beginnings of the Roosevelt administration.

But now Kennedy needed those files, and he had a hunch Hoover would label them obscene.

Kennedy opened the file, and was shocked to see Richard Nixon's name on the sheets inside. Kennedy thumbed through quickly, not caring what dirt they'd found on that loser. Nixon couldn't win an election after his defeat in 1960. He'd even told the press after he lost a California race that they wouldn't have him to kick around any more.

Yet Hoover had kept the files, just to be safe.

That old bastard really and truly had known where all the bodies were buried. And it wouldn't be easy to find them.

Kennedy took a deep breath. He stood, shoved his hands in his pockets, and surveyed the walls of files. It would take days to search each folder. He didn't have days. He probably didn't have hours.

But he was Hoover's immediate supervisor, whether the old man had recognized it or not. Hoover answered to him. Which meant that the files belonged to the Justice Department, of which the FBI was only one small part.

He glanced at his watch. No one pounded on the door. He probably had until dawn before someone tried to stop him. If he was really lucky, no one would think of the files until mid-morning.

He went to the door and beckoned Haskell inside.

"We're taking the files to my office," he said.

"All of them, sir?"

"All of them. These first, then whatever is in Hoover's office, and then any other confidential files you can find."

Haskell looked up the wall as if he couldn't believe the command. "That'll take some time, sir."

"Not if you get a lot of people to help."

"Sir, I thought you wanted to keep this secret."

He did. But it wouldn't remain secret for long. So he had to control when the information got out—just like he had to control the information itself.

"Get this done as quickly as possible," he said.

Haskell nodded and turned the doorknob, but Kennedy stopped him before he went out.

"These are filed by code," he said. "Do you know where the key is?"

"I was told that Miss Gandy had the keys to everything from codes to offices," Haskell said.

Kennedy felt a shiver run through him. Knowing Hoover, he would have made sure he had the key to the attorney general's office as well.

"Do you have any idea where she might have kept the code keys?" Kennedy asked.

"No," Haskell said. "I wasn't part of the need-to-know group. I already knew too much."

Kennedy nodded. He appreciated how much Haskell knew. It had gotten him this far.

"On your way out," Kennedy said, "call building maintenance and have them change all the locks in my office."

"Yes, sir." Haskell kept his hand on the doorknob. "Are you sure you want to do this, sir? Couldn't you just change the locks here? Wouldn't that secure everything for the President?"

"Everyone in Washington wants these files," Kennedy said. "They're going to come to this office suite. They won't think of mine."

"Until they heard that you moved everything."

Kennedy nodded. "And then they'll know how futile their quest really is."

The final crime scene was a mess. The bodies were already gone— probably inside the coroner's van that blocked the alley a few blocks back. It had taken Bryce nearly a half an hour to find someone who knew what the scene had looked like when the police had first arrived.

That someone was Officer Ralph Voight. He was tall and trim, with a pristine uniform despite the fact that he'd been on duty all night.

O'Reilly was the one who convinced him to talk with Bryce. Voight was the first to show the traditional animosity between the NYPD and the FBI, but that was because Voight didn't know who had died only a few blocks away.

Bryce had Voight walk him through the crime scene. The buildings on this street were boarded up, and the lights burned out. Broken glass littered the sidewalk—and it hadn't come from this particular crime. Rusted beer cans, half buried in the ice piles, cluttered each stoop like passed-out drunks.

"Okay," Voight said, using his flashlight as a pointer, "we come up on these two cars first."

The two sedans were parked against the curb, one behind the other. The sedans were too nice for the neighborhood—new, black, without a dent. Bryce recognized them as FBI issue—he had access to a sedan like that himself when he needed it.

He patted his pocket, was disgusted to realize he'd left his notebook at the apartment, and turned to O'Reilly. "You got paper? I need those plates."

O'Reilly nodded. He pulled out a notebook and wrote down the plate numbers.

"They just looked wrong," Voight was saying. "So we stopped, figuring maybe someone needed assistance."

He pointed the flashlight across the street. The squad had stopped directly across from the two cars.

"That's when we seen the first body."

He walked them to the middle of the street. This part of the city hadn't been plowed regularly and a layer of ice had built over the pavement. A large pool of blood had melted through that ice, leaving its edges reddish black and revealing the pavement below.

"The guy was face down, hands out like he'd tried to catch himself."

"Face gone?" Bryce asked, thinking maybe it was a head shot like the others.

"No. Turns out he was shot in the back."

Bryce glanced at O'Reilly, whose lips had thinned. This one was different. Because it was the first? Or because it was unrelated?

"We pull our weapons, scan to see if we see anyone else, which we don't. The door's open on the first sedan, but we didn't see anyone in the dome light. And we didn't see anyone obvious on the street, but it's really dark here and the flashlights don't reach far." Voight turned his light toward the block with the parked limousine, but neither the car nor the sidewalk was visible from this distance.

"So we go to the cars, careful now, and find the other body right there."

He flashed his light on the curb beside the door to the first sedan. "This one's on his back and the door is open. We figure he was getting out when he got plugged. Then the other guy—maybe he was outside his car trying to help this guy with I don't know what, some car trouble or something, then his buddy gets hit, so he runs for cover across the street and gets nailed. End of story."

"Did you check to see if the cars start?" O'Reilly asked. Bryce nodded; that was going to be his next question as well.

"I'm not supposed to touch the scene, sir," Voight said with some resentment. "We secured the area, figured everything was okay, then called it in."

"Did you hear the other shots?"

"No," Voight said. "I know we got three more up there, and you'd think I'd've heard the shooting if something happened, but I didn't. And as you can tell, it's damn quiet around here at night."

Bryce could tell. He didn't like the silence in the middle of the city. Neighborhoods that got quiet like this so close to dawn were usually among the worst. The early morning maintenance workers and the delivery drivers stayed away whenever they could.

He peered in the sedan, then pulled the door open. The interior light went on, and there was blood all over the front seat and steering wheel. There were Styrofoam coffee cups on both sides of the little rise between the seats. And the keys were in the ignition. Like all Bureau issue, the car was an automatic.

Carefully, so that he wouldn't disturb anything important in the scene, he turned the key. The sedan purred to life, sounding well-tuned just like it was supposed to.

"Check to see if there are other problems," Bryce said to O'Reilly. "A flat maybe."

Although Bryce knew there wouldn't be one. He shut off the ignition.

"You didn't see the interior light when you pulled up?" he asked Voight.

"Yeah, but it was dim," Voight said. "That's why I figured there was car problems. I figured they left the lights on so they could see."

Bryce nodded. He understood the assumption. He backed out of the sedan, then walked around it, shining his own flashlight at the hole in the ice, and then back at the first sedan.

Directly across.

He walked to the second sedan. Its interior was clean—no Styrofoam cups, no wadded up food containers, no notebooks. Not even some tools hastily pulled to help the other drivers in need.

He let out a small sigh. He finally figured out what was bothering him.

"You find weapons on the two men?" he asked Voight.

"Yes, sir."

"Holstered?"

"The guy by the car. The other one had his in his right hand. We figured we just happened on the scene or someone would have taken the weapon."

Or not. People tended to hide for a while after shots were fired, particularly if they had nothing to do with the shootings but might get blamed anyway.

Bryce tried to open the passenger door on the second sedan, but it was locked. He walked around to the driver's door. Locked as well.

"No one looked inside this car?"

"No, sir. We figured crime scene would do it."

"But they haven't been here yet?" Bryce asked.

"It's the neighborhood, sir. Right there—" Voight aimed his flashlight at stairs heading down to a lower level, "—is one of those men-only clubs, you know? The kind that you go to when you're... you know... looking for other men."

Bryce felt a flash of irritation. He'd been running into this all night. "Okay. What I'm hearing in a sideways way from every representative of the NYPD on this scene is that crimes in this neighborhood don't get investigated."

Voight sputtered. "They get investigated—"

"They get investigated," O'Reilly said, "enough to tell the families they probably want to back off. You heard Brunner. That's what most in the department call it. The rest of us, we call them lifestyle kills. And we get in trouble if we waste too many resources on them."

"Lovely," Bryce said dryly. His philosophy, which had gotten him in trouble with the Bureau more than once, was that all crimes deserved investigation, no matter how distasteful you found the victims. Which was why he kept getting moved, from communists to reviewing wiretaps to digging dirt on other agents.

And that was probably why he was here. He was expendable.

"Did you find car keys on either of the victims?" Bryce asked.

"No, sir," Voight said. "And I helped the coroner when he first arrived."

"Then start looking. See if they got dropped in the struggle."

Although Bryce doubted they had.

"I got something to jimmy the lock in my car," O'Reilly said.

Bryce nodded. Then he stood back, surveying the whole thing. He didn't like how he was thinking. It was making his heartburn grow worse.

But it was the only thing that made sense.

Agents worked HooverWatch in pairs. There were two dead agents and two cars. If the second sedan was back-up, there should have been four agents and two cars.

But it didn't look that way. It looked like someone had pulled up behind the HooverWatch vehicle, and got out, carefully locking the door.

Then he went to the door of the HooverWatch car. The driver had got out to talk to him, and the new guy shot him.

At that point, the second HooverWatch agent was an easy target. He scrambled out of the car, grabbed his own weapon, and headed across the street—maybe shooting as he went. The shooter got him, and then casually walked up the street to the limo, which he had to know was there even though he couldn't see it.

As he approached the limo, the limo driver lowered his window. He would have recognized the approaching man, and thought he was going to report on the danger.

Instead, the man shot him, then went to lie in wait for Hoover and Tolson.

Bryce shivered. It would have happened very fast, and long before the beat cops showed up.

The guy in the street had time to bleed out. The limo driver couldn't warn his boss. And the beat cops hadn't heard the shots in the alley, which they would have on such a quiet night.

O'Reilly brought the jimmy, shoved it into the space between the window and the lock, and flipped the lock up with a single movement. Then he opened the door.

No keys in the ignition.

Bryce flipped open the glove box. Nothing inside but the vehicle registration. Which, as he expected, identified it as an FBI vehicle.

The shooter had planned to come back. He'd planned to drive away in this car. But he got delayed. And by the time he got here, the two beat cops were on scene. He couldn't get his car.

He had to improvise. So he probably walked away or took the subway, hoping the cops would think the extra car belonged to one of the victims.

And that was his mistake.

"How come you guys were here in the middle of the night?" Bryce asked Voight.

Voight swallowed. It was the first sign of nervousness he'd shown. "This is part of our beat."

"But?" Bryce asked.

Voight looked away. "We're supposed to go up Central Park West."

"And you don't."

"Yeah, we do. Just not every time."

"Because?"

"Because I figure, you know, when the bars let out, we could, you know, let our presence be known."

"Prevent a lifestyle kill."

"Yes, sir."

"And you care about this because...?"

"Everyone should," Voight snapped. "Serve and protect, right, sir?"

Voight was touchy. He thought Bryce was accusing him of protecting the lifestyle because he lived it.

"Does your partner like this drive?" Bryce asked.

"He complains, sir, but he lets me do it."

"Have you stopped any crimes?"

"Broken up a few fights," Voight said.

"But not something like this."

"No, sir."

"You don't patrol every night, do you, Voight?"

"No, sir. We get different regions different nights."

"Do you think our killer would have thought that this street was unprotected?"

"It usually is, sir."

O'Reilly was frowning, but not at Voight. At Bryce. "You think this was planned?" O'Reilly asked.

Bryce didn't answer. This was a Bureau matter, and he wasn't sure how the Bureau would handle it.

But he did think the killing was planned. And he had a hunch it would be easy to solve because of the abandoned sedan.

And that abandoned sedan bothered him more than he wanted to admit. Because the presence of that sedan meant only one thing: that the person who had shot all five FBI agents was—almost without a doubt—an FBI agent himself.

Kennedy looked at the bins and the filing cabinets stacked around his office and allowed himself one moment to feel overwhelmed. People ribbed him about the office; he had taken the reception area and made it his, rather than use the standard-size office in the back.

As a result, his office was as long as a football field, with stunning windows along the walls. The watercolors painted by his children had been covered by the cabinets. His furniture was pushed aside to make room for the bins, and for the first time, this space felt small.

He put his hands on his hips and wondered how to begin.

Since six agents began moving the filing cabinets across the corridor more than an hour ago, Kennedy had received five phone calls from LBJ's chief of staff. Kennedy hadn't taken one of them. The last had been a direct order to come to the Oval Office.

Kennedy ignored it.

He also ignored the ringing telephone—the White House line—and the messages his own assistant (called in after a short night's sleep) had been bringing to him.

Helen Gandy stood in the corridor, arms crossed, her purse hanging off her wrist, and watching with deep disapproval. Haskell was trying to find out if there were remaining files and where they were. But Kennedy had found the one thing he was looking for: the key.

It was in a large, innocuous index file box inside the lowest drawer of Helen Gandy's desk. Kennedy had brought it into his office and was thumbing through it, hoping to understand it before he got interrupted again.

A man from building maintenance had changed the lock on the door leading into the interior offices, and was working on the main doors now that the files were all inside. Kennedy figured he'd have his own office secure by seven am.

Then he heard a rustling in the hallway, a lot of startled, "Mr. President, sir!" followed by official, "Make way for the President," and instinctively he turned toward the door. The maintenance man was leaning out of it, the doorknob loose in his hand.

"Where the fuck is that bastard?" Lyndon Baines Johnson's voice echoed from the corridor. "Doesn't anyone in this building have balls enough to tell him that he works for me?"

Even though the question was rhetorical, someone tried to answer. Kennedy heard something about "your orders, sir."

"Horseshit!" Then LBJ stood in the doorway. Two secret service agents flanked him. He motioned with one hand at the maintenance man. "I suggest you get out."

The man didn't have to be told twice. He scurried away, still carrying the doorknob. LBJ came inside alone, pushed the door closed, then grimaced as it popped back open. He grabbed a chair and set it in front of the door, then glared at Kennedy.

The glare was effective in that hangdog face, despite LBJ's attire. He wore a plaid silk pajama top stuffed into a pair of suit pants, finished with dress shoes and no socks. His hair—what remained of it—hadn't been Brylcreemed down like usual, and stood up on the sides and the back.

"I get a phone call from some weasel underling of that old cocksucker, informing me that he's dead, and you're stealing from his tomb. I try to contact you, find out that you are indeed removing files from the Director's office, and that you won't take my calls. Now, I should've sent one of my boys over here, but I figured they're still walking on tip-toe around you because you're in fucking mourning, and this don't require tip-toe. Especially since you got to be wondering about now what the hell you did to deserve all of this."

"Deserve what?" Kennedy had expected LBJ's anger, but he hadn't expected it so soon. He also hadn't expected it here, in his office, instead of in the Oval Office a day or so later.

"Well, there's only two things that tie J. Edgar and your brother. The first is that someone was gunning for them and succeeded. The second is that they went after the mob on your bidding. There's a lot of shit running around here that says your brother's shooting was a mob hit, and I know personally that J. Edgar was doing his best to make it seem like that Oswald character acted alone. But now Edgar is dead and Jack is dead and the only tie they have is the way they kowtowed to your stupid prosecution of the men that got your brother elected."

Kennedy felt lightheaded. He hadn't even thought that the deaths of his brother and J. Edgar were connected. But LBJ had a point. Maybe there was a conspiracy to kill government officials. Maybe the mob was showing its power. He'd had warning.

Hell, he'd had suspicions. He hadn't let himself look at any of the evidence in his brother's assassination, not after he secured the body and prevented a disastrous autopsy in Texas. If those doctors at Parkland had done their job, they would've seen just how advanced Jack's Addison's disease was. The best kept secret of the Kennedy Administration—an administration full of secrets—was how close Jack was to incapacitation and death.

Kennedy clutched the file box. But LBJ knew that. He knew a lot of the secrets—had even promised to keep a few of them. And he wanted the files as badly as Kennedy did.

There had to be a lot in here on LBJ too. Not just the women, which was something he had in common with Jack, but other things, from his days in Congress.

"From what I heard," Kennedy said, making certain his voice was calm even though he wasn't, "all they know is someone shot Hoover. Did you get more details than that? Something that mentions organized crime in particular?"

"I'm sure it'll come out," LBJ said.

"You're sure that saying such things would upset me," Kennedy said. "You're after the files."

"Damn straight," LBJ said. "I'm the head of this government. Those files are mine."

"You're the head of this government for another year. Next January, someone'll take the oath of office and it might not be you. Do you really want to claim these in the name of the presidency? Because you might be handing them over to Goldwater come January."

LBJ blanched.

Someone knocked on the door, and startled both men. Kennedy frowned. He couldn't think of anyone who would have enough nerve to interrupt him when he was getting shouted at by LBJ. But someone had.

LBJ pulled the door open. Helen Gandy stood there.

"You boys can be heard in the hallway," she said, sweeping in as if the Leader of the Free World wasn't holding the door for her. "And it's embarrassing. It was precisely this kind of thing the Director hoped to avoid."

Then she nodded at LBJ. Kennedy watched her. The dragon lady. Jack, as usual, had been right with his jibes. Only the dragon lady would walk in here as if she were the most important person in the room.

"Mr. President," she said, "these files are the Director's personal business. He wanted me to take care of them, and get them out of the office, where they do not belong."

"Personal files, Miss Gandy?" LBJ asked. "These are his secret files."

"If they were secret, Mr. President, then you wouldn't be here. Mr. Hoover kept his secrets."

Mr. Hoover used his secrets, Kennedy thought, but didn't say.

"These are just his confidential files," Miss Gandy was saying. "Let me take care of them and they won't be here to tempt anyone. That's what the Director wanted."

"These are government property," LBJ said with a sly look at Kennedy. For the first time, Kennedy realized his Goldwater argument had gotten through. "They belong here. I do thank you for your time and concern, though, ma'am."

Then he gave her a courtly little bow, put his hand on the small of her back, and propelled her out of the room.

Despite himself Kennedy was impressed. He'd never seen anyone handle the dragon lady that efficiently before.

LBJ grabbed one of the cabinets and slid it in front of the door he had just closed. Kennedy had forgotten how strong the man was. He had invited Kennedy down to his Texas ranch before the election, trying to find out what Kennedy was made of, and instead, Kennedy had realized just what LBJ was made of—strength, not bluster, brains *and* brawn.

He'd do well to remember that.

"All right," LBJ said as he turned around. "Here's what I'm gonna offer. You can have your family's files. You can watch while we search for them and you can have everything. Just give me the rest."

Kennedy raised his eyebrows. He hadn't felt this alive since November. "No."

"I can fire your ass in five minutes, put someone else in this fancy office, and then you can't do a goddamn thing," LBJ said. "I'm being kind."

"There's historical precedent for a cabinet member barricading himself in his office after he got fired," Kennedy said. "Seems to me it happened to a previous President named Johnson. While I'm barricaded in, I'll just go through the files and find out everything I need to know."

LBJ crossed his arms.

It was a standoff and neither of them had a good play. They only had a guess as to what was in those files—not just theirs but all of the others as well. They did know that whatever was in those files had given Hoover enough power to last in the office for more than forty years.

The files had brought down Presidents. They could bring down congressmen, Supreme Court justices, and maybe even the current President. In that way, Helen Gandy was right.

The best solution was to destroy everything.

Only Kennedy wouldn't. Just like he knew LBJ wouldn't. There was too much history here, too much knowledge.

And too much power.

"These are our files," Kennedy said after a moment, although the word "our" galled him, "yours and mine. Right now we control them."

LBJ nodded, almost imperceptibly. "What do you want?"

What did he want? To be left alone? To have his family left alone? At midnight, he might have said that. But now, his old self was reasserting itself. He felt like the man who had gone after the corrupt leaders of the Teamsters, not the man who had accidentally gotten his brother murdered.

Besides, there might be things in that file that could head off other problems in the future. Other murders. Other manipulations.

He needed a bulletproof position. LBJ was right: the attorney general could be fired. But there was one position, constitutionally, that the President couldn't touch.

"I want to be your vice President," Kennedy said. "And in 1972, when you can't run again, I want your endorsement. I want you to back me for the nomination."

LBJ swallowed hard. Color suffused his face and for a moment, Kennedy thought he was going to shout again.

But he didn't.

Instead he said, "And what happens if we don't win?"

"We move these to a location of our choosing. And we do it with trusted associates. We get this stuff out of here."

LBJ glanced at the door. He was clearly thinking of what Helen Gandy had said, how it was better to be rid of all of this than it was to have it corrupting the office, endangering everyone.

But if LBJ and Kennedy controlled the entire cache, they also controlled their own files. LBJ could destroy his and Kennedy could preserve his family's legacy.

If it weren't for the fact that LBJ hated him almost as much as Kennedy hated LBJ, the decision would be easy.

"You'd trust me to a gentleman's agreement?" LBJ asked, not disguising the sarcasm in his tone. He knew Kennedy thought he was too uncouth to ever be considered a gentleman.

"You know where your interests lie. Just like I do," Kennedy said. "If we don't let Miss Gandy have the files, then this is the only choice."

LBJ sighed. "I hoped to be rid of the Kennedys by inauguration day."

"And what if I planned to run against you?" Kennedy asked, even though he knew he wouldn't. Already the party stalwarts had been approaching him about a 1964 Presidential bid, and he had put them off. He had been too shaky, too emotionally fragile.

He didn't feel fragile now.

LBJ didn't answer that question. Instead, he said, "You can be an incautious asshole. Why should I trust you?"

"Because I saved Jack's ass more times than you can count," Kennedy said. "I'm saving yours too."

"How do you figure?" LBJ asked.

"Your fear of those files brought you to me, Mr. President." Kennedy put an emphasis on the title, which he usually avoided using around LBJ. "If I barricade myself in here, I'll have the keys to the kingdom and no qualms about letting the information free when I go free. If you work with me, your secrets remain just secrets."

"You're a son of bitch, you know that?" LBJ asked.

Kennedy nodded. "The hell of it is you are too or you wouldn't've brought up Jack's death before we knew what really happened to Hoover. So let's control the presidency for the next sixteen years. By then the information in these files will probably be worthless."

LBJ stared at him. It took Kennedy a minute to realize that although he'd won the argument, he wouldn't get an agreement from LBJ, not if Kennedy didn't make the first move.

Kennedy held out his hand. "Deal?"

LBJ stared at Kennedy's extended hand for a long moment before taking it in his own big clammy one.

"You goddamn son of a bitch," LBJ said. "You've got a deal."

It took Bryce only one phone call. The guy who ran the motor pool told him who checked out the sedan without asking why Bryce wanted to know. And Bryce, as he leaned in the cold telephone booth half a block from the first crime scene, instantly understood what had happened and why.

The agent who checked out the sedan was Walter Cain. He should've been on extended leave. Bryce had recommended it after he had told Cain that his ex-fiancée had tried to commit suicide. On getting the news, Cain had just had that look, that blank, my-life-is-over look.

And it had scared Bryce. Scared him enough that he asked Cain be put on indefinite leave. How long ago had that been? Less than twelve hours.

More than enough time to get rid of the morals police—the one man who made all the rules at the FBI. The man who had no morals himself.

J. Edgar Hoover.

Bryce had spent the past week studying Cain's file. Cain had had HooverWatch off and on throughout the past year. Cain knew the procedure, and he knew how to thwart it.

He'd killed five agents.

Because no one would listen to Bryce about that vacant look in Cain's eye.

Bryce let himself out of the phone booth. He walked back to the coroner's van. If he didn't have back-up by now, he'd call for some all over again. They couldn't leave him hanging on this. They had to let him know, if nothing else, what to do with the Director's body.

But he needn't've worried. When he got back to the alley, he saw five more sedans, all FBI issue. And as he stepped into the alley proper, the first person he saw was his boss, crouching over Hoover's corpse.

"I thought I told you to secure the scene," said the SAC for the District of New York, Eugene Hart. "In fact, I ordered you to do it."

"The scene extends over six blocks. I'm just one guy," Bryce said.

Hart walked over to him. He looked tired.

"I need to speak to you," Bryce said. He walked Hart back to the two sedans, explained what he'd learned, and watched Hart's face.

The man flinched, then, to Bryce's surprise, put his hand on Bryce's shoulder. "It's good work."

Bryce didn't thank him. He was worried that Hart hadn't asked any questions. "I'd heard Cain bitch more than once about Hoover setting the moral values for the office. And with what happened this week—"

"I know." Hart squeezed his shoulder. "We'll take care of it."

Bryce turned so quickly that he made Hart lose his grip. "You're going to cover it up."

Hart closed his eyes.

"You weren't hanging me out to dry. You were trying to figure out how to handle this. Son of bitch. And you're going to let Cain walk."

"He won't walk," Hart said. "He'll just... be guilty of something else."

"You can't cover this up. It's too important. So soon after President Kennedy—"

"That's precisely why we're going to handle it," Hart said. "We don't want a panic."

"And you don't want anyone to know where Hoover and Tolson were found. What're you going to say? That they died of natural causes in their beds? Their *separate* beds?"

"It's not your concern," Hart said. "You've done well for us. You'll be rewarded."

"If I keep my mouth shut."

Hart sighed. He didn't seem to have the energy to glare. "I don't honestly care. I'm glad to have the old man gone. But I'm not in charge of this. We've got orders now, and everything'll get taken care of at a much higher level than either you or me. You should be grateful for that."

Bryce supposed he should be. It took the political pressure off him. It also took the personal pressure off.

But he couldn't help feeling if someone had listened to him before, if someone had paid attention, then none of this would have happened.

No one cared that an FBI agent was going to marry a former prostitute. If the Bureau knew, and it did, then not even the KGB could use that as blackmail.

It was all about appearances. It would always be about appearances. Hoover had designed a damn booklet about appearances, and it hadn't stopped him from getting shot in a back alley after a party he would never admit attending.

Hoover had been so worried about people using secrets against each other, he hadn't even realized how his own secrets could be used against him.

Bryce looked at Hart. They were both tired. It had been a long night. And it would be an even longer few weeks for Hart. Bryce would get some don't-tell promotion and he'd stay there for as long as he had to. He had to make sure that Cain got prosecuted for something, that he paid for five deaths.

Then Bryce would resign.

He didn't need the Bureau, any more than he had needed Mary, his own pre-approved wife. Maybe he'd talk to O'Reilly, see if he could put in a good word with the NYPD. At least the NYPD occasionally investigated cases.

If they happened in the right neighborhood.

To the right people.

Bryce shoved his hands in his pockets and walked back to his apartment. Hart didn't try to stop him. They both knew Bryce's work on this case was done. He wouldn't even have to write a report.

In fact, he didn't dare write a report, didn't dare put any of this on paper where someone else might discover it. The wrong someone. Someone who didn't care about handling and the proper information.

Someone who would use that information to his own benefit.

Like the Director had.

For more than forty-five years.

Bryce shook the thought off. It wasn't his concern. He no longer had concerns. Except getting a good night's sleep.

And somehow he knew that he wouldn't get one of those for a long, long time.

Sacrifice

Mary Rosenblum

From 1999 to 2002, Mary Rosenblum wrote the "Gardening Mysteries" novels under the name Mary Freeman. But she began her career as a science fiction author, and it's to science fiction she has now returned. She is a Hugo Award finalist, an Endeavour Award finalist, a winner of the Compton Crook Award and the Asimov's Readers Award, and her short fiction has been collected in several Year's Best anthologies. This is my first time working with Mary. It won't be my last.

"Gerard? Wake up. Hurry!"

The hissing whisper dragged me out of a dream of Song's smile and the scent of spring prairie grass. I sat up, groggy, on my mat, wondering if it would ever stop hurting. "Who?" A faint hint of gray light seeped in through the window. "Avery?" He crouched on the tile floor by my mat, shivering in the pre-dawn chill. "What are you doing here? What's wrong?"

"I need money. Please?" The Irishman twisted his hands together, his expression invisible in the dim light. "I'm in trouble, Gerard. I need to go north. Right now."

"Did you get drunk again? I warned you." Wide awake now, I tossed my quilt aside. "The Ciuacoatl cuts foreigners some slack, but you're going to end up a slave if you don't..."

"Just loan me the money. Whatever you can." He cut me off, his young face haggard in the faint light. "I'll pay you back. I promise."

"I'll help you out. Of course. But tell me what's going on." I scrambled to my feet, knelt in front of my petlacalli, throwing back the wicker lid and digging through my stored clothes. "Maybe I can do something?"

"You can't." His voice was flat and emotionless. "I'm heading up to Columbia. The Spaniards will hand an Englishman over to the Aztecs in a heartbeat, but I can catch a Hudson's Bay trader heading up the coast. If anyone asks, you haven't seen me, okay?"

"Here." I handed him three gold quachtli. "I wish you'd tell me what happened."

He shook his head, darted to the door of my one-room house. Paused there and looked back, a black outline against the gray light. "I didn't do it, Gerard." And then he was gone, the soft slap of his sandals fading in the distance.

I stared after him, worried. I had taken the young poet under my wing when he had first arrived here from St. Augustine, the eastern capital of New Spain. He was a dreamer, that one. I don't know how he had survived this long on his wanderings. The first flat claps from the wooden gongs atop the Temple of the Sun shattered the quiet. A moment later, the conch shells trumpeted the start of the day from the Temple of Quetzalcoatl. Frowning, I folded my cotton quilt and left it neatly on my mat, which would annoy Ten Reed, my slave. A warrior before he had been accused of murder, he took his current slave status as seriously as he had taken his warrior career. I was not supposed to fold things.

What had Avery done? I couldn't imagine. I said a small prayer to Tezcatlipoca, the local god of night and youth, to keep the dreamer safe and shivered in the chilly dawn air. Xitllali, the chocolatl vendor would have her brazier burning by now. I needed chocolate with some of those kava beans imported from the Byzantines. I pulled on cotton pants and wrapped my tilmatli around me, fastening it with one of the imported brooches that were all the rage now, and stepped into the bustle of a Tenochtitlan morning.

My assigned house was in the huge palace complex and bordered one of The Quetzal's gardens—this one planted in Hot Land species and full of the big, noisy red and blue birds from the Mayan jungles.

So even if they didn't bang gongs in the morning, nobody would sleep in around here. But my teaching time with The Quetzal's daughter, Malinal, was early anyway. I headed for the chocolatl vendor's stand just outside the palace's southern gate past the street sweepers with their reed brooms, their hair braided in the sweepers' knot and woven with blue to honor their favorite god Ometeotl. Xitllali was already frothing a bowl for me as I turned the corner into the wide main thoroughfare, smoke from her brazier sharp in the cool morning air. Her booth bordered the canal, not far from the public latrine barges gathering their loads of night soil. The location assured her a brisk morning business and strands of jade beads around her neck attested to her success.

"The Spaniards are banging their shutters again." She grinned and handed me the bowl. "Ahexoti says they light up two hands' worth of lamps every night. If they slept when it was dark, they would get up early, eh?" She slipped the small quachtli I handed her into the bag beneath her long blouse and winked.

"They're just angry because the high priest wouldn't give up their captain is all. Ah, that's good." She had not only mixed in some of the Byzantine kava beans, but also some hot chili. Europe couldn't get past the ritual sacrifice thing although the Sioux nation understood it completely. Usually, after a certain amount of negotiation and "gifts," the priests would give up foreign transgressors to their consulate, but in this case, a high-ranking Spanish official had lost his temper while he was drunk and had stabbed a feather-mosaic artist in front of witnesses. Someone of his rank was just too valuable a treat for the bloodthirsty Aztec gods. And for all their bloody reputation, the Aztecs did not tolerate crime, especially not murder. Rumor was that the Spanish delegation had appealed to the Chinese Ambassador, but the Chinese Ambassador had refused to meet with them.

Which probably had a lot to do with the current trade squabble between China and Spain over the North African trade routes. World politics were never dull. And the city on the lake was a good place to hear it all. The Aztecs loved gossip as much as they loved blood. I leaned against the huge, carved doorposts of the palace's east gate and watched the bearers trotting across the huge central square bent into their forehead straps, balancing huge loads on their backs as they dodged pedestrians and street sweepers. Oh, you saw more and more of the wheeled carts and rickshaws introduced by the Chinese, and many of the nobles owned horses now, but the Brotherhood of Bearers still carried most cargo. Although The Quetzal was listening seriously to news of the fire-fueled engine that had supposedly carried a thousand pounds on its back, over in the Germanic Federation. I finished the last of my spicy chocolatl. I doubted a steam engine would ever run along the Ixtapalapan causeway here. The Brotherhood of Bearers had way too much power.

The lake mist was rising, thickened with the smoke from the cooking braziers and the big central market was already in full swing. I crossed the square to where the vendors' stalls formed a miniature city, picking my way through the narrow alleys between the stalls past cages of bright birds, bundles of feathers, gobbling turkeys with their feet bound, piles of cinnamon bark and vanilla beans brought up from the Hot Lands, exotic woods, making my way to the street of flowers where I bought a fat bunch of yellow sunflowers.

Malinal, The Quetzal's favorite daughter, had a suite of three rooms that opened into his favorite garden, the one with a waterfall fed by the aqueduct from Chapultepec that splashed into a mosaic-tiled pool. We always had our lessons beside the pool unless it was raining. She was waiting for me as usual, sitting on her mat beside the low table carved from dark African wood, dressed in a white cotton blouse and skirt hemmed with intricate feather work in blue, red, and green. She raised her finely drawn eyebrows, her dark eyes sparkling as she eyed my armful of yellow blossoms.

"Tell me the story of these flowers." She smiled up at me and for a moment, my wife, Spring Wind Song, looked from her eyes.

I had to make a fuss over arranging the blossoms on the table until I could speak normally. "There is no story." I managed a smile as I sat down on my mat, arranging my tilmatli over my thighs because it was still cool here in the breath of the waterfall. "They were my wife's favorite flower and this is her birthday."

"I am honored." She paused for a moment, those dark eyes so like Song's fixed on my face. "It is a deep love that lasts three hands of years beyond death."

"Seventeen years," I said automatically, in English.

She bent her head, her jade earrings tinkling slightly with her movement. "So what is our lesson to be today, Teacher of Foreign Thought?" She shifted smoothly into English.

I was still worrying about Avery and my nebulous plan for today's lesson had taken flight like a white heron from the lake. "Why don't you begin with a question?"

"Why is sacrifice to the gods so terrible to the French when it is considered honorable to cut the bowels from a man on a battlefield and leave him to die in the sun?" Her dark eyes bored into me. "That death has no more meaning than cutting the throat of a hare for the pot. It devalues the warrior. According to the Ambassador from France, three hundred warriors died like that in their latest battle with England."

I sighed. "So what did the Ambassador from France say at the state dinner last night that stung, oh feathered daughter?"

"He said nothing to *me*." She lifted one shoulder in a delicate shrug, then frowned. "My maid told me after that he had brought an application for marriage from the king of France on behalf of his youngest son. For me, of course. He was... condescending. And he was not pleased with my father's answer to him." She tilted her head. "At dinner that night he stared at me and then he left the table. I saw... pity in his face, Gerard. I feel... insulted." Her dark eyes were deep as pools and old as I was, young as she was, I felt as if I teetered on the brink, as if I could fall in. And drown.

"How could he *pity* me? How dare he?"

"He doesn't understand." I had a hard time getting the words out. "It is hard... for someone who is not of your race to understand your choice. He believed you are a victim, that this is not really your choice."

"You don't understand it either." Her voice was gentle. "Even after all your years here."

"It's hard." I fixed my eyes on the water that sparkled like Arabian diamond as it shattered on the rocks above the mosaic pool. "It's hard to... teach you, to see your brilliance and know that in less than a year..."

"How could I be less than the best I can be, when I go before the gods?" She lifted a carved pendant of rosy jade that she wore around her neck. "I can smash this jade with a hammer; the earth could shake down the very Temple of the Sun tomorrow. There is no certainty in life; all is ephemeral. What offering can we give the gods that has any real meaning? Gold, jade, even diamonds." She took the delicate golden chain from around her neck, held it out. "Nothing has any permanent value." With a flick of her wrist, she tossed the necklace into the pool. The gold caught the sunlight, delicate as a spider web as it sparkled, then plopped into the water, leaving tiny, widening rings behind it. "What gift can one give the gods save the enduring ephemera of the human soul?"

I just shook my head. I did understand—intellectually at least. I had seen the barbarity on the battlefields as a boy when the Sioux Nation repulsed the land-hungry settlers of New Britannia. Barbarity had been about equal on both sides. And the Choctaw had been largely destroyed, whole villages massacred to the last infant. War, for the Three Peoples was mostly about taking prisoners. Some were sacrificed, others bartered back. But when I watched the bright sparkle in Malinal's eyes as she recounted the conversation at a state dinner and deftly dissected the political undercurrents... I didn't understand her choice at all.

Two slaves bustled in, carrying a tray of food and dishes. Startled I looked up at the climbing sun. Mid-morning already. I nodded thanks as one slave set a bowl of atolli, sweet maize porridge, on the table beside a plate of sliced melon. Compared to the table of the factor of Hudson Bay Company or the minister of New Britannia, The Quetzal's Chinese porcelain dishes and the food they held were simple. The Aztecs had never acquired a taste for ostentation, although they had decorated the guest quarters more to European standards of luxury at my suggestion. Europeans did not sleep well on mats, even thick ones like mine, which made Ten Reed curl his lip.

"This is Ixchac's last day of servitude." Malinal smiled up at the tall, skinny man with streaks of gray in his hair. "I thank you for your service."

The older slave bowed, grinning and carried the empty tray from the garden. The Aztec penal system was a practical one. Nearly all transgressions earned you time as a slave, longer or shorter, depending on the severity of your crime. The most severe crimes made you the gods' meat. The legal slaves were auctioned every week in a small court in the central market. When I had first come to live in Tenochtitlan, I had been amazed at how well the system worked. A slave could accuse a master of abuse and the master could be... and often was... punished. Slaves were rarely confined in any way and simply paid off their legal debt. At the end of that time, a grateful and generous master or mistress might reward the freed slave with a gift. Or they might not. The system was hardly perfect and ugly incidents occurred, but I often thought that the system worked better than the stocks and whipping post in New Britannia or New Spain's barbarous punishments left over from their Inquisition.

As the slaves reached the garden gate, they both stepped backward off the path, bowing, fist to forehead.

The Quetzal walked in. Dressed in the antique maxtlatl knotted about his loins, draped with a short, formal cloak of exquisite feather-mosaic work, his sandals ornamented with jade, he nodded as both Malinal and I stood and bowed.

"Father." Malinal held out her hands. "I thought you were meeting with the trade delegation from Palenque this morning."

"They are examining the small model of the fire-horse that we've received from our delegation in England." He smiled. "You know the Maya. They love machines."

"I should go," I said.

"No." He lifted a hand. "I came looking for you."

I spread my hands and bowed again. It's hard not to be impressed by The Quetzal. He must be pushing sixty but he has welded the southern half of the twin-continents into a power that not even the Europeans with all their navies can challenge. Of course the Chinese and their gunpowder back him, but even there, he has managed to keep that alliance a partnership of equals—no mean feat. Once Avery told me that if the Chinese hadn't arrived here first and given the Three Peoples guns, Europe would have overrun the entire twin-continent. I find that hard to believe.

"I have heard of your interference in legal matters in the past." He was staring at me, his dark eyes as readable as chips of obsidian. "Most notably, of course, you proved the innocence of that young Mayan diplomat when he was accused of murder, and I have also heard that the slave who tends you does so of his own choice, in payment for exonerating him when he was accused of killing the aurianime he had hired for a night's entertainment. It appears that you have favor with Tezcatlipoca. He gives you clearer eyes than most, eh?"

"I am only a searcher after truth," I told him. "Tezcatlipoca doesn't whisper in my ear... at least not that I understand."

"The gods find many ways to speak when they choose to do so." The Quetzal waved a dismissive hand, the thick bracelet of gold on his wrist winking in the sunlight. "I have a truth for you to find." His obsidian eyes pinned me. "In the dark hours of the night, the first son of the Chinese consul was killed, without honor. He had a visitor that evening, the watchman attests to it. That visitor was just captured as he tried to escape the city."

"The truth seems very obvious here," I murmured.

"It does, does it not?" The Quetzal smiled, but his eyes were thoughtful. "A foreigner did this. I am disgraced, that I could not protect a guest in my city from an outside assassin." He paused, his strong lips curving downward until his face resembled one of the faces of the old warrior-kings carved on the ball court walls. "I want to be assured of the truth. Can you do that for me?"

"I can certainly try."

"I did not ask you to try." Those obsidian eyes bored into me.

"I can only do the best that I can." I forced myself not to look away. "To guarantee otherwise would be to imply fraud."

He frowned at me for a moment longer, and that look made my guts squirm. He was The Quetzal. He could assign me a starring role in the next sacrifice on the Sun Temple's steps with a snap of his fingers. The moment stretched between us, then he jerked his chin in a brief nod. "I will assign you whatever assistance you require. What do you need?"

"I would like the place of the killing to be guarded. So that none can enter." I frowned. "And I would like to speak to the accused. Or has he been given to the Chinese?" If that was the case, it was probably too late to do much. They would wring a confession out of him for sure. The Chinese could be as barbaric as the Spaniards that way, if more subtly. But The Quetzal nodded. "One of my personal guards has secured the room. The accused man is being held in the Hall of Justice." He lifted a hand and a slave in a loincloth ornamented with a jade tassel appeared in the doorway.

I followed the slave into the complex of main buildings near the palace gates. The lower floors were used for civic business and the courts. The upper floors housed The Quetzal's extended family. As we entered the ancient stone building that held the Hall of Justice, the slave offered a small scroll to the doorkeeper. He took the scroll and bustled away, his sandals slapping briskly on the beaten-earth floor. I had been here many times, for many reasons. The age of the place leaned on me like a weight. It had been standing before the first Chinese ship appeared on the horizon. Not one hint of modernity ornamented the whitewashed walls and earthen floors, no kiln-fired tile, no colorful silk hangings, even the tilmatli of the ministers and judges were knotted in the old style rather than fastened with the new brooches. Resinous ocotl flickered and smoked on the walls. No whale oil lamps here and not one tiny shard of the glass that was the new fad in the city.

A minister bustled up, his hair shaved at the forehead and twisted into the intricate knot that denoted high rank. He frowned at me, then handed back The Quetzal's scroll and gestured me to follow him. The cells for holding prisoners were in the bowels of the building, lit only by narrow slits high up in the outer wall. As the heavy wooden door creaked open, I made out a slender man face down on the thin mat. An earthenware pot for night soil stood in one corner and a water-gourd sat precisely in the middle of the floor. The wretch on the mat lifted his head, blinking as the rush light pierced the gloom.

"Avery!"

He scrambled to his knees, staring up at me, his face haggard. "Gerard? Are they going to let me go?"

He was so afraid. I knelt beside him, put a hand on his shoulder. He was shivering and the building was still cool with night's chill. His cloak, bordered with elegant feather mosaic work, lay in a heap on the floor. I picked it up, draped it around his shoulders. "Avery, what happened? The Quetzal has asked me to find out the truth."

"The truth is I didn't kill him. Shin Li." White ringed his eyes. "We played chess. We played chess every week. Gerard, they're going to give me to the Chinese." His voice rose. "Do you know what they'll do to me?"

"Stop." I took him by the arm, my fingers denting his flesh. "Help me, Avery. I need to know every detail of what happened if I'm going to save you. Don't leave anything out. How did you get to be friends with the consul's son?"

"I met him in the Garden of Small Trees, east of the central market. I was playing chess with a friend of mine there, and he challenged me to a game. I had met him before, at one of the palace functions—Mal... The Quetzal's daughter had invited me to read my poetry. I'm... not invited to the palace."

I nodded. The Quetzal had no use for any poet who was not Nahuatl.

"Shin Li was a strong player and we played weekly." Avery gave me a crooked smile. "A much better player than you, Gerard."

"That's hardly high praise." I rolled my eyes.

"That night... last night... I went to his room to play. I had started going there because he liked to talk and the Garden of Small Trees was too public."

"Did you notice anything different?"

"No." Avery frowned. "Well, maybe. He... shared something with me. We had been talking politics—he thought his father was too 'old school,' unwilling to deal with the Three Peoples as equals. He wanted to abolish some of the trade restrictions. He told me his father was in line for a court appointment and he had talked about leaving Li in charge when he returned to Beijing. To prove his theories correct, he said."

Suddenly The Quetzal's interest in this case made more sense.

"So you played chess. Then what happened?"

"We... we finished the game. It was a stalemate." Avery swallowed. "We drank some of their god-awful rice brandy and talked. Li told me that the Chinese compound used to be a brothel—for high-ranking ministers and diplomats. It offended his father that The Quetzal had housed them there. Don't look at me like that." Avery grimaced. "I wasn't drunk."

"I'm glad to hear that," I said rather dryly. "Who saw you leave?"

"The watchman did." He shrugged. "He sits on a stool by the courtyard entrance. Shin Li was alive then."

"Where did you go afterward?"

"Home." Avery didn't meet my eyes. "To bed. It was late."

He was a lousy liar. I stood. "I'm going to go look at the murder scene and talk to the watchman."

"Are you going to help me, Gerard?" Kneeling on the thin mat, Avery clutched at my knee. "You can prove that I didn't do it, can't you?"

"I can try." It bothered me that he hadn't told me the truth. I didn't try to sound very hopeful. Let him stew for a while and think about how much he wanted to hide from me.

The Quetzal's slave waited outside and I told him that I wanted to visit the room where the consul's son had died.

This turned out to be a bit more difficult than visiting the Hall of Justice. The watchman at the gate of the compound ushered us into the interior garden but there we were stalled while a Chinese servant or slave hurried off to fetch someone with more rank and he fetched his boss and so on until finally a young man in blue, brocaded silk stitched with gold arrived. The consul's younger son. I recognized him from some court function or other and couldn't remember his name.

"I have sent a message to The Quetzal." He barely inclined his head. "I see no reason for this disturbance of our grief, or the guard at my elder brother's room. The circumstances of my brother's foul murder are clear as well water."

I have seen some very muddy well water in my time. I merely bowed and enjoyed the shade beneath the carefully pruned and shaped tree that decorated this courtyard.

The sun stood straight overhead by the time the Chinese messenger returned from the palace to bow and hand the consul's younger son a small scroll. The contents made him scowl and he crumpled the fine agave-fiber paper gracelessly. "All right." He jerked his chin at the watchman. "Show them what they want. You are responsible for them." He turned on his heel and disappeared through a silk-hung doorway.

Rude. The Quetzal's slave looked down his arched nose after the young man. People were not rude here. Not even when they killed you. "Were you the man who was here last night?" I asked him.

"Yes." A stocky man in his middle years with the shaved forehead of a warrior, he nodded. "I was told that someone would speak with me. About last night."

The servants knew more than the masters, but that's the city for you. "Tell me what you saw," I said.

"I record all visitors." He reached into a small alcove behind the carved wooden stool where he sat, retrieved a bundle of reeds. "I record everyone who enters and leaves. See?" He extracted a long reed and waved it at me. "This one is yesterday. At the first hour after dawn, three bearers bringing fresh produce from the market and the water merchant's bearers, refilling the cistern." His blunt nail pointed out the marks, one by one. "A servant from the palace, a masseuse for the consul..." I frowned as that thumbnail ticked off the many visitors to the bustling consulate.

"The poet—this is him." The watchman dug his nail into that mark. And see? Here he leaves."

"When did you find the body?"

"Oh, much later." The nail moved on. "The consul had a late dinner and five people arrived for that. Then a servant came to the rooms of both sons. They were supposed to attend the dinner. She woke the younger son and then went to the older one's room. She screeched." The watchman shrugged. "I went to see what was wrong and he was there, lying dead on the floor behind the chess board where the poet had killed him. He still had a chess piece in his hand." The watchman nodded. "The poet seems very soft, but he knew right where to put the blade to pierce the heart."

He sounded approving. I sighed. "What then?"

The watchman shrugged. "The girl had run off to tell everyone. I went to see if he still lived, although you could tell from where the blade went in that he must have died."

"Did you move him?"

"I lifted his hand. That's when I saw he was holding the chess piece. It rolled onto the floor."

I frowned. "How so? Wasn't his hand stiff?"

"No." The watchman shrugged. "No more stiff than when you sleep."

My heart leaped. "You will swear to that on the steps of the Sun Temple?"

"Of course." He blinked at me, then his eyes narrowed. "Ah. It was a long time after the poet left. I did not think of that." He frowned. "No one else went into that room. I can see the doorway from where I sit. I never left my stool."

I could suggest that someone might have slipped through the shadows of the courtyard and into that room as the watchmen greeted one of the arriving guests, but the guests would be staring right at him. "I wish to see the room," I told my informant.

He took me, eager now.

It was an elegant room if not overly large, but that was not surprising if this had once been a brothel as Avery had said. I reflected briefly on The Quetzal's subtlety here. He was aware of the current consul's attitude toward the Three Peoples. He thought they were savages. Brocaded hangings crawled with gilded dragons and mother of pearl inlays gleamed on the intricately carved wooden furniture, including a wide bed thick with silken cushions. Imported rugs from the Byzantine warmed the tile floor and a carved wooden screen set into a tall, narrow window allowed the blossom-scented breath of a garden to cool the room. I pushed on the screen but it was set firmly in place, not designed to open. No other doorway opened into the room. I lifted the lid of one of the carved chests, eyed the pile of folded silk garments. A small rusty stain, no larger than the nail of my little finger marked one of the ivory colored tiles in front of the chest. I closed the lid and studied the chessboard. One piece was missing. That would be the piece the dead Shin Li had been clutching. The inlaid wooden chair lay on its side and flies buzzed about the dark bloodstain in the small but richly woven rug that the chair must have stood upon. Apparently the son of the consul did not like to chill his feet on the bare tiles as he played.

It was hot as I walked back to the Hall of Justice. The streets were empty, even the sweepers were resting in the shade, waiting for the cool of early evening. The market had shut down for the day and the stragglers were making their way home with remnants of unsold goods or were resting in the shade of their canopied stalls. In the dim, cool cell, Avery scrambled to his feet as the door opened.

"What did you find out?"

"That you didn't kill Shin Li."

"I told you that." Some color had come back into Avery's face. "Are they going to let me out?"

"I need to know where you were. After you left Shin Li."

"Home. In bed."

"You weren't." I kept my voice conversational. "You need to prove that you were somewhere else when the murder was committed, Avery. You need an alibi. So tell me where you were and who can swear on the Sun Temple steps that you were there."

He looked away from me and I watched a muscle jump in his jaw.

"If I can't solve this, The Quetzal will give you to the Chinese." I said it harshly, watched him go pale. But he shook his head. "I was at home. In bed."

And that was all I could get out of him. Well, maybe he deserved the Chinese. I went home, followed by The Quetzal's slave because I didn't yet know what other doors I might need to have him open. Ten Reed was working in the small garden although what he found to do when he never allowed a leaf to be out of place, I couldn't tell. I sent him to give The Quetzal's slave food and something to drink and a mat so he could rest and I seated myself in the shade on a thick petlatl that Ten Reed disapproved of as too comfortable, to listen to the birds in the big garden beyond the wall.

When Ten Reed returned with a tray of golden maize tlaxcalli, turkey seethed with chilis, and melon, I gestured to him to join me. Of course the tray held two bowls. Ten Reed reads me more accurately than anyone I have ever known. "Do you believe in ghosts?" I asked him as I scooped up turkey with a golden disk of tlaxcalli. "Ghosts that are strong enough to stab someone with a knife?"

Ten Reed chewed, frowning slightly. Swallowed. "I have never encountered a ghost that did damage directly. Someone else always saw it." He raised one eyebrow. "Perhaps the ghost possessed a mortal hand?"

"Perhaps indeed." I reached for another tlaxcalli. "But the mortal hand is not as adept as a ghost at slipping through solid walls."

"The appearance is not always the reality."

"Very profound." I smiled at Ten Reed. "So what is the gossip about the murder in the Chinese quarters?"

Ten Reed pulled at the sparse hairs growing on his chin, his broad face thoughtful. "That it was the Drunken Poet." He shrugged. "He was seen leaving, after the killing. He tried to flee." Ten Reed shrugged. "What can you expect of a drunk?" His tone was disapproving.

Yes, in many ways, Avery was the perfect suspect for this. Every resident of Tenochtitlan would expect the worst. He was a drunk. What, after all, can you expect from a drunk? I steepled my fingers and listened to one of the big red and blue Hot Land birds shriek. "Tell me about the compound where the Chinese consul lives."

Ten Reed pursed his lips. "It was built only four hands of years ago, for the son of the previous Quetzal. He was... notorious. When he finally chose to become a sacrifice it was rumored that he had had no choice. Everybody knew about his parties." Ten Reed shook his head. "My mother's cousin was the builder. He designed many houses for the nobles." Ten Reed smiled. "My uncle took me through it as he laid out the rooms. It was very challenging. The son of The Quetzal had many requests."

So it wasn't quite the brothel Avery had said. "What kinds of requests?"

Ten Reed shrugged. "The son of the previous Quetzal had... many appetites. And he wished to satisfy them privately. My uncle still talks about that building." Ten Reed chuckled. "He was very proud of how he solved all the challenges set for him by the son." He gave me a sideways look. "I found it interesting that The Quetzal gave the compound to the Chinese as a gift."

"A piece of cracked jade?"

"The Chinese do not forget that they brought us gunpowder and helped us defeat the Europeans when they first came looking for gold," Ten Reed said thoughtfully. "Sometimes it seems as if they have not noticed that we are no longer those same people."

"The Chinese are very sure of their place in the world. I would like to talk to your uncle." I bit into a slice of melon, suddenly very hungry.

"He has retired from building." Ten Reed was looking at me very closely. "He has a small plot of land west of the city in Aztacalco, where he grows flowers for his amusement. We could visit him in the morning, if you wish."

"I wish," I told him and ate a last slice of melon. "I am going for a stroll. I will eat dinner in one of the eating-houses. No need to fix anything for me tonight.

"And The Quetzal's slave?"

"I will need him tomorrow. This afternoon, he can take a message to The Quetzal's daughter, Malinal, that I will have to miss our morning tutoring session." I went to my room to fetch a roll of paper, an inkstone, and a brush. Then I headed out into the late afternoon heat.

Ten Reed woke me before the first birds chirped, and by the time the wooden gong and the conch shell blasts woke the city, we were beyond the west gate. I like the city suburbs with their dusty roads and sleepy little whitewashed houses, each with its central garden full of turkeys and playing children. Houseboats floated in a sea of reed-mat gardens planted to market produce or floating among the tall green spears of Chinese rice in the mud-fenced paddies.

Ten Reed's uncle occupied one of the small, whitewashed houses and we sat in his little garden beneath a fig tree that had been a gift from the previous Quetzal, eating the sticky fruits and drinking Chinese tea. He showed us his gardens, neatly planted to the bright, colorful flowers like the ones that filled the Street of Flowers stalls in the central market. One by one he pointed out each variety and described how he had obtained it. Ten Reed looked on with a fond resignation, but I found the old man's knowledge of botany to be quite up to date. Sure enough, when we entered the main room of his house to escape the heat of the day, I spied a heavy volume of *Systema Naturae* by the Swede, Carolus Linnaeus. Botany was clearly his passion these days and it took me some time to finally turn the conversation to building and the Chinese consul's building in particular. But my time was rewarded because Ten Reed had been right. The old man was still quite proud of his accomplishments there and the drawing I had made of Shin Li's room and that section of the complex turned out to be very useful.

"So," Ten Reed asked me as we walked home through the golden evening light. "Did you find your ghost?"

"I found the hand," I told him.

The next morning, I asked The Quetzal's slave to bring me to him. He led me quickly through the maze of tiled streets, dwellings, and gardens to The Quetzal's private ball court. A game was in progress and I caught a glimpse of the bronze, oiled figures as they raced across the court after the hard ball.

The Aztecs were crazy about their ball games. The whole city turned out for the big, public games. Sure enough, The Quetzal was seated beneath a fine-woven cotton canopy with a group of guests, intent on the game. I assumed from the dress that these were the Palenque visitors and perhaps some local dignitaries. The slave scurried up the steps to bow and speak to one of the servants standing around the group and a moment later, The Quetzal nodded in my direction. He excused himself from his guests, strolled over to the strip of shade cast by the whitewashed wall, and gestured me over.

"You are swift with your truth." He glanced at the ball court as the crowd cheered.

"The truth was not hard to guess. Finding proof for all eyes was more difficult." I watched as a small, wiry youth caught the ball on his padded hip, sent it arrowing across the stone-flagged court to his teammate.

"And your truth is?" The Quetzal kept his face turned to the court, but I could see that he was no longer paying attention to the game.

"I would... prefer to show you." I bowed. "At the Chinese consulate. In the room where the consul's son was murdered. Perhaps your daughter, Malinal, would care to join you there? It will be instructive." I kept my face still as he bent his dark gaze on me.

"I will invite her." He started to turn away. "I will send a runner to the consul about our arrival."

"I would not do that."

He gave me one quick glance and I saw a brief flicker of satisfaction there. Or perhaps I imagined it.

We made our way to the Chinese complex in the hot time of day. Slaves carried a blue canopy on long poles as we walked through the palace gate and across the square to the Street of Nobles and the Chinese consul's residence. The watchman there bowed us through, the same man who had found Shin Li's body. The consul hurried out, of course, his sandals shushing on the tiles of the courtyard in his haste to greet The Quetzal.

The Quetzal brushed aside his offers of hospitality. "This man will tell you who has killed your son and how it could happen, here in my city." He jerked his chin at me.

The consul gave me a cold look that made me glad to have The Quetzal as a protector. We all marched together across the spacious courtyard and a small icy snake curled in my gut. If I was wrong...

I tried not to think about that. Malinal was giving me wary glances that made me think I was not wrong. The Quetzal's guard still stood at the door, eagle-eyed, his atlatl at his side. He saluted and stood aside for The Quetzal to enter first.

Nothing had been touched. The bloodstain on the carpet had dried to a rusty brown and it gave the room a faint odor reminiscent of the Sun Temple. They were all looking at me now, like shoppers in the market watching one of the fire-eaters or the serpent dancers. Faintly I heard the sound of flutes and drums. Some ceremony at one of the temples? A hushed quiet had filled the room, thick as the blood smell.

"Avery is called the drunken poet for a good reason," I said. "Everyone knows that only luck and the generosity of The Quetzal toward a foreigner have saved him from serving as a slave. Who will believe the words of a drunkard?" I spread my hands. The consul was scowling agreement, Malinal looked troubled, and The Quetzal revealed nothing. "I asked him to tell me what had happened on the night Shin Li was murdered. He told me they played chess, that it had ended in a stalemate, that he had left. Later, when the watchman at the gate told me about finding the body, he mentioned that Shin Li's hand was soft. Pliable." I watched The Quetzal's eyes narrow with instant understanding. The consul did not, but then the consul probably didn't have as much personal familiarity with death. "That means the man had just died," I explained. "A body stiffens quickly after death. Yet the watchman saw Avery leave long before the body was found."

"He was mistaken," the consul snapped.

"He records all people who pass through the gate," I told him mildly. "You can ask to see his records and he will explain them to you."

"Someone sneaked in." Malinal spoke up.

"I thought of that." I nodded. "But you can see this doorway from the watchman's stool. Only tradesfolk came through the gate until just before the murder was discovered. The watchmen would not greet a water carrier or bearer, just note that person's passing on his record. He would have turned his back on the doorway to greet the honored guests of the consul, but those guests could see if someone emerged from Shin Li's rooms as they entered, and none of them saw anything, is that not so?"

"That's so." The consul's voice creaked like old wood.

The Quetzal was watching me narrowly.

"I found a few peculiarities when I examined the room." I gestured to the chessboard. "Notice the game? It is not a stalemate. The board is full of pieces. The game has barely begun."

"What does that mean?" The consul spoke angrily. "Who can trust—"

"The words of a drunk?" I nodded. "But why lie to me about the game? And look here." I pointed to a faint stain in front of the carved chest. "Let us suppose that Shin Li knelt in front of the chest on a rug. He was stabbed there and fell onto the rug. The murderer moved the body to the chess table to make it look as if he had been killed while playing chess. Of course he had to move the rug, too, and didn't notice that a small amount of blood had soaked through to the tiles. I suspect if you ask the woman who cleans this room you will discover that the rug normally lies in front of the chest, so that one kneels on softness to search through the chest. Its position in front of the table does not really make sense."

"The position of a rug in a room is meaningless," snapped the consul. "And you have already explained that it would be impossible for anyone to come into this room at the time you believe he died. Your logic is flawed."

"No." I shook my head. "My logic is not flawed. We do not yet have all the information we need." I walked over to the carved screen. "Tell me about the garden beyond this screen."

"It is a small private garden." The consul shrugged. "It is shared by my sleeping room along with this room and one other. But the screens block access to the garden. You have to go in through a door and that door opens only to my private sitting room. That is where I was entertaining my guests. I was there all evening. No one came though there and no one could get through this screen anyway."

I walked over and slid my fingers along the carved frame of the screen. Nothing. Sweat prickled my armpits. What if I had the wrong room... what if he had remembered wrongly? The Quetzal cleared his throat.

Left, I thought. Right. He had mixed up the two. Quickly I ran my fingers along the frame on the other side. Aha! I felt the tiny lever, pressed on it. With the tiniest of "clicks" the screen sprang free and swung silently inward. "The son of the former Quetzal liked women and young men and his father did not approve of his behaviors," I said. "When he built this house, he had the builder include these clever windows. He could house 'guests' in these rooms and visit them by night. Not even the servants could know and word would not get back to his father. Shall we?" I stepped through the screen.

The Quetzal followed with the consul and Malinal at his heels. I had expected the consul to protest, but he was silent and when I glanced back at him, his face was the color of old ivory. Well, he was the father, after all. "Notice the hinges and the latch." I pointed to the dark stains on the wood. "They have been recently oiled." I stepped through flowering shrubs that smelled of cinnamon to another, identical screen. Across the small garden I could see a third screen next to a carved door. That would be the consul's chambers. I ran my fingers down the correct side of this screen and it swung silently inward. The consul's younger son lay asleep on the silk coverlet of the bed. He startled awake as I stepped into the room. "According to the watchman, your younger son was in his room until the maid came to call him to your private dinner."

"This is scandal. Ridiculous!" The consul's face had gone even paler and twin spots of red stained his cheeks. "What do you insinuate here? You have taken the side of a drunk, built a house of feathers in your accusations..."

"I suspect that if you search the room, you will find the blade that killed your son. Unless he hid it in the garden."

"What are you saying?" The young man's eyes had gone wide. "What are you accusing me of? How dare you, you... savage!"

The consul turned away from his son. "You may search." His tone was leaden, without expression. "My son and I will wait in my rooms."

* * *

The Quetzal called in his private guard to do the searching and summoned a minister from the Hall of Justice to oversee it. He spoke with the minister at length, then joined Malinal and myself in the small garden where we sat on stone benches. Servants brought cups of delicate tea and small sweet rice cakes.

"You have presented me with a truth," The Quetzal said. "But perhaps not all of that truth. Where did the drunken poet go after the chess game? The consul will want to know and so do I. Before I can release him, I must know that he had nothing to do with this."

I looked at Malinal. She was staring at the ground.

"He was in my garden." Her voice was low, but she raised her head and met her father's stare. "I enjoy his poetry, father."

"He is a drunk." The Quetzal's tone was flat and cold. "You were without a chaperone?"

"Of course I was. You forbade me to invite him to the palace." She flushed. "Nothing improper occurred." She held his gaze, didn't look away.

I'm not sure I could do that.

The Quetzal said nothing.

One of the searchers appeared, a lanky young man with a narrow face and beaked nose. He held a long, slender knife. A golden dragon's head formed the hilt, set with blood-colored rubies for eyes.

"My father gave that knife to my older son." The consul had emerged from his chambers. He seemed to have shrunk, as if he had aged ten years. "This is a family matter. I have accepted a post in the emperor's court. I will dispatch a communication to the emperor and he will select a replacement for me. My younger son is not fit to assume my duties." The words fell from his lips like dry stones. "He will be punished."

"I will permit your son to depart with you." The Quetzal inclined his head. "As you say, this is a family matter. We are a civilized people who understand family." He watched the consul cross the garden and disappear into his chambers, walking with the faltering steps of an old man. "And the gods do not appreciate a flawed sacrifice." He turned to face me.

"You are a finder of truth." The Quetzal's eyes bored into mine. "A very wise man." A hint of a smile flickered at the corners of his mouth. "On the day of your choosing, I will be honored to sacrifice you on the altar in the Temple of the Sun."

"I am... honored."

"You are horrified, but you are a European." The smile came and went again. "Is it better to grow old, witless, blind, a burden to all?" He turned to Malinal. "One of my guards will escort you back to the palace when you are ready." He left the garden, followed by two guards bearing their atlatls.

The sun was setting. Birds began their evening song in the garden's trees and I could hear the raucous shrieks of the Hot Lands birds.

"He offered you a great honor, you know." Malinal's voice was bitter.

"I know."

"The priests will not accept my sacrifice now. I knew the risk." She sighed. "But it was innocent and I love the music of his words."

"There are many ways to serve the gods," I said.

"So my father says."

She left the garden then. She will make a good ruler, after The Quetzal lies down on the altar stone. Whenever that is.

He has ruled the Three Peoples for three decades now and made them powerful among the world nations. Of all his children, Malinal, with my Spring Wind Song's eyes, is the one who is most like him.

The Quetzal has his priorities.

So the Chinese consul who does not think much of the Aztecs will leave in disgrace and perhaps his replacement will have more respect. Malinal will honor the gods by becoming an even better ruler than her father. Since she can no longer honor the gods with her blood. Avery will leave Tenochtitlan before he makes a fatal mistake.

How does my guilt measure up in all this?

I left the garden as the shadows lengthened. The watchman had been assigned to the consul personally by The Quetzal. As a gift. Ten Reed found that out for me. The carved chest had plenty of room for a slender man to hide. The women who clean—also a gift from The Quetzal—would know where the dagger with the ruby eyes was kept. And they could oil the old hinges on the screens.

Ten Reed's uncle had been surprised by my curiosity about the consul's house. The Quetzal's emissary had asked him to draw up detailed plans the month before The Quetzal had given the house to the consul.

I will never play chess with The Quetzal.

I went home through the darkening streets. They still don't use street lamps here. The night streets belong to Tezcatlipoca and I felt his breath tonight. Ten Reed will have dinner waiting for me. When they release Avery, I will convince him to go north as quickly as possible. I recognized the exquisite feather border on his cloak as one created by Malinal's personal feather artist. I should go with him, too, I suppose. But I will not. My knees twinge on some of these cold mornings and I am starting to feel old. Who knows? One day, The Quetzal's honor may look like a good choice. But meanwhile, I want to watch Malinal learn to rule.

Murder in Geektopia

Paul Di Filippo

Paul Di Filippo is my secret weapon. No, really, that's all you need to know. Anything else one can think to say about this gonzo maverick, who always surprises and who seems to snort the zeitgeist and regurgitate works of brilliant and hysterical relevance, would still fall short of the total gestalt of Di Filippo goodness. He is a genius in a field of geniuses.

Max Moritz is the moniker on my NC license, and, yes, I've heard all the obvious allusive wisecracks already.

"Funny, you don't look Prankish."

"I heard you keep all your cats in jam jars."

"What strength monofilament you use for chickens?"

"Did your mama stick dirks in her bush?"

But of course I haven't let smartmouth cracks like those bug me since I was twelve years old, and just finishing my third-level synergetics course at GBS Ideotorium Number 521. (Our school motto that year, picked by the students of course: "A fool's brain digests philosophy into folly, science into superstition, and art into pedantry. Hence University education." From one of my favorite Shaw and Raymond pictonovels, *Major Barbara versus Ming the Merciless.*)

And of course after I left GBSI Number 521 that year for my extended wanderjahr before declaring my major and minor passions, I fell in with a variety of older people who politely resisted the impulse to joke about my name.

Except when they didn't.

But that's just the Geek Way, anyplace you go.

Still, I wasn't about to change Moritz to something else. Family pride, and all that. Would've killed my mother, who had worked hard with my pop (and alone after his death) to make the family business a success. Moritz Cosplay was known worldwide for its staging of large-scale (ten thousand players and up) recreational scenarios, everything from US Civil War to Barsoom to Fruits Basket, and Mom—Helena Moritz—regarded our surname as a valuable trademark, to be proudly displayed at all times, for maximum publicity value.

Not that I was part of the firm any longer—not since five years ago, when I had told Mom, with much trepidation, that I was leaving for a different trade.

Mom was in her office, solido-conferencing with the head of some big hotel chain and negotiating for better rates for her clients, when I finally got up the courage to inform her of my decision. I waited till she flicked off the solido, and then said, "Mom, I'm switching jobs."

She looked at me coolly with that gesture familiar from my childhood, as if she were peering over the rims of her reading glasses. But she hadn't worn eyeglasses since 1963, when she had gotten laser-eye surgery to correct her far-sightedness. Then out the glasses went, faster than Clark Kent had gotten rid of his in *Action Comics* #2036. (But Lois Lang still didn't recognize Clark as Superman, since Clark grew a mustache at the same time, which was really a very small shapeshifting organism, a cousin of Proty's, who could attach and detach from the Kryptonian's upper lip at will to help preserve Supe's secret identity.)

Anyway, I had made my decision and announcement and wasn't about to quail under a little parental glare.

"What're you planning on doing?" Mom asked.

"I've just gotten my NC license. I've been studying in secret for the past six months."

"You? A nick carter? Max, I respect your intelligence highly, but it's just not the Sherlock-Holmes-Father-Brown-Lincoln-Powell variety. You had trouble finding clean socks in your sock drawer until you were ten."

"I aced the exam."

Mom looked slightly impressed, but still had an objection or two. "What about the physical angle? You're hardly a slan in the strength department. What if you get mixed up with some roughnecks?"

"Roughnecks? Shazam, Mom! What century are you living in? There hasn't been any real prevalence of 'roughnecks' in the general population since before I was born. At GBSI Five-twenty-one, one of the patternmasters spent half a day trying to explain what a 'bully' was. The incidence of sociopathic violence and aggressive behavior has been dropping at a rate of one-point-five percent ever since President Hearst's first term—and that was nearly three-quarters-of-a-century ago."

"Still, the world isn't perfect yet. There's bad people out there who wouldn't hesitate—"

"Mom, I also got my concealed weapons license."

Mom had a technical interest in weapons, after hosting so many SCA tournaments and live-action RPG events. "Really? What did you train on?"

"Nothing fancy. Just a standard blaster."

I didn't tell Mom that I had picked a blaster because on wide-angle setting the geyser of charged particles from the mini-cyclotron in the gun's handle totally compensated for my lack of aiming abilities. But I suspected she knew anyhow.

Mom got up from her chair and gave me a big hug. "Well, all right, Max, if this is really what you've got your heart set on. Just go out there and uphold the Moritz name."

So that's how, on August 16, 1970 (Hugo Gernsback's eighty-sixth birthday, by coincidence; I recall watching the national celebration via public spy-ray), I moved out of the family home and hung up my shingle in a cheap office on McCay Street in Centropolis.

Now, five years later, after a somewhat slow start, I had a flourishing little business, mostly in the area of thwarting industrial espionage.

All Mom's fears about me getting into danger had failed to come true.

Until the morning Polly Jean Hornbine walked through the door.

Business was slow that day. I had just unexpectedly solved a case for ERB Industries faster than I had anticipated. (The employee dropping spoilers on the ansible-net about ERBI's new line of Tarzan toys had been a drone in the shipping department.) So I had no new work immediately lined up.

I was sitting in my office, reading the latest copy of *Global Heritage* magazine. I had always been interested in history, but didn't have much Copious Spare Time these days to indulge in any deep reading. So the light-and-glossy coverage of *GH* provided a fast-food substitute.

I skipped past the guest editorial, a topical poem written by Global Data Manager Gene McCarthy himself. Where he found the time to churn out all these poems while shepherding the daily affairs of billions of people around the planet, I had no idea. Everyone else, myself included, bright and ambitious as one might be, looked like a lazy underachiever next to our GDM.

Beyond the editorial, the first article was a seventy-fifth anniversary retrospective on President Hearst's first term of office, 1901–1905. Even though the material was mostly familiar, it made for a lively, almost unbelievable story: the story of a personal transformation so intense that it had completely remade, first, one man's life, and then the collective life of the whole world.

Few people recalled that William Randolph Hearst had been a money-grubbing, war-mongering, unscrupulous newspaper publisher in the year 1898. A less likely person to become a pacifist politician and reformer would be hard to imagine. But there was a key in the rusty heart of the man, a key that would soon be turned.

And that key was Hearst's son.

In 1879, at age twenty-six, Hearst had been vacationing in England. There, through mutual friends, he met a poor but beautiful woman named Edith Nesbit, aged twenty-one. The American and the Englishwoman fell in love and married. The couple returned to America. The next year saw the birth of their son, George Randolph Hearst.

In 1898, spurred on by his father's jingoist rhetoric, the teenaged boy enlisted in the Army and went off to Cuba to fight in the very conflict his father was so ardently promoting, the Spanish–American War.

And there young George Randolph Hearst died, most miserably, on the point of a bayonet and subsequent peritonitis.

The death of their son first shattered, then galvanized William and Edith. Recanting all his past beliefs, Hearst vowed on his son's grave to use all his skills and resources to bring an end to armed conflict on the planet. A titanic task. But he would be aided immensely by Edith. Her hitherto undisclosed writing talents and keen political sensibilities were brought to their joint cause.

In early 1899, Hearst and Edith formed the US branch of the Fabian Society, based on the parent UK organization that Edith had ties to. Backed by his media empire, Hearst ran a feverish, spend-thrift campaign for the presidency of the United States under that banner, and indeed defeated both McKinley and Bryan.

And that's when Hearst started changing the world—

My robot annunciator interrupted my downtime reading then. "Chum Moritz, you have a client in the reception room."

I swung my feet off my desk, and checked my appearance in a mirror hanging on the back of the door to reception.

My blue T-shirt bearing the image of Krazy Kat and Ignatz with the legend "Hairy, man!" was relatively clean. A small cluster of pinback buttons on my chest displayed the logos or faces of Green Lantern, Frank Buck, Li'l Abner, Les Paul, Freeman Dyson, Dash Hammett, Bunny Yeager, Jean Harlow (still gorgeous at age sixty-four), and the Zulu Nation. The pockets of my khaki cargo shorts were stuffed with the tools of my trade. My high-top tennis shoes were fresh kicks.

There was nothing I could do about my perpetually unruly cowlick or thin hairy shanks, so out I went.

A pretty woman under thirty—roughly my own age—stood up as I entered. Her thick auburn hair crested at her shoulders and curled inward and upward, and her wide mouth was limned in that year's hot color, Sheena's Tiger Blood. She wore a green short-sleeved cashmere top that echoed her green eyes, and a felted poodle skirt that featured a snarling Krypto. Black tights, ballet slippers. She looked like a page of Good Girl Art by Bergey come to life.

She extended her hand forthrightly, a somber expression on her sweet face. "My name's Polly Jean Hornbine, and I'm here because the police don't believe someone murdered my father."

Her grip was strong and honest. I got a good feeling from her, despite her unlikely introductory claim. "Let's go into my office, Ms. Hornbine."

"Call me P.J., please. That's... that's what Dad—"

And then she began to weep.

Putting my arm around her slim shoulders, I conducted her into my office, got her some tissues and a spaceman's bulb of diet Moxie (I took a Nehi for myself out of the Stirling-engine fridge), and had her sit. After a minute or so, she had composed herself enough to tell me her story.

"My father is—was—Doctor Harold Hornbine. He was head of pediatric surgery at David H. Keller Memorial. Until he was murdered! The authorities all claim he died of natural causes—heart failure—but I know that's just not true!"

"What leads you to believe his death was murder, P.J.?"

"Dad had just undergone his annual physical, and his T-ray charts revealed he had the physiology of a man much younger. He followed the Macfadden–Kellog Regimen religiously. All his organs were in tip-top shape. There was no way his heart would just stop like it did, without some kind of fatal intervention."

"An autopsy—"

"Showed nothing!"

This woman's case was starting to sound more and more delusional. I tried to reason with her gently. "Even with current diagnostic technology, some cardiac conditions still go undetected. For instance, I was just reading—"

"No! Listen to me! I might have agreed with you, except for one thing. Just days before Dad died he confided in me that he had discovered a scandal at the hospital. Something in his department that had much more widespread implications. He claimed that the wrongdoing at Keller would implicate people all the way up to the GDM himself!"

"I find that hard to believe, P.J. In nearly thirty years, Global Data Management hasn't experienced any scandal worse than the use of some public monies to buy a few first editions for the private libraries of the occasional greedy sub-manager. And even that was resolved with simple tensegrity counseling. No, the GDM is just too perfect a governmental system to harbor any major glitch—especially not something that would involve murder!"

P.J. stood up determinedly, a certain savagery burning in her expression. I was reminded immediately of Samantha Eggar playing Clarrissa MacDougall in 1959's *Children of the Lens*. I found my initial attraction to her redoubling. I hadn't felt like this since I fell in love with Diana Rigg (playing opposite Peter Cushing) when I first saw her onscreen in *Phantom Lady Versus the Red Skull* when I was fifteen.

P.J.'s voice was quavering but stern. "I can see that you're not the man for this job, Max. I'll be going now—"

I reached out to stop her. I couldn't let her leave.

"No, wait, I'll take the case. If only to put your mind at ease—"

"It's not me I'm concerned about. I want you to find the people who killed my father!"

"If that's where the trail leads, I promise I'll run them down."

A thought suddenly occurred to me. "How's your mother figure in all this? Mrs. Hornbine. What's she got to say about your father's death?"

P.J. softened. "Mom isn't with us anymore. She died five years ago, on the way home from Venus Equilateral."

I whistled. "Your mom was Jenny Milano?"

P.J. nodded.

Now I could see where P.J. got her spunk.

Jenny Milano had managed to nurse the leaky reactor of her crippled spaceship, the GDM *Big Otaku*, for thousands of miles until she finally achieved Earth orbit and spared the planet from a deadly accidental nuclear strike. Today her ship currently circled the planet as a radioactive memorial to her courage and skills.

According to P.J., Dr. Hornbine hadn't been conducting any independent research prior to his demise. And he didn't see any private patients outside the clinical environment. Therefore, whatever scandal he had uncovered had to originate at David H. Keller Memorial itself. At first, I assumed that to learn anything I'd have to go undercover at the hospital. But how? I certainly couldn't masquerade as a doctor. Even if I managed to get some kind of lowly orderly job, I'd hardly be in any position to poke around in odd corners, or solicit information from leet personnel.

So I abandoned that instinctive first approach and decided to go in for a little social engineering.

I'd try to infiltrate one of Dr. Hornbine's karasses. Maybe amongst those who shared his sinookas, I'd learn something he had let slip, a clue to whatever secret nasty stuff was going on at the hospital.

Assuming the beautiful P.J. Hornbine wasn't as loony as Daffy Duck.

Hopping onto the a-net, I quickly learned what constituted the doc's passions.

He had been a member of the Barbershop Harmony Society.

No way I could join that, since I could carry a tune about as well as Garfield.

The doc had also belonged to the Toonerville Folks, a society dedicated to riding every municipal trolley line in North, Central, and South America, a life-quest which few members actually managed to achieve, given the huge number of such lines. (The old joke about the kid who parlayed a single five-cent transfer for a ride from Halifax to Tierra del Fuego, arriving an old man, came readily to mind.)

But this karass mainly encouraged solitary activity, save for its annual national conventions. No good to me.

Pop Hornbine also collected antique Meccano sets.

Again, that wasn't going to put me into social situations where I could pump people for dirt.

But at last I hit gold, like Flash discovering Earth-Two.

Harold Hornbine was also known as Balkpraetore, common footpad and strangler.

The Centropolis sept of the Children of Cimmeria called itself the Pigeons from Hell. That was Balkpraetore's crowd. Every weekend they had a melee with other regional groups. These were the tight friends with whom Hornbine would have shared thoughts on what had been troubling him, even if he hadn't ventured into full disclosure.

This group I could infiltrate. No reason I had to assume warrior guise. I could go as a bard or mage or tavern-keeper.

Today was Thursday. That gave me plenty of time to prepare.

So that sunny Saturday morning found me riding the Roger Lapin trolley line out to the Frank Reade Playing Fields, several hundred acres in the heart of Centropolis devoted to cosplay, recreations, re-enactments, live RPG, and other pursuits of that nature. I was dressed like a priest who might have been Thulsa Doom's wimpy mouse-worshipping cousin. I figured nobody would want to waste a sword-stroke on me. I didn't stick out particularly amongst my fellow passengers, as half of them were attired in similar outfits. And besides, most were busy reading books or zines or pictonovels, or watching movies and cartoons on their pocket-solido sets.

After I boarded at the Dunsany Towers stop, a little nervous at carrying out this imposture, I dug out that issue of *Global Heritage* that I had been reading when P.J. first showed up.

Once in the Oval Office, President Hearst quickly assembled an official cabinet—and a semi-secret cabal of assistants and advisors—who could help him carry out his radical disarmament and re-education program. The list leaned heavily toward scientists and reformers and what passed for media people in those days, deliberately excluding the tired old politicians. Hearst hired Havelock Ellis and Thomas Edison. Mrs. Frank Leslie and Nikola Tesla. Edward Stratemeyer and Margaret Sanger. Frank Munsey and Percival Lowell. Lee de Forest and even old rival Joseph Pulitzer.

(Cabinets during Hearst's subsequent six terms as President would include a new generation of younger luminaries such as Buckminster Fuller, Huck Gernsback, Major Malcolm Wheeler-Nicholson, Robert Goddard, B.F. Skinner, Thomas Merton, Vannevar Bush, David Ogilvy, Marshall McLuhan, Claude Shannon, Dorothy Day and A.A. Wyn. Service in the Hearst administration became a badge of honor, and produced a catalogue of America's greatest names.)

These men and women set about dismantling the cultural foundations of belligerence, both domestic and international, substituting a philosophy of intellectual passions, encouraged by education and new laws.

And one of their prime weapons in this initially subliminal war was the same yellow journalism that had once fomented violence.

Specifically, the Funnypaper Boys.

Hearst wanted to reach the largest percentage of the population with his message of reform. But there was no radio then, no spy-rays or ansible-net or ether-vision or movies. Mass media as we know it today, in 1975, was rudimentary, save for zines and news-papers.

And most importantly, the newspaper comics.

The funny pages. Already immensely popular, comprehensible even by the nation's many semi-literate citizens, able to deliver con-cealed subtextual messages behind entertaining facades.

Thus were born the Funnypaper Boys, artists who were really secret agents for Hearst's program.

Outcault, Herriman, Dirks, McManus, McCay, King, Opper, Schultze, Fisher, Swinnerton, Kahle, Briggs, and a dozen others. They were motivated by Hearst's grandiose humanistic dreams to create a Golden Age of activist art, full of humorous fantastical con-ceits.

No one could deny the power and influence of such other even-tual Hearst allies as pulpzines and Hollywood. But the Funnypaper Boys were first, the Founding Fathers of a republic soon informally dubbed Geektopia. ("Geek" became the in-term for the fanatics who followed the Funnypaper Boys due to Winsor McCay's associ-ation with carnival culture, where the word had a rather different meaning.) Their utopian artwork swept the nation—and the globe. American comics proved to be potent exports, with or without translation, and were adopted wholeheartedly by other cultures, carrying their reformist messages intact and sparking similar native movements.

(America's oldest and staunchest ally, Britain, was the first to fully join the Hearst movement. The Fabians, Shaw, Bertrand Russell, Wells, Stapledon, Haldane, the many brilliant Huxleys, publisher Alfred Harmsworth, Edward Linley Sambourne and his fellow car-toonists at *Punch*—They soon had complete control of the reins of governmental power.)

Reprint books of newspaper strips began to appear in America. And then the original pictonovel was born. That's when the tipping point was reached—

And my trolley had reached its destination as well, as the con-ductor announced over a clanging bell.

I left my *GH* magazine behind on the seat and climbed down the stairs to join the costumed crowds surging into the Frank Reade Playing Fields.

Past fragrant food carts and knick-knack booths and bookstalls, costume-repair tents and armories, taverns and daycare corrals, I strolled, heading toward the fields assigned to the Children of Cimmeria. (My Mom's business had a hand in running all this, of course.)

I decided to take a shortcut down a dusty path that angled across the vast acreage, and there I encountered a startling sight.

In a tiny lot, mostly concealed by a tall untrimmed privet hedge, a few people were playing what I think was a game once called "football." They wore shabby-looking leather helmets and padding, obviously homemade. The object of their contention was a lopsided, ill-stuffed pigskin.

I chanced upon the game when it was temporarily suspended, and I spoke to one of the players.

"Are you guys seriously into this antique 'sports' stuff?"

The player made a typically Geekish noise indicative of derisive exasperation. "Of course not! This is a *simulation* of sports, not *real* sports! Frank Merriwell stuff. We're just trying to recreate a vanished era like everyone else. But it gets harder and harder to find re-enactors. This sports stuff never really made much sense to begin with, even when it wasn't dead media."

I left the football players behind and soon arrived at the dusty turf allotted to the Conan recreators. I registered with the gamemasters and quickly inserted myself into the action.

For the next several hours I ministered in my priestly role to the dead and dying on the mock battlefield, liberally bestowing prayers and invocations I had learned off the a-net on their hauberked torsos and helmeted heads. For a big he-man guy, Conan's creator Thomas Wolfe sure had a way with the frilly, jaw-wrenching poetry.

It was hot and sweaty work, and I was grateful at last to hit the nearby grog tent for some shade and mead. While listening to a gal in a chainmail bikini sing some Geeksongs about the joint adventures of Birdalone and the Gray Mouser, I spotted the Pigeons from Hell crowd, recognizable from their a-net profiles. One of them was

Ted Harmon, an anesthesiologist compatriot of Hornbine. As he wasn't engaged in conversation, I went up to him.

"Hey, Ted—I mean, Volacante. Neat ruckus. I saw you get in some wicked sword thrusts."

Ted looked at me for a moment as if to say, *Do I know you?* But his weariness and the mead and my compliments and the congenial setting disarmed any suspicions.

"Thanks. Been practising a lot."

"I just wish old Balkpraetore could've been here to see your display of talent. Shame about his death."

We clinked flagons in honor of Dr. Hornbine. Then Ted said, "Yeah, a damn shame. You know, when I first heard about him kicking it, I thought—"

"Thought what?"

"Oh, nothing…"

"C'mon, now you got me curious."

Ted leaned in closer. "Well, he was just so nervous the last time I saw him. Something was obviously bothering him. It was almost as if he expected something bad to happen to him."

"Oh, he was always like that."

"Are you serious? You never saw Balkpraetore without a grin and a joke. It was only after he had that visit at the hospital—"

"Visit?"

"Yeah, from a drug rep. Guy named, uh, Greenstock. From MetamorPharma. I remember the rep's name because it reminded me of the Green Man. The Green Man's always been a minor passion of mine. You see, it all started with a Henry Treece novel when I was twelve—"

I cut Ted off in a practiced Geek manner. I couldn't indulge him in a passion-rant now. "Queue it up. Back to Greenstock. What do you think he proposed? Something shady?"

"I don't know, but it freaked Hornbine out."

"Some kind of bribery scheme maybe, to get a certain line of drugs into the hospital?"

"Maybe. But it seemed more threatening than that, almost like Greenstock could compel the doc to do something bad against his will."

I wanted to press for more information, but Ted began to turn a bit suspicious.

"Why're we chewing up this old gossip? Tell me more about the slick way I took down that bastard Numendonia..."

I always tried to honor an individual's passions as much as the next Geek, but sometimes it's hard work pretending to be interested. Especially when I was suddenly aching to tell P.J. what I had learned.

Our waitress wore a transparent plastic carapace molded to her naked breasts and torso, black lurex panties, tights and musketeer boots. Her hair was pouffed up and her makeup could've sustained a platoon of Calder gynoids. She carried an outrageously baroque toy blaster holstered at her hip. I didn't know where to put my eyes.

I had decided to take Polly Jean Hornbine out for supper, rather than relay my news in my office. I chose the nearest franchise of *La Semaine de Suzette*, because it was a fairly classy low-budget place, and I was in the mood for French food.

The restaurant chain was named after one of the French zines that had gotten behind Hearst and his program shortly after the Brits came onboard. The French *bande dessinée* artists (and their Belgian *stripverhalen* peers) had joined the ranks of the utopian Funnypaper Boys with awesome enthusiasm and international solidarity. And in Germany, artists like Rodolphe Töpffer and Lyonel Feininger, and zines like *Simplicissimus*, *Humoristische Blätter*, and *Ulk* weren't far behind. And when the Japanese invented manga—

But like all Geeks, I digress.

I knew that the waitresses at *La Semaine de Suzette* dressed like characters from their namesake zine. But during all my previous visits, their outfits had mimicked those of Bécassine and Bleuette, modest schoolgirls.

What I didn't realize was that *La Semaine de Suzette* had also published *Barbarella*, starting in 1962, and that the waitress uniforms went in and out of rotation.

No matter how much you knew, it was never everything.

So now Polly Jean and I had to place our orders with a half-naked interstellar libertine.

It was enough to make Emma Frost blush.

Somehow we stammered out our choices. After Barbarella had sashayed away, I attempted to recover my aplomb and relate the revelations I had picked up from Ted Harmon.

P.J. absorbed the information with dispassionate intensity, and once again I was taken with her quick intelligence. Not to mention her adorable face. When I finished, she said, "So a visit to this fellow Greenstock is next, I take it?"

I began sawing into my Chicken Kiev, which was a little tough. The chain keeps prices down by using vat-grown chicken, which is generally tender and tasty, but this meat must've been made on a Monday.

"That's right. If we're lucky, the trail will end there."

She shook her head. "I can't see it. If this were just a simple case of Dad refusing a bribe, there'd be no call for murder."

"If it was murder—"

P.J.'s temper flared again. "It was! And that could only mean a big deal, bigger than Greenstock and his company. You've got to find out who's behind them!"

"I'm not leaving any tern unstoned, as the nasty little kid said when he was pitching pebbles at the shore birds."

P.J. relented and smiled at my bad joke. "Did you actually imagine I had never heard that one before?"

"No. But I did imagine that you would imagine that I would never be dumb enough to say it. And so it made you smile anyhow."

"Touché..."

"Now let's finish up. I'm going to take you to a show."

"Which one?"

"The touring version of *Metropolis*."

"With Bernadette Peters as Maria?"

"The one and only."

"Let's go!"

Was it cheating to have looked up P.J.'s passions on the a-net? If so, I joined millions of other romance-seeking Geeks.

After the show we ended up on the observation deck of the Agberg Tower of Glass. All of Centropolis lay spread out below us, a lattice of lights, and I felt the same epiphany experienced by Oedipa Maas in Thomas Pynchon's *The Cryonics of Blot 49*, when she envisioned the alien spaceport as pure information.

This high, the air was chilly, and P.J. huddled naturally into my embrace. We kissed for a long time before our lips parted, and she said wistfully, "This tower is the fourth-highest in the world."

"But only," I whispered, "until the completion of the Atreides Pylon in Dubai."

The next day I took the trolley to the intersection of Kirby Avenue and Lee Street, to the HQ of MetamorPharma. Built in the classic Rhizomatic style pioneered twenty years ago by the firm of Fuller, Soleri, and Wright, the building resembled an enormous fennel bulb topped with ten-story stylized fronds. The fronds were solar collectors, of course.

Inside at reception, where giant murals featuring the corporate cartoon—the famed multicolored element man—dominated the walls, I used the annunciator to rouse Taft Greenstock, sales rep, from whatever office drudgery he had been performing. In a few moments, he emerged to greet me.

Greenstock was a black man of enormous girth and height, sporting scraggly facial hair and an Afro modeled on Luke Cage's, and wearing a polychromatic caftan and sandals. As he got closer, I smelled significant B.O. and booze. Aside from his sheer size, he was hardly intimidating. I had expected some kind of hard-nosed Octopus or Joker or Moriarty, the instrument of Hornbine's murder, and instead had gotten a fourth-rate Giles Habibula.

I had been planning to show Greenstock a fake ID and profile I had set up on the a-net, and feed him a line of foma. But taking his measure as an unwitting proxy who might be frightened into spilling some beans, I shifted plans. After we shook hands and I showed him my NC license, I just braced him with the truth.

"Chum Greenstock, I'm here about the death of Dr. Harold Hornbine. We have cause to believe he was murdered."

Greenstock looked confused, and began to sweat. I could smell metabolized gin. People passing in the lobby glanced at us curiously.

"I don't know anything about that. He was just a customer. I deal with hundreds of medicos every week. He was fine the last time I saw him—"

"And what did you discuss with him during that visit?"

"A new product. A vaccine. KannerMax."

"What's KannerMax inoculate against?"

"It's not for every child. It's only recommended for those with certain chromosomal defects. I don't know the hard scientific data, I'm just a salesman. I left him all the literature and a sample—"

Greenstock looked like he was about to collapse. I quit pushing.

"All right, that's fine. You've helped me a lot, Chum Greenstock. I'll be back if I have any further questions."

I had a name of the compound that had seemingly been the catalyst in Hornbine's murder. And murder I now indeed believed it to be. Greenstock's visit introducing this new vaccine synchronized too well with Hornbine's "heart attack." The doc must've learned something upon examination of the vaccine that earned him a death sentence.

Leaving the building, I knew just where to turn next.

Dinky Allepo.

Wonder Woman was sitting in Doc Savage's lap, while Atom Boy rested on her shoulders. Godzilla was destroying Jonestown, home to the wacky Stimsons clan, while Maggie and Jiggs and Li'l Abner and Daisy Mae applauded. Mutt and Jeff were herding approximately a dozen Felix the Cats toward the maw of Cthulhu. And my namesakes, Max and Moritz, were duking it out with Skeezix and Little Lulu.

These scenes of extreme cognitive dissonance comprised the smallest part of Dinky Allepo's many thousands of disparately sized action figures. They covered every available tabletop and shelf, much of the furniture, and a good portion of the floor. I had to walk as if through a minefield of sharp plastic shrapnel.

Having let myself in, I found Dinky in front of his a-net terminal, his usual habitat. He was surrounded by a midden of fast-food debris. On the walls of his study hung various film posters, mostly featuring busty, scantily clad scream queens: Tura Satana in *The Female Man*; Elke Sommer in *The Left Hand of Darkness*; June Wilkinson in *Motherlines*.

Dinky's long greasy hair hung at an acute angle as he tipped his head back to drain a can of Brazilian guarana drink. His soiled T-shirt was printed with the molecular structure of caffeine.

"Em *und* Em, how can I help you today? Need some more dope on who's ripping off whom in the exciting world of playware?"

"No, Dink, it's something more serious this time..."

I explained to him everything I had on the Hornbine case. His dilated pupils widened even further with interest.

"KannerMax, huh? Let me see what I can learn..."

Dinky swung back to his a-net node and got to work.

Dinky Aleppo was one of the top fifty Nexialists in the GDM. If his synthesizing skills couldn't connect the pieces of this puzzle, I wouldn't know where else to turn.

Not wanting to disturb his work, I left the room.

Dinky's den held a big ether-vision set, whose remote I grabbed. I dropped down into a chair and immediately sprang up with a shout. My left buttock had not taken kindly to being pierced by the spear held by Alley Oop. For a moment I was frozen in Geekish reverie. I thought about how "Alley Oop" was a near anagram of "Aleppo," and how if you added in the name of the caveman's dinosaur, "Dinny," you could almost get "Dinky" as well. Then I threw the action figure across the room.

The set came alive to a broadcast of *Ziegfeld Follies of 1975*. God bless our quondam President Hearst! He had loved chorus girls even after his marriage and spiritual reformation, and endowed the Follies as a subsidized National Treasure. But I wasn't in the mood for all the leggy dancework, and I switched to one of the fifteen major history channels.

I arrived in the middle of a documentary on the 1930s.

After the gradual pacification of the world in the first two decades of the century, the Thirties had been a march of progress unparalleled in history. Scientific, economic, artistic—that decade had seen the true flowering of Geek culture as it spread across the globe. The first generation of True Geeks, their sensibilities fostered by twenty years of the Funnypaper Boys and other creators, had finally supplanted any remnant of old-school barbarism. The creation of Centropolis as the new capital of the nation had been the crowning achievement of that era, surpassed only by the establishment in the Forties of Global Data Management as the civic superego of national governments.

I was just enjoying some old newsreels of Tsarevich Alexei Nikolaevich judging an Atlantic City beauty pageant awarding the title of "Sexiest Wilma Deering of 1939" (Alex was a healthy young man then thanks to the hemophilia cure invented by Linus Pauling), when Dinky called my name. I shut off the set and rejoined him.

"Have you ever heard of Kannerism before?" he demanded.

"No."

"Well, neither had I. But his name in this new MetamorPharma 'vaccine' led me to him. Leo Kanner was a doctor in the 1930s, a specialist in child psychiatry. He had a theory about a certain kind of developmental glitch in the juvenile brain that would lead to a supposedly 'aberrant' personality type. He said such individuals were suffering from 'Kannerism.'"

"What'd Kannerism consist of?"

"Oh, stuff like the ability to focus intensely on whatever your main areas of interest were. Your passions, in other words. Then you possibly got hypersensitivity to certain inputs. Some sensory integration problems."

"What else?"

"Maybe some self-stimulating behaviors. Kannerist kids might also have difficulty interpreting facial expressions and other social cues. But they also had enhanced mental focus, excellent memory abilities, superior spatial skills, and an intuitive understanding of logical systems."

I was baffled. "But—but that's just a description of your average Geek."

"Pre-diddily-cisely. Kanner chose to unveil his theory just when the whole world was adapting a new standard of sanity, new Geekcentric paradigms of mature adult behavior. All the very qualities Kanner identified as defects were being hailed as the salvation of the species. Kanner was trying to define the new normal as crazy, and he got laughed into an early grave. Only one other researcher, some guy named Hans Asperger, took his side, and he soon met a similar fate."

"This vaccine, KannerMax—what's it do?"

"I got all the specs. It's not a vaccine per se. That's bullshit from MetamorPharma, to convince the medical establishment to introduce the drug to the right age cohort. This stuff regulates gene expression. It targets the chromosomes that seem most closely linked with Kannerism."

A horrifying image walloped me then, of a planet reverting over the span of the next generation to the bad old violent days of pre-Geekdom. "Let me guess—it shuts them off."

Dinky gave a sardonic grin. "Nope. It ramps them up."

My jaw dropped like Dippy Dawg's upon seeing Clarabelle Cow in the nude. "What!"

"This drug is a recipe for the production of super-Geeks. But it only works if administered to those younger than three. Otherwise I'd be brewing some up for myself right now."

"But who's behind this? I can't see a small firm like MetamorPharma as the masterminds behind such a scheme."

"They're not. The research program was initiated by Global Data Management. Specifically, the head of the Bureau of Cultural Innovations."

"Zarthar," I said.

That night I met P.J. at a branch of Tige and Buster's convenient to both our residences. I didn't want anyone overhearing our conversation, and knew the noise of the videogame arcade within the restaurant would shield us from both local and spy-ray eavesdroppers.

Our waiter, of course, was a midget dressed as Buster Brown, accompanied by a real dog. We had to practically shout above the screams of pixel-addled kids to order.

Once the little person left, I disclosed everything to P.J.

She sniffled a bit at this confirmation of her worst fears, but then bucked up, her intellect fastening on assembling a chain of deductions.

"So something made Dad mistrust MetamorPharma. He analyzed KannerMax and figured out what it would do. Dad was always a helluva good molecular biologist. He obviously disagreed with the ethics of injecting this stuff without informed parental consent. So he contacted the guy behind it all—and was murdered!"

"Gee, do you want to come onboard Moritz Investigations as a junior partner?"

"Max, this is my dad's murder we're discussing, remember!"

"Sorry, sorry. Please forgive."

The words weren't just *pro forma*. I realized I *was* sorry, and *wanted* her forgiveness. Because I couldn't imagine being happy with P.J. angry at me, or being happy at all without her in my life somehow.

P.J. must have sensed my emotions, because she reached across the table and gripped my hand. But whatever romantic response she might have been about to utter just then got postponed to our hypothetical future together, because one of the Tiges wandering by chose that moment to piss on her foot.

Once we got that mess cleaned up, P.J. was all business again.

"You're going to see Zarthar, right?"

"Yup."

"And I'm coming with you."

Centropolis being the capital of both the USA and the GDM, the city was full of offices and officeholders.

The Bureau of Cultural Innovations was an impressive, civic temple-style building that occupied two square blocks bounded by Disney and Iwerks. P.J. and I climbed its broad marble steps and passed between its wide columns to its brazen doors and entered the vast, well-populated lobby.

I had to surrender my blaster to security, and P.J. confessed to carrying a vibrablade, which surprised me.

Once we were beyond the checkpoint and on our way up to Zarthar's office, she volunteered: "Some Geeks go way beyond grabby hands, you know."

"Admitted."

The GDM is open-source government. Citizens are encouraged to participate at all levels. Which is why we had been able to get a quick appointment with Zarthar himself.

I wasn't exactly certain how we were going to confront the mastermind behind this secret scheme to produce überGeeks, but I figured some gameplan would present itself.

And then the door of Zarthar's office opened to our annunciated arrival.

"All Geeks are Geeky, but some Geeks are Geekier than others." Everyone knows George Orwell's famous line from his novel *Server Farm*. But you haven't really experienced it until you meet someone in that leet minority like Zarthar.

Zarthar had been born Dennis LaTulippe, but had refashioned his entire persona somewhere around age sixteen, when he was already well over six feet tall. He legally changed his name, permanently depilated his head and tattooed it with a Wally Wood space panorama, grew a Fu-Manchu mustache, adopted sandals and flowing floor-length robes of various eye-popping hues as his only attire, and declared his major passion to be Situationist Bongo Playing. (This was circa 1956, twenty years ago, when beat-zeks like Jack Kerouac, Allen Ginsberg, and Doris Day were all the rage.) He revolutionized his chosen field, and his career since then had been successive triumphs across many passions, resulting in his appointment to his current position.

Zarthar's voice resonated like Boris Karloff's. "Chum Hornbine, Chum Moritz, please come in."

We entered tentatively. I had just begun to take in the furnishings of Zarthar's ultra-modern office when P.J. hurled herself at the man!

"You killed my father! You killed him! Admit it!"

Attempting to choke Zarthar, P.J. made about as much progress as Judy Canova might've made wrestling with Haystack Calhoun. And when multiple ports in the walls snicked open and the muzzles of automated neural disrupters poked out, she wisely ceased entirely.

Zarthar composed himself with aplomb, smoothing his robes. His next words did not immediately address P.J.'s accusation.

"My friends, have you ever considered the problems our world still faces? To the average citizen, it seems we occupy a utopia. And granted, two-thirds of the world—the portion under GDM—deserves that designation. But that still leaves millions of people living in pre-Geek darkness. And these seething populations are actively anti-GDM, seeking constantly for ways to undermine and topple what we've created. They are ruthless and violent and cunning. All we have to oppose them is our brains and special Geek insights.

"I realize that you've learned about my plan to create a new generation of ultra-Geeks, especially talented individuals who could develop new strategies, new ways of looking at the world that would extend the GDM way of life to those benighted portions of the planet. If you just stop a moment and reflect, you'll see that this program is a dire necessity, not anything I do out of personal aggrandizement."

"But why the secrecy?" I said. "Surely you'd find plenty of parents willing to enroll their kids in such a program."

"KannerMax is still highly experimental. We can't predict whether those who undergo the treatment will emerge as geniuses or idiots. Results point to the first outcome, with a large percentage of certainty, but still... If parents were to enroll their young children who can't decide for themselves, and the lives of these children were ruined, the parents would recriminate themselves endlessly. Better for one man to shoulder that responsibility, I thought."

P.J. and I contemplated this for a while. Zarthar seemed sincere, and his dreams had merit. But there remained one obstacle to our endorsement of his plan.

"Dr. Hornbine—" I began.

"Committed suicide. A self-administered dose of potassium chloride stopped his heart. You can see him inject it here."

Zarthar activated a monitor, and an obvious spy-ray recording, time-and-date-stamped with the GDM logo, showed Dr. Hornbine alone in his office. He tied off his arm with surgical tubing to raise a vein, picked up a hypodermic—

"No, stop it!" P.J. yelled.

Zarthar flicked off the recording. P.J. sobbed loudly for a time, and when she had finished, Zarthar spoke.

"After contacting me, your father was so despondent that KannerMax would not work on adults—that he himself would be deprived of its benefits—that he chose not to live in a world where he would soon be Darwinically superseded. And this is another reason for secrecy. So as not to instill a similar mass despondency in the population. Let everyone think that these bright new stars are random mutations. It's more merciful that way."

I had come here ready to bring Zarthar down in the media with a public shaming. But now I found myself ready to enlist in his cause. I looked to P.J., who raised her red-rimmed eyes to mine, and saw that she felt the same.

And then I knew that our children would rule the sevagram.

Chicago

Jon Courtenay Grimwood

Jon Courtenay Grimwood has won the British Science Fiction Association Award, and been short-listed for the John W. Campbell Memorial Award, the Arthur C. Clarke Award, and the August Derleth Award. And it is my assertion that anybody and everybody who enjoys fusions of science fiction and mystery should read his brilliant San Francisco novel, 9Tail Fox, *and then work their way through his backlist. Many of Jon's novels are set in "alternate futures," future settings derived from a point of departure from somewhere in our shared past. For example, his Arabesk trilogy,* Pashazade, Effendi, *and* Felaheen, *is set in an Islamic Ottoman North Africa of the Twenty-First Century that branched from our history in 1915. As with many contributors to this anthology, I've wanted to work with him for some time, and I hope this is only the beginning.*

It took Jack Cogan five days to hunt me down. I don't know why because I was where anyone with half a brain would expect me to be. In my office. At the back table in Finnegan's, drinking New York sours and watching some old film on screen. You know the kind; girl meets boy, boy gets killed, girl saves every cent to bring him back to life, boy goes off with someone else...

Finnegan had turned down the lights; instantly lowering the ceiling and sending the wall into shadow. The place smelt of cigar smoke, whiskey, and cologne. The way you would expect a Chicago speakeasy to smell.

The bar stools held memories of those who'd already left. Little Pete, who overflowed everything except a four-seater settee; a whore I knew from somewhere else; a couple of soldiers; and a man who spent half an hour watching me before glancing away when I held his stare.

He left shortly afterwards.

Maybe he had another appointment, and maybe pulling back my jacket to reveal a Colt .45 in my belt made him decide to leave me alone. That's what I thought at the time. When Jack Cogan came blustering into Finnegan's with his shoulders rolling and his belly jutting proudly, I knew the watcher was one of Jack's sneaks.

"Take a seat," I said.

"Yeah," said Cogan. "I just did."

Leaning forward, he let his jacket drop open.

"Sweet rig," I said, looking at his double holster. "Where d'you get it. Wal-Mart?"

Jack Cogan scowled. "From Lucky himself."

That was Lucky Luciano XI, unless it was Lucky Luciano X. They had a high attrition rate in that family. Since gang positions became hereditary, we'd seen some weird shit in this godforsaken city; like thirteen-year-old *capos* running whole districts and a seven-year-old pimp managing a stable of hookers without knowing what the punters were buying.

"You're a hard man to find."

"Can't have been looking hard enough."

Jack was broad and barrel-chested, running to fat. At the moment his chest was larger than his gut, but it was only a matter of time. He tipped his head to one side, inviting me to explain.

"It's been a bad year. This is the only bar I'm not banned." Glancing at the door, I noticed two plainclothes officers. They weren't clients for sure. They owned all their own teeth, wore clean clothes, and were sober. One of those was possible, two at a stretch...

But all three?

"I'm touched," I said. "You brought backup."

Jack Cogan flushed.

You can probably tell, the police captain and I go way back. In fact, we go back so far that I can remember when he was thin and he can remember when I was rich, successful, and kept the key that wound his boss.

"Al..." he said, and his use of my first name killed my grin faster than a gun ever could. "I need to know. Where were you between two and three o'clock this morning?"

"Can't remember."

"Listen to me..."

"Mean it," I said. "Had my memory wipe this morning. Last three days. Shit, I guess. Must have been, or I wouldn't have bothered to wipe then." Pulled an envelope from my pocket, then pushed it across.

You would think it was poisonous from the way Jack Cogan hesitated to touch it. Although it might have been the color, which was purple.

"Classy," he said.

A young woman I couldn't remember told me she didn't want to see me again. She told me this in childlike writing with tear splotches crinkling the page. So I guess we'd gone from romance to break up in fewer than three days. Impressive, even by my standards.

"You're in trouble." Jack Cogan was saying.

"Guess I am," I said. "If her brothers or father ever catch up with me."

"No," said Cogan. "I mean you're in real trouble."

"And you're bringing me in?"

"Yeah," he said. "Felt I owed you that." The captain nodded at my screen. "Watched any news recently?" His sigh answered his own question. "Guess not, or you wouldn't be sitting round here drinking those."

Without asking, he leant over and flicked channels.

My face stared back at me. Only it was me as I might have been; if I were sober and my hair was clean and I'd bothered to shave any time in the last week. This version of me wore a pinstriped suit, with a fancy waistcoat and patent leather shoes. He was carrying a tommy gun, the traditional mark of a recognized gang boss. The gun looked old, but it wasn't. Not really. My grandfather had it made the day he moved up from *consigliore* to *capo*.

"You might want to turn up the sound."

I did as Jack suggested, and discovered what a bit of me already guessed. The other Al had checked out with a shot to his head.

"Professional," said the presenter.

A thin woman came on to talk about Chicago traditions and that particular MO. She talked about stuff that hadn't happened as well. Gut shots, blindings, slashes to the throat, tongues ripped out, testicles removed and sewn into the mouth; nothing everybody hadn't heard three hundred times before.

Round here the bosses appointed the mayor, and they helped choose the governor, and the governor helps choose the President. It was the system that had been in place since the President realized only the bosses could make prohibition stick, because only they had a cast-iron gold-plated reason for wanting it to stick. It was what made them rich.

"So," said the presenter. "You're saying this is *capo a capo*, right?"

The woman hesitated. "It's what that particular MO would suggest, but there's another rumor..."

"What's all this got to do with me?" I demanded.

Something like sympathy showed in Jack Cogan's eyes. "We need you down the station," he said.

"We've got your fingerprints," said the man. "Your DNA and your ugly face on tape. All you got, do is sign." Picking up a rubber hose, he slashed me across my hip and grinned when pain forced its way between my teeth.

He and his companion had me naked and tied to a chair, with blood filling my mouth and three of my teeth shining like cheap ivory on the cell floor. I'd already watched myself limp down a corridor onscreen, slowly open a door, and slip through it. Exactly 180 seconds later came the sound of a shot; exactly 15 seconds after that I limped back through the door, shut it quietly behind me, and shuffled my way downstairs.

I came out of yesterday's memory wipe with one knee broken. Don't know how it happened any more than anything else that happened in those three days.

"You listening?"

"Yeah," I said. "I'm listening."

He hit me again anyway; swing the hose to make me listen harder. I knew him from my old life. While the other enforcer looked like the kid of someone I used to know. Probably was. As I said, all gang jobs are hereditary.

One point troubled me though. I'd expected Jack Cogan to do the dirty work and here I was with a couple of high-level enforcers doing it themselves. Made no sense. At least, not to me.

"Why not leave this to Jack?" I asked.

For a moment, I thought the two men were going to tell me *they asked the questions*. But the man with the rubber hose grabbed a chair, flipped it round, and straddled it, pushing his face close to mine. "Only three people it can be," he said. "Freddy, Machine Gun, or you. Now my boss knows it's not him. And Mickey's boss knows it's not him. So that just leaves you..."

Digging into his pocket, he extracted a pair of pliers, a switchblade, a lighter, and something that looked like cotton thread, and laid the first three on the table. In the time it took me to realize the fourth was not cotton; he'd wrapped it round my ear and tugged.

"Fuck..."

Then he reached for my other ear. "Come on Al," he said. It was a day for people calling me by my first name. "You know how it goes. We slice off your ears. We sever your fingers. We crush your toes and then we crush your balls. Assuming you're too stupid to have signed before then."

The other enforcer snorted.

"So," he said. "Agree to sign and we'll get you a doctor. It's late, we're all tired, and we all know you're going to confess eventually."

The judge had a face like a sucked lemon or maybe he was constipated. Either way, he twisted his lips and shuffled in his seat; every *moue* of distaste and twitch of discomfort captured on camera. And there were a lot of cameras, journalists, and members of the public. The demand for seats for my trial had been so great the city had held a lottery.

Now, I'm sure there are prosecution lawyers who are polite, intelligent, quietly spoken, and understated. The small man who stalked out into the well of the court was not one of them. Glancing around him, Mr. Dalkin stopped when his eyes reached the jury box and he gazed at each juror sympathetically. *I don't know why he didn't just confess,* his expression said. *I don't know why you're being put through this.* And then he turned to me.

"Tell me," he demanded. "Why you refused to take a lie detector test."

"I didn't."

Mr. Dalkin rolled his eyes at the jury and turned to where I stood behind bulletproof glass. "Then why are the results of that test not entered with the court?"

I shrugged.

"You don't have an answer?"

"I took the test," I told him. "But the results prove nothing."

"How is that possible?" he said. "How can they not show anything?"

"Because I had a memory wipe the morning of the murder."

He grinned smugly and flicked his gaze toward the judge, to check that he was paying attention. He was, leaning forward to catch the prosecutor's reply. "Are you telling me that's a coincidence?" he said. "That you just happened to have a memory wipe that morning?"

I nodded.

"The defendant will answer the question," the judge ordered.

"Yes," I said. "It's just coincidence."

"And when was the last occasion you had a memory wipe before this?" The prosecutor demanded. He was smiling.

"Eight days earlier."

That was true and the police had already checked. In the last five years I'd had seventy-three memory wipes. Jack Cogan made the bank double-check the figure, and when they told him it was correct, he went to the clinic himself to check this was true.

"But why?" Cogan had asked me.

"Because I get bored."

"And memory wipes stop you getting bored?"

"No," I said. "They stop me remembering what I'm bored about."

He'd sighed, offered me a coffee, and muttered that he was sorry. We both knew what he meant. Jack Cogan was sorry he had to hand me over to the enforcers. He was sorry he couldn't fix the jury. He was sorry he couldn't have the machine guns that would kill me loaded with blanks and give me an exploding vest.

It wouldn't be the first time that happened.

When Mr. Dalkin kept pushing the memory wipe angle, I told him how many I'd had in the last five years and suggested he confirm this with the police. He decided to move on to other things after that.

"What you're going to see," he told the jury, "is horrific. If I could spare you this, I would. If the man in the dock had any decency..." The little man paused to glare at me. "He would spare you having to see this by pleading guilty. But then, if he had any decency he wouldn't have done what you're about to see."

The lights went down, the shutters were closed, and a screen on a sidewall began to flicker and then clear as the clerk of the court played back the house security tape from that night. At first none of us could see anything. We were looking at the wrought-iron gates to a mansion and we were looking at them from inside. From a camera just above the front door to judge from the angle of the picture onscreen.

I hadn't seen this section of tape before. I'd seen shots of the body, close-ups of the bullet wound meant to make me confess out of horror for what I had done. But everything I'd seen began with the corridor outside the boss's study. This was outside the house itself, and at the moment the killer was a shadow outside the gate.

He limped up to the gate, slapped his hand on the lock, and blinked as a flash of light read his palm and lit up his face. A hundred people, maybe a hundred and fifty filled the court, and all of them turned to stare at me.

A click announced the gate had unlocked and a shuffle of gravel could be heard as the killer made his way toward the front steps. An automated machine gun bolted to a gatepost followed him and a tiny gun satellite dropped into view, skimmed once around his head, and then slipped away.

As the killer approached the front door, it clicked open for him. "Welcome," said the house AI.

The killer nodded absentmindedly.

In the light from the hallway, his face could be seen more clearly than ever. It was my face. His hair was dirty and his face unshaven.

A tatty overcoat hid a Colt .45 in a shoulder holster that became visible as he turned toward the stairs and his coat swung open slightly.

He checked his watch.

And the entire court glanced at my wrist. I wondered why the guards had given me back my Omega before letting me into court, and now I knew. The heavy black ring around its dial and the fat metal links of its strap were unmistakable.

He took the steps clumsily, obviously troubled by his bad leg. All the same, he knew where he was going and that, in itself, was significant. On the landing, he looked once in a mirror to adjust his hair, brushing it out of his eyes. Then he pulled the Colt from its holster and dropped out the clip, checked it was fully loaded, and slipped it back, flicking the safety catch and jacking the slide.

After which, he extracted a silencer from his side pocket and began to screw it onto the muzzle of the gun. Something made him change his mind, because he shrugged, in exactly the way I'd shrug, unscrewed the silencer, and dropped it back into his pocket. A few seconds later he was approaching the study door.

As we watched, the screen froze.

"What did you say to him?" demanded the prosecutor. "In those three minutes when he was staring death in the face. Did you mock him? Tell him he had it coming?"

"It wasn't me."

But I knew all the things I would have wanted to say.

In the old days when you talked to yourself it was inside your own head. These days...? One of me was dead, the other stood here. I had no idea who the third man was because I'd only ever had myself cloned once and look at the trouble that got me into.

At a nod from Mr. Dalkin, the screen came back to life and I watched myself step out of the door and shut it behind me. I was smiling. It was a self-satisfied smile.

"Notice the complete lack of remorse," he demanded, turning to the jury. Obediently, they did exactly as told. A bunch of sheep the lot of them, although I was the lamb to their slaughter.

Whatever glamour my own attorney once had was reduced to a tired-looking flower in her buttonhole. The rest of her was a washed-out ghost in a cheap black dress. She was court appointed, which tells you all you need to know. And the entire court—including the judge—had decided that I was guilty as sin long before she even stood up to defend the indefensible.

When I smiled at her, she looked away.

I'd been wondering what defense she'd been planning to use. Insanity, drunkenness, unhappy childhood. We could have used any of those. But someone would have had to talk to me first to extract some facts and no one had bothered.

She fell back on dramatics.

"Tell me," she said, flinging out one arm. "Can a man really stand trial for murdering himself?"

The prosecutor was out of his seat and hopping up and down before my counsel had drawn breath to begin her next sentence. He needn't have bothered. The judge announced that yes, a man could.

Mr. Dalkin sat down.

My counsel looked around her, noticed the number of cameras and the size of the crowd, and decided she had to do more than just stand there opening and shutting her mouth. "This man," she said, pointing at me. "Used to be a gang boss. Until he was sued by his own clone. For reckless endangerment. Sued successfully."

I was sure the jury got that bit.

Because I was the man standing in the dock wearing a tatty jacket and being defended by her. And they'd buried the other me in a new silk suit and smothered his grave in enough orchids to fill a rainforest.

She made a half-dozen mistakes in my life story but no one bothered to correct her, including me. The basics were there. Gang boss discovers he's due to be hit and grows clone to take the bullet instead. Clone stops off on his way to the hit, calls the police, the media, and a lawyer he gets from a small ad in the back of that day's paper. The police and the lawyer could have been handled. The police, the lawyer, *and* the media was one problem too many. Particularly as it was the out-of-state media my clone called.

The assassin was arrested.

I was sued by my clone. As my defense counsel said, successfully.

He took everything. The house, control of the gang, my bank accounts, my contacts book, and a web of connections I'd spent most of my life building up. A dozen gangs had rolled over in the time I was boss; moving me up the ranks toward being boss of bosses. All the gangs got their autonomy back. Mostly it was the previous boss who simply stepped back into his old shoes. Sometimes his son, where an old boss had died in mysterious circumstances. Once it was the grandson; but that was the Lucianos and they were notoriously unlucky.

The map of the city went back to where it was before I came in. Jack Cogan kept me alive. That is, he let it be known he'd not be bought off or intimidated if anything happened to me and the best way to make sure nothing bad happened was to keep me alive. I don't doubt I owe him. Equally, I don't doubt that at some point, he'd intended to collect.

Sighing deeply, my counsel retook her seat.

Whatever she'd been saying, it didn't look like the jury were convinced. A couple were even shaking their heads, as if they didn't know why she'd wasted her time trying to defend me in the first place. Only Jack Cogan was looking at me.

He nodded at the screen.

Then he glanced at his watch. When I shrugged, he did it again.

Maybe he had an appointment? A whore and a bottle of whiskey waiting for him in some police apartment somewhere? I hoped so, one of us deserved to enjoy this afternoon and it didn't look it was going to be me. Although there was probably someone out there sick enough to look forward to a couple of dozen machine-gun slugs to the chest. There are some sick people in this city.

And then, and this was weird, Jack Cogan stood up from his table and limped toward the restroom. Now Jack doesn't have a limp. I do, courtesy of whatever happened in those lost three days.

His leg was fine when he walked back to his seat.

It was my turn to speak. At least I assumed it was, from the way everyone was staring at me when I looked up from the dock.

"Well," said the judge. "Do you have anything to say before I pass sentence?"

By this point Jack Cogan was almost purple with... It was hard to tell with what. I've only ever seen Jack with three expressions: angry, more angry, and angrier still, and all of these involved scowling. Now he looked almost anxious.

"Well?" the judge demanded.

"Yes," I said. "Can I see that tape again?"

You could tell from the judge's expression that he just thought I was digging myself into a deeper hole. The sneer on his face said he had no problems with me doing just that. As for Mr. Dalkin, he was nodding like a toy dog before the judge even turned to him.

"No objections," he said.

Jack Cogan, he was looking relieved. Which told me what I needed to know. At least, it told me I was meant to know something and that something was on this tape. So I watched the killer walk to the gate, slap his hand on the palm reader, and listened to the gate click open.

"Sir," I said. "Can I see that again...?"

The judge sighed, but he let the clerk of the court rerun the sequence. As the killer tapped his hand to the plate, I tapped mine to the bulletproof glass in front of me, trying to mimic his movements.

He limped across the gravel, and he'd almost reached the front door before I realized the obvious. A glance round the court told me no one else had noticed it. So I kept silent as the front door opened itself and the killer made his way upstairs and along the corridor. I watched him drop his clip from the gun, check his watch, and decide against using a silencer.

We heard the shot and watched the man make his way back to the front door, shut it behind him, and let himself through the gates, vanishing into the darkness beyond.

"And the tape stops after that?"

The prosecution lawyer looked up sharply, and the judge looked at the chief of police, who nodded reluctantly. My defense looked blank. No one had bothered to tell her. Why would they? And for the amount she was being paid, she hadn't bothered to ask.

"How long for?"

"Mr. O'Brian?" The judge was staring at the police chief.

"An hour, your honor."

"And when the tape comes back on?"

Judges are not meant to ask questions like that. They're meant to leave it to the lawyers. But this was Judge Mallory's court and he'd obviously decided he was going to do what he wanted.

"Nothing, sir. It's all silent."

"How did you know?" Judge Mallory demanded. He was talking to me this time. "And what relevance does it have?"

"That's not me on film," I told him. "That's the clone."

Uproar filled the court. It was a big room and its ceiling was high and its walls were paneled in oak that muffled speech so effectively the main players were miked for sound. All the same, the noise of the crowd echoed off those oak walls and I watched at least a dozen sound men wince before turning down their dials.

"He's wearing his watch on the wrong wrist."

"You could have done that," shouted the prosecution lawyer. "You did do it. A cheap attempt to establish an alibi."

"And his hair's parted on the wrong side."

"Once again..."

The judge waved the prosecution into silence. "Anything else?" he demanded, smiling sourly.

"He's limping on the wrong side."

"Run the bloody tape again," the judge told his clerk.

So the clerk did, and then the judge made me limp across the courtroom while everyone watched. He checked that my hair did indeed part on the other side, that I habitually wore my watch on a different wrist. He asked who could confirm this and Jack Cogan put up his hand.

"And the limp?"

"Recent," said the captain. "We had it examined. A cracked kneecap. It looks like a fall downstairs."

"In your opinion," the judge said. "How do you read what we've got here?"

Jack glanced toward the chief of police.

"I'm over here," the judge told Jack.

"Sorry, sir."

The judge grunted. "So," he said. "Talk me through what you think we've got. That is if your chief has no objections."

Chief O'Brian scowled.

"The killer used a photograph of the defendant to perfect his disguise. Only he dressed himself in the mirror and forgot to allow for things like the watch being on the opposite side. So when he came to faking the limp..."

"He dragged the wrong foot."

Jack Cogan nodded. "Yes, sir. That's my reading."

"But he got through the gate and the front door and none of the weapons targeted him. That means..."

"He shared DNA with the man in the dock."

"I know what it means," the judge said sharply. "You need to find out if there's a second clone."

There wasn't, and no one could come up with a reason why the first clone might want to commit suicide, or decide to take me with him when he did.

The next time I saw Jack Cogan he had gold braid on his uniform and arrived at the restaurant in a bulletproof sedan with *police* stenciled discreetly on the side. A driver so young he was barely out of diapers rushed to open the door.

"Chief," I said.

"Mr. Capone..."

We shook hands while his driver took up position beside the restaurant's front door and my bodyguards went round to protect the back. I owned the place and had chosen its staff myself. That was a while ago. All of them had since assured me, hand on heart, that they were delighted to see me back.

"The usual?" I asked Chief Cogan.

He nodded, unfolding his napkin and tucking one corner into his collar. In the three weeks since the court case his chest had lost its epic battle with his girth and resigned itself to losing. We ate squid, the little ones dropped into batter and dusted with paprika. Then we ate linguine and clams and washed it down with a bottle from my own vineyard in California. And then we ate whatever those little cakes are that are doused in rum and rolled in sugar.

"You had me scared," he said, when coffee finally arrived.

I waited for him to explain.

"Al..." he said. "You had me scared. I thought you'd forgotten the plan and the man was about to send you down." He sat back and huffed like a horse. "Guess that's why I'm me and you're you. I don't have that kind of nerve."

He ate the sweet biscuit I passed him and reached into his pocket for a folded piece of paper. I let him reach. The chief had been searched long before he came into my presence.

"Thought you'd like to see this," he said.

It was a note from the city coroner. Three mob bosses had died, fallen to their deaths from three different windows. The two goons who beat me up on arrest had saved everyone the trouble and shot themselves the afternoon the trial ended. The old chief of police was still alive, but he'd decided to leave town.

"You know where he's gone?" I asked.

Chief Cogan nodded.

"Good, then let it be known it wouldn't be good for his health to come back. Anything else?"

"Usual stuff," he said. "Clubs wanting licenses, drive-bys in the ghetto, an unlicensed pimp trying to take over three blocks in the east city." He dumped his notes in front of me and listened intently as I told him what I wanted done in each case.

"You clear on that?"

"Sure thing," he said. "Completely clear."

So I glanced at my famous watch to show it was okay if he wanted to take his stomach somewhere else now. In fact, it would be good, because I had stuff to oversee. And Jack Cogan took the hint and pushed back his chair, dipping forward at the last minute to grab a chunk of bread that had been hiding in a basket under a napkin. After stopping to butter it, he nodded apologetically and headed for the exit.

At the door, he turned back. "Can I ask you something?"

"Sure," I said. "Who knows? I might even answer."

"That night you came by my house and told me to smash your right knee. I thought you'd lost it." Chief Cogan shook his head at the memory. "But you had it planned, didn't you? Right from the start. All that getting drunk and being thrown out of bars. All those memory wipes. You were setting it up, so no one could say you'd had your memory wiped only the one time it mattered. After... after..."

"The other Mr. Capone shot himself?"

"Yeah," said the chief, wiping sweat from his forehead. "After that."

"Maybe," I said.

Jack Cogan grinned. He knew that was all he was going to get. The chief let himself out and left me wondering. Maybe I had set it all up that carefully. Left myself little notes on the earlier occasions.

Worked it all out down to the last memory wipe, wrong parting, misworn watch, and shuffle of the wrong foot.

And maybe I hadn't. I couldn't remember.

The Sultan's Emissary

Theodore Judson

Theodore Judson is the author of Tom Wedderburn's Life, Fitzpatrick's War, *and* The Martian General's Daughter, *the latter of which it was my distinct privilege to edit. Speaking of* The Martian General's Daughter, *a future history detailing the fall of a society with certain parallels to the last days of our own Roman Antonine Caesars, Judson says, "I re-write history like this not because I believe history repeats itself, but that humans inevitably repeat the triumphs and mistakes of those who have gone before them."*

The lord chamberlain dared not wake the king at that late hour. As much as he hated yoking himself to a fanatic of Lord Cromwell's ilk in any undertaking, Lord Thomas Fairfax decided he had to go at once to the general's residence near St. James's Palace, for Fairfax knew there was no more loyal defender of the Holy Catholic Church and the Stewart monarchy than the ferocious commoner from East Anglia. Besides, most of the other mighty men in the realm had gone home for the spring planting. Fairfax gathered a score of his servants, and saw that each had a torch and a sidearm before he set out through the darkened streets of 1650 London. A light rain was falling that April morning, as it had fallen early every morning that month. While not quite as pious as most prominent men in Britain were, Fairfax saw the hand of Providence in the foul weather, as if God were lowering a protecting hand upon the island, the last sanctuary for his faith in all the wide world.

"Bad weather has long been our homeland's most stalwart defender, Hugh," he commented to one of his men, a man who had been shivering under his cloak as the group progressed through the cobblestone streets. "We should not curse it."

"A cold-hearted defender it is, my lord," said Hugh. "It beats on us as true as it will on them what's against us."

"Sanctuaries are found in difficult climes, Tom," said Fairfax, who could always console himself with the knowledge he had seen worse and would one day see worse once more. "We should love our land's wind and rain; they caress us like kisses when set against the blows of the Saracens."

As an educated man, Fairfax appreciated that Britain had been Europe's sanctuary for the faithful since the ancient days of the Fifth Century, when Attila's Huns had defeated the combined Roman and Visigoth army at Chalons in Gaul; hundreds of thousands had then fled the Christian Roman Empire along with the great Pope Leo for the sanctuary of island Britain as the Huns proceeded to conquer Italy and then to destroy the armies of Theodosius the Second and the entire eastern empire. The patchwork of barbarian tribes the Huns had left in their wake had offered only feeble resistance to the Muslim tide that washed over the European mainland in the eighth and Ninth Centuries, and only the British Isles, the pagan Vikings of Scandinavia, and the even fiercer pagans of Lithuania remained outside the Caliphate, a development that had brought yet more refugees to the home of Fairfax's ancestors. After the Norse converted to Islam in the Twelfth Century and had become the sultan's military vanguard, Britain and her sometime allies in Lithuania had managed to survive by artfully playing the Shiites against the Sunnis and the Arabs against the Turks, by paying discrete bribes first to the Seljuks and later to members of the Ottoman court, and by giving refuge to any learned Christian or Jew who might help them perfect the technologies of naval warfare. Because out of necessity she had developed better ships than the land-loving Arabs and Turks, Britain had been first to cross the Atlantic and to discover both North and South Cabotland, and had planted a string of colonies on the eastern coastline of the former continent. But because the far more numerous Ottomans had also in time crossed the Atlantic and had conquered the Aztec and Inca empires, they now ruled everything in South Cabotland and claimed everything in North Cabotland west of the Appalachian Mountains. Then two years ago in 1648, the greatest disaster of all befallen what was left of Christendom: the Turks had won the Thirty Years War and had utterly conquered Lithuania and the once invincible White Knights of Vilnius. The small expeditionary force Britain had sent to Eastern Europe under the command of the foppish Prince Rupert had availed nothing. Now in 1650 only economic bad times brought on by a cooler climate and the reappearance of the Black Death on the mainland along with the 400 ships Britain could still put upon the sea were all that kept the Turks at bay. Spies had been sending word to London for years that Mehmed the Fourth, the Ottoman sultan who from his throne in Rum ruled everything from the Gates of Hercules to the Ural Mountains and all from Lapland to the Sahara, was contemplating an invasion. The terrible news Fairfax was carrying that evening could only give the sultan another excuse for launching his attack.

Lord Cromwell's servants answered the door. One of their number went to wake the master while others made China tea which they brought to Fairfax's men in the front room. Cromwell himself charged downstairs in his dressing gown, his long hair uncombed, a blazing candelabra in his hand, and his state of mind in its usual grim condition.

"Sir Thomas," he barked at Fairfax, "either the king is dead or a Mussulman army has landed at Dover, or else you have imposed upon me sorely."

"I bring report almost as dire, my lord," said Fairfax. "Selim al Ibrahim, the sultan's emissary, has been found dead fourteen houses hence. A marksman has clearly shot him through the window of an upstairs bedroom. I am having a surgeon remove the bullet from the dead man's side, but the wound is from a rifle, I warrant it. You know I beheld many such wounds when you and I were on campaign together in the Low Countries."

Cromwell set down heavily on one of the foyer's bare benches. He gave the lit candelabra to a servant and sat in silence for a moment as he mused upon what Fairfax had said.

"We must pray," he decided after a pause.

The general at once fell upon his knees and began to say the rosary. His servants immediately followed his example, and Fairfax soon found himself surrounded by kneeling people offering up their prayers to God.

"Ahem, Sir Oliver," said Fairfax, vainly attempting to get the general's attention, "I don't want to sound as if I do not hold the Lord Christ in the highest esteem, but we are statesmen, sir, not servants of the Pope in Dublin."

"Silence!" roared Cromwell and continued his prayers.

Fairfax sighed deeply and resolved to wait for his moment. Out of deference to the king's chief general he knelt and pretended to count beads in his hands when in fact Fairfax had only a few coins he passed from palm to palm. Sir Thomas at times entertained sentiments he dared not utter, and there were instances, such as when he was in the company of a fervent Papist of Cromwell's sort, when Sir Thomas wished the Lollards had triumphed in times past and so created a less rigid, less orthodox form of Christianity. As a student of history, he realized he was a citizen of a nation ever on the verge of extermination and such a nation as his had to cling to its traditions, its beliefs, and its mores with a steel grip. Lax standards were something only the Moslems could afford, for they not only governed half the world from the seat of the Caesars, they had the Caesars' wealth and thus the Caesars' confidence.

"Were the emissary shot by rifle, why did not I or any in my household hear the report of a rifle?" asked Cromwell, rising to his feet and bringing everyone else upright with him. "Nor did anyone passing on the street bring us news of this deed."

"That is part of the mystery, my Lord," explained Fairfax, also jumping up. "The emissary's guardsmen themselves heard nothing. A manservant, one of those poor eunuchs the Turks employ, was in the chamber at the time his master was shot. This same man swears he heard the glass break and nothing more."

"The assassin had an air rifle, perhaps," suggested Cromwell, mentioning a weapon Francis Bacon had developed decades earlier. (As was characteristic of the general, when was not at his prayers or orating to a gathering, he was pacing the floor as he now was.) "Certainly a Christian weapon, Sir Thomas; the Turks themselves have no lack of powder. Or else his men could be telling us false. The armed men about him, they are Vargarians?"

Varangians or Vikings was yet the term the British used to name the elite Norse soldiers within the sultan's army. In contrast to the highly civilized Turks, who were admired in the city as much as they were feared, everyone in London abhorred the uncouth Norsemen, the products of a civilization that had communicated with the rest of humanity only with swords until the day the Ottomans conquered them. The late al Ibrahim had been famous for his mastery of the English tongue and for the charity he distributed to the city's numerous and truly wretched poor on both Christian and Moslem holidays. The Norse in his employ were a shaggy, heavily armed lot, well known for their propensity to break open the heads of any who dared get in their way. Like the recent converts to any religion, the Varangians were more fanatical in their faith than were their Turkish masters, for the Turks were often paying fines and making apologies for misdeeds their guardsmen had committed.

"They are the usual hairy men," said Fairfax. "One of their number, one Abdul Erickson, brought me the news of the murder. He presented me with this."

He took from his pocket a cockleshell and gave it to Cromwell. The lord general examined it while Fairfax told him Erickson claimed to have found the item on the porch of the emissary's house.

"The symbol of St. James the Greater," said Cromwell and momentarily put the shell on the collar of his dressing gown, for pilgrims to St. James's tomb in Compostela had worn similar shells on their outer garments back before the Ottomans had conquered the last of northern Hispania and the journey to that sacred site was yet possible. "James was the patron saint of Spain. Perhaps one of the Spaniards the king has quartered in the Mews did this."

"Or someone wishes us to believe so," said Fairfax.

The Mews were of course once the royal stables, which Queen Mary had converted to the residences of the European mainland's displaced nobility, although some who dwelt there had but dubious claims to a noble lineage. As the area once housed the king's animals, London's many wags had spoken many creative insults in regards to those currently living in the same location.

"I have the man in the Mews to assist us," suggested Cromwell in one of his characteristic outbursts of enthusiasm strangers often misinterpreted as fits of anger. "Jean Baptist Colbert; he is attendant upon the Capet family, the scions of an ancient Gallic line."

"Another of your priests?" asked Fairfax.

"No, he is some manner of banker," said Cromwell. "Colbert thinks as logically as you and I, but he likewise understands the mind of the devious, a subject alien to us."

Fairfax lifted an astonished eyebrow and half expected the lord general to laugh at his own remark. He quickly remembered this was Cromwell, the most humorless man left in Christendom, and apparently the general's talent for deception was so great he had even deceived himself.

Within the hour Cromwell was properly dressed in his black coat and cape, and he and Fairfax and twenty of their retainers were standing inside the crowded space of the first floor of the aforementioned Jean Baptist Colbert's residence. The home was made of uncovered brick and rough-hewn timbers, but Mr. Colbert in the flesh was as handsome as spring and several times as gaudy. Dressed in scarlet cloak and cape and sporting a well-trimmed Van Dyke beard the young dandy must have fussed over every morning, the perfumed Mr. Colbert was as cheerful as the lord general was glum. Watching the young banker and Cromwell from a distance while Colbert was informed of the facts of the case, Fairfax remarked how Colbert's animated cheerfulness and his dark eyes and hair contrasted with the solemn and very blond Cromwell. Sir Thomas would soon also deduce that Colbert and Cromwell were identical twins when it came to energy, for both men were equally driven toward achieving whatever goals they aspired to, and it was this bond of both wanting to achieve in the shortest possible time that made the two of them better workmates than one would at first expect.

"The cockleshell, the English rifle, the familiarity the killer must have had with the neighborhood," declared young Colbert when had heard the preliminary details; "these point toward a murderer who has long dwelt in London."

"I suspect one of the Spaniards the king has here in the Mews," said Cromwell and nodded his agreement with what Colbert had said, and all of the retainers murmured similar sentiments.

Sir Thomas cleared his throat to gain the others' attention and said: "Be that as it may, gentlemen, and I do not challenge any of your assertions, I have to say, before we dive further into this matter, that our object here is not merely to punish the guilty. We must additionally strive not to create a reason for the Turks to attack us."

"Let them come!" boomed Cromwell. "Those our navy does not drown will perish before our New Model Army!"

"There does have to be a resolution someday, Sir Thomas," added Colbert. "Better we fight the infidels in this generation than wait till they are more numerous still."

Fairfax had heard this sort of warmongering language before. Both British patriots and the many, many descendants of mainland refugees often gave themselves up to talk of slaughtering the tens of millions within the Ottoman Empire, despite the hard truth that the Turks could put ten men on the battlefield for every one Britain could. The lord chamberlain was thankful that he and the easily persuaded king were in charge of the kingdom's affairs and not men sharing the opinions of the stalwarts standing before him.

The group of them went first to the emissary's quarters and examined the dead man's corpse, which by then had been removed to another portion of the house. The physician, one Dr. Collins, had arrived to examine the body while Fairfax was fetching Cromwell and Colbert. The team of investigators found the good doctor standing beside the shrouded corpse, surrounded by no fewer than fourteen Varangians. The Norsemen wore turbans similar to those of their Turkish masters, but they otherwise attired themselves in the fashion of their pirate ancestors; they each had large straight swords attached to their belts and had several dueling pistols stuck in the leather bandoliers crossing their chests. Dr. Collins looked uncomfortable stranded among the cluster of hirsute and angry men, and he was relieved to have some armed British company.

Dr. Collins showed Colbert and Cromwell the lead slug he had removed from the emissary's heart and the small hole it had made in the plump, middle-aged man's side.

"Not as wide as a barn door, yet will do," commented Fairfax.

Cromwell recognized Fairfax's words as coming from a play, and he took the opportunity to condemn all diversions that did not edify as well as entertain. Colbert said he never had time for any diversions because of the work he did for the Capet family and the British crown. The emissary's guardsmen, who had reluctantly retreated a step to give the eminent men room enough to get near the body, meanwhile made some angry grunts to one another, no doubt calling down curses upon these Christians they blamed for their master's death.

"The thing is as clean a missile as I ever seen fired from a gun," said Dr. Collins while Cromwell and Colbert examined the slug. "I would swear it has never actually been shot."

"That is the effect of an air rifle," said Colbert. "Pressure of the atmosphere inside the weapon propels the bullet rather than an explosion. The marksman cranks the pressure as high as it can go," (he showed in pantomime how it was done) "and then he releases the compressed air when he pulls the trigger."

"Where is the one called Abdul Erickson? I mean the one I spoke to earlier?" Fairfax asked the Norsemen, for he could not see that most ferocious guardsman present. "And the eunuch who was with the emissary when he was struck; where is he?"

Through gesture and some broken English the guardsmen explained that the manservant was awaiting them upstairs in the bedroom. "Abdul go to send message," said one of the hairy men, meaning that Erickson had gone to send a letter across the Channel, informing his Turkish cohorts that the emissary had been murdered.

"God's wounds!" swore Fairfax. "Then we are short on time. We have to move along, gentlemen."

Fairfax led Cromwell and Colbert to the bedroom and showed them the broken windowpane and the bloody spot on the floor left where the emissary had fallen. The still terrified manservant explained he had been undressing his master when he heard the glass break. "Selim fall," he said in his high-pitched voice. "Magic."

"We are on an upper floor," noted Colbert, looking out the damaged window. "The shot could not have come from the street. The assassin had to be hidden in the building opposite. Do you know what that place is, Lord Fairfax?"

"There is a public house on the ground floor," said the lord chamberlain. "Its entrance is on the other side of the structure. The upper story is divided into rooms the landlord lets out to travelers with public business here in London. The rooms are not as squalid as one might suppose. A member of Commons keeps his city residence in one of them. How far across would you say the second story over there is, Mr. Colbert?"

"Thirty, forty paces," guessed the handsome young banker.

"And then the bullet had to pass through a heavy glass pane before it struck the emissary," added Fairfax. "These air rifles, if this were an air rifle, are accurate to perhaps a hundred feet. Would you allow one of your soldiers to use such a weapon in battle, General Cromwell?"

The lord general scowled and shook his head.

"An air rifle is a toy, sir," he said. "Boys use them to kill small birds. To give one to a man on the battlefield would be to send him forward unarmed. But I see your point, my lord," said Cromwell, going to the window to have a look of his own. "There cannot be six men in the kingdom capable of making such a shot."

"I doubt there are as many as six," said Fairfax. "This was done by a rare marksman."

"I beg to disagree," said Colbert, sounding rather too pleased to be disagreeable. "Some of the displaced aristocracy in the Mews hunt with nothing other than air rifles, as they cannot afford the powder the king sets aside for the army and navy."

"He speaks the truth," said Cromwell.

"Some of these starving kings and their retainers in the Mews can hit a mark at two hundred paces with such a rifle," proclaimed Colbert.

"Are you one of these marksmen, sir?" asked Fairfax in a not overly friendly manner.

"But no, my lord," said the handsome man of Frankish lineage. "I never have time for sport. Now I think we should examine the room directly across the street from this one. There, as you yourself have said, is where the killer must have lain in wait."

Another fifteen minutes passed, and the innkeeper had been roused and had opened the door of what must have been the assassin's room for the group of investigations, which by now included several of the hairy Norsemen, who had tagged along with Cromwell and Fairfax's group and were following what was said as well as they could. The window opposite the emissary's residence had been left slightly ajar. A chair was still sitting at the same window, and a stack of boxes had been piled beneath the sill, giving the marksman a place to steady his weapon. The avid Colbert sat himself in the chair and demonstrated once more in pantomime what the killer must have done; he laid an imaginary rifle across the boxes and pulled an invisible trigger.

"The matter is as plain as day," said Cromwell.

"Yes, I am amazed at the progress we are making," noted Lord Fairfax.

"Good man," said Colbert to the innkeeper, "to whom did you rent this room tonight?"

The poor fellow shook with fear to be in the dangerous presence of so many prominent men.

"I don't know his name, your lordships," he said, trembling. "He paid in coin. He said his name was Charlie. He's a tall, sickly-looking gentleman. His skin's as yellow as old paper. My wife says he's one of the ex-royals from the Europe side what the king has put up in the Mews. I can't tell why he would want a room here tonight when his own home is so close."

"I say, I may know this fellow!" declared Colbert, rising from his chair. "Is he slender as well as tall?"

"Yes, your lordship," said the innkeeper. "He's as thin as a scarecrow."

"Does he go about in dirty, white leggings?"

"Why, yes, your lordship."

"Long, prematurely white hair and sallow skin?"

"His hair's white alright. I can't tell if it's *pro-mat-turic*. And his skin's yellow, not that other thing."

"It is Charles Habsburg!" Colbert proclaimed to the others. "I swear: that's the very image of him. He is German, of course, but his family claims a connection to some obscure and long dead king and queen who were supposedly the rightful rulers of Spain."

"Which would explain the cockleshell," chimed in Cromwell. "Saint James was the patron saint of the Spaniards. The man must have killed the emissary out of some misplaced effort to win a measure of revenge. I warrant we will find the weapon at his home if we search it immediately."

"I have no doubt you will," said Fairfax, although the irony in his voice was wasted upon Cromwell and Colbert.

The sun had not completely risen before they had proceeded to the shabby row house of Mr. Charles Habsburg and had roused the poor man and his family onto the street while Cromwell's men ransacked the building in search of the air rifle. Watching the sickly man shiver in the cold while his fat wife cursed the out-of-uniform soldiers in the lord general's employment, Lord Fairfax doubted Mr. Habsburg had the strength to climb the stairs to a second story, let alone turn the crank on a powerful weapon. Certainly this pale figure had not been out of doors often enough to learn how to shoot. The troopers had been within the house for only a half an hour ere they triumphantly emerged, one of them carrying above his head a large air rifle like a trophy.

"That isn't mine!" protested the hapless Mr. Habsburg.

Nonetheless, Cromwell's agents fell upon him and were prepared to carry the unfortunate man away when Fairfax intervened.

"We will retire to my rooms in Parliament, gentlemen," he announced. "There we will resolve this matter to my satisfaction."

"But, my lord," started Colbert, "the matter is as clear as day: this man—"

"This sorrowful man no more shot the emissary than I did," said Fairfax. "But we will bring him to my rooms in Parliament. He looks to be in need of a full breakfast, and we can feed him there. Come along."

So they progressed to the Parliament Building, whereat Fairfax had Mr. Habsburg and his family sent to the servants' quarters and given something warm to eat.

"Let him set by a fire," Fairfax instructed his men. "The man looks as though he might perish if not handled with the gentlest care."

"We must keep a guard on him," said Cromwell.

"If that eases your concerns," allowed Fairfax. "Now," he said to those who remained in the small chamber wherein the lord chamberlain did most of his paperwork, "before I make my report to the king, I will need to speak to the man who assisted our feeble suspect in this murder."

"Of whom do you speak, sir?" asked Cromwell, although the general should have let Colbert speak for him, as the young man simulated surprise better than he could.

"Whoever fired the fatal shot across the street knew when and in which room the emissary would be this past night as he prepared for bed," explained Lord Fairfax. "Only a member of the emissary's household could have provided the assassin with that information. Indeed, I suspect only a trained warrior, such as the emissary's guardsmen, could have made the shot. The first man in my suspicions is this Abdul Erickson, who alone of the emissary's retinue has fled the city. I suspect if we were to search this man Erickson's belongs—or his person when he is overtaken—we will find this man has possession of more gold than an honest guard could earn in five years of duty."

"The man you speak of is, regrettably, gone, sir," said Cromwell, his hands on his hips and tone, like his pose, in a defiant mode.

"Then send your fastest horsemen, General. He has only a few hours' head start."

"He was bound to Dover," said Cromwell. "He may be on board a vessel and at sea before we can overtake him."

"A ship does not leave Dover every day, sir," said Fairfax, sounding equally defiant. "If he is gone by the time you reach the shore, send another boat after him. He cannot slip away so easily. When he is in your custody, my lord, bring him here that we may question him as to the identity of his cohorts. Send your riders, sir, or I will dispatch my own men, and *they* will be the ones to interrogate him."

Cromwell paused for several seconds in the middle of the small room. He looked at Fairfax with an anger few present could understand.

"When we served together, Sir Thomas—" he started to say.

"When we last served together," said Fairfax, "I was your superior, as I am yet, sir. Now please do as you have been commanded."

The lord general reluctantly left the room. He would not return until that afternoon. In the long meantime, Mr. Colbert and several of the chamberlain's retainers remained in the unadorned chamber with Sir Thomas. While they waited for news from Dover, Sir Thomas delved into the stacks of documents that each day needed his attention. Servants brought some cheese and bread at noon, and everyone had a bite to eat and a glass of the rather foxy wine from the New York colony in America.

"This is what Mohammed has forced us to drink after his followers conquered Gaul," said Fairfax and grimaced as he took a long swallow of the tart nectar. "Our soldiers and working men have the good sense to drink porter."

"May I leave you, sir?" Colbert asked him, and would ask him such on several occasions that day.

"You may, young man, but then you would miss the great moment when this affair is resolved," said Fairfax, not looking up from his work. "I would like to have you here then, sir."

When Cromwell returned at half past four that afternoon, he and several of his men were splattered with mud from the trail to the coast.

"The one called Abdul Erickson is dead by his own hand," announced the lord general. "We spied him immediately beyond Gravesend. Seeing the seven of us and knowing his sins, he pulled out a pistol and fired the same into his skull. We took this from his body."

The general tossed a leather bag of gold coins on Fairfax's table.

"He did not have time to make a full confession?" asked the lord chamberlain.

"He did not," said the lord general.

"Then I need you to find one, sir," said Fairfax. "Suitably, this suicide's last missive to the world will be composed in his Norse tongue and will state that he alone was responsible for the emissary's death. His motive arose from a dispute over money. No, wait, they argued over a woman. There needs to be a woman in the story. Most importantly, the king in London and the sultan in Rum must know this murder was committed by a Muslim member of the emissary's household, and thus this horrible crime cannot be a cause for war."

Cromwell was aghast at the suggestion.

"What of this Habsburg man?!" he demanded.

"He is innocent, as you and your helpful Mr. Colbert are well aware, sir," said Sir Thomas. "Oh, and I need this Erickson's letter today. I must make a report to the king tonight, you understand. Please see to it that I have a note to show him."

The enraged general turned on his heels and stormed from the room. Mr. Colbert would have followed after him, but Sir Thomas made another "ahem" into his fist when Colbert moved toward the door, signaling the young man he should stay a while longer.

"There is nothing to be done in regards to Sir Oliver Cromwell, lord general of the king's army, defender of the Holy Catholic Church," said Fairfax, ever busy with his paperwork. "He must be endured till God calls either him or me to our reward. You, sir, are another man entirely. You can be dealt with."

Unlike Cromwell, Mr. Colbert did not lose his temper. He smiled at Fairfax as gamely as he would have had the story ended with his triumph.

"When did you know, sir?" he asked the chamberlain.

"Everything was too convenient," said Fairfax. "The cockleshell Erickson found, the rare weapon, you, the innkeeper and his story, and you knowing of Mr. Habsburg; they all directed me to the same conclusion. I do not know why you despise this Charles Habsburg and would want to put the murder weapon inside his quarters—"

"He is a parasite," said Colbert. "He and the others in the Mews live on the king's charity. Why waste treasure upon them when money is needed to buy arms, to train soldiers, to—"

"To fight a war," suggested Fairfax.

"Yes, why not? We in Christendom beat the Turks when they sent their giant fleet against this island in Queen Bess's time. We can do the same again."

Colbert was referring to the victory of 1588, when Drake and the other sea dogs had defeated the so-called Armata that Sultan Suleiman the Lesser had sent to invade Britain.

"Why tempt fate?" said Fairfax. "I have every reason to hope we could fight off another Turkish invasion. We have, after many centuries of trial and error, developed fighting ships superior to theirs. The Turks remain, however, far more numerous than we, and there is ever the danger they would wear us down in any prolonged conflict."

"Then you are one of those resigned to letting Britain drop like ripened fruit into the hands of the sultan? A struggle might be lost, so why risk it?"

"I am one who hears the grass grow, sir," said Fairfax, at last setting aside his work and looking up. "I have listeners positioned around the world, young man, and they tell me the sultan's empire has grown too large and its divisions are too many. Persia is on the move against the Ottomans. The newly liberated Marathas of Hindustan are on the move against the Persians and the Afghans. The Arabs in North Africa have already rebelled twice in the last two decades."

"And been put down twice," inserted Colbert.

"They will rebel again, sir, and again, and will do so until the Turks are gone from their lands. The Red Men of North Cabotland already, after a mere 200 years of the Ottomans' presence, favor us over them. You see, the Turks rule a thousand varied peoples, and each wants to cast off the Ottoman rule. You were able to find compatriots among the Norsemen in the emissary's household only because the shaggy men of the north also hate their Turkish masters and are willing to join forces with unbelievers for a few coins and the chance to kill an important Turk."

"Yet when the time comes that they expel the Ottomans from their lands, will not these thousand separate peoples remain followers of Mohammed?" asked Colbert.

"What makes them different from us gives us a solidarity which will not grow old before God visits another flood upon us," said Fairfax with an unforced smile. "The inhabitants of these islands may settle in lands upon the other side of the globe, but for safety's sake these wayward Englishmen will remain married to the Crown, lest they fall victim to the scimitar of the fearful alien constantly so close at hand. The lands the Turks presently rule will, on the other hand, never be completely free of each other. Their shared religion guarantees the weak nations and the strong will be forever involved in the affairs of each other, and they will grow weak while they squabble as our small country grows constantly stronger while it stands apart."

He handed a sealed paper to Colbert.

"You will present this to the captain of the H.M.S. *Falcon*, sir," explained the lord chamberlain. "The ship sails from Plymouth for Virginia in two weeks. I am certain you will find work to occupy you there. Perhaps you will be allowed to make war upon the Red Natives, if fighting is what you desire. I do not know, sir, if you or this Erickson person shot the emissary, or if you were on the scene at all. I do know you and Cromwell were part of the conspiracy. I cannot send the lord general away, but you I can. Do hurry your journey, Mr. Colbert. Your continued presence in the city might be inconvenient to Sir Oliver and irksome to me. Good day, sir."

One of the chamberlain's servants showed Mr. Colbert the way out of the Parliament building.

Worlds of Possibilities

Pat Cadigan

X-Files star Gillian Anderson once pronounced Pat Cadigan "the queen of science fiction," and no less than William Gibson proclaimed her as a "major talent." She has won the Arthur C. Clarke Award more than once, as well as the World Fantasy Award and the Locus Award, and been nominated for the Hugo and the Philip K. Dick. Often identified with the cyberpunk genre, she has written horror, dark fantasy, and science fiction. When I met her a few years ago in London and asked how she was, she replied, "I'm fabulous. But then I'm always fabulous." She wasn't lying.

...for all your mystic needs.

If she had been just a little more paranoid, Detective Ruby Tsung thought as she climbed out of her ancient Geo, she would have read the antique gold letters on the display window as a taunt. And why not? This morning she had woken up feeling as if something about the size and shape of a hockey puck had congealed just under her breastbone and was slowly twisting her insides into a misshapen mass. Or mess.

The return of the Dread; she had known it would happen eventually but that didn't make it any easier. This time there had been no warning, no gradual onset, and so no chance to talk to her partner

Rafe Pasco about why the near-overwhelming sense of impending doom that he had told her was actually a kind of allergy had come back. She had intended to call him but even as she was reaching for the phone, Ostertag had rung with orders to proceed directly to this address on the other side of the downtown business district. Do not pass the squad room; do not collect 200 calories of doughnut.

She had arrived to find half the block cordoned off and a small army of uniformed police trying to look purposeful and on the case and not at all like they were milling around drinking coffee and gossiping. That would be down to Ostertag's presence. The lieutenant only showed when there was something majorly unfortunate. Usually this involved someone high up in city or state government and an underage person. They didn't get many of those calls, however, and none of them in Ruby's experience had ever been found at a store that sold tarot cards, crystals, and incense. Maybe this was a massage parlor in disguise? She frowned at the window again. *Worlds of Possibilities;* there were stranger ones—worlds and possibilities both.

"Hey, Rube," said the uniform on the front door, smiling and in spite of the Dread, she managed to smile back at him. Dave Maqsood had been one of her classmates at the academy, umpty years ago.

"So what's it like in there?" she asked, clipping her badge to the breast pocket of her jacket.

"Very spiritual and mystic." He leaned toward the open doorway and took a deep breath in through his nose. "The manager lit a lot of incense while he was waiting for us to show. Sandalwood and something else. I don't know what it is but I think it's in my wife's favorite cologne. It's nice. Almost covers the db stink. Almost."

She poked her head in and looked around. There were even more uniforms inside, some taking photos. "Jesus, who died—the mayor? Or does he just own the place?"

"He might as well own everything in a ten-block radius. Or didn't you notice how much this area's been pimped out lately? Redevelopment. The old warehouses are loft condos, they turned the old handbag factory into an art gallery, and there's two designer coffee joints on this block alone, one at each end. Serious money's getting poured in here and nothing fucks that up like murder, you know?"

Ruby nodded. "Yeah, there goes the neighborhood." She peered in through the doorway again. None of the glass cabinets or display tables seemed to be disturbed even slightly. "So where *is* this dead body?"

"*Two* dbs," Maqsood corrected her, "and they're in one of the treatment rooms in the back." He pointed; at the far end of the room to her left, she saw a doorway with a multicolored beaded curtain currently tied up out of the way. Just above it was a sign that said *Treatment Rooms* in flowery script.

"Treatment Rooms?" Ruby made a pained face. "What kind of treatments are we talking about?"

"Don't ask me, I don't even work here." Maqsood chuckled. "Your partner's back there with Lieutenant Ostertag. DiCenzo and Semente are talking to the employees who found the bodies and now that you're here, the party can really begin."

"You didn't get a chance to talk to anyone, did you?" Ruby asked as the Dread pressed harder on her stomach.

Maqsood shook his head. "Sorry, Rube. Rivard and Goldie were the responding officers. Jean and I came in on the second wave by request."

"Anything you *can* tell me?" she said without much hope.

"Whoever's in there has made Ostertag very unhappy." He leaned in a bit closer. "I heard the word 'mob.'"

Ruby blinked at him. "Really."

"If you heard it, too, it wasn't from me. Necessarily." He spread his hands. "Sorry, Rube, that's the best I can do."

"I hear you," she said and started to go in.

"No, I feel you."

"Pardon?" She paused, looking at him in surprise.

"That's what they say now. Not 'I hear you' but 'I feel you.'"

"Great. That's all I need is everybody *feeling* me. Jesus wept."

Maqsood's laughter followed her as she went inside.

She spotted Tommy DiCenzo and his partner Lou Semente talking with three very distraught people. DiCenzo excused himself from the group and came over to her.

"You look like hell," he said with a grim half-smile.

She winced. "Why, you silver-tongued devil, always with the flattery."

"Sorry. You coming down with something or was the traffic that bad?"

"The traffic's always bad in this part of town. It's because the highway's all screwy. I swear to God, the exit and entrance ramps make a square knot." She nodded toward the people with Semente. "They find the bodies?"

"Yeah. The older guy's the manager, Clement Odell. The taller woman with the black hair's named Joan Klein, the short one's a Candy Lovelace and as you can probably see, she's pretty freaked out." Candy Lovelace was huddled between the manager and the other woman with her arms wrapped tightly around herself, her head bowed and her shoulders up around her ears. Ruby could see she was crying. "I called an ambulance," DiCenzo added. "Maybe it'll get here before she melts down altogether."

Ruby nodded absently. "And what's the story with these treatment rooms?"

DiCenzo shrugged. "Manager says they just used them for private appointments with psychics. I didn't see any massage tables or baby oil or anything."

"Okay, whatever." She frowned. "Do they still say 'whatever' or is it something else now like 'I feel it?'"

DiCenzo gave her a sideways look. "Who are 'they' and what are 'they' feeling?"

"Don't ask."

She made her way across the store, nodding at the various uniformed officers. Just outside the doorway leading to the rooms in the back, she paused for a look at a long glass display case filled with a large collection of semi-precious gemstones in a multitude of colors, shapes, and sizes. Ruby knew nothing about any sort of gems but she was fairly sure that unless these were all fakes made out of plastic, there was a small fortune laid out glittering under those tiny bright lights in the case. But again, as far as she could tell, nothing had been disturbed. The stones were grouped by color, dark alternating with light, in a way that made her think of one of those pictures made up of thousands of smaller pictures—you could only see the larger picture at a distance.

And why would she think that, she wondered, frowning. Then the Dread throbbed inside her, a reminder that everything was wrong and would continue to be wrong until further notice.

The so-called treatment rooms had been dressing rooms in a previous lifetime; Ruby could tell by the doors. They had been repainted a rich, midnight blue and decorated here and there with tiny gold suns and crescent moons and comets but they still had panels with adjustable shutters. Cheaper than getting rid of them but they must have been a bitch to paint, Ruby thought.

However many rooms there had been originally, the area had been remodeled so that there were now only three. Two smaller ones on her left faced a larger one across a narrow passageway; at the far end was a door marked *Employees Only.*

Abruptly, her partner Rafe Pasco poked his head out of the larger room on her right, his honey-colored dreadlocks swinging with the motion. "Door number three for the win."

"And today's prize is?" She followed him into the room.

"My ulcer," said Ostertag. He was crouched at the foot of two bodies, a man and a woman, laid out side by side. Both had been shot several times in the chest, leaving their faces untouched.

"I didn't know you had an ulcer," Ruby said, unconsciously pressing one hand to her own midsection where the feeling of impending doom had gone up another few notches.

"I don't. Yet," the lieutenant said. "It's the one I'm going to have by lunchtime. Between the mayor and the city council and the press, it'll be a doozy, too."

"Does anyone still say 'doozy?'" she said before she could think better of it.

Ostertag was apparently too deep in his study of the bodies to hear her. The woman was blonde, medium build, in her late twenties or early thirties, wearing a long, gauzy white garment that made the manner of her death all the more vivid. It wasn't really a dress, Ruby thought; it looked more like it was supposed to be a ceremonial robe. Perhaps the sort of thing the well-dressed psychic wore on the job these days.

By contrast, the man had met his end in a very expensive suit, possibly made to order, along with the silk shirt. No tie—either he hadn't been wearing one or someone had taken a souvenir. Ruby estimated that he was about her own age, making him perhaps twenty years older than the woman next to him, dark-haired and a bit heavy-set, as if he had just started to put on weight. There was something familiar about his face but she couldn't place him.

"Do we know who they are?" she asked.

"The manager ID'ed her as Emmeline Lilliana, professional psychic. The other two employees confirm that," Pasco told her. "None of them recognized the man."

Ruby frowned, thinking. "I could swear I've seen him somewhere before—"

"You have," said Ostertag, pushing himself to his feet. Ruby waited for him to continue. Instead he began walking slowly in a wide circle around the bodies. She turned to Rafe Pasco; his face was carefully composed, impossible to read. The irritation she would have felt was all but completely overridden by the Dread, the awful feeling of utter certainty that she was about to find herself at the mercy of something unstoppable, unbearable, and incurable. Because one or both of the dead people on the floor didn't belong here. She wished Ostertag would go off and have his ulcer somewhere else so she could talk to her partner alone.

All at once she noticed that Ostertag had several faint shadows radiating in all directions and looked up. The original ceiling had been raised several feet and track lighting installed; four tracks, with a lot more lights than the room really needed. Ruby looked around and there was also an indirect lighting system running along the perimeter of both the floor and ceiling.

"Is it me," she said, "or is it warm in here?"

Ostertag glanced at her but didn't answer.

"Seriously," she prodded, "what's with all the lights?"

The lieutenant still didn't say anything. He had finished his circuit of the bodies and was now standing at their feet again with his hands in his pockets.

"Okay," she said, taking out her notebook and pen. "We've got an ID on the woman but nobody knows who the guy is—"

"I didn't say that." Ostertag eyed her darkly. "The manager and the other two don't know who he is. But *I* do. That's Phil Cannizzarro. Career criminal, convicted felon. Family man."

Ruby had to think for a couple of seconds before she remembered. "I thought Phil Cannizzarro died four or five years ago while he was serving time for bribery."

"I know he did," Ostertag said. "I saw the body myself."

"Then this is just some guy who looks like—"

"I don't want anyone talking about who he is or isn't or who he looks like," Ostertag added, going on as if she hadn't spoken. "I told DiCenzo and Semente and the uniforms who saw the body the same thing. That's four other people besides you two and me. I don't want anyone else in here who hasn't been in here already."

"What about the coroner's office?" Ruby asked. "How long do you think they'll keep a lid on it?"

"Long enough to prove this isn't Phil Cannizzarro."

"That'll be easy. One DNA test, end of story."

Ostertag's mouth twitched. "It better be," he said. "Because I don't know how I'll take it if it turns out Phil Cannizzarro has an evil twin. Or an even more evil twin."

"*Had* a twin," Ruby corrected him. "Evil or more evil, he's dead now, too. It's still end of story."

Ostertag shook his head slowly and emphatically. "It'd be an evil omen."

Ruby's eyebrows went up; in the eight years she had known him, Ostertag had never shown any sign of being superstitious. She turned to her partner who was studying a palmtop computer with a deeply furrowed brow. Before she could say anything to him, Ostertag's cell phone rang, sounding exactly like the phones from a certain TV series about a counter-terrorist agency that her grandkids were crazy about.

Ostertag noticed her reaction and said, "My daughters" before answering. He left the room with the cell clamped to the side of his head.

"He didn't even say hello," she said.

"Probably didn't have to," Pasco replied. He was taking photos of the bodies from several different angles with his palmtop. "By the time this is over, he'll have to have his phone surgically removed from his ear. Someone ought to tell him about Bluetooth."

"Someone did," said Ruby. "He's got a thing about walking around talking to nobody." She let out a long breath. "So this is why I woke up feeling like shit this morning."

Pasco finished taking pictures and thumbed the small keypad with the expert rapidity that made Ruby feel old and in the way every time she saw it. Except for today, of course; nothing trumped the Dread.

"What kind of identity theft is this?" she asked, just for the sake of saying anything at all instead of standing silently in a room with two corpses and the Dread growing inside her like a tumor on fast-forward.

Pasco's attention was still on his palmtop. "Not the usual. Maybe not even mainly identity theft." He glanced up at her briefly. "Sorry, I'm looking up some..." His voice trailed off before his lips stopped moving. Ruby waited. In the eleven months since he had transferred to homicide from cybercrime—the Geek Squad, as everyone called it, including the people in it—she had gotten used to him. To say that he was nothing like her old partner Rita Castillo was an under-statement. When Ostertag had assigned him to her after Rita's retirement, she'd had a few misgivings and they were as much about her own ability to adapt to working with somebody her son's age as they were about Pasco's being able to switch from virtual crime to real violence with real blood and guts and worse.

But there was more to it than that. His arrival in homicide had coincided with the arrival of the Dread, which hadn't actually been a coincidence at all. And from there—well, she might not have believed any of it, not even what she saw with her own eyes. Except for the Dread. It was like a mix of every bad feeling she had ever experienced, heavily salted with the certainty that there was worse to come. In fifty-four years of life (fifty-five next October), she had never had any idea that it was possible to feel so awful and not be in physical pain.

Regret, Rafe Pasco had told her, was like that.

She took his word for it; regret was something she had never allowed herself to give into, not in any serious way, not even when the Dread took hold of her. Because when the Dread did take hold of her, the regret trying to find its way into her wasn't exactly her own. Pasco had told her that, too and she wouldn't have believed it except for Rita Castillo—not the one who had been her partner for so many years but the one who had worked out of some other precinct and had never met her at all.

Her gaze fell on the corpses again and she felt her stomach do a slow forward roll. "Aw, shit," she groaned.

Pasco looked up from his palmtop, mildly surprised. "I know, but anything in particular?"

"This is just what we need,' Ruby said. "The Mob working an angle with identity theft. Evil twins, more evil twins, terrifyingly evil twins—who knows, maybe even *good* twins. That would really be something. This is like a dream come true for them. They can alibi each other, dump bodies, tamper with evidence, witnesses, juries—" She made a disgusted noise, wiping one hand over her face. "Once they really get their hooks in, they'll have everything so fucked up we won't know what world—system—universe—we belong in. They'll take over the best ones and force people to pay them to live in it. Jesus, I better put in for my retirement while I still know which end is up."

Her partner started to say something when they heard a terrified scream from someone out in the main part of the store. She automatically reached for her gun but Pasco put his hand on her arm and shook his head.

Several voices were talking at once; she could hear DiCenzo telling someone to calm down, *calm down* and come over here, please come over here right now and sit down while a man's voice said *Omigod, Omigod, Omigod* over and over with the same inflection, like a machine. Underneath the commotion, Dave Maqsood was asking someone to step outside, please just step outside for a few minutes and a woman wanted to know what had happened. Keeping her hand on her weapon, Ruby went out to see what was going on.

On one side of the store, DiCenzo was trying to calm the manager who was gesturing at the door and then toward the treatment rooms. The other two employees were in a far corner with some uniformed officers; Ruby could hear the rapid whooping pant of someone hyperventilating. She looked around, caught the eye of Dave Maqsood's partner Jean Fletcher; Jean shook her head and shrugged.

Pasco tapped her on the shoulder and pointed at the display window. Through the glass, she could see Maqsood talking calmly but firmly to someone whom he was preventing from coming into the store. Ruby moved closer and saw that it was a young blonde woman dressed in a yellow sleeveless top and a ruffly peasant skirt; draped over one arm was something long and white, covered in plastic from a local drycleaner.

Ruby turned to Pasco, mystified.

"Who said anything about the Mob?" He chuckled. "What we've got is a case of job sharing without the employer's knowledge or permission, by a con artist running a psychic scam."

Ruby stared at him flatly.

"Although I will admit that the presence of a Mob figure is definitely disturbing," he added.

"Oh, no shit, Sherlock?" Ruby gave a single, mirthless laugh.

"Still, *she's* at the center of this," Pasco insisted. "Not him."

"What makes you so sure?" Ruby asked, still skeptical.

"Because if she weren't, there'd be two identical women back there."

Ruby wanted to appreciate the sight of Ostertag looking as bad as she felt, possibly even worse, except it did nothing to relieve the Dread weighing her down.

"I give him points for not going back to the precinct and hiding out in his office," Pasco said as they watched him directing the cops outside to tighten the cordon from where they stood near the front door.

"Are you kidding?" Ruby said. "In case you hadn't noticed, he calls confrontation a lifestyle. And he's not gonna let go of this Phil Cannizzarro thing until he gets some answers."

Pasco's faint smile was wry. "If he gets any, you think he'll believe them?"

"I have no idea." Ruby sighed. "It depends on what they are, I guess." She saw Ostertag pause at the back door of the ambulance where the hysterical employee was now lying down. A paramedic came out to have a few words with the lieutenant, then went back inside. The ambulance had arrived at the same time as the crime scene techs who were now crawling all over the back rooms, including the one marked *Employees Only;* Ruby had managed to get a quick look at it before they had chased her out complaining about contamination. Half the room served as the employee lounge with a couple of cheap vinyl sofas and a dented coffee urn; the other half was the manager's office. Not what she'd have called a great arrangement. She tried to imagine having to take coffee breaks in Ostertag's office and felt nothing but the Dread.

"Here, look at this," Pasco said, giving her a nudge. He was holding the palmtop in front of her. She had to lower it six inches and when that didn't help, made him wait while she took out her reading glasses.

"What am I looking for?" Her eyes focused on a mug shot of a woman. She was dark-haired and very disheveled, with a swollen lower lip and the start of a black eye but Ruby recognized her. "Okay, is that the dead one or—" she looked around, spotted DiCenzo with the manager in the astrology section but no one else.

"Semente is babysitting her over in the self-help corner," Pasco told her. "I thought we might ask her that."

"Fine, but I'd like to know if *you* know," Ruby said. "I think at least one of us should know if she's lying."

"You don't think you'd be able to tell?"

Ruby frowned. "What, if she doesn't belong here I'll feel worse? I didn't think it worked that way."

"Once you know what to look for, you can see the differences."

"Fine. *You* look for the differences. I'll back you up."

"All right," said Pasco genially.

The self-help corner was furnished with several wicker chairs. Semente and the woman might have been two customers having a chat about biorhythms or some other mystical thing except that Semente had positioned himself so she had no unobstructed avenue of escape. As soon as he saw Ruby and Pasco, he excused himself. The woman watched them with wide, anxious eyes as they sat down, Pasco taking Semente's place. Ruby had to force herself not to push her own chair farther away. If the Dread was any worse, she couldn't tell; it certainly wasn't any better.

"Why won't anyone tell me what's going on?" the woman said, looking from Pasco in front of her to Ruby on her right. "What happened?"

"You're Emmeline Lilliana?" Pasco said, glancing down at his palmtop.

The woman looked at him, then at Ruby with her notebook and pen. "Yes. Is someone ever going to write that down? You people keep asking me that."

"Is that your real name?"

Now she frowned at Pasco, offended. "What kind of a question is that?"

"Is that your real name, or is that just the name you do business under as a psychic?"

She glanced at Ruby. "It's my legal name. My full legal name."

"Actually, that comes up as an alias," Pasco told her, almost sounding apologetic. "Along with Emily LaDue, Lilly LeFevre, Lillian Emerson, and Emma Casey."

The woman took a deep put-upon breath and let it out again. "Don't you think it's a waste of time to ask me questions you already know the answers to?"

"Just want to see if your answers match ours."

"Okay, whatever. Look, I'm not trying to be difficult or disrespect you or anything but I just got here. I thought I was coming into work like I would on any other day and instead the street's blocked off, there are cops everywhere and as soon as Carol lays eyes on me, she goes bananas and has to get sedated. And no one will tell me what's going on."

Pasco shook his head. "Come on, you must have picked up on something."

She gave Pasco and Ruby dirty looks. "Yes, all right, I can figure out something really bad's happened. Someone's been hurt—killed?"

Pasco shrugged, glancing at Ruby; she put up a hand, fingers spread.

"There wouldn't be so many cops here if it wasn't a murder," the woman said after a long moment. "Right?"

Pasco shrugged again.

"Come on, yes or no," she prodded.

"I didn't think you'd have to ask," said Pasco. "You *are* psychic, aren't you?"

The woman looked heavenward. "I can't believe I walked into that one again. I never learn."

"I figured that out from your record." Pasco chuckled, glancing at Ruby again. "That you never learn, I mean."

"If you were planning on telling the owners of this place about my record, don't bother. They already know. I didn't even have to explain. They know the torment that skeptics visit on the sensitive."

"Do they," Ruby said.

Emily Lilliana's half-closed eyes swiveled to look at her. "Of course. Both you and your partner must know what it's like to be picked on just because you're different. How many other Chinese kids did you go to school with, dear? Did they call you 'kung fu' or 'ching chong,' pull the corners of their eyes up? Make jokes about slanty-eyed rice-burning cars?"

"Those are Japanese cars," Ruby corrected her.

"As if they knew the difference." Emmeline Lilliana sniffed and turned back to Pasco. "And you—did you grow up with the black parent or were you forced to try fitting into a world full of people who looked nothing like you? Or are both your parents black and you were the little genetic surprise that no one knew what to make of. What *did* your father think of those freckles?"

"What's your point?" asked Ruby. "Other than antagonizing the people who are trying to decide whether to arrest you or not?"

"Arrest me? What for?" Emmeline Lilliana looked hurt. "For being psychic? I can't help that any more than you can help those freckles, officer—"

"Detective," Pasco said.

"Of course, detective. My bad—"

"Do they still say 'my bad?'" Ruby said, doing her part to keep the woman off-guard in spite of the increasing pressure of the Dread in her chest.

"I don't see any arrests on your record for being psychic," Pasco told the woman as he studied his palmtop. "A lot for fraud, though. And larceny, of course. A couple of assaults here, too. You're not going to get violent, are you?"

"I have never been violent in my life," the woman said, offended. "All of those charges are complete fabrications. As are the fraud charges. It's a sad world where you can be thrown in jail for someone else's lack of faith."

"And the two dead people in the back room—is that why they were killed?" Pasco said. "Or was it something else?"

"I don't know anything about the people back there."

"Even though you're psychic."

Emmeline Lilliana huffed. "It's not a trick. I'm not a dove-puller. It doesn't work that way."

"'Dove-puller?'" Ruby almost laughed.

"A stage magician," the woman said, her lips curling with contempt. "Abracadabra, hocus pocus, hey, presto, I found a quarter in your ear. You know, whenever you see one of those flash-bang tricks where a dove disappears in a sudden flame and a puff of smoke, the bird gets killed. And the magician always gets away with it; you never arrest him for animal cruelty. Meanwhile I'm not hurting a soul, animal or not, and I've got cops jumping on me just because of who I am."

"Well, that's because it's illegal to pretend you're getting messages from people's dead friends and relatives and then charge them money for them," Pasco told her.

"I don't *pretend* anything. I'm sensitive—I receive messages from a realm beyond this one. The people they're intended for identify them as being from loved ones no longer on this plane of existence. They insist—quite forcefully, in fact. I can't argue with them; after all, they know their loved ones. I don't. And I don't charge anyone anything. The grateful reward me as they see fit."

"You've got it all figured out," Pasco said.

The woman dipped her head, shrugging one shoulder. "If you don't believe me, that's your right. But that's hardly grounds for arrest."

"There's the problem of two dead people, though."

"That has nothing to do with me."

"I think it does."

The woman turned to Ruby, looking blank. "What is it with your partner? He's got my record literally in the palm of his hand with that gadget. You read it, you'll see I've never—"

"I think messages from the dead weren't lucrative enough," Pasco went on, talking over her. "Especially after someone showed you how to cross from one line to another. You saw a few differences and decided to use them to your own advantage. Did Phil Cannizzarro even know where you were taking him? What did you tell him to get him here?"

The woman looked down at her hands folded in her lap and didn't answer.

"How hard was it to get his old crew here?" Pasco went on. "Did you try to run the messages-from-the-dead scam on them or did you tell them that Cannizzarro was really still alive?" He sat forward. "How long did it take, even with a connection you could exploit? Was it your connection, or did you have to go through several different lines?"

"Pardon me for saying so but I'm not following you at all." The woman kept her gaze fixed on her hands.

"What am I thinking?" Pasco said, hitting his forehead lightly with the heel of his hand. "Of course it wouldn't be your connection. You wouldn't want to get all mobbed up in your own line. It's very dangerous, getting into bed with the Mob. Tends to shorten your life expectancy. Like the poor woman in the back. Your co-workers all thought it was you."

Ruby turned to him sharply, frowning. At the same time, the woman looked up, her face the picture of innocent bafflement. "Obviously it's not me. But just because they thought it was doesn't mean that I have any connection—"

Pasco got up and pulled her out of the chair by one arm. "Tell you what," he said, propelling her through the store toward the treatment rooms, "instead of arguing about it, you can see for yourself and then tell me what you think."

The woman stumbled along, trying to pull away and protesting that she didn't want to look at any dead bodies, especially murder victims. Unsure of what to do, Ruby followed, wondering what her partner thought he was going to accomplish. She had been known to shove gory crime scene photos at suspects or their accomplices or even material witnesses who were reluctant to make a statement but this was something entirely different. Even some of the uniformed cops looked shocked as they watched Pasco force the woman through the doorway to the back.

"See, this is what we've been discussing," he said, shoving her into the room.

She twisted out of his grasp and tried to push past him to leave. Pasco spun her around, grabbed the back of her head, and held her in place.

For a long moment, they stayed like that, as still and silent as statues. Just behind them on the threshold, Ruby waited, not daring to breathe, waiting for the woman to scream or try to run. But the moment stretched out and continued to stretch and still no one moved or spoke. Because of the lights, Ruby thought, feeling surreal; too many lights and no proper shadows.

Then she heard the woman say, "Uh-oh," and everything unfroze.

"Yeah," Pasco said. "'Uh-oh.' Houston, we've got a problem for sure."

The woman turned to him, her face tight with fear and more than a little desperation. "I didn't set this up. It was someone else. One of the others."

Pasco glanced at Ruby. "Why should we believe you?"

"Because she said they wouldn't have faces."

"Pardon?" Ruby said, although she was pretty sure she knew exactly what the woman meant.

"Because of the way they'd be killed," the woman said, desperation rising. "She said the way they'd be killed, they wouldn't have faces. There'd be nothing left, not even enough for dental records." She looked from Pasco to Ruby. "Hey, I didn't want to go along with it but she made it pretty clear that if I didn't, it would be me on the floor instead of—well, you know. A different one."

Ruby swallowed hard and took a steadying breath. "Does she belong here or do you?"

"I do," the woman said quickly. "*I* belong here. She's from the same place as *him*." She made a gesture at the bodies without looking at them and shuddered.

"And which scam were you running—messages from the dead or manifesting spirits?"

The woman's mouth opened and closed a few times silently.

"Come on, if you want to stay alive, I have to know," Pasco snapped.

"Manifestation," she said, her voice small. She looked at Ruby, her eyes pleading. "That wasn't my idea, I wanted to stay with just the messages. But she said if we could actually show them the dear departed, the money would roll in like—well—"

"Did Phil Cannizzarro know he was coming back from the dead?"

"Sometimes. I—we—didn't always use the same one."

The Dread had acquired an almost sharp edge now; Ruby pressed her lips together, trying to keep her face impassive.

"What about this one?" Pasco said. "Was he in on it?"

"I—I'm not sure. I'm *not!*" she added in response to the look Pasco gave her. "She set it all up. I—we just had to make the appointment, she said she'd take care of everything else, getting all the right people together."

"And you knew it was going to be a hit," Ruby said. There was more of an edge in her voice than she had expected.

"She didn't give me a choice. She said either I went along with it and she'd split the money with me or she'd make an appointment for me, too."

"The money?"

"Like a finder's fee. For finding out he was alive and getting him here."

Pasco turned to Ruby, one eyebrow raised. She shook her head.

"Did you tell them how Cannizzarro faked his death in prison? Or did you just show them photos of him alive?"

"She did all that, handled all the details."

"And where is *she* now?" Ruby asked.

"I don't know," the woman said. "Not here, obviously, since she left me holding the bag." She looked nervously from Pasco to Ruby and back several times. "What happens now?"

"We take you into custody, of course," Pasco said. "What did you think?"

"But what about *her?*"

Pasco shrugged. "*You're* her. Case closed."

"But I'm not! I wouldn't do something like this—"

"I wouldn't know." Pasco dragged her back to the main part of the store and told a couple of uniforms to take her into custody.

"I don't suppose you've figured out how we can write this up so that it makes sense," Ruby said, watching as the cops cuffed her and took her out.

"Hey, we just arrest them—we don't explain them." Pasco smiled. "As she makes her way through the system, she'll wind up taking a detour which will take her where she belongs. The appropriate law enforcement agency will take over and you'll stop feeling the effects of your, ah, allergy."

"And I assume there'll be a plausible explanation or cover story for all of it?" Ruby said. "Something that'll keep Ostertag's head from exploding?"

"Ruby, it's the *system*. That's all the explanation anybody's going to need. Especially Ostertag."

She didn't understand until a week later, when Ostertag made a passing mention of a murder victim who had borne an extremely strong resemblance to a dead Mob figure.

"Do *not* try to talk me out of this," she said, shaking her retirement papers in Pasco's face. "It's all getting too loose and runny."

"I understand," he said. "Fortunately, not all of you retired. There's one—"

"Shut *up!*" She whacked him over the head; papers flew in every direction and she refused to let him help her pick them up again.

A Murder in Eddsford

S.M. Stirling

S.M. Stirling is a king of alternate history, with several widely read series to his credit. He is perhaps best know for his Nantucket series, which began with Island in the Sea of Time, *in which the island of Nantucket is inexplicably transported from March 1998 to 1250 BC. Recently, he has embarked on The Lords of Creation series, beginning with* The Sky People, *and detailing a Cold War-era world where the pulp visions of Mars and Venus are surprisingly accurate. The story that follows is set in the world of his best-selling Emberverse series, which began with the trilogy of* Dies the Fire, The Proctor's War, *and* A Meeting at Corvallis *and continues in a second trilogy with* The Sunrise Lands, The Scourge of God, *and* The Sword of the Lady. *Despite his productivity, readers coming in to Stirling's work cold will be just fine. You're in the hands of a master, and I'm sure you'll want to see his sleuths in action again. Fortunately, you can.*

Detective Inspector Ingmar Rutherston of New New Scotland Yard's Criminal Investigation Department looked up from his copy of the preliminary report as the coach began to slow; he'd had the vehicle to himself for the last three stops. The document was signed *Corporal Bramble, Ox. & Bucks Light Infantry,* but it was as well written, terse and concise as most constables could have managed. The description of the dead man's condition made Rutherston's brows rise; the soldier's dismay showed through the flat official prose, as well.

"Peaceful country to all appearances," he mused to himself, forcing his mind to stop worrying the scanty data. "But this Jon Wooton is very dead indeed. Beyond that, there's nothing to be done until I've some fresh information."

He tucked the semaphore-telegraph form into a pocket of his jacket and focused on the view out the window instead. It was a warm afternoon turning into evening, late in August this year of grace AD 2049. A little white dust smoked up from under the hard rubber treads of the wheels, but the vehicle was well sprung on good Shropshire steel. The coach was the weekly from the capital, Winchester, to sleepy little Dover over in Kent, much slower than the British Rail pedal-car but stopping at places not so served... such as his destination, the Hampshire village of Eddsford.

The landscape of the Downs passed by at a good round trot, long shadows falling from the roadside trees as the sun declined toward the west; rolling chalk hills, green close-cropped pasture dotted with off-white sheep, fields of grass and clover and reaped grain on the lower slopes, beech-plantations and coppice-woods and low-trimmed hedges where red admiral and peacock and tortoiseshell butterflies fluttered. An occasional white-walled farmhouse stood in a sheltered spot, thatched in golden straw, surrounded by barn and stable and cart-shed, wool-store, stock-pond and whirling wind-pump and gnarled orchards.

Looking about, you'd never dream that the trackless tangled wildwood of Andredesweald lay only a few miles eastward, home to boar and wolf and the odd tiger down from the Wild Lands, and perhaps an outlaw or highwayman now and then. The New Forest to the west was almost as savage, more than it had ever been in the Conqueror's time. Here the nearest to nature in the raw were hovering kestrels and a buzzard now and then, and flocks of swallows and house martins crowding the uppermost branches of trees, getting ready for their migration to Africa.

Rutherston smiled at the sight; his father had never seen that without reminiscing about how they'd used the wires strung from pole to pole for roosting when *he* was a young boy in the Old Days.

The detective rolled the window down the rest of the way and peered out, welcoming the fresh air and the scents of baked earth and growing things with the slightly faded, tattered smell that said summer was past its peak and autumn rains might hit at any moment. A farmer and his workers in the field beyond the roadside hedge were pitching the last of the wheat-sheaves into a wagon drawn by two big chestnut Shires. Men and women and horses alike stopped to look at the high-stepping black geldings that drew the coach, male farmhands with stolid sunburned faces above their smock-frocks, and women in loose pants and blouses and some-times canvas field-aprons.

A straw-covered jug went from hand to hand as the coach pulled away, and then the pitchforks went back to work. The road dipped down toward the valley of the Rother, showing a glint of sun-struck water in the distance and flatter country southward. Partridges whirred up from the roadside verge...

"No, y' daft rassgat!" the driver cursed; probably his assistant leveling her crossbow—she was young and enthusiastic. "Just *your* luck there'd be some kiddie behind a bush!"

The top of the south-facing slope was planted in undulating rows of shaggy goblet-trained grapevines; beyond, the village proper was bowered in trees and followed the riverbank at a cautious distance, separated by water-meadows and a low bank against spring floods.

And that's the miller's house where the body was discovered, he thought, looking north. *There's the roof through the trees, and you can just see the water from the millrace.*

The assistant tooted again and again on her brass horn, and the driver pulled up to a walk with a *woah-woah, there!* to his team; children and dogs and chickens and the odd passer-by afoot or on a bicycle or on horseback made way, and the usual curious crowd started to gather at the inn. The houses were mostly white-walled, roofed in shingle or thatch, slate or tile, along a street still paved with old-style asphalt and lined with big beeches and horse chest-nuts.

The lane opened out into a green at the other end, with the tav-ern on one side and a stretch of grass in the center, and a church further on near the water-meadows. It was unique in the ordinary manner—a handsome battlemented tower of flint and stone obligingly labeled *AD 1599* over the west door, and other parts that looked to be anything from Victorian to Norman; a Georgian brick rectory stood a little to one side, nearly hidden in oaks and beeches.

The inn was long and low and rambling, plaster over brick with a higher two-story section in its middle, and an irregular studding of chimneys through its mossy shingles. A brass plaque with the royal arms by the door proclaimed that it was a mail inn, where the coaches stopped for a change of teams and to drop and pick up letters and parcels—usually a profitable sideline for the innkeeper. Three or four shops stood across the green; so did the village post office, flanked by a reading-room and small public library marked by its sign and extravagant stretch of window.

A sign also swung from an iron bracket over the main entrance of the inn, showing a Moor's severed head on a silver platter, and a branch of dried holly above it. There was a smell of wood smoke and cooking as households prepared their evening meal, mingling with the homely aroma of middens and the odd whiff from pigs kept behind cottages. A toddler tried to climb into a horse-trough by the side of the street, and a harassed-looking woman in an apron ran out of the door and pulled him inside, smacking him smartly on the bottom while she did.

The gate to the inn's courtyard opened, and an ostler in a leather apron came out, ready to lead out the fresh team. The driver's assistant unspanned her crossbow with a sharp *tunnggg*, racked it and jumped down from the seat to open the door as the coach came to a halt. Rutherston sprang down without waiting for the folding step, ignoring a slight twinge where the old wound in his right leg reminded him of that evening in the foothills of the Riff Atlas. She handed down his carpetbags and took a sixpence with a bob of her head before turning to unload the mail-sack and several parcels labeled *Eddsford, Hants*. The ostler and the driver unharnessed the team and led it over into the courtyard.

And a stout man with a waistcoat straining over a considerable belly and graying muttonchops came out of the front door, smiling and fingering the chain of his watch. The taverner's experienced eye flicked up and down the detective's long lanky form and saturnine beak-nosed face; quietly expensive but well-worn traveling tweeds and half-cloak, wide-brimmed panama hat, light cravat of white Irish linen, longsword and belt of good quality but plain and worn, half-boots. Just a touch of gray in at the temples of the yellow hair. And two carpetbags, but no valet...

Rutherston smiled to himself as he saw the quick expert evaluation running through the man's guileless blue eyes:

Gentleman, but not rich; still, better than a bagsman or commercial traveler. Not a professor, or a doctor, nor a merchant, surely; and not stopping at the Hall with the Squire. Some King's Man out of Winchester, perhaps, or an officer on leave? Not here for the fishing, though, nei rods...

It was accurate enough, and he spoke with precisely calculated deference:

"Mark Eyvindsson," he pronounced it *Evinson,* in the modern manner, "at your service, sir. I'm landlord of the Moor's Head. Will you be wanting a room for the night then?"

In fact what he said sounded more like: *Oi'm the laandlorrd o' the Moo-er's 'Ead. Will ye be wantin' a room fer the noight, then?*

If he'd been born in Winchester instead of just living there the last ten years the detective might have suspected the innkeeper of deliberately coming it the heavy rustic. But Rutherston had been born in Short Compton in the Cotswolds himself, about a hundred miles north and a little west of here, where the local dialect was just as heavy and only slightly different.

"Detective Inspector Ingmar Rutherston, of the Yard," he replied crisply. "I would like a room; for several days, at least."

The innkeeper managed not to look too startled; several of the oldsters sitting with their pints along the bench beside the inn's door gaped at him; a pipe nearly fell out of one wrinkled mouth. A babble of voices rose and died away.

"Ah, you'll be here about young Jon Wooton; quick work for you to get here so soon, all the way from Winchester. A bad business, sir, a very bad business."

"It usually is, when a man's murdered," Rutherston said grimly.

* * *

The interior of the inn's main room was L-shaped: a long space with tables, a hearth—swept and garnished with pots of flowers now—and a row of windows that looked down on a water-meadow and a stretch of the Rother flowing slowly between willows beyond.

There was a fair scattering of regulars trickling in for a pint or two—it *was* after harvest, after all, the high point of a laborer's year... and pocket. A man in a good country suit was talking business with some obvious farmers in cords in the snug, and there were a scattering of everything from cottagers in smocks to tradesmen and their families.

The ones that caught his eye obviously weren't locals: five army troopers and a corporal, hobelars in green-enameled chain-mail shirts and leather breeches and riding-boots, with their open-faced sallet helms propped on tables. The longbows and quivers, sword-belts and bucklers hung on pegs by the door. They all had mugs of beer before them, and they all looked dusty and tired, as if they'd been on road patrol, which they probably had.

Rutherston walked over to their table as the innkeeper and his staff saw to the baggage and took his hat and half-cloak and his own sword—even on a murder investigation, he wasn't going to wear a long blade inside the village. The soldiers looked up, polite but not more than that—they were the King-Emperor's men, after all. Then he reached into his coat-pocket and flipped open the wallet to show his Warrant Card, and handed their squad-leader his letter of authorization from the War Office.

That brought them to their feet, saluting smartly amidst a scrape of chairs. The troopers were ordinary enough, strong-built youngsters with open countrymen's faces, distinguished only by one's startling red roach of hair or another's freckles and jug ears. The corporal with the chevrons riveted to the short sleeve of his mail shirt was a few years older than his men. He was about six feet—Rutherston's own height—but broader, with dark blunt features unusual for an Englishman and curly hair so black it had highlights like a raven's feathers.

"Corporal Bramble, Oxfordshire and Buckinghamshire Light Infantry, currently out of Castle Aldershot," he said in a deep rumbling voice

The accent was a strong yokel burr but with a slight trace of something different, a yawny-drawly lilt that had a teasing half-familiarity. Then he placed it.

Ah, I've heard something like that from Jamaican sailors in Portsmouth and Bristol, Rutherston thought. *Though he's definitely English born and bred; yeoman-farmer's son, I'd say.*

He'd half-expected a southern-provinces twang; those looks could be Gibraltarian, but a touch of Caribbean a couple of generations back would account for it just as well.

The noncom went on: "We were told to expect you. I'm to assume this is aid-to-the-civil-power, sir?"

"You are, corporal; dull work, probably, I'm afraid. Your commanding officer has been informed I'd commandeer you; it saves time and trouble. I'll want to talk to you later tonight. You can quarter your men here at the Moor's Head, and I'll handle the requisition slips."

None of the hobelars looked unhappy about it. They'd be spared fatigues and drills, the food and drink would be free but much better than ration-issue, and the chance of finding a girl interested in the glamour of a uniform rather than hard cash was distinctly better here than near a garrison town like Aldershot.

"Thank you, sir. I've a man at the miller's house, of course, guarding the place where we found the body. I'll rotate the duty."

"Good work, that, corporal," Rutherston said, nodding.

It had saved him an undignified scramble, and he had reasons for not heading straight to the scene of the—possible—crime.

"Permission to ask a question?" the noncom said.

The detective nodded, raising a brow.

"You were army yourself, sir, weren't you?"

Rutherston smiled thinly. *Good. He has a sharp eye, this one.*

He nodded. "Yes; in the Blues and Royals. Tours in the Principality on the Provoland border, and out of Rabat and Marrakech. It still shows, eh?"

"It does, inspector."

"And you're not from this shire, are you, corporal? A bit further north and east, I'd say."

"My dad's place is just north of Woburn, sir; Jamaica Farm, it's called, after Granddad. Near Wavendon, if you know Buckinghamshire."

"I do," he said.

Better and better, he thought

That area was northerly and a little wild, though not quite on the frontier of settlement any more; that ran just south of Nottingham these days.

But still close to the Wild Lands, and still a smuggler's paradise, up the Ouse from the Wash.

The Moor's Head wasn't large, but it had all the modern conveniences you'd expect so close to Winchester and right next to a good trout-and-salmon stream; running water in the bathroom on the first floor brought up by a hydraulic ram from the river, flush toilets, and a big copper boiler that supplied plentiful hot water. The maid had unpacked his bags, all but a small locked case set on the table, and the sitting room had a pleasant view of the Rother; the detective found his two rooms to be very comfortable in a country-inn fashion. Both smelled of clean linen and dried-lavender sachets, and the alcohol lanterns were bright enough for reading, even to one accustomed to the capital's incandescent-mantle gaslights.

Rutherston wallowed gratefully in a tub of the hot water—at thirty-two, sitting all day in a coach was no longer perfectly comfortable—and set out his boots and traveling suit to be taken and dealt with. He took a moment to write a letter as well; Janice was in her eighth month and naturally hadn't wanted him to leave town just then.

Then he dressed and came down to an excellent dinner: grilled trout right out of the river, a pie of veal and ham and truffles, sprouts, raudkál, salad, chips, followed by a fruit tart with cream. There was a glass of a perfectly acceptable local Cabernet Franc to go with it.

Bramble's troopers were plowing their way through much the same, with a roast chicken each added. It reminded Rutherston of the sort of appetite you had when you were twenty years old and spending ten hours a day in the saddle or marching on your own feet under seventy pounds of armor and gear. Instead of his more recent fate, having a city's pavements under his boots, or worse still, an office chair beneath his backside while he filled out endless reports.

Most of the patrons were quiet, talking with their heads together, but the soldiers were merry enough; it wasn't their village, after all. He even caught a snatch of song from them:

"For forty shillings on the drum
Who'll 'list and volunteer to come?
And stand and face the foe today:
It's over the hills and far away..."

When he'd finished his own meal, he signed Corporal Bramble over.

"Sit, man. I'm an officer in the police now, not the Blues."

"Inspector."

The big soldier sat, and Rutherston raised his hand for the barmaid—a statuesque blonde a decade younger than himself, with a forty-inch bust displayed to advantage by her low-cut blouse and a pouting lower lip that might have been promising under other circumstances, along with the lack of a wedding-band.

But you do have one on now, Ingmar, at long last. Keep it in mind. Janice can't see you but God can.

He'd spent a long time as a footloose and fancy-free bachelor, and shedding the habits came a little hard sometimes despite a happy marriage; they crept back while you weren't looking, especially away from home.

"Now," he said, opening his notebook. "Let's get the details. Your report was informative, but short."

"You won't be questioning anyone else tonight, sir?" Bramble asked.

Rutherston nodded. "Why am I sitting on my arse waiting for the villains to scarper, you mean?" he said, and smiled at the look of blank innocence the noncom put on. "What I'm doing, corporal, is letting them get good and nervous. Winchester has seventy thousand people, but here in Eddsford there are six-hundred-fifty-odd and they all know each other. If anyone runs, they identify themselves for me. If they don't, they'll probably make other mistakes."

"Hmmm, *the guilty flee where nei man pursueth*, eh, sir? My dad's a deacon in our parish," he added in an aside. "You're letting them come ripe, as it were."

"Quite. Tell me what you've seen and heard. Then tell me what you think of it."

The barmaid returned with their mugs. She smiled at the policeman as she put them down, then turned the full wattage on Bramble when it didn't bring any result. He grinned back at her reflexively—he was, after all, still several years short of thirty himself—and then cleared his throat and returned to business.

"Yessir." Bramble's face went blank as he replayed memories in his mind's eye. "My men and I 'ave been on standard road patrol along the South Downs; we vary the route unpredictable-like."

Rutherston nodded as he took a sip of the cool, nutty-bitter ale; it didn't do to make things easy for a would-be Dick Turpin. Open lawlessness like that wasn't likely around here any more, but it honed field-craft and helped hold edge-dulling boredom at bay. He took his gunmetal cigarette-case out of his jacket and flipped it open, offering it across the table.

"No thank you, sir. Never got the habit."

Rutherston lit one himself. They were rum-flavored *Embiricos* cigarillos from Barbados, and he found the rich smooth taste soothed and helped him concentrate. The old-timers said tobacco was bad for you, but then living was ultimately always fatal and they seemed to have been a bunch of damned old women back then anyway.

"Go on," he said, and opened his notebook to begin jotting down the points.

"We were passing the Mill here on our way back to base—"

"This was early this morning?"

"Yessir, about eight hundred hours. We'd been out since midnight, not seen nothing more dangerous than a badger or a barn owl, the usual. A woman—the old miller's widow, name of Kristin Wooton—ran out and grabbed me stirrup; there was a man behind her, a wringin' of his hands. She screamed out that her son Jon was dying, and we should get him help. Well, I sent young Jones—that's him, sir, the one with the ears like a bat—back into the village for the District Nurse, then went in to see what I could do."

Corporal Bramble looked hard enough to drive horseshoe-nails with his knuckles, but his strong-boned face was uneasy as he went on.

"The man was dying, right enough. Never seen anything like it, sir, and I've seen men die before... been stationed over most of the Empire these last ten years. It was like he was *rotting*, sir; hair comin' out in clumps, sores all over his hide. Bleeding from everywhere too, eyes, nose, gums—even his arsehole, begging your pardon, inspector."

"I've heard the word before, corporal."

A broad white smile, and the man drained half his mug as if trying to wash away a bad taste. His voice was impersonal as he went on:

"Looked like poison to me, sir, and his mother was swearing that he'd been fine the day before, or maybe just a bit peaked. So I sent McAllister—he's the one with the hair like a new penny—over north to the line of rail, they've a semaphore station. Just about then the poor unfortunate bugger *did* die, and Major Grimsson sent back that I was to hold in place until someone arrived, so I had the body put in keeping, the man's room sealed and a guard put on it. And then I waited until you got here. Which was quick work on your part, sir."

Rutherston looked down at his notes, tapping the pen on the metal coil at the top of the pad. "It does sound like possible foul play," he said thoughtfully. "The first in this parish since 2012... and *that* was a drunken swain using a hay-knife when he caught his ladylove where she shouldn't have been."

"I don't have any great acquaintance here in Eddsford, sir, but I've heard little good of Jon Wooton. Nothing specific... but reading between the lines, like." A pause for another pull at the beer. "Still, you'd 'ave to hate a man right hard to do *that* to him."

Rutherston nodded and finished his beer. "See that your men get a good night's rest," he said.

Meaning, this isn't a weekend pass so see that they go to bed sober; but there's nei need to say that aloud.

Bramble nodded in turn, obviously following his meaning effortlessly. He'd never met the corporal before but he knew the type, a reliable long-service non-commissioned man, steady as a rock in any situation he understood.

What's uncertain is how much imagination he has, but offhand I think he has plenty, just doesn't show it much.

"Tomorrow we'll start doing the rounds," he said aloud.

Bramble hesitated. "If you don't mind my asking, sir, why do you need me and the lads?"

Rutherston closed the notebook. "I very well may not," he said. "On the other hand, if there's something nastier than a simple impulse killing... or someone may run, in which case I'd rather have help quicker on their feet than the usual part-time village Special Constable."

Bramble nodded and grinned. "The one here, name of Edward Mukeriji... runs the tobacconists and sweet-shop, sir, and he was fair stuttering. I see your point."

"And while this may not be your village, you might see things that I don't."

"Ah," Bramble said. "That's a point too, sir."

The words were uninformative, but Rutherston felt that he'd passed some test.

St. Swithun's School For Girls was not far from Eddsford, having been moved out of town when it started up again in the resettlement; a few young ladies in the dark-blue frocks with pleated skirts and white blouses of that revered institution were walking through the village, overseen by a nun in a gray habit.

"Dullafullt," one of them said to a friend, rolling her eyes.

Rutherston had to admit that to a youngster Eddsford might indeed seem a little boring, particularly if you'd been stuck there by your parents during the holidays when the other boarders went home. That had happened to him several times, though Winchester College was admittedly much closer to the heart of things.

I'd quite like Eddsford myself if I weren't here to investigate a murder, he thought, taking a deep breath of the cool morning air; it was still fresh at eight o'clock, but he thought it would be another warm day. *It reminds me of home.*

Corporal Bramble stood inconspicuously by his elbow as he used the brass knocker on the door of the clinic, or as inconspicuously as a sixteen-stone man in armor with a longbow and quiver over his shoulder could.

The clinic was just down the lane from the village green; Eddsford wasn't quite large enough to rate a doctor of its own, though one came by weekly from Petersfield, and could be fetched at need. There was a polished plate by the door, also brass, that read: *District Nurse Delia Medford, SRN,* and a modern bicycle with a rather heavy tubular frame and solid-rubber wheels in a stand by the entryway. Roses bloomed in a trellis along one wall, and there were colorful impatiens in the window boxes.

Delia Medford opened the door and responded with a dryly courteous nod to the detective's slight bow. She was a tallish, slender woman in her thirties with blue eyes and brown hair drawn back in a bun and a no-nonsense expression, and a stethoscope tucked into the breast pocket of her jacket. There was another with her enough alike to be her older sister.

"Detective Inspector Ingmar Rutherston, ladies," he said, removing his hat and showing his Warrant Card. "Corporal Bramble here is assisting me."

The soldier tucked his helmet under one arm and rumbled "Ma'am," twice.

The nurse gave Rutherston's hand a quick firm shake. "My sister, Mrs. Alice Purkiss," she said, after she'd introduced herself.

The widow Purkiss was a decade older and otherwise very like her sibling, apart from the fact that she wore a conservative knee-length skirt rather than cord riding breeches; the other main difference was her shoes, which *weren't* graced with thick rubber soles.

"I was Jon Wooton's teacher at our little school, Inspector Rutherston," she said. "We thought it would save you time and effort if I came along first thing. I'm retired from teaching now, but I'm still postmistress and run the Eddsford reading room and lending-library."

Ah, excellent, Rutherston thought.

He wanted to put off seeing the Wootons until he'd gotten a feel for how the rest of the village regarded them; and these two probably knew everyone's family history since the resettlement, just for starters. Doubtless they were pillars of half a dozen Church organizations and ran the local Whig election committee with an iron hand as well.

Like most such, the office had a waiting room with chairs, a table, and ancient copies of several magazines—*The Illustrated*

Winchester News, the *Church Times,* the *British Agriculturalist,* and rather surprisingly the *Boy's and Girl's Own Paper.*

There was also the inevitable Bible, a tall antique clock ticking in one corner and hanging pictures of King-Emperor Charles IV, Queen Thóra, the Pope, and the Cardinal-Archbishop of Winchester. A consulting room gave off it and there were several storage areas in the back; presumably Delia Medford lived over the shop, judging from the selection of Wellingtons, umbrellas, and mackintoshes at the bottom of the hall stairs, and the tabby-cat looking down curiously from the top.

The body was in one of the storerooms, a tile-floored one with two roll-out compartments for cadavers against the wall, and an ingenious icebox-like arrangement for keeping them cold.

"Sir James sends me down ice when I need it," she explained, as she pulled on a pair of thick rubber gloves.

Rutherston took up her offer of another pair, a bib-apron and a mask that smelled strongly of disinfectant, and a little jar of a strong-smelling ointment. He rubbed a touch of that below his nose and handed it around, and was glad of it when she pulled out the tray—decay had been quicker than he would have expected, given the refrigeration.

Odd, he thought. *The marks are almost like* burns, *rather than* sores. *Blister marks running with clear fluid. As if he'd been touched with a red-hot... no, there's no charring. As if he'd been touched with something supremely* cold *instead.*

The nurse might have been examining a gutted chicken at the butcher's, but Corporal Bramble went a little gray beneath his olive tan, and Mrs. Purkiss looked at the ceiling; both stood well back. Rutherston sympathized. The postmortem had left the corpse as gruesome as anything on a battlefield, if neater, and whatever the man had died of was ghastly. Sections of the back peeled away as she moved the corpse.

"I conducted the autopsy," she said. "I usually do them here and pass on the reports to the County Coroner. I confess I was tempted to send for Dr. Kvaran from Petersfield this time, but honestly I don't think Gudrun could have made head nor tail of it either."

"I'd have brought a forensic surgeon from Winchester if one had been available, but I agree that it's quite baffling," Rutherston said. "May I see your notes?"

"By all means," she said, handing him a clipboard.

Wooton, Jon: age, 27, single male, height 5ft 11 inches, weight eleven stone, hair, dark brown, eyes, green...

Jon Wooton had been a fairly average modern Englishman... if you subtracted the gruesome lesions that had killed him. The small photograph attached showed him in his late teens, scowling and slouching in a coat with extravagant lapels, but with a certain crude Heathcliffian handsomeness to him. Even allowing for the circumstances, the ensuing decade hadn't been kind.

Rutherston got out his own notebook and began sketching and making observations of the body; he'd seen a good many corpses himself in both his careers, and this one had certain features you didn't often find in a Home Counties' village mortuary. After a moment he tapped his pen in the air above the left shoulder.

"Notice that, corporal?" he said, pointing to a white scar on the triceps.

Bramble nodded. "Not before, sir; I was sort of distracted. But you're right—he didn't get 'is buckler up in time that round," he said.

Then the noncom followed the pen with his comments: "That's an arrow-wound... so's that... or a square-headed crossbow-bolt... sword-scars on the right arm. Nasty cut to the leg—he was lucky that time. That there could be a spear'ead. He didn't get that lot being quarrelsome in the pub of a Saturday night. Not even a pub in Portsmouth or Bristol."

"No record of military service," Rutherston said thoughtfully.

"No, not beyond the usual militia training," the District Nurse confirmed. "He did *say* he'd shipped out overseas as a merchant seaman several times, to Asia and America and the African coast."

"So he *might* have got those fighting off pirates. But," Rutherston said, and turned over the man's right hand.

Even with the skin damage, the hands were definitely wrong for a seaman. Hauling on tarred hemp and sisal and fisting up canvas gave you a layer like cracked horn all across your palms, and you didn't lose it quickly either; he'd seen that often enough. Jon Wooton's right hand was if anything less callused than Rutherston's own, which bore the marks of life-long work with the sword. It did share the "swordsman's ring," a circle of hard skin around the outer side of the forefinger and the inner side of the thumb. There were other scars, too, ones that looked as if they'd been caused by hot metal or acid.

Odd, Rutherston thought. *Those look like blacksmith's marks, or even what someone working in a bleach-powder plant might get. With nothing else to go by, I'd put these as the hands of an artisan in some skilled trade.*

"But he *was* away from home for a good long time?" the detective said.

"More often than not, since he turned twenty. Usually about half the year, a month or two at a time; more in the winter than the summer."

"Hmmm. Did he have money?"

"Nothing formal, but he didn't seem to lack for it. Of course, the Wootons are fairly well-to-do; the family have held the lease of the mill since the resettlement."

"Cause of death?"

"Proximate cause was massive exsanguination due to internal bleeding," Miss Medford said.

She unfastened the clips and opened the body cavity. Her sister looked aside slightly, and Corporal Bramble more than that.

"You see?" she said. "The pattern of tissue degeneration is quite unlike anything I've seen before; very severe mercury poisoning, perhaps—that would account for some of the sores—but there's nei evidence of mercury in the amount you would need. And that should have taken longer. I passed him in the street the day before yesterday, and he was healthy enough to scowl and spit then; perhaps a bit pale, but no more. And note how there's no inflammation around the lesions? Simple cellular collapse, I think. There's been no bacterial action to speak of."

"You don't think it was an infectious agent, then?"

"Probably not. I've read of African viruses with similar effects in the old days, and he might have come in contact with those on a voyage, but it's a month's sailing time between Britain and the Guinea coast, and they acted *quickly.* And the *Journal of the Royal Medical Society* lists no known cases since the Change; I have a complete series."

"Had you treated Jon Wooton before?"

"Apart from the usual childhood complaints? Yes." She sniffed audibly. "For a social disease, twice: gonorrhea. Cured by a course of antibiotics from the National Health Center. One tries to be forgiving, but I cautioned him that I would report any further occurrences to the Ministry of Health."

She slid the tray closed with a snap. They stripped off their gloves and washed up in the stainless-steel sink with strong medical soap, then repaired to a sitting-room to one side of the business part of the building; Rutherston took a seat, and Bramble stood next to the door, shrewd dark eyes taking everything in. The furniture was in excellent if subdued and rather plain taste, with a picture on the wall that Rutherston thought might be French Impressionist—salvage art—and a landscape showing Eddsford from the Downs, done in the fashionable neo-Pre-Raphaelite style with a certain amateurish attractiveness. Miss Medford rang a small handbell.

"Tea, please, Aud," she said.

Inwardly, Rutherston raised a brow as a pretty young woman in a dark dress and white apron bustled in and then returned with a tray that had obviously been kept in near-readiness; usually a District Nurse's salary wouldn't run to a housemaid, and he noticed that Mrs. Purkiss seemed a little constrained. When the tea came—in a beautiful salvaged set of Wedgewood, rather than modern manufacture—he could tell by the scent that it was the genuine black-leaf article from Hinduraj or Sri Lanka, rather than the herbal substitutes most people still used. Asian tea wasn't quite a luxury reserved for the wealthy any more, but it was expensive even in these days of prosperity, peace and growing trade, like the cubes of white refined cane sugar in their silver bowl.

He took out his cigarette case and raised a brow. Miss Medford raised her high-bridged nose in turn.

"Not in here, if you please, inspector," she said in clipped tones. "It's a filthy habit and I don't encourage it."

He sighed slightly and slipped the gunmetal case back into its pocket; he could have used one now... or a stiff whiskey-and-soda, despite the hour. Winchester was a city of 70,000, and they might have as many as four or five homicides a year, but none like *that*.

She went on: "How do you take your tea?"

"Two lumps and milk, thank you," he said, sipped appreciatively, then buttered one of the fresh muffins. His notebook went on his knee. "You taught Mr. Wooton, Mrs. Purkiss?"

"Yes; for six years—he left school at fourteen."

That was the minimum legal age, and usually the maximum for ordinary countryfolk. Rutherston made another note. He'd have expected a miller's son to take another two years; the rural middle classes, farmers and craftsmen and shopkeepers, usually did. Primary education was free to that level, if not compulsory; and a miller, even if he rented rather than owning the machinery, was usually prosperous enough that he didn't depend on a teenage son's labor to keep the family eating.

The retired schoolteacher seemed to sense his question. "Jon's father died when he was twelve—fell into the gears. His elder brother Eric took over the mill, young as he was. Sir James wanted to keep it in the family."

"What sort of a student was Jon Wooton?"

Mrs. Purkiss lips thinned until they were bloodless. "Quite talented," she said in a tone that tried for clinical and nearly achieved it. "And he continued to study after he'd left school; requested books on interlibrary loan through our reading room here."

"Quite the scholar, then? His interests were?"

"Late-period pre-Change history, and the sciences. He enjoyed reading, too, which I'm sure you know isn't all that common, particularly if it's not just romances and adventure stories. Very intelligent; even brilliant, perhaps. With more application and self-discipline, I would have recommended him for a Royal and Imperial Scholarship. Father Frances thought the same."

"You liked him, then?" Rutherston said neutrally.

The pinched look grew stronger. "He was a detestable little boy and did *not* improve with age. A sneak, bullied until he got his growth, and a vile bully himself afterwards. When he was quite little he would try to look in the..."

She flushed a little and set her cup down sharply.

"...the girl's privy."

"Unpopular?" Rutherston asked. "As an older boy, or a young man."

"With all but the *worst* element, louts and... girls of questionable taste. He had his cronies. And he would do *unspeakable* things to library books! I had to speak very sharply to him about that, and impose fines."

"Ah," Rutherston said, with an inward sigh.

Unpopular with the respectable element, and the village Bad Boy. Probably got a girl or two pregnant, too, or gave her Cupid's Measles, and skipped out on some of his trips to avoid the avenging relatives and the Squire and the parish priest.

When they'd left the clinic, the detective put his hat back on—the sun was bright in a sky with only a few piled white clouds—before he snapped the notebook shut and turned to Bramble with a silent question.

"Bad apple, that one," Bramble said. "Knew some wide lads like that back home, but none so bad. From the looks of the knocks he took—and lived afterwards—I'd judge he was a hard man and nei mistake, not just your High Street ruffler ready with his fists or a quarterstaff. Smuggler, probably—treasure trove."

Rutherston nodded. Ruins within the Empire of Greater Britain—which included western Europe to the old German and Italian borders, the Mahgreb west of the Sicilian settlements around Tunis and Bizerte, and theoretically the Atlantic coast of what had been the United States—were in law Crown property. Salvage for ordinary materials went on by firms making competitive bids for the rights to a given area, and control of exports gave Winchester influence with the King of Ashante and the Sultan of Zanzibar and his ilk.

Certain types of salvage goods, bullion and jewelry and artwork, were still more tightly controlled. Licenses for searching the dead cities for those were dependent on good character, and the government kept the Royal Third. That made violating the law potentially very profitable for interlopers... and in the vast tangled wilderness of the Wild Lands northward and on the Continent outside the English settlements, very hard for the authorities to stop. The whole army wouldn't be able to surround the jungled wreck of Paris or Madrid alone.

If the wilderness hadn't been so dangerous, with remnant tribes of Brushwood Men ready to kill and rob unknowing unwary travelers—and sometimes, still, to eat them—the problem would have been even worse.

Bramble went on slowly: "There was something a bit odd about the way those two talked about him, sir. Miss Medford didn't like him—not half! You could tell that, but she gave him penicillin for the clap, *twice,* without reporting him."

"That *is* odd, corporal. Not technically *very* illegal, but odd. She'd have to mention it, it would be in the NHS disbursement records..."

Bramble frowned as they walked toward the church. "Something rum there. You don't suppose... you don't suppose he was having it away with 'er, or something of that sort, sir? She struck me as a born old maid, though."

Rutherston started to wave a dismissive hand, checked himself, and spoke slowly in turn, stroking his jaw: "No... but you're right, there's more there than meets the eye." He thought for a moment. "And by the way, do ask questions if you think it would help. I need you for another viewpoint, not just to look formidable."

He sighed. "The usual procedures are of little use here. *Everyone* had access to the victim, if it is a poisoning case. There's no clear time element with slipping something into a man's beer, the way there is with bashing him over the head."

The churchyard was well kept behind its wrought-iron fence, even the older graves from the last century. Like most here in Hampshire, the new sections started with a marble slab on a long mound for the bodies found when the area was resettled from the Isle of Wight in the spring of 1999. By then the dead in Britain had outnumbered the living by around three hundred to one...

It bore a simple: *For the unnumbered and nameless whom we could not aid: Father forgive us. Lord have mercy. Christ have mercy.*

The fifty-two years since showed the usual pattern, a burst in the first years of terrible struggle, then four or five annually, then more again as population built up and the last survivors of the old days approached their three score-and-ten—according to the *Hampshire Gazetteer,* the village had about 600 people now, and the parish as a whole twice that. A sexton in his shirtsleeves with his suspenders dangling was digging a new grave for Jon

Wooton, not far from a spreading yew whose dark foliage seemed to drink the sunlight.

The notice-board beside the doors of St. Mary the Virgin gave the times for services—Mass Tuesdays, Thursdays, and Sunday mornings of course, as well as the holy days—and the usual exhortations to parishioners to make sure that they confessed and were absolved before partaking. Below that were listed meetings of the vestry, the choral society, the Harvest Festival Committee, the Mothers' Union, the guilds—a dozen organizations altogether, some like the Sunday School chaired by the vicar's wife.

Rutherston and the soldier removed their headgear and walked through the open door into the cool gloom, with beams of light shining through the stained glass of the windows overhead and a small side-altar to Our Lady of Walsingham. They touched their fingers to the holy water in the font, signed themselves, and genuflected to the altar and the image of the Blessed Mother, waiting for their eyes to adjust. A half-dozen other people were in the church: the usual volunteer middle-aged women and elderly men cleaning and polishing and doing minor repairs, an organist running her fingers through a hymn with the pumps disconnected, a few at silent prayer in the pews, and the vicar himself talking to a deacon.

The detective smiled to himself; together with the sweetness of cut grass from the churchyard it all had the wax-incense-hassocks-and-choirboy smell of Anglican Rite rural piety; not much different from St. Wilfred's back in Short Compton, where he'd been born. He thought of himself as an unsentimental man, but the scent did take him back to the summer Sundays of his boyhood. Janice and he had been back just this Lammas, to watch the Loaf and the corn dolly being carried in and to share a niece's First Communion.

The priest here was a different story from old Father Johnson, though. He nodded to the deacon and came striding over, the skirts of his black cassock swirling around stout walking shoes; Father Frances Broxby was a vigorous man in his mid-thirties, not tall but bull-chested and broad-shouldered, with reddish muttonchop whiskers and an athlete's corded neck under the clerical dog-collar.

Squire's younger brother, Rutherston reminded himself as they shook hands; he'd consulted *Burke's Peerage and Landed Gentry,* and the *Church Registry*, of course. The grip was not only strong, but callused like a laborer's or a smith's.

That's a bit surprising too. This parish is a reasonably good living.

Topped up by the major landowner, and at his encouragement by donations from the yeomanry and tradesmen. In theory the Church didn't allow lay patronage, but in practice the bishop always consulted about local appointments with someone like Sir James, who owned about half the parish. The everyday work of the church required the leading family's cooperation.

Frances Broxby has an Oxford Divinity degree, too, but he's not ambitious; he wouldn't have married before he was ordained if he was.

Married men could be ordained in the Anglican Rite and be parish priests, but not those who aimed at episcopal rank, or of course monastics; it was much the same arrangement as for the Ruthenian Catholics though on a vastly larger scale.

"Come, walk with me, my sons," the priest said. "I think I know what you wish to speak of. A painful duty grows nei easier if we put it off."

Rutherston blinked in the sunlight behind the churchyard. The long meadow there was part of the glebe—the land a parish priest used to graze his necessary horses and a milch-cow for his household, and cut hay; the sweet scent from the two fresh stacks was overwhelming. It was also the site where the militia practised with their longbows once a week; the tattered-looking wooden target shaped like a Moorish corsair with a scimitar stood down by the hedge and bank at the end, along with a row of thick shield-shaped wedges of wood on stakes. Two Irish setters trotted up grinning and lolling their tongues; the priest bent to ruffle their ears and then led on at a brisk pace until they were on the embankment.

The tree-lined stream-bank stood on the other side, with the Rother's surface glittering through the willows where a few last blackbirds and song thrushes were greeting the morning, and there was a pathway along the top of the earth mound.

"I knew Jon Wooton fairly well," Frances said. "And I regarded him as one of my major failures as a priest."

"Bit of a wild one, Father?" Bramble said. "We get a fair number of those in the army. They do well enough, mostly, with some discipline."

Frances looked a little surprised. "Not just that, corporal. Wild young men are common enough, as you say. It was..." he hesitated, obviously groping for words. "It was the fact that he was so *intelligent*. So able in many ways. And yet the *character* was the sticking point. Come."

He turned and walked briskly toward the manse. Rutherston and Bramble exchanged a look that said *this one would do well on a route march* as they followed him to a long shed-like building behind the brick house, one with skylights of salvage glass.

Frances unlocked it and threw the door open, with a sharp *sit* to keep the dogs outside.

Rutherston felt his eyebrows rise; his nose tingled to strange metallic scents, oily and sharp and pungent. The inside was fitted out as a laboratory-cum-machine-shop. Shapes of brass and steel and glass shone with the gleam of well-cared-for equipment; the detective recognized lathes and drill presses, a still, racks of chemicals, draughtsman's tables, and one corner held a library of several hundred books.

"I supervise a club for some of the parish boys—and a few girls— who are interested in mechanical things, and in the sciences," he said. "It's a healthy hobby, better than drink, fornication, and poaching, or even an excess of cricket and Morris dancing, and God did not make everyone to work the soil. For that matter, all the land in this area has been taken up and there are as many laborers as there is employment on the farms. I've been able to find apprenticeships, and a few engineering scholarships, for some of the most able of our young people."

"A worthy effort, Padre," Rutherston acknowledged sincerely. "I presume Jon Wooton was one of your club members?"

"The best of them!" Frances said. "And one of the first. It was the first time he or any of his family took an interest in anything involved with the church, too."

"Ah," Rutherston said, opening his notebook. "Lutherans or Anti-Reunionists?"

"Nei, we've hardly any Dissenters in the parish, not enough for a meeting-house, and none at all in the village. Well, there's Jack Hordursson, our cobbler, but he's an atheist... loudly. And the Norbits, they're Buddhists—they got it out of a book. Nei, the Wootons are just indifferent for the most part."

"So you were surprised when Jon Wooton joined the..."

"Philomath's Club. Here, let me show you. This is all his work."

He led them over to a bench. Several photographs were pinned above it. Rutherston nodded. They were excellent work; one of the priest, another a family group in front of a water mill, and still another of the District Nurse and her housemaid in front of the clinic.

"Jon Wooton made the camera, and developed the negatives. He made several cameras, in fact, some of them every bit as good as one from a factory in Winchester."

Several model machines were racked against the wall, including a small telescope. Another had a brass tube like a miniature hot-water boiler set over a spirit-lamp, with an affair of levers and pistons in an arrangement like a grasshopper's legs. The priest undid a cap, poured in water, lit the lamp, and worked valves. After a minute the machine began to hiss... and then, slowly at first, the levers began to work up and down, and the flywheel to spin with a smooth, alien motion.

Bramble took a step back and crossed himself, his eyes going wide. The priest smiled and made a soothing gesture. "Nothing but natural law at work, my son."

"But... that sort of thing doesn't work nei more! Not since the Change!"

"Actually it does, corporal," Rutherston said briskly. "If it isn't the type that needs high pressures. But an... what's the phrase, Padre? I should have paid more attention in Classics... *they* work."

"A Watt-style steam engine, that functions by creating a vacuum and then using the pressure of the air to push the piston—an atmospheric engine. Wooton made this himself, when he was sixteen, just from the plans in a book. And it worked the *first* time."

"That's rare?"

"Take my word for it. *Very* rare."

Rutherston nodded. "There's a few large ones in dockyards to pump out dry docks, and in coal mines up the Severn for drainage. They're not of much use otherwise; they weigh too much and take too much fuel for the work they do. For most purposes, an ordinary waterwheel or windmill is far better."

Frances pointed to several places where the brass rods of the little engine had been bent and then carefully repaired.

"There you have Jon Wooton's genius, and his failing—when I told him that nei great use could be made of the engine under modern conditions, he smashed it and stormed away."

"And who fixed it, Padre?"

Frances passed a hand over his face and sighed. "He did. I had expelled him from the club—and from the sacraments—nine years ago, for reasons which must remain confidential. Then just two years past he came back to Eddsford from his longest trip abroad. He'd made a little money, it seems, as a sailor—"

Bramble rolled his eyes slightly toward the ceiling. *Too holy for his own good, this one,* the expression said. Rutherston gave an almost imperceptible nod.

"—and he convinced me that he had mended his ways. Among other things, he offered to help instruct at the Philomath Club here. And did so... brilliantly. Until I found him in a compromising position with one of the girls who was a member."

He shook his head. "And he absconded with... oh, nothing of value. Some fanciful plans he'd drawn up, and a few books—old works, on technologies that definitely do *not* operate since the Change."

Rutherston nodded. "Evidently the young man was a disappointment to most people who knew him, Padre. Do you think anyone was disappointed enough to kill him?"

The priest bit his lip. "Inspector, you put me in a very difficult position."

"Oh, I realize that you have to respect the confidences of the—"

The vicar of Eddsford surprised him by chuckling. "No, it's not so much that. It's that there were so *many* people here in Eddsford who... ah... very strongly disliked Jon Wooton. I hope I'm Christian enough to forgive those who wrong me, but my brother—"

"Frances!"

The voice came from beyond the door; a woman in a good plain dress hurried in with a leather box in her hands; it had a buckled flap with a golden cross embossed on it. "Frances! Mrs. Thordarsson—oh, pardon me."

"Inspector, corporal, my wife Hrefna Broxby," he said, pronouncing it more like *Refna*. "Yes, dear?"

"Mrs. Thordarsson is failing."

"Ah, then I'll have to leave you, I'm afraid, inspector," he said briskly, taking the leather box. "Their farm is on the edge of the parish and time presses. Very much a pleasure and do feel free to call on me at any time."

A youngster in his teens outside was holding the reins of a rather thickset horse in the shafts of a light two-wheeled carriage; it looked like a prosperous farmer's Sunday showpiece. The priest walked out at the same quick pace, stepped into the seat, gave the other a hand up, flourished the whip, and started off at a brisk trot.

The vicar's wife watched him leave with a smile, then turned to the two men: "Oh, detective inspector," she said. "Sir James asked me to pass on his invitation to visit this afternoon."

After they'd left the churchyard, Bramble nodded slowly to himself. "Think I've got a bit of a handle on this Wooton fellow, sir," he said.

"Yes?"

"Well, he was a right clever lad, eh? And thought he should be a big man... and maybe he should have been."

Rutherston frowned. "Then why in God's name didn't he *leave?* Miller is the best thing he could hope for here, in a settled county like Hampshire. And he wasn't even the heir to the lease; there's an elder brother."

"But," Bramble made a sweeping gesture, "he kept coming *back,* you see? He wanted to make his mark here; not in Winchester or Portsmouth or Bristol or the colonies, but *here.* Where he grew up and with all the people *here,* where it really counts, sir."

"Ah," the detective said. "Now I see your point."

He glanced up at the sun; it was an hour or so to noon. "Let us repair to the Moor's Head until luncheon. If there's anyone in town who knows the gossip, it's an innkeeper."

"Then the Squire," Bramble said. He smiled. "Better you than me, sir."

The park around the manor wasn't particularly large, probably because labor had been scarce until the last few decades, but

Rutherston stopped to admire the sight of a herd of fallow deer grazing beneath a beech. They ambled away across greensward studded with crimson poppies and golden corn marigolds as he and Bramble walked in past the gatehouse; the laneway was flanked by clipped shapes of golden yew as it curved around an ornamental pool of several acres, and then through a screen of timber and over a ha-ha into the house gardens, velvety lawns and tall chestnuts and cedars, and banks ablaze with phlox, penstemon, black-eyed Susan, and more. A few gardeners stared or waved tentatively as the two King's Men walked toward the entrance.

Royston Hall itself was Seventeenth Century work for the most part, a rectangular block done in pale stone and four stories high. The gray-haired butler opened the door before he could knock and took the card he offered.

"You're expected, sir," he said, not deigning to notice Bramble. "If you'll follow me?"

And I don't think he's been a butler all his life, Rutherston thought. *Men rarely have half their left ear chopped off in that line of work. Or get a limp quite like that.*

There was a suit of armor inside the door at the entrance to the hall, a modern man-at-arm's outfit of head-to-toe articulated plate. The model had been Fifteenth Century, but the metal was considerably better than any available to medieval smiths.

The detective and the corporal gave it identical considering glances as they went by. It took a good deal of effort to batter good alloy-steel armor into that sort of shape, and it wouldn't be at all healthy for the man inside; the shoulder-flash of the Cordoba Lancers was barely visible, and the visor of the sallet helm had been cut nearly in half, which must have taken a two-handed blow with a heavy axe or a halberd. The butler led them into a room with bay windows overlooking a walled garden; they were open, and a scent of lavender and cut grass drifted in, along with a country-house smell compounded of faint traces of lamp and dog and woodsmoke, tobacco, the old walls…

Sir James Broxby was a man of medium height, still slender and lithe at fifty, with amber-colored hair and mustache liberally streaked with gray. He would have been handsome if it hadn't been for the slash that had taken his left eye and furrowed the brow above and the cheek below; as it was he wore the black patch with distinction, and the other eye was bright blue and shrewd beneath the shaggy brow. Rutherston heard Bramble make an *mmmm* sound behind him, and the same thought occurred to him as they shook hands:

Well, that's what happened to the suit of plate.

"A pleasure, Sir James," he told the baronet.

"Mutual, inspector... just a moment... Rutherston... the Short Compton Rutherstons? The Blues?"

"Yes, Sir James, twice. On the retired list at present, and making my way in the CID—younger son, and all that. Youngest of four sons, actually."

"Ingmar Rutherston... the Military Medal down in Morocco some time ago?"

The detective shrugged. "Medals came up from the rear with the rations, and everybody deserved one," he said.

That brought a short laugh and a nod; not precisely agreement, but a meeting of minds on matters that others without their shared experience could never really know. Rutherston opened his cigarette case and offered it.

"Ah, *Embiricos*," Sir James said, taking one. "These alone made the cost of resettling Barbados worthwhile, and damn the Whigs and their Babbage Engine project."

He cocked an eye at Bramble. "You can sit too, corporal."

"I'll stand, if it's all the same, sir," Bramble said, taking a position behind the sofa where Rutherston sat; it was rather like having a bear behind the flowered chintz, but reassuring for all that.

"The corporal has been assisting me, and doing rather a good job of it," Rutherston said.

"I'm not surprised."

The baronet rang a bell, and a housemaid slid into the room. "Gin and tonic, please, Martha," he said. "And you, inspector?"

"The same, thank you. It is a warm day."

They made small talk—the weather (good), the state of the just-completed harvest (excellent), the trends in wheat and wool prices (deplorable), Sir James's former command in the resettled areas of southern Spain (great potential)—until the drinks came. Rutherston sipped at his, enjoying the tart astringency, and then opened his notebook as a hint.

Sir James sighed. "Unpleasant business this, all 'round. I confess I wouldn't have been even the least upset if young Wooton had come to grief somewhere abroad, but to have him murdered in my own village..."

Rutherston nodded sympathetically. "The Wootons are an old family here?"

The other man laughed shortly and drank, smoothing his mustache with a knuckle. "*Very* old. Gaffer Wooton... Jon's grandfather... lived here before the Change. So did my family... nearby, at least."

Rutherston's brows went up. That *was* unusual. The rescue parties had swept up selected people from all over Southern England that first year and taken them to the Isle of Wight Refuge to wait out the inevitable die-off after the machines stopped. Most had been farmers, and the others craftsmen or skilled workers of high value. Thatchers, weavers, and blacksmiths and the like... and to be sure, the families of commanders and of their soldiers and of persons of influence on the Refuge. The men in charge had saved civilization here where nearly everything on the Continent from Normandy to Iran had gone down in utter wreck... but they'd still been only human, and their power had been near absolute for a while.

The Squire of Royston Hall sighed again. "I don't know how much background you want—"

"The more the better, Sir James."

"Well, the Wootons got the lease on the mill as soon as this area was resettled in the spring of 1999—my grandfather was commandant of the region under the Emergency Regulations and got a substantial grant of land when things were privatized, the usual arrangement. Old Tom Wooton did a splendid job; he'd been in the Life Guards with my grandfather, driving one of those... what where they called? Not automobiles or trucks, moving steel fort things on bands of metal..."

"*Tanks*, I believe."

"Yes. One called after a sword, a 'scimitar,' I think. Old Tom was handy with machinery, and so he was put in charge of renovating the mill—it hadn't been operational before the Change, just kept for appearances, they did a lot of that sort of foolishness then of course. He married an Icelandic woman—"

Rutherston nodded; that was also common. It had been encouraged, in fact, when the refugees from the northern isles were welcomed into a land gone empty in the second and third years.

"—And his son extended it, added a fulling section."

The detective closed his eyes for a second to search his memory. The mill was on the fringe of the village, but he hadn't heard the distinctive sound of wet woolen cloth pounded by wooden hammers. At his unspoken question, Sir James went on:

"We closed it down about nine years ago. There's not as much weaving here as there was in my father's time—just rough homespun and blankets, that sort of thing. The cloth trade's been moving off to the West Country and north into your bailiwick lately and it's cheaper to buy the finer grades. Our Rother really doesn't have enough water power for manufacturing."

True enough, Rutherston thought. *Though I wouldn't call Dursley and Stroud and Chalsford our bailiwick, precisely; we just sell them our farmers' wool and wheat and flax.*

He'd never liked the mill-towns. They were too big—Stroud was the most monstrously overgrown and had four *thousand* people nowadays—and they didn't really fit into the Cotswold country he loved.

Winchester and Bristol and Portsmouth are cities, he thought. *Eddsford and Short Compton are villages. Those places are neither fish nor fowl nor good red meat.*

"I turned it into a winery instead, and loaned a few of my tenants the money for planting more vines. There we have some chance of competing, what with haulage costs from the colonies. In any case, young Jon took it hard. He'd been full of plans for making the fulling operation more efficient—even adding a spinning mill. That we *definitely* wouldn't have had the water power for, but Jon was a trifle unbalanced on the subject. We had words on the matter when I pointed out that it *was* my property and the decision was mine. In fact, we both lost our tempers. He swore he'd buy the mill and the freehold of it and I... well, I'm afraid I laughed and said he was welcome to do it, any time he had a thousand pounds in cash about him."

Rutherston winced slightly, and felt Bramble do the same at some subliminal level. A thousand pounds was what Rutherston made in five years or a corporal in fifteen. There were places, not here in Hampshire but not necessarily right out on the frontiers either, where you could buy and stock a good farm with that much.

Sir James looked at the end of his cigarillo, finished his gin and tonic, and then sighed.

"Well, two years ago... by God, he did it."

Rutherston felt his jaw start to drop, and the Squire of Eddsford nodded.

"Yes, quite a surprise. But I'd given my word, even if I meant it as a joke, and... there he was with a thousand in good Bank of England notes. I had absolutely nei desire to sell family land, but what could I do? It was a fair price, after all; better than fair, even if I did have to put up a new winery. I felt lucky he didn't insist on making a public parade of it; he was always one to kick a man when he had him down, was our Jon."

The detective's pen scribbled over his pad. Unwillingly, he felt a certain admiration for the late Jon Wooton's sheer gall. To come home and beard the Squire that way... although it said something reasonably favorable about the landowner, too. If Sir James wanted to he could make living here impossible for anyone he took against, since he was the largest landowner, the major employer directly and through his tenant-farmers, and Justice of the Peace and militia captain to boot. Nobody apart from his own mother seemed to have liked Jon Wooton much either, which would have made his position that much worse.

Just then the door crashed open. A woman stood in it, dressed in black silk. It clashed horribly with her graying ginger hair, which escaped in wisps about her long and rather horsey face; she had mismatched features that might have been charming if she smiled, but he had an instant and distinct impression that she didn't do that very often, even apart from whatever was bothering her now.

Relative of the Squire, Rutherston thought instantly. *Close relative. Sister, probably.*

Her eyes were red as if from prolonged weeping, but she glared at Sir James Broxby with open rage.

"You *killed* him, James! How could you!"

The accused man sighed again, closed his eyes for a second, and stood. "I'm rather busy now, Vigdis—"

She turned to Rutherston, who'd also stood by automatic reflex. "Arrest him! He killed Jon because he couldn't *stand* the thought of my being happy, of having a home of my own—"

Something in the detective's face stopped her; she started to weep again, then snatched something from a shelf and threw it. The porcelain shattered against a window, which broke itself; then she turned and stormed out again.

The baronet sat again. "Good *God*," he said quietly. "I apologize for subjecting you to that, inspector."

Rutherston sat as well. "No need to apologize, Sir James. In my line of work one often sees people when they... ah... aren't at their best."

His host rang the bell again. "Another gin and tonic, Martha," he said. "Much gin, little tonic, nei ice. Another, inspector? Nei? Well, *I* need it, by God!"

He shook his head and went on: "I've been lucky in my wife, my sons and daughters, my brother and our other sisters... but Vigdis is, as you can see, a consummately silly woman. And Jon Wooton was rather a swine with women of all classes. Whether you believe me or not, I wouldn't have objected if I'd thought he *would* give her some happiness, but... it wouldn't have mattered if Wooton had *ten thousand* pounds coming in every year and a seat in the Lords."

"Of course, Sir James," Rutherston said; quite sincerely, on the whole.

By God, it's a good thing that being a copper is a cure for embarrassment; otherwise I'd be dropping dead of the English Disease right here. I suspect Corporal Bramble is willing his vital functions to cease immediately.

"Now," he continued. "Jon Wooton bought the mill two years ago?"

"Yes, and that made his brother Eric *his* tenant," Broxby said, escaping to—relatively—impersonal matters with relief. "Another reason I hated to sell; Eric's been a perfectly sound man. Jon immediately cleared out the winery equipment, and began extending the old mill building, which at least gave some of our Eddsford people employment. In fact, he swore he'd put in spinning machines as well, even power-looms."

Rutherston snorted. He might not like Stroud, but having it close by as he grew had taught him *something* about the economics of the textile trade. Nobody used power-looms. Power *spinning*, yes, and some of the processing parts of the fine-cloth trade were mechanized, but when so many cottagers had good treadle-looms and needed work in the off-seasons of the farming year it just didn't pay, especially when people willing to work in factories were so scarce and could demand high wages. Master-spinners put the thread out for weaving through the cooperative guilds, then bought back the cloth for finishing.

"I thought you said there wasn't much spare power from your river?"

"None!" Broxby said, then: "Ah, thank you, Martha," and knocked back his drink as if it were neat whiskey. "In fact, there's a Catchment Order enjoining anyone on this stretch from building more dams or weirs. To preserve the fishing, you see. But Wooton would have it that he could install a *steam engine,* of all things! In Hampshire, with not a pound of coal within fifty miles! And they don't pay for anything but pumping out mines even up the Severn, where it's cheap."

Rutherston started to snort again, then remembered the vicar and his Philomath Club, and the little model.

But that makes even less sense. He was nei fool, our Jon, and he knew you couldn't get useful work out of one of those machines. Not without a coalmine right beneath it, so the fuel was free! And they took most of the coal in the Old Days; we're working their leavings, or seams too small to be worth noticing back then.

That was the basic lesson of the Change; under the laws of nature as they'd applied since that March 17th of 1998, you couldn't get mechanical work out of heat, not in any really useful amount. Not in an engine, not in a firearm. The detective shook his head. He'd learned the details of it in school, though it had been boringly abstract, especially the bits about electricity—you could visualize a steam engine in your head, but not force flowing in wires.

What really puzzled him was that Jon Wooton, in his own personal and repulsive fashion, was acting as if he was seventy years old and *remembered* the Old World, and missed it enough to keep scheming to find a way around the Change. Sir James Broxby braced his elbows on the arms of his chair and steepled his fingers. When he looked over them at Rutherston he was once again the forceful man he'd first met.

"I'm afraid we've presented you with a puzzle, inspector. You have to determine who *didn't* want to kill Jon Wooton."

"Starting with the District Nurse and his schoolteacher," Rutherston said ruefully.

For a moment he wished he'd accepted the second drink.

The brow over Sir James's single eye went up. "Them? They *have* been handling his business correspondence with that firm in Portsmouth," he said. "So they can't loathe him quite as much as the remainder of us."

"No, not all as it seems," Bramble said, frowning intently, as they walked back down the lane to the park gate.

Rutherston nodded. *He's been caught up in the puzzle of it,* he thought, amused. *Natural huntsman, I suppose.*

The big noncom went on: "If Sir James was going to kill a man, he'd do it face-to-face; Jon was younger and knew how to use a blade, too, sir."

Dueling wasn't legal. On the other hand, it wasn't absolutely unknown, either, in the last generation or so.

"There's his sister," the detective pointed out. "The most honorable of men could lose control... still..."

Bramble cleared his throat apologetically. "No disrespect to the Squire's sister, but Jon was a man with an eye for the girls from all we've heard, and you'd have to be right desperate to fancy waking up next to her for the rest of your mortal days. *And* he was a good ten years younger."

"Unless it was for revenge."

"Then he wouldn't string her along. Having it away and then dumping her public-like would be revenge in plenty."

"Hmmm," Rutherston said. "I see what you mean. He probably did mean to marry her then... and be a rich man here in Eddsford, with the Squire's sister too. That *might* be enough to overcome Sir James's scruples."

"More likely one of his men's. Did you see that butler, sir?"

Rutherston shot him a glance, and got that guileless expression once more.

"Yes, I did. Yes, you're right, corporal, he might be the sort to quietly take care of something the master wouldn't or couldn't... but I don't think he'd use poison. Quick stab to the kidneys, and then the body never found, that would be more like it."

"Something to that. But *someone* did it... and it would have to have a bit of spite behind it, inspector. He died hard, did our Jon. Very hard."

Rutherston nodded. "That's the way we have to approach this. Usually we look for motive and opportunity..."

"But everyone in this sodding village hated Jon Wooton, and they all had the opportunity to drop sommat in his beer."

"Exactly. Therefore we'll have to focus on the *means*. Time to go see what may be seen at the Wootons.'"

The mill was at the other side of the village; they walked back through the green and along the single long lane, since Eddsford had more length than breadth. With the harvest in the farm-workers who made up most of the people here were taking time to do repairs and tidying up; they passed half a dozen parties of thatchers, with householders tossing up bundles of the golden straw to be pegged and trimmed. The trades and crafts were busier than ever, though; they went past a shoemaker—who from the sign also repaired harness and saddles—tapping away with his family working around him, a smithy with its blast of heat and inevitable hangers-on and iron clangor, a tailor's where the treadle-powered sewing machines hummed.

Children were running about, enjoying their last weeks of freedom before the school year started. A mob of the older boys came by kicking a football; one of them sent it across the path of the two men. Bramble stopped it with his foot, bounced it expertly into the air with his toe, bumped it up with his knee and then head-butted it unerringly to the gangling youth who'd kicked it to him. The tow-headed boy grinned back and then led his shouting mob down a laneway toward the water-meadows.

Rutherston caught a look of mild enjoyment on the noncom's face before it gave way to his usual seriousness.

"You may have found His Majesty a recruit there," he said.

"Worse things than going for a soldier, sir," Bramble said. "If you've the inclination."

"True enough."

They passed out of the village proper; beyond it were the allotments—plots of a few acres came along with the rental of a cottage. Many of the villagers were at work there, hoeing and weeding, or harvesting vegetables and fruit into woven-withe baskets. Some of them nodded to the two outsiders; others just glanced at them.

"You or I would be grockles in Eddsford if we lived here thirty years, married local girls and were buried in the churchyard," Rutherston said.

"Probably, sir. Not quite as bad as that where I come from; we weren't resettled until a decade or so later. Still had new folk moving in until around the time I was born."

A few two-wheeled carts went by, loaded high with billets of firewood cut in the coppices; this was the season to start laying it in for the winter. It was also the season for milling some of the recently harvested grain, of course, though not all of it; besides taking time to thresh, it kept better in the kernel. The tall overshot steel wheel was turning as water dropped onto the curved metal vanes from the millrace. That wound out of sight along the hillside and into a patch of dense forest.

Ah, Rutherston thought, looking at a series of heavy metal shapes, forged steel and cast iron; they rested by the newer section of the long rectangular building. *That will be the parts Sir James mentioned from Portsmouth. Odd that Miss Medford didn't mention doing Jon's correspondence.*

In mourning for a brother or no, the world's work had to go on; as they approached, a sling full of the sacks was hoisted up to the top story, to be poured into the hopper and eventually emerge as flour—and sacks of *that* were being unloaded into empty wagons from a doorway lower down. The groaning sound of burr millstones turning on each other ran under the rush of the water and the rumble of the big gearwheels meshing. There was a mealy, dusty smell in the air, despite the dampness.

A tall man with thinning sandy hair was overseeing operations. He turned as Rutherston and Bramble approached and nodded at them:

"Been expecting you. I've a bit t' do furst, sir." Then he shouted upwards at his workmen: "Awroi, keep her running! Light on the lever! There's nei way for even biyani like you t' bugger it up now, so don't!"

Rutherston introduced them; the miller had a hand like something carved from bacon-rind, and a gravely respectful manner that *might* be hiding resentment... or possibly relief. He led them into the rambling ivy-covered house that stood near the mill and offered refreshment—*nammit* was the word he used for the pound-cake and rosehip tea that his wife brought in and slammed down with a nervous irritation that made the husband wince.

"Where's mother?" he said to her. "And the kids?"

"*She's* in Jon's room, with his things," she said with a waspish note.

Eric Wooton looked surprised. "How'd she get in? It's locked! There's the guard! She were fussing about it all yesterday, and yelling at the so'jer."

"The squaddie's asleep, and she used a strip of tin!"

Oh, my, Rutherston thought, and exchanged a glance with Bramble as they both rose.

Mrs. Wooton the younger was a woman of about her husband's age, somewhere between thirty and forty, with bright blonde hair and sharp intelligent features and tourmaline-green eyes. She went on with a snap:

"Margrethe and Sally and Tom are staying with Jenny. And that's where *I'm* going now. Call me when your Jon isn't mucking up our lives any more. I didn't marry *him,* you know."

Eric Wooton winced as the door slammed, and went on as he trailed after the two King's Men down a corridor toward the stairs.

"Jenny's her sister..." he sighed, then went on: "You talked with the Squire, I suppose, inspector? Jon... ee allus was a strange boy, off alone with his books or fiddling with some bit of gearwork, but he changed when the Squire closed the fulling mill. First he goes off to sea; then he comes back with money and big plans, talking all fess about how he'd settle everyone who ever crossed him, and then he goes and buys the mill!"

"Which will be yours now, I suppose, Mr. Wooton?" Rutherston said over his shoulder, as they came to a landing.

The square Saxon face went slack. "I hadn't thought!"

The detective blinked. He'd been on the receiving end of a great many attempts at innocence, and that was the real thing if he'd ever seen it.

And now the poor fellow has more guilt to add to the relief he's trying not to feel, Rutherston thought; the Wootons had ratcheted up two steps on the local social ladder. *Now, how to interrupt his mother...*

Eric Wooton visibly put the dawning realization that he now had his beloved mill in fee simple and rent-free aside and continued:

"I didn't think any good would come of it, nor of those friends of his."

Aha, Rutherston thought. *That's new.*

"Friends?" he said.

"Foreign," Eric Wooton said shortly.

The problem is, foreign *could just mean someone from Warwickshire, or even Winchester,* Rutherston thought. *I doubt they were from outside the Empire.*

"And they came by night. Jon would go out and talk to 'em, I suppose he went with them on his trips away, but he wouldn't bring them into the house—not that I wasn't glad of it. Wouldn't want them around my kids. Then when they left he'd have more—"

Suddenly he stopped and sniffed the air. Rutherston did too; there was a hint of smoke, not likely from a hearth in this season, but it could be from the iron stove in the kitchen.

"*Mother!*" Wooton bellowed, and tried to bolt past them.

Bramble had his sword out. Rutherston made a gesture and the noncom sheathed it as they went pounding up the last flight of stairs. The trooper who'd been on guard lay slackly on the floor with a cup beside him; drugged, not drunk or asleep, but Rutherston didn't envy him when he eventually met Corporal Bramble again in his official capacity.

The door had been locked once more; the miller rattled the handle and shouted incoherent pleas, threats, and curses at his mother. Smoke leaked underneath it; Rutherston shoulder-checked the agitated man neatly out of the way, and Bramble hit the oak planks with his shoulder tucked in. That was practical, if you had a lot of bone and muscle behind the shove, and a mail-coat and padding to protect it. The lock tore out of the jamb with a crunch, and the door banged open.

"No!" a woman screeched.

That was probably Kristin Wooton; at least she was stout and middle-aged. She went for Rutherston with a creditable tackle, but he dodged aside—he'd been a very good rugby fly-half once—and picked up a jug of water by the side of an unmade bed still marked with the dried blood and fluids of Jon Wooton's hard dying. Smoke turned to steam as he threw it into a metal box where flames ran. Behind him Bramble had the mother in an unbreakable grip—despite her attempts to kick and gouge—and Eric Wooton was...

A wringin' of his hands, Rutherston thought, as he opened a window and waved a pillowcase to disperse the smoke. *If I had to pick a recruit for a commando operation, I'd take Eric's mother Kristin over him any day of the week.*

The basket held charred papers. And charred photographs as well. The detective picked one up between thumb and forefinger.

For a moment the shapes made no sense. Then his brows rose as he mentally untangled the interlocked limbs and saw what was going where; he hadn't seen anything like it since a handful of pre-Change magazines were handed eagerly around after lights-out in the dormitory at Winchester College... Then the brows rose again, to an almost painful level. Those photographs were modern, and not posed; they'd been taken at some distance, through an open window—with a camera hooked up to a telescope. It took him a moment to recognize Delia Medford, and a moment more to identify pretty Aud; facial features weren't the most immediately apparent part of the overall composition.

No wonder his mother had wanted to burn them! Rutherston thought. *And no wonder that Delia Medford was willing to handle his business correspondence... and she certainly had a motive for murder.*

"Good God almighty," Bramble said in reverent tones.

Rutherston turned, automatically holding the photograph closer to his chest with the back outwards. A large trunk stood by the bed—evidently pulled from beneath it, and with the large, complex and extremely strong-looking lock hammered off. At a guess, Jon Wooton's mother had done it when she realized that the police were on the doorstep. Part of the contents had gone into the metal waste-basket and been set on fire; the rest had been tossed on the bed. They included some diagrams... and several neat bundles of ban-knotes, with many noughts in their numbers. Buying the mill and ordering equipment from Portsmouth hadn't exhausted young Jon's profits from his putative illegal salvage trips by any means.

"I don't want the money!" Kristin screeched. "Take the money! Just don't you slander my Jon! Jon was a good boy!"

No, he was a man, and a very bad one, Rutherston thought. *But that doesn't mean it was all right to murder him.*

Then he looked at the plans. *A steam engine, right enough,* he thought. There was the big rocking beam, the circular boiler, the huge six-foot piston, and the separate condenser. The rest of it made less sense. The channels for water were labeled *cooling system.* Surely the point was to heat the water up, though? And there was no provision for a coal store; simply a rectangular object with pipes running through it labeled *heat source.* And a weird geared arrangement to lower rods into it from above, each fitting neatly into a cylinder.

They were neatly titled *control rods,* with *graphite* in brackets after that and a note: *test composition? Add fuel elements gradual-ly to check necessary mass.*

"This doesn't make any sense," he said to himself, baffled. "But Jon was brilliant at mechanical things; it's the one virtue he had, and everyone agrees on it. What could—"

He felt his face go pale. "That's *impossible,*" he added.

No, he realized after a moment. *It's just very implausible. Anything* else *is impossible.*

"Dammit, I should have known better!" he said softly.

Kristin Wooton's screeches had subsided into sobs. Bramble heard the older man's words.

"Sir?" he said.

"Known that you see what you expect to find!"

"What was it you expected, exactly?" said Bramble, letting the woman down on her feet; she stumbled to a chair and dropped her face into her hands.

"I expected to find a murder."

* * *

"The trail's as plain as plain, sir," Bramble said. "Now that we've got one end of it, I can follow it."

The olive face was phlegmatic as usual, but there was a slight sheen of sweat on it. It was near sunset, and they'd been quartering the hanger north-east of Eddsford's mill all afternoon. Half the corporal's squad were helping—the ones with the best field-craft, as Bramble put it.

Or the ones that did the most poaching, Rutherston thought mordantly.

"Best get the rest of them out, then," he said aloud. "We don't need numbers to check on something."

The detective and the non-commissioned officer looked at each other in perfect unspoken understanding; if you were a leader of King's Men you didn't send them where you wouldn't go yourself. Or send them at all instead of going yourself, if accomplishing the mission was simply a matter of one man walking into danger. He'd been honor-bound to tell the corporal what he thought they were looking for. Corporal Bramble wouldn't let him go in after it alone.

It felt eerily strange to walk through an English beechwood with the smooth gray bark dappled by the sun and feel this way. You were meant to feel like this amid a landscape of arid rock, knowing that hating black eyes were peering at you and quivering-eager hands gripped spears, while the armor was like a vise around your chest and the long clatter of boots and hooves on rock echoed back from the sides of the wadi. His hand ached for the hilt of his longsword, but there was nothing here from which a sword could protect him.

"Here," he said.

Whatever-it-was had been buried skillfully, but you couldn't sink a dozen boxes bigger than coffins into the dirt without leaving *some* trace. Rutherston forced his mind and memory back from a time more than a decade distant, swallowed, cleared his throat.

"This one," he said.

They scrabbled at the duff with their gloved hands. The steel top of the box was still covered in chipped, faded olive-green paint, with faint black traces where words and code-sequences had been stenciled on. The rope handle was modern, though. Rutherston licked his lips again and bent to pull at it. The effort made him stagger,

taken off-guard; the weight was far greater than a four-by-three section of stamped steel should be. Bramble stepped nearer and gave
him a hand; there was room for both on the loop of hemp.

The lid began to creak upwards. As soon as it was open at all he
could see that the chest had been lined with thick plates of lead and
then something else—graphite, he thought. Then he saw what was
within, dull-shining metallic wedges, and he jumped back. Bramble
did an instant later, and the lid fell back with an echoing *whump*.
The softness of the sound meant that the fit must be very good, seal-
ing the boxes airtight.

Thank God for Jon Wooton's clever hands, Rutherston thought,
scraping the back of one hand across his face. *And damn him for a
lunatic!*

"Corporal, get your man out to the semaphore line. Code Seven-
Seven-Eight, and send it *emergency priority.*"

"Yes *sir!*"

That gave Bramble a reason to run. Rutherston turned and
walked instead. He couldn't outrun what waited in those lead-lined
boxes behind him... and you could never really outrun fear, anyway.

"He wanted to *what?*" Sir James said.

"Build a steam engine," Ingmar Rutherston said.

He looked around the parlor in Royston Hall. Only the essential
people were there: the Squire, his brother the vicar, and District
Nurse Delia Medford, SRN. And Corporal Bramble, of course. The
sheer *normalcy* of it was inexpressibly comforting, down to the tea-
tray the maid had left, and the sheen on the mahogany of the table,
the leather of the sofa and chairs and the large and rather bad oil of
William the Great's victory over the Moors at Tenerife that hung by
the door.

"That is mad!" the Reverend Frances Broxby said.

The nurse stirred her cup, genteelly holding out the little finger of
that hand. She nodded as the detective went on:

"Not if he had the right fuel," Rutherston said. He lit one of his
cigarillos and leaned an elbow on the mantelpiece. "Plutonium, I
believe it was called, Father?"

The scholarly priest shook his head. "Plutonium—you're all
familiar with the name?—plutonium won't *explode* any more. Even

if the chemical explosives to drive the pieces together would work, or the electronic control mechanisms functioned. It won't even get hot enough to melt. And thank God for that. Otherwise it would have poisoned half of England as it burned through the containment structures."

"Thank God indeed. From my dimly recalled lessons one sort turns into another sort as it runs down, somehow, and only God and a few boffins know what it is by now."

"Radium, cobalt-60, other decay products," the priest said quietly. "Wooton's chests probably came from an old power station. Whoever dug it out probably did so under duress, and died very quickly."

Rutherston nodded; even if the slave laborers had been Wild Lands savages, it was an unpleasant thought. He went on:

"As you say, Padre. But though it won't melt down, in concentrated form it will sit there and glow at about seven hundred degrees... which is quite hot enough to boil water, and to keep doing so for a very long time. I remember that from a course on the Dangerous Substances Act. Generally we leave the old reactors strictly alone—they're safer repositories for the stuff than anything we can build now."

He could see that the priest followed him, and Delia Medford was unsurprisingly unsurprised; it took Sir James a little longer.

"You mean... you mean it would have *worked?*" he said at last, blinking his one eye.

"In theory. In practice, no, and Jon Wooton would have killed everyone in Eddsford trying. It's been looked into exhaustively, back around the turn of the century, though the studies were kept secret. The resources of the whole realm couldn't do it, not with the machines we can make. That stuff is hellish dangerous."

"Good God," the baronet said, and drank blindly from his cup, looking as if he'd prefer something much stronger.

"Fortunately, the disposal squad says that nothing significant escaped. The boxes will be put in larger boxes, those will be encased in seamless lead castings, and the whole will be cast into very deep parts of the sea. What the boffins call a subduction zone, where evidently we won't have to worry about it again this side of doomsday."

Father Frances crossed himself. "So there *was* no murder here in Eddsford," he said slowly. "Thank God indeed! Jon Wooton simply killed himself... by accident."

All those present signed themselves as well, as the cleric murmured *"Amen."*

"And no harm done to the village or the people," Sir James said, with a gusty sigh. "I think, Frances, that a thanksgiving mass is in order... not that we need be too specific about the cause." He looked at Rutherston. "And no crime was committed after all."

"Oh, there were several crimes: smuggling, violation of the Treasure Trove Act, the Dangerous And Prohibited Substances Act... but all by the very late, and extremely unlamented, Jon Wooton. So my report will make plain."

There will *be an investigation, but not here and, thank God, by the Special Branch, not me.* Aloud he went on:

"I don't think any of you will be bothered further. Officially this will be simply a matter of a dead smuggler's buried treasure being confiscated—sensational enough to satisfy village gossip. *Provided* everyone here is discreet."

There were smiles and handshakes all around; Rutherston firmly declined the Squire's invitation to dinner.

"My wife expects me back just as soon as possible, Sir James. Otherwise our first child might be born in the absence of his or her father, and I'd never hear the end of it."

"I could lend you a phaeton and some fast horses..."

"Many thanks, but I think I can impose on the military for a pedalcab to Winchester along the line of rail. Miss Medford, shall I walk you home on my way to the Moor's Head?"

Bramble fell discreetly behind as they walked down the drive from Royston Hall. Casually, Rutherston drew an envelope from his jacket and handed it to her.

"I suggest you burn these, Miss Medford," he said. "I glanced at the first, but very briefly."

The spare handsome face of the nurse was calm as she accepted the package. "You don't feel obliged to include them in your report?"

Rutherston lit another cigarillo. "Why should I?" he said with a shrug. "There's no indication of anything illegal... on your part; Jon

Wooton was evidently a blackmailer, among his many other sins, but that will go with him to the grave. Nothing illegal, or in Winchester even cause for much remark. I'm a detective, not a priest."

"But Eddsford is my home, and where my work is, and I very much wish to continue living here," she said. "Thank you very much, inspector." She drew a breath: "About the money—"

"Dear lady, I *am* a policeman. Intelligent blackmailers usually try to have as many strings on a victim as possible. It would be just like Jon Wooton to force you to accept part of his smuggling profits. If you feel you should donate to charity, that's none of my affair either."

"Thank you very much, inspector." They came to the door of the clinic. "And you should stop smoking those things. They'll kill you."

Small children followed the two King's Men as they walked toward the inn, and there was a ripple of nods and smiles from the adults; everyone was happy to have the *murder* settled so quickly and nobody in their tight-knit little world brought up before the law. The ostler of the Moor's Head had his employer's trap ready, with a good-looking horse between the shafts; it would be an hour's travel to the semaphore station on the rail line, and then perhaps two back to Winchester. Rutherston smiled contentedly and drew the smoke into his lungs.

"She scragged 'im, of course, sir," Bramble said quietly.

"No names, no pack drill," Rutherston said. "Yes, of course. At a guess, she gave him some worthless placebo and assured him it would protect him from the radiation, then told him to pick the pieces up and measure them against some part he'd ordered from Portsmouth, or something of that order. From someone who'd healed his illnesses since he was a child, he'd believe it."

"She'd have grassed him up before much longer, any rate," Bramble said thoughtfully. "Don't blame her for waiting 'till the last minute, sir, either."

"Not at all," Rutherston agreed.

The two men turned and faced each other. The detective held out his hand; they gave a single firm grip, no squeezing nonsense, but a mutual recognition of strength.

"You were of the greatest possible help, Corporal Bramble, and I will say so in my report."

"Thank you kindly, sir."

"And Bramble... have you considered what you'll be doing after your current enlistment ends? Promotion is slow in peacetime."

Bramble's square face went a little slack for an instant. "Hadn't thought much, sir... might take up a farm in Spain, p'raps. Under me own vine and fig tree. Though farming's a mite too much like 'ard work, when you come to think about it."

"Have you considered the police? A good many ex-servicemen do... myself, for example."

Bramble chuckled. "Honestly, sir, I can't see meself in a leather bobby's 'elmet, rattling the doors of an evening and chatting up housemaids."

"I meant the detective branch, of course. The pay and pension are reasonable, we can always use good men—and you'd be protecting King and Country just as surely as you would in that tin shirt."

He held out his card. "Take this, think it over, and drop me a line if you want to talk it over a bit more."

Bramble took the card, turning it over in his thick fingers. "I will give it a thought, sir."

Then he grinned. "It hasn't been as boring as road patrol, inspector, I'll give you that."

Rutherston put a hand on the side of the trap and vaulted into the seat. He tipped his hat to the corporal, and waved to the crowd of villagers. They were still waving back as the horse broke into a trot, hooves falling hollow as it trod the shadows of tree and cottage into the roadway.

The detective settled back as the ostler whistled to his horse, smiling as the long peace of Eddsford fell behind and the blue-shadowed line of the Downs rose ahead. The church bell rang as they crested the first hill above the river, calling the villagers to give thanks for God's protecting hand.

And it's no slight privilege, to share the work with Him.

Conspiracies: A Very Condensed 937-Page Novel

Mike Resnick & Eric Flint

I could listen to Mike Resnick tell stories about the business all night. I just couldn't repeat any of them here. In addition to being an all-around good guy, Mike is just a natural born storyteller, as his status as the most awarded short story writer, living or dead, in the history of the science fiction field attests (ranked as compiled by Locus).

Eric Flint is the best-selling author of, among many things, the 1632 series, about a small American town that finds itself transported back to Germany, May 1631. When they told me they were collaborating on a story, I got excited. When they told me they guaranteed it wouldn't be like anything else I had in the book, I got scared. When I started reading it, I got delighted.

Prologue

If you go to the northern end of Praslin Island in the Seychelles, a thousand miles off the coast of East Africa, there's every likelihood that you'll chance upon a pudgy, gray-haired man holding a cigar in one hand and a cold drink in the other. You can nod a greeting to him, but if you try to start up a conversation, you may find yourself spending the next few years in a jail on Mahe, the main island in the chain.

So we figure it's our job to tell you who he is and what he's doing there.

1

"It was a dark and stormy night."

The alien lapsed into silence thereafter. It seemed sullen and brooding, simply staring at a blank wall of the chamber with its peculiarly small eyes.

After a while, Fuyd turned to the interrogator. "What is the meaning of 'stormy?' I thought it referred to a tempest."

"It does, more or less."

Fuyd looked back at the lumpy, ugly creature. "That makes no sense at all. How can the simple effect of a planet's rotation be tempestuous?"

The interrogator rippled its neck in the manner by which his species indicated uncertainty. Fuyd found the gesture vaguely unsettling. But then, she found much about the gnuzzit unsettling. It didn't help that their names were unpronounceable by her species. By any other species, actually.

"This human seems prone to obfuscation, Mistress Fuyd. Very little that it tells us seems to convey any sensible meaning."

"Try again," Fuyd commanded. "More severely."

The gnuzzit interrogator joggled a lever. The torture device's arm stretched out and began twisting the slender body parts growing out of the human's head. Some sort of feeding cilia, obviously. The pattern was not an uncommon one. They would be acutely sensitive to pain.

The brutish creature's eyes seemed to narrow. Other than that... Nothing.

Quite an astonishing pain threshold. Fuyd was tempted to order an anatomical analysis of the monster, on the remote chance its body type was unique among its species. But that would be in clear contravention to the Drasspunt Accord, and the matter simply wasn't important enough to risk an altercation with the liucuz, and certainly not with the always-belligerent jatts.

Frustrated, she leaned forward and hissed at the creature. "Why did you murder the first Kennedy one? Did the jatts pay you to do so?"

They were the most likely culprits. The liucuz and the kly—not to mention the miserable flappa—were equally aggressive players of the Great Game, but were not prone to such crude and direct methods.

The human creature answered. But again the reply made no sense.

"Snoopy's on the doghouse and his bowl is empty."

Other than the term "Snoopy"—perhaps it was a name—all of the words were recognizable, even the peculiar "doghouse" with its odd connotations. But the statement as a whole conveyed no sensible meaning.

"Perhaps," suggested the gnuzzit, "it is implicating the first Kennedy's spouse. 'On the doghouse' might be a reference to marital tensions. Perhaps she was his direct employer, recruited by the jatts because of her animosity and acting on their behalf."

Fuyd considered the scenario. Unlikely, but...

There was no reason not to investigate. The Drasspunt Accord carried no prohibition against testing for trace elements. Not even the excessively legalistic tlatla advanced such a claim. Naturally, there was no prohibition against violating the quaint customs and taboos of playee species. Their anatomies could not be probed, but their reliquaries could.

"Disinter the first Kennedy spouse and examine the corpse for trace elements of our opponents."

2

The newly elected President of the United States had expected any number of surprises once he assumed office. He'd even made a joke to his wife that maybe he'd finally know the truth about Roswell and Area 51.

It had been a *joke*.

He stared at the national security adviser—not *the* National Security Adviser, who was just as new as he was to her post and whose eyes were as round with surprise as his own—but at the wrinkled little man who seemed to be at least eighty years old and was apparently the official keeper of the nation's deepest secrets. His name was H. Saddler. Just "H." It seemed that not even the President of the US was cleared to know his first name. Nor his actual title.

"Do you mean to tell me," the President said, managing not to splutter outright, "that *we* abducted Jimmy Hoffa?"

The little old man seemed to wince. At least, two or three more wrinkles appeared on his face.

"Please, Mr. President. *We* did not abduct Hoffa. The aliens did. We simply fingered him to them. On account of the Kennedy assassination and what he might know about it, which we'd just as soon he didn't talk about."

"Which might be *what*?" demanded Janet Dailey, the new NSA. "You told us not more than an hour ago that the nation's security specialists were certain there was no conspiracy to assassinate John Kennedy."

"There wasn't," came the firm reply. "Lee Harvey Oswald acted on his own, sure enough. But there were a lot of conspiracies *around* the whole JFK business, if you know what I mean. Most of which involved us versus the Cubans—very delicate stuff, you understand—and it's almost certain Hoffa had his thumb in at least one of them." The old man's expression grew pious. "Being as how he had it in for Mr. Kennedy on account of him being a crook and the Kennedys being the bane of his life. That's why Robert Kennedy got assassinated, we're pretty sure."

The President thought his head might start spinning. "*Hoffa* ordered RFK murdered? Sirhan Sirhan was supposed to have been acting alone also."

"Well, sure, he was. Guy was a complete fruitcake. And I didn't say Jimmy Hoffa did it. Would have been a neat trick, since he was still in prison at the time. What I meant was that we're almost certain Sirhan Sirhan was abducted and brainwashed by the aliens—a different set, we think—so that by killing Robert Kennedy they could cast suspicion on Jimmy Hoffa."

Now, the President's head *did* feel like it was spinning.

"That makes no sense at all, Mr. Saddler," protested the National Security Adviser.

"I know that, Ms. Dailey." The old man's tone was lugubrious. "They're *aliens*, like I said. We're not sure if they're actually stupid or just barking mad. I'm inclined to the latter suspicion myself, seeing as how the whole thing apparently started with the Lincoln assassination, 'way back a hundred and fifty years ago."

"*Lincoln* was assassinated by aliens?"

"No, ma'am." Saddler gave her a reproachful look. "Abraham Lincoln was assassinated by John Wilkes Booth. Everyone knows that. But after what happened at Roswell—that's tomorrow's briefing—"

"I can't wait," muttered the President.

"—we got suspicious about some of the inconsistencies and ordered the disinterment of Edwin Booth's body from where it was buried in Massachusetts, as well as all of his relatives that we could find." Somehow, the pattern of wrinkles exuded triumph. "Sure enough. John Wilkes Booth's older brother was not human. Close, mind you, but no cigar. The body had too many bones in the feet. Which means he wasn't actually his brother at all."

The President and the NSA stared at Saddler. The old man shrugged. "We don't think the older Booth brother himself—or *it*self, maybe—had anything to do with the Lincoln assassination. Which, like I said, we don't actually have any suspicions was anything other than it looked to be. But we're now dead certain that Edwin Booth—maybe his alien confederates—must have brooded about the matter afterward. And that's why they assassinated Garfield and McKinley."

"You're referring to *Presidents* Garfield and McKinley," said Janet Dailey. Her voice sounded a little feeble.

"Well, sure. Garfield the cat's still alive and he isn't real anyway. We're not positive about the Garfield business, I need to add by way of caution, on account of the only parts of his assassin Guiteau's body we could get hold of were his skeleton, brain, and spleen. They kept them in a jar, so to speak, at the museum at Walter Reed Hospital. The spleen's suspiciously large, but that's not much to go on. There's no question about the McKinley assassination, though. First, because Leon Frank Czolgosz—he was the assassin—was just about the silliest caricature of an anarchist you can imagine. He actually voted Republican! The stated motive didn't make any sense at all."

Apparently, unlike the President himself, Ms. Dailey was beginning to make sense out of this lunacy. "Another case of alien abduction and brainwashing, you're saying?"

Mr. Saddler smiled at her approvingly. "Yes, ma'am. It's obvious. Sulfuric acid and lye were thrown into his coffin, you know, and all of his possessions were burned. Letters, clothes, the lot. There's only one logical reason to do that: cover up the evidence."

Forcibly, the President reminded himself that he had been elected not only by a landslide in the electoral college but by almost 56 percent of the popular vote. Leadership was called for here.

"You're contradicting yourself, Mr. Saddler," he said sternly, trying to sound as if he were following the logic instead of thinking he'd fallen into a rabbit hole. "If Cholo—whatever his name was—had to have his body destroyed, then presumably he was an alien himself. Not an—ah—*abductee.*"

Saddler went back to his lugubrious head-shaking. "No, sir. They would have destroyed the body and the possessions to eliminate any traces of their own DNA—or whatever they have instead of DNA. Like with the feet, it's close but no cigar. In fact, we're almost sure there are at least three species of aliens involved, from the stuff we found at the Roswell crash. From the sets of almost-like-DNA traces, you understand. As I'll explain tomorrow. Well, tomorrow and the day afterward. It's pretty complicated stuff."

The President and the NSA stared at him again. Eventually, the President said: "This is sheer lunacy."

Mr. Saddler nodded his head. "That's what the Rand people think. The gist of every one of their analyses is that all these aliens are just plain bonkers. I have to admit there are times I almost think they're right, especially when I go back over the Alydar case. Can't call it a murder, of course."

Seeing the blank look on the President's face, he added: "Alydar was a race horse, Mr. President. Pretty famous one, if you're a racing fan. He got euthanized after breaking his leg twice in a stall when he was the leading sire in the country. Foul play was suspected on account of the insurance involved—there was a tidy forty-five million dollar payout, and eventually there was even a conviction. But we dug up the carcass and, once again, there are just too many damn bones. But why would aliens kill a horse, unless they were simply insane?"

"This is *all* 'simply insane,'" snarled the President. "Mr. Saddler, I have to tell you—"

There was an interruption, as one of the President's staff entered the Oval Office.

"Excuse me, Mr. President," Raul Sanchez said apologetically. "This isn't normally something I imagine you'd—well—"

The young man seemed nonplussed. That wasn't perhaps surprising since he was just as new to his post as almost everyone in the White House, starting with the President himself. Sanchez didn't really have any more of an idea what was "normally something" than anyone else.

"Well," he concluded diffidently, "I thought you'd want to see it anyway."

He laid the newspaper he was holding down on the desk, the front page facing up.

It was the morning edition of the *Washington Post*. The President stared down at the blaring headline.

JACKIE O'S GRAVE DESECRATED
President Kennedy's grave left untouched by vandals

Mr. Sattler rose from his chair just enough to read the title. Then, looking very self-satisfied, slouched back into it. "Like I said, Mr. President."

3

"In other words, you got no rights at all."

The gnuzzit interrogator wriggled its neck. "What are 'rights,' Master Hoffa?"

The squat little human shook its head. "Just call me Jimmy, willya? I'm a labor man. Can't organize your way out of a paper bag, you insist on formalities."

The Hoffa human reached up and scratched its head. It could do that because after Mistress Fuyd had left the chamber, the gnuzzit had released the shackles on the human's upper limbs.

Dubiously, the interrogator eyed the head-scratching. The cilia were being given a treatment almost as rough as they'd gotten from the torture device.

"That is not painful?"

"Meaning no offense, Jock, but you guys aren't exactly the sharpest pencils in the box. That includes Missus Toadstool."

The phrase about pencils made little sense. Neither did the cognomen "Jock," which was not even an approximation of the interrogator's name. But the gnuzzit had come to understand by now that the Hoffa human was two things.

First, it was peculiar. Second, it was extremely intelligent. Much more so than the interrogator, and certainly more so than Mistress Fuyd.

So, the Hoffa human was worth listening to. The gnuzzit was still puzzled by "rights," but it had no trouble at all understanding the concept of "grievances," which Hoffa had introduced the first time Mistress Fuyd left the interrogation chamber.

"So, if I've got this right, if you guys tried to fight for a decent contract, the other side would just refuse to negotiate."

"What is 'negotiate?'" asked the gnuzzit. "Whatever it is, the bluipta don't do it. Neither do the jatts or the liucuz or the kly or the flappa. Not even the fussy tlatla. If any of the servant species fail to perform as expected, any of the master species will have the offender exterminated."

"Right." Hoffa lowered its hand. The creature's thick chest rose and fell in a peculiar manner the gnuzzit had noticed before. It was more pronounced than the human's regular breathing. Perhaps that indicated frustration or aggravation. It was hard to know, of course, with such a bizarre life-form. The gnuzzit still found it upsetting to watch the creature move about on only two legs.

"Right," the human repeated. "So we gotta start with the ABCs. Damn, I wish you'd snatched Farrell Dobbs too. I never held with his commie ideas, but he'd sure be handy in this situation. Guy knew his stuff."

"What is 'commie?'" asked the gnuzzit.

For the first time since he'd met the human, Hoffa's face expressed something other than stolidity. It would have been extremely alarming, actually, except the teeth displayed were so blunt.

"You are," said the human, its voice seeming to gurgle a bit. "Regular Bolshies, all of you downtrodden gnuzzit, starting from this moment forward."

"What is 'regular Bolsh—?'"

"We'll get to that," interrupted Hoffa. "First, I gotta explain some of the basic ingredients. We'll start with 'general strike.' Then we'll move on to 'insurrection.'"

4

As he always did when he came into Roswell, Ken Phipps grinned at the sign just outside the town limits. The Chamber of Commerce put up the billboards, in a feeble attempt to maintain a semblance of respectability.

WELCOME TO ROSWELL!
Dairy Capital of the Southwest

Ken drove past the billboard, looking for the first signs of the town's true principal industry. They started appearing almost immediately. Every other storefront, one way or another, was hawking something related to aliens. The pious and stodgy Chamber of Commerce notwithstanding, Roswell's real business was milking tourists, not cows. If he didn't know better, Ken would have suspected the whole thing was a hoax invented by some of the town's more ingenious inhabitants.

As he usually did unless he was in a real hurry, Ken stopped for lunch at the big restaurant located at the town's main intersection. The *Cover-Up Café*, that was, whose menu was a faithful reflection of the name. Beneath the clever plays on aliens and cover-ups, of course, the food just amounted to the standard burger-and-fries fare one found in any small American town. Still, it tickled Ken's fancy.

After paying the bill and leaving a generous tip, he wandered down Main Street, window-shopping as if he were any tourist. Eventually, satisfied that no one was following him, he slipped into one of the more nondescript gift shops on the street.

"Hi, Jock," he said to the proprietor, who was sitting on a stool behind the cash register. "How's tricks?"

The proprietor frowned—tried to, anyway; he still didn't really have the expression right. "I do not understand the relevance of 'tricks' to the question. And my name is not Jock, as you know."

There was no heat to the complaint. This was an old routine, by now. Ken simply shrugged.

"Nobody can pronounce your name. And that means *nobody*, according to you."

"We are a much oppressed people," said the proprietor sullenly. For a moment, he lost control and his neck did a little wriggle that would have instantly alerted anyone not in the know that this was no human being in front of them.

"Yeah, that's what they all say," replied Ken. "Life's hard and all that. Mr. Henderson still wants to know why you're short-changing him." He mustered his best gangster glower—which was in fact very good. Given that he was a no-fooling gangster, that was hardly surprising.

The gnuzzit managed an actual sneer. Ken was impressed.

"Fucking coyotes." The alien had mastered essential gerunds and participles early on in their acquaintance. "We have decided to discontinue paying Mr. Henderson his smuggling fees. They are unconscionably high. Besides, we have decided to adopt a different course of action."

Ken's sneer was way better, of course. "'Unconscionably,' no less. Listen, snake-neck. It costs money to smuggle aliens into the United States, especially no-fooling alien aliens. Mr. Henderson even provides them with jobs."

"Washing dishes. Making beds. Mowing grass."

Ken shrugged. "You got no other skills. Other than running spaceships and things like that that don't exist here. Whaddaya expect?"

The store proprietor—which he was, too; even legitimately—pushed a button on the cash register. A little chime sounded.

Stalling for time, obviously. Ken did his best gangster-threatening hunch, which was every bit as good as his glower. "And enough already. I'm warning you, Jock, Mr. Henderson's not a man to waste time arguing. He'll just—"

He felt himself seized, as if by a giant pair of hands. Then, lifted into midair.

"Hey! What are you up to?" He twisted his neck, but couldn't see anyone behind him.

"You are being abducted," said the gnuzzit. "The man wants to talk to you."

5

"You can't be Jimmy Hoffa," Ken protested. "You disappeared more'n thirty years ago—and you wasn't no spring chicken then. You'd have to be... jeez..."

"What's the date?" asked the square-headed man sitting across from Ken at what seemed like a table except Ken couldn't see any legs holding it up.

The man *did* look like Jimmy Hoffa, from a few photos Ken remembered.

"What's the date?" the man repeated.

"Uh... Well, I don't know how much time passed since they... uh..."

"The *date*, asshole!"

Now he really did look like Hoffa. *The* Hoffa.

"It was August 2 on Thursday."

"What year?"

"Huh?"

"Jesus, they snatched me a dimwit," muttered Hoffa to himself. "I told 'em I needed muscle, but I didn't mean between the ears."

Ken wasn't even offended, for some reason. "2007."

Hoffa nodded. "I was born in 1913. February 14, Valentine's Day. Means I'd be ninety-four and a half years old." He grinned, very coldly. "Funny how time flies. Last time I looked in a mirror—which they ain't got on this ship—I didn't look a day over sixty."

Ken stared at him. The truth was, Hoffa *didn't* look much over sixty.

The burly labor leader—ex-labor leader?—shrugged. "What I can tell, the way these alien ships move around, there's some kind of time tricks involved. I think Einstein explained it once."

Actually, Ken had some serious problems with the Special Theory of Relativity, but nobody wanted a hit man who could quote Shakespeare and argue quantum mechanics, so he put on his most thuggish expression and tried to remember not to use any three-syllable words.

"So, okay. What do you want, Mr. Hoffa?"

Finally, there came a smile. "Call me Jimmy, why dontcha? Never been much of one for formalities."

6

"And you're Kenny, right?" continued Hoffa, making an easy transition from the previous chapter.

"Kenneth, actually."

"Kenny, right," repeated Hoffa. "And you were brought here by a guzzler."

"A gnuzzit," Ken corrected him.

"Yeah, a guzzler," agreed Hoffa. "Stupid race, even for godless aliens."

"You believe in God, Mr... Jimmy?"

"Fucking-A right I do!" said Hoffa firmly. "But you could fill a book with what God doesn't know about organizing." Suddenly he smiled. "In fact, I think someone has. Called *The Capital*."

"You mean *Das Kapital*?"

"Yeah, that's what I said. Anyway, we got us some work to do, you and me, kid."

It had been a long time since anyone had called Ken a kid, but he decided not to mention it. Even up here, you didn't mess around with Jimmy Hoffa.

"So what, exactly, am I here for?"

Hoffa stared at him. Ken felt like the burly man was staring *through* him.

"Why dontcha ask what you really want to know?"

"I beg your pardon?" said Ken.

"Don't," admonished Hoffa. "It's a sign of weakness. Now ask."

"Okay," said Ken. "What does the job pay?"

Hoffa grinned. "That's more like it."

Ken waited a moment, then said, "Well?"

"Quiet, Kenny. I'm doing the math." Hoffa closed his eyes, frowned, moved his lips almost imperceptibly, and then looked at Ken. "Here's the deal. First, you get to live."

"Was that ever in doubt?" asked Ken, suddenly nervous.

"Don't interrupt. Second, you get five percent of my rake-off." A brief pause. "Ah, hell—make that seven percent. You're probably the only human-type person I'm going to be dealing with. And third, when we're done, I'll give you a planet of your own. You can be king of the kbajics, or muscha-muscha of the silky spaxxora." Hoffa leaned forward. "What do you say, Kenny?"

"My own planet?"

"Your own planet," replied Hoffa. "Of course, you'll have to pay your annual dues to the Brotherhood."

"What Brotherhood?" asked Ken.

"The one you're here to help me organize," answered Hoffa. "The United Brotherhood of Godless Alien Scum."

"It needs a more dignified name," suggested Ken. "Sir," he added quickly.

Hoffa frowned. "You really think so?"

"Absolutely."

"Maybe you got a point, Kenny." A thoughtful pause. "How about the Federated League of Godless Alien Heathen?"

7

In Chapter 7 Ken stumbles into an orgy involving a jatt, three flappas, a kly, a fussy tlatla, an underage gnuzzit, two liucuz of the Southern variety, and Paris Hilton. It breaks the tension and serves as comic relief, as everyone knows you need at least five flappas— one of each gender—for any kind of sexual encounter at all, but since it would take fourteen pages to set up the scene, even in this condensed form, we elected to leave it to the reader's—and Ken's— imagination.

8

"He's up to something, that much seems clear," said the gnuzzit.

"How can he be?" replied Mistress Fuyd. "I mean, after all, he's our prisoner, isn't he? At this point in the interrogation, he should be a pushover."

"The Kennedy creature thought he was a pushover too," remarked the gnuzzit.

"Which Kennedy creature was that?"

"The one with too much hair who couldn't keep his hands off females."

"Oh," she said, ashamed of her ignorance. "*That* one. Of course."

"I wonder why the Hoffa requested this other human, this Ken thing?" continued the gnuzzit. "He seems obsequious, yet we know from our background check that there is no crime of which he is not guilty, possibly excepting bestiality."

"Possibly?"

"You didn't see his last bedmate," answered the gnuzzit.

"What do we propose to do about him—or is it *them*?"

"We'll keep a watchful four or five eyes on Hoffa, and if he tries anything deleterious to the ship or those aboard it, we'll torture him."

"That could be fun," she said. Then she frowned—as much as an animated fignewton *can* frown—and said: "We'll have to apply new methods. Cutting the cilia from his head and chin elicited no reaction whatsoever."

"I know," answered the gnuzzit. "But I've been observing him carefully. Have you seen those hardened protrusions at the end of his mandibles—you know, the ten manipulative tentacles? I may just take something sharp and cut off a sixteenth of an inch or so. *That* will have him screaming in agony."

"Can I watch?" asked Mistress Fuyd eagerly.

9

"Now, you got that straight, Kenny?" said Hoffa.

"I contact all the gnuzzits and wichtigos..."

"All the gonzos and witches, right."

"And I tell them that if they're tired of working long hours for short pay and taking orders from the bluiptas and the rest of them, they should meet in your room after dark."

"You left out the part about owning a full and equal share of the ship, a percentage of all the trade with Earth, and regaining their self-respect and being able to walk with their heads held high."

"Jimmy, have you gotten a good look at the wichtigos? Both of their heads are on top of their feet. You get one of them to walk with his head held high and it means he's been decapitated."

"So think of something else to say. Don't hassle me with details, Kenny. I've got my eye on the big picture."

"Well, there's one more detail I have to bring up," said Ken.

"Yeah? What?"

"You want everyone to meet in your room after dark."

"That's what I said."

"Yeah, well, where we are, it's been after dark for ten billion years, give or take a month."

Hoffa looked out a viewport. "Okay," he said. "When you're right, you're right." His expression became threatening. "Don't be right around me too often, unless you're agreeing with me. Got it, kid?"

"Got it." Ken paused. "So when should I tell them to show up?"

Hoffa pondered the question for a moment. "Tell them to show up when they're sick of things as they are, and want their rights, their self-respect, and especially a sizeable piece of the action. Then stand aside so you don't get trampled."

"They're aliens, Jimmy," said Ken. "Do they *care* about that stuff?"

"Kid, there are three truisms in the universe. Two of them have to do with women. This is the third. Trust old Jimmy on this."

Ken had planned to tell every member of the crew below the rank of *quaslodit*. But after he told the first dozen aliens he met, he had to flatten himself against a bulkhead to avoid the mad dash to Jimmy Hoffa's room.

10

"Do you really think it'll work?" asked Mistress Fuyd.

"It worked every time I tried it back home," said Hoffa. "Maybe the bliptas and the floppies and them others call the shots, but *you* carry the mail."

"All of our mail is electronic," the gnuzzit pointed out.

"Don't interrupt," said Hoffa. "Like I said, you carry the cargo— even if the cargo is nothing but a bunch of bloodthirsty gonzo and witch scum, meaning no offense. If you go on strike, commerce and conquest both come to a stop. The wheels don't roll."

"We don't have wheels," pointed out another gnuzzit.

"Shut up," said Hoffa. "The wheels don't roll, the wings don't flap, the nuclears don't pile. Choose whatever fits."

"What do we do when the bluipta or the fussy tlatla come after us with a punishment party?" asked Mistress Fuyd.

"How are they gonna get here? You control the ships. You control the gas pumps."

"We don't use gas."

"Okay, you control the plutonium pumps. Don't hassle me with details." He looked around the room. "Think about it. How are they going to *make* you go to work?"

"They'll threaten to torture and kill us," answered the gnuzzit.

"See?" said Hoffa with a triumphant smile. "A dead man can't fly a ship! You've won already."

"So they'll stick to torture," said the gnuzzit.

"How are you gonna read a chart if they gouge out your eyes? If they cut off all your hands, do they think you're going to push all these little buttons with your nose?"

"Actually, we could," said another gnuzzit.

"That's defeatist talk!" snapped Hoffa. "I'm telling you, we can bring the galaxy to a standstill. Maybe even the whole solar system."

"Somehow I think there must be more to it than just killing our engines and demanding better treatment."

"Right," agreed Hoffa. "The very first thing we need is a pension fund. Since none of you have had any experience in that area, I'll take the job myself, onerous as it is." He paused once more. "All right," he continued. "Now it's time to elect a leader, someone who will call the shots. I modestly put myself forth as a candidate. Are there any others?"

One of the wichtigos seemed about to step forward. Ken immediately walked over to it and let it see that his hand was gripping the hilt of a knife he had in his pocket.

"None?" said Hoffa. "Then I guess I'm elected."

"And you're *sure* that a general strike always succeeds?" asked Mistress Fuyd.

"Always."

"And unions are always successful?"

"Every single time," answered Hoffa.

"I have checked your record," said Mistress Fuyd, "and your own race incarcerated you."

"Pure jealousy," answered Hoffa. "And if you checked *all* the records, you'll see that the Teamsters continued to run even while I was in stir. *That's* why I offered to be your leader. I'll take the heat, and you'll keep on truckin'. Or jettin'. Or whatever."

A wichtigo stepped forward. "Why are you here at all?" it asked. "Why aren't you back on Earth, organizing strikes and pension funds and whatever else it is that you do?"

"You want the truth?" asked Hoffa.

"Please."

"I'm a modest man, and I was so popular people wouldn't leave me alone. Gorgeous oversexed women kept breaking into my house to thank me for helping them obtain full dental care. Politicians from both parties kept asking me to run for President. *Fortune* and *Business Week* were always after me for interviews, and the *Christian Science Monitor* wanted me to write a daily column on the strong moral code that led me to become such a successful man of the people." He paused and shrugged. "What could I do? They had become too dependent upon me. So I faked my own death, took just enough money from the pension fund to meet my modest needs, and I was leading a humble incognito life under an assumed name in the presidential suite of the Hong Kong Hilton when one of your gonzos—"

"Gnuzzits."

"Gezundheit," said Hoffa. "Anyone, a gonzo snatched me and brought me up here."

"And all that is absolutely true?" said the wichtigo dubiously.

"As God is my witness," said Hoffa, holding his right hand up.

"I guess we'll take your word for it," said the wichtigo. "For now."

"You don't take anything at face value," said Hoffa. "I like that in a man—or a whatever-you-are. You got a name, son?"

"Mercortule."

"I'll remember it," promised Hoffa. "Anyway, I think this has been a successful first meeting. My vice chairman Kenny here will let you know when we're having the next one. But I got a good feeling about this. I wouldn't want to be a floppy stockbroker a month from now."

"Flappa," Mistress Fuyd corrected him.

"Flappa to you, too," said Hoffa, shaking what passed for her hand. "Thank you all for coming." After they had filed out, Ken approached Hoffa.

"So you faked your death!" he said. "Everyone always wondered."

"The feds wanted me dead, the Mafia wanted me dead, even the Teamsters wanted me dead. I figured the only way I was gonna survive my murder was if I committed it myself." He looked around to make sure the room was empty. "Now to business. You know that little bastard, Mercantile?"

"You mean Mercortule?"

Hoffa nodded. "When everyone's asleep, find an airlock and put him in orbit." He grimaced. "If there's one thing I hate, it's a lippy alien."

11

It took seven months for the Brotherhood of Enlightened Aliens to bring the galactic economy to a screeching halt.

It took two weeks of negotiations before the races that ruled the Sevagram, or at least the Spiral Arm of the Milky Way, agreed to supply medical and dental care to the gnuzzits, the wichtigos, and the other oppressed races of the sector, as well as vacation time, sick leave, personal days, profit sharing, and 401Ks. They dug their heels in—not that any of them actually *had* any heels—at committing never to deal with a non-union shop, especially since there was only one union, but after another general strike they capitulated.

Things went swimmingly—which is probably a poor way of stating it, since there were a lot of things in the galaxy, and many of them spent their entire lives immersed in water or more noxious liquids, coming to the surface only to chat with fishermen, sing folk songs, and sign up for the union. Let us say, then, that things went smoothly— yes, that's the word: smoothly—for the better part of a year. Everyone, even the toothless raxiia, received dental care; everyone, even the muskagogees, who laid 4,000 eggs a month, got paternity leave. Everyone worked, everyone got a handsome pay raise, everyone looked forward to a retirement in which every need was taken care of thanks to astute management of the union's assets.

And then one day the pension fund was gone, and so was Jimmy Hoffa.

12

The President followed H. Saddler into the small fourth-floor room in the Executive Office Building. It was 4:05am, and there was no one there except a lone guard who was totally loyal, to Saddler if not the President. Even the Secret Service had been ordered to remain in the underground passageway leading to the White House.

"Are you sure this is necessary?" asked the President.

"Mr. President, it is more than necessary. It is essential. Even if you weren't at a twenty-three percent approval rating in the polls, this is an opportunity you can't pass up."

"It's not my fault!" muttered the President. "Paraguay and Uraguay sound so much alike! Someone should have corrected me when I gave the order to attack."

"That's in the past," said Saddler. "As is Uraguay, alas. But what you're doing now will make you the most important President since—"

"Truman?" interrupted the President hopefully.

"Think bigger."

"The Roosevelts?"

"Bigger still."

"Honest Abe himself?"

Saddler nodded.

"And you're saying this one meeting will accomplish that?"

"This one meeting will be the first step toward accomplishing that."

"And how did you hear about this, Mr. Saddler?" asked the President. He wanted to be informal, to call the man by his first name, but he didn't know his first name, and it seemed awkward to just called him "H."

"I have my sources." Saddler looked at his wristwatch. "He's due here any minute."

"It occurs to me that the guards will never let him in."

"Then it's fortunate that I sent them all home, isn't it?"

"But... but what if some thief sneaks into the building while they're gone?"

Saddler smiled. "This is the Executive Office Building, Mr. President. You don't really think there's anything worth stealing here, do you?"

The President considered it. "No, I suppose not."

"When you get right down to it, the most valuable thing here is a list of the better escort services in Washington DC—and even if someone steals a copy, there are four hundred more in the building."

There was a knock at the door.

"Come in," said Saddler.

Jimmy Hoffa entered the room, peering into the darkened corners to make sure no one besides Saddler and the President was there.

"Mr. President, say hello to Mr. Hoffa."

"*The* Mr. Hoffa?" asked the President.

"Call me Jimmy," said Hoffa, pulling up a chair.

"Mr. Hoffa has a proposition that I think will meet with your approval, sir," said Saddler. "Jimmy?"

"Right," said Hoffa. "I've spent the last few years... well, *elsewhere*. And in the process I learned a lot of things that affect the security of the United States, which I love as if it was my own country."

"It *is* your own country," said the President.

"Don't interrupt," said Hoffa. "Anyway, I had to leave my last position in a hurry, and I have reason to believe some of my former associates are gunning for me—especially one called Kenny."

"Should I know why?" asked the President.

"It's not important," said Saddler. "Go on, Jimmy."

"Anyway, I didn't come back empty-handed," said Hoffa. "I'm prepared to make a deal."

"What have you got that we could possibly want?" asked the President.

"A list of every illegal alien in the country—names, addresses, IDs, everything."

"And in exchange?"

"You get me the best plastic surgeon on the East Coast, give me a new face and a new identity, and put me in the witness protection program."

"All that, just for identifying a few illegal aliens?" said the President dubiously.

"There are more than a few," said Hoffa.

"Even so, they're just illegals. We've got fifteen million of them."

"These guys are a little more."

The President looked confused. "More illegal?"

"More alien."

"Where is this list?" asked the President.

"In a safe place," said Hoffa. "Now, do we have a deal?"

The President looked at Saddler, who nodded almost imperceptibly.

"We have a deal," said the President.

And that is the story, true in every detail, of how Jimmy Hoffa faked his own death a second time and saved America from an alien invasion, the magnitude of which had not been seen since the prior year along the Mexican border.

Epilogue

Praslin Island really isn't known for much except the Coco de Mer, and since this is a G-rated story, or at least PG, we're not at liberty to tell you why all the Victorian explorers were fascinated by it. (But it's a really neat story. Remember to ask us about it over drinks. Your treat.)

Still, it's a relatively untouched tropical paradise, and one of the things that remains most untouched is the burly, gray-haired gentleman with the brand-new face who spends most of his time lounging on the northern beach under a huge umbrella, his every need catered to by three unbelievably gorgeous bikini-clad women whose signet rings identify them as members of the most secret branch of the CIA.

Occasionally some tourist finds himself within a couple of hundred yards of the burly gentleman, and is promptly carted away for questioning, then released on neighboring La Digue island with just enough time left on his visa to get home.

Only one visitor is ever allowed to come closer. He usually carries a briefcase, and his suit and tie show him to be a stranger to the tropics. His passport displays only an initial for his first name, but no one ever challenges it.

He was there again just the other day. The burly man welcomed him, had one of the girls fetch a pair of beers, and lit up a cigar.

"What is it this time?"

"Your information about the Kennedy brothers, John Lennon, James Dean, Amelia Earhart, and Alydar checked out, but I still have a couple of questions about the Garfield assassination. Can you point me in the right direction?"

"Sure can," said the man.

"What is it going to cost this time?"

"I don't know," said the burly man, leaning forward and smiling. "Let's negotiate."

The People's Machine

Tobias S. Buckell

Tobias S. Buckell is the author of three very fine books, Crystal Rain, Ragamuffin, *and* Sly Mongoose, *stand-alone but linked adventure tales that collectively bring a refreshingly different Caribbean flavor to the science fiction genre. Aztecs and airships factor in to these stories as well, as they do in the tale that follows—though not the* same *Aztecs and airships, mind you. I first met Tobias before any of his books let the wider world in on his talent, in San Jose in 2002, the same year that he was nominated for the John W. Campbell Award for Best New SF Writer, and to hear him tell it my inclusion of his story in this anthology makes good on a promise of working together I made five years ago at that time. Given the adventure that follows, I'd say it was worth the wait.*

Inquisitor, warrior, and priest, Ixtli's fast-paced journey by airship began in Tenochtitlan, facing the solemn row of white-robed pipiltin. The rulers of the grandest city of the world had roused him from his house, burly Jaguar Scouts with rifles throwing open his doors and shouting him awake.

"I'm to go to New Amsterdam?" Ixtli could hardly keep the distaste out of his voice. The colonies were cold now, and filthy, and smelly.

Mecatl, the eldest of the pipiltin and rumored favorite of the Steel Emperor, explained. "There has been a murder there."

"And have the British lost the ability to police their own?" Ixtli had little love for the far north.

"The murder is of a young man. His heart has been removed in what looks like an Eagle sacrifice. Find out the truth of the matter, and whether apostate priests have immigrated to New Amsterdam."

This was news to Ixtli. Followers of the sacrifice usually inhabited borderlands between cities, scattered and un-united. None of them tried to keep the old ways in any Mexica city.

But in the chaos of a savage, foreign city like New Amsterdam, maybe they could rebuild their followers.

"And if I find it's so?" Ixtli asked the pipiltin.

"Find the truth," they told him. "If it is true, then we will have to root out the heresy from a distance. But if it is not true, we need to find out what is happening."

And seven hours later Ixtli was passing out of his father country and into the great swathe of territory the French called Louisiana, the large airship he'd booked passage on powering hard against the winds. After a refueling stop at the end of the first day's travel it was over the Indian lands, and then, finally, they touched down on the edges of New Amsterdam airfield. Two days. The world was shrinking, Ixtli thought, and he did not know if that was a good thing.

Pale faces looked up at Ixtli, colonials dressed in little more than rags, tying off the airship's ropes as they fell down toward the trampled grass. They shouted in guttural languages: English, Dutch, French. Ixtli knew many of them from his days along the Mexica coast, fighting them all during the invasions of '89.

The airship's gondola finally kissed the earth, and ramps were pulled out.

Ixtli walked off, porters following with his suitcases. The cold hit him and he shivered in his purple and red robes, the feather in his carefully tied hair twisted in the biting wind.

A bulbous-nosed man in a thick wool cape and earmuffs strode confidently forward, his hand extended. "Gordon Doyle, sir, at your service!"

Ixtli looked down and did not take the man's hand in his own, but gave him a slight nod of his head. "I am Ixtli."

"Splendid, what's your last name?"

"I am just Ixtli." He stared at Gordon, who rubbed his hand on his cape and fumbled around with a pipe.

"Well, Ixtli, I just arrived from London the day before it happened. Scotland Yard needed me over here to find the Albany Rapist. Bad series of events, that. Poor urchins, bad way to end it, very sensational, all over the papers."

Gordon was a jittery man. "Did you solve it?" Ixtli asked.

"Um, no, not yet. But come, I have a hansom waiting."

The murder site was in the Colonial Museum, a massive neo-Dutch structure embedded in the east side of New Amsterdam's Central Park. The driver whipped the massive beast of a horse up to speed and took them down the Manhattan thoroughfares.

"It's such a vibrant city, this," Gordon said, the acrid smell of his pipe wafting across over the smell of horseshit and garbage. The city, as packed and heavy with people as it was, placed its garbage on the streets to be picked up.

At least the city had sewers.

Ixtli leaned back, looking up at the buildings. This island was denser than Tenochtitlan. Large buildings, some over ten stories high and made of brick, lined the road on his left. Greenery and park, with cook fires and shantytowns that dotted it, lined his right.

Gordon noticed Ixtli looking. "Revolutionaries. This year's batch anyway. The Crown recently seized the land of the 'Americans.' Think they would have learned their lesson from the last time. Damn terrorists."

"You let them camp on your public lands?"

"Well, the homeless are always a problem in big cities. They skulk around here hoping one day to rise up again."

The cab lurched to a stop and the horse farted. Ixtli leapt down into the mud and walked up to the giant, imposing steps of the Colonial Museum. He was chilled to the core and wanted to get out of the wind. "Have you investigated any of the revolutionaries in the park?"

Gordon cleared his throat loudly. "Dear God, man, what do you take me for, a simpleton? Of course."

Ixtli ignored the reaction and stepped through the brass doorframes and into the museum past waiting policemen. Come see the original colonial declaration of secession, a poster proclaimed, next to an encased poster that showed a snake cut in thirteen pieces.

"Let's see this."

The young man in question had been left for two days at the request of the Mexica via telegraph. There was the telltale sign of faint bloating. Both Gordon and Ixtli held handkerchiefs to their noses as they approached the body.

Ixtli peered in at the body, then looked around. "The room has not been touched, or the floor cleaned? Was there blood on the floor apart from what the body pooled out?"

"None of that nature," Gordon confirmed.

"The manner in which the chest has been split, while similar, is done in a much more calculated manner than any normal ceremonial practice. And then there is one other thing."

"Entrails are still in his body." Gordon stabbed the air with his pipe. "Usually both are burnt, are they not?"

"There is also no blood on this floor, from ripping them out. This was done in a surgical manner, with the heart being removed and taken out in a waterproof container. No doubt to sensationalize and excite people in New Amsterdam," Ixtli said. "This is not the work of a warrior priest."

And that was a relief.

Gordon did not look as relieved, however. He made a face. "Well, I guess that rather leaves it all up in the air."

"Do you have any other leads?"

"Nothing of any particular sorts," Gordon said. "You were our best, as it would have allowed us to start questioning around certain areas."

Ixtli shook his head. "Round up the brown skinned?"

Gordon at least had the decency of looking somewhat embarrassed. "One of the guards saw someone."

"Dark skinned."

"Red, is actually what he said." Gordon hailed a hansom. Ixtli looked over at the curb, where a small group of dirty urchins had melted out of the bush to stare at them. Cold hard stares, devoid of curiosity.

One of them held a small, stiff piece of paper in his left hand, fingering it reverently.

"Red like me?" They melted back into the bushes of Central Park under Ixtli's stare.

The hansom shook as Gordon stepped in. "We didn't pull out an artist's palette and paints. When your embassy found the headline and details, and said they were sending you over, we had hoped they might know something. The method of death is... unique." Gordon tapped the driver perched on the rear of the cab and gave him directions to the hotel Ixtli would be staying at.

"Ah, you talk about the past, Mr. Doyle, and nothing but the past. You should know better."

And on this note, Gordon smiled. "And yet you are here, sir. So speedily. So sanctioned by your country. It suggests that there may have been something."

The man, Ixtli thought, didn't miss much. "Do you know what I am, Mr. Doyle?"

"I have my suspicions."

"I am no spy. I am an inquisitor. It is my job to find heretics. It is my job to find them and stop their heresy." They clip-clopped their way down into the maze of New Amsterdam's chaotic business. "When your people invaded—"

"The Spanish, sir, the Spanish, not us..."

Ixtli shrugged. To him one European was just like another. "They had several advantages against us. Guns, steel, disease, but most importantly, the numbers and fighters of Tlaxcala who hated our taxes and loss of life to the blade of the priest. When Cortez took our leader hostage and Moctezuma stood before our city and told us to bow to the Spanish, we stoned him to death and elected a new leader, and drove the white men from our city. We fought back and forth, dying of disease, but fighting for our existence.

"We'd already killed our emperor. We were bound by tradition, and religion, but it kept hindering us. The living city leaders decided only radical new ways of thinking could save us, and the first was to renounce our taxes on tributary cities, and claim that we would no longer sacrifice the unwilling to our gods. And we made good with actions. It was bloody and long, Gordon, but an idea, an idea is something amazing. Particularly when it spreads.

"So what I do is help that idea. That blood sacrifice isn't required, that people are equal under the Mexica, and that we are an alternative to the way of the invaders. And those who want the old religions, the old ways, I hunt them down, Mr. Doyle, I hunt them down and exact a terrible price from them."

"And you are here to make sure your image as past savages isn't continued?"

"Something like that." The Mexica made a point of stealing the brightest heretics from Europe over the last 300 years. You wouldn't get burned in Tenochtitlan, you could print your seditions against European thought there, and anything useful, anything invented, all benefited the Mexica.

Anything that faulted that haven needed to be destroyed.

That was Ixtli's job.

In the sitting room of the cramped, smelly, dank hotel room that professed to be properly heated, Ixtli removed his colorful cape, hung the gold armband of his profession up, and sighed.

Gordon Doyle followed him in and looked around. "Grand, this. I had a last thing. You never asked if we had identified the body."

"I had assumed you would tell me when you felt it was important. Is it?"

"Important. Somewhat. The grandson of one of the prominent revolutionaries." Gordon stood there, waiting for some reaction.

"I have no theories, certainly there is no reason I know that my country would need some dissident killed in a way that makes us look culpable." Ixtli shivered. This was like standing up on a mountain. "Isn't our business over, now? You can go find some other brown-skinned people as your suspects."

With a tap of a finger on his awkwardly sized hat Gordon backed out the door. "I'll give you a ride in the morning to the airfield."

"My thanks."

Ixtli sat near the heater for a while, trying to warm up, and then finally gave up the attempt as futile and crawled under the thick and scratchy woolen blankets.

His feet never seemed to stop aching, but after a while he relaxed and fell into a light sleep with the odd shiver or two spaced a few minutes apart.

That was until he heard a foot creak on a nearby floorboard.

Ixtli rolled off and under his bed just as a large club smacked into his pillow. Just as quickly he rolled back out and swept the attacker off his feet with one good kick to the nearest kneecap and a sweeping motion with his other leg.

He was rewarded with a half-hearted jab to his thigh with the club. Stone chips ripped at his skin.

It was a macehuitl, the club.

What on earth was someone doing with a museum piece like that?

But it was just a feint. The attacker grabbed him for a takedown, and they were both on the floor, rolling around, Ixtli realizing that the man's heavy weight lent him a major advantage.

It was a scraping, heaving, bloody bashing fight that resembled something between a Grecian wrestling match and a cock fight, and it ended only when Ixtli wrestled the macehuitl away and clubbed the man in his face.

Ixtli looked something like a stereotype when Gordon responded to his urgent message, delivered to the concierge by the pneumatic speaking tube in his room: he sat on his bed, still holding the squat fighting club with the sharp stone bits embedded on its sides, blood dripping, the vanquished foe by his feet.

"Dear God!" Gordon said.

"He isn't Mexica," Ixtli said.

"Well, someone is working awfully hard to make sure it looks like that."

Ixtli looked down at the man and bent to rifle his pockets. No papers of any sort. Except for a stiff, beige card with holes poked through it. Ixtli held it up. "But we do have something here."

Gordon looked at it. "A loom card?"

Ixtli nodded. "It's your best clue yet, they didn't count on an Ambassador being a skilled warrior. Find out who makes it, or even who purchased it. We don't have much time before they find out their man is dead."

"I'll get right on it. I'll send some men up to get the body. They'll also stay and keep guard in a new room that we'll be getting you into."

"Thank you." But Ixtli didn't think he would be sleeping.

He called down to the concierge to pass on the message that he would not be taking the next airship home.

Ixtli would see this to its end.

Gordon found him in the restaurant before sunbreak poring over hot coffee, the closest thing Ixtli could get to cacoa. It warmed him.

"I heard you weren't returning to your homeland?" Gordon asked.

"News travels quickly." Ixtli stirred in honey. "I want to know who wants me dead. A professional courtesy, I had hoped you would understand."

"A case could take weeks, or months, to crack. It's not a case of roughing up the bystanders and accusing people of crimes. It's a methodical thing, filled with suppositions and theories that need to be validated or checked. One must be cool and moderate, and uninvolved."

"By then your trail will have gone cold." Ixtli sipped the coffee. Passable. Very passable. He smiled for the first time in the last two days. "I think, Mr. Doyle, that you and I have something in common."

"What's that?"

"We're both children of the enlightenment."

Gordon stiffened. "I wouldn't say that around here. French revolutionaries and colonialist terrorists were the children of the enlightenment."

Ixtli laughed. "Not politically. I am speaking of your reverence for the truth, the interest in where the trail will lead. And now I have the greatest mystery in front of me: someone wants me dead. I admit, I'm very curious."

Gordon didn't look so sure. Ixtli kept a mask of geniality on. It was not quite true, what he'd said. Underneath he simmered to find the true assassin behind all this.

"Okay," Gordon said. "But you are unarmed, right? I don't want you causing any trouble."

"I am unarmed." Ixtli spread his arms.

Gordon slapped the loom card on the table. "Then we visit the makers of this. And tonight we'll switch you to a new hotel."

* * *

The giant brick building near the docks of New Amsterdam, chimneys looming overhead, was called the HOLLERITH MACHINE COMPANY. A Mr. Jason Finesson waited for them, resplendent in tails and a tall hat, spectacles clamped down over his nose hard enough to leave a welt.

"Detective." He shook Gordon's hand, and then turned to Ixtli. "And sir."

Ixtli gave a nod of the head and turned to Gordon, who pulled out the offending card. Ixtli wasn't sure why they were at a machining company, but he declined to say anything out loud. If a card could control a loom for weavers, maybe it could control other kinds of machines.

"Ah." Mr. Finesson looked at the card. "A punch card. Your message; you do say you found it at a crime scene?"

Gordon nodded. "Yes."

"How curious." Finesson held it up to the gaslight in the corner of the room. A bored-looking secretary with perfectly slicked back hair in a black suit sat poring over a ledger laid out across his desk by the entrance. "Well, I can tell you the very machine it was made on."

"Excellent." Gordon looked elated. The thrill of the hunt.

"But that won't help you much," Finesson continued. "Our customers use these in bulk for all sorts of things. I couldn't tell you which customer this comes from."

Ixtli had been staring at the man. He looked assured, confident, as if he were telling the truth. "You are the manager here?"

"Yes."

"What exactly do your customers use these things for?"

"Ah, let me show you."

Finesson escorted them back through the dim hallways of the building into a large room several stories high that looked like it was the lovechild of a Swiss watchmaker and a train engineer. Massive gears and wheels strained, clicking away on bearings the size of a man. All throughout pulleys and shafts spun, and a massive steam boiler, fit to power a trans-Atlantic ship, squatted in the center of the room, steam hissing lazily out the pipes connected to it.

"Last summer we were commissioned to count the census of the colonies, sirs. Since then we've processed merchant accounts, calculated the mysteries of the universe for leading scientists, and been available for engineers."

"That's a mechanical adding machine," Ixtli said. "I've heard of these."

Finesson pranced around the entryway like a circus grandmaster. "Oh, but it's so much more. Complex maths, instructions, this is a computing machine, gentleman. One of only four or five like it in the world! I'll wager you, sirs, that if you could take the mathematics of policing, and reduce it to calculations and variables and insert it into this machine, we could run your police force."

"Another child of the enlightenment I presume," Gordon said out of the side of his mouth to Ixtli, who was still gaping at the machine.

"Even better," said Finesson. "I've talked to your counterparts, the Dutch constabulary here in New Amsterdam. Yes the British do an excellent job of co-ruling this tiny island, but why be so reactive? You know the study of physiognomy, wherein you can determine a person's character merely by studying their unique facial characteristics?"

Both Ixtli and Gordon nodded.

"Indeed, well I suggested to his Excellency Mr. Van Ostrand that, were we to take sketches of all the criminals encountered by his forces, load them into our device to find points of similarity, and then begin sketching in all manner of our population to load into our machine, we could find criminals *before* they commit their crimes. It would revolutionize your jobs, men."

Gordon and Ixtli glanced at each other. Ixtli spoke first. "And what if you were fingered by the device?"

"What? I'm no criminal," Finesson said. "How dare you! I have nothing to fear."

"I take it the Dutch have not invested in this idea?" Gordon changed the subject quickly.

"No," Finesson looked down at his shoe. "More's the pity."

"Indeed." Ixtli picked up a stray punch card and looked at it. It made no apparent sense to him, hundreds and hundreds of tiny pockmarks.

A man sitting behind the table on which the punchcards were stacked leaned forward and snatched the card back from Ixtli. "Please don't disturb the cards. The order in which we feed them into the machine is important, it tells them what to do."

"Well Mr. Finesson, we would like your customers records."

"And do you have a writ?"

Ixtli glanced at Gordon, who shook his head. "Not yet, sir."

"If my customers found out I turned over my books so easily, I could lose a great deal of business. There are forms and numbers and calculations being done by businesses here that would not want their information spread about the city."

"I understand."

And with that, a frustrated Gordon and Ixtli were back out, headed back to the hotel.

"That was a waste," Gordon said, stuffing a new pipe and looking annoyed. "Physiognomy..."

"Maybe that isn't so." Ixtli held a mirror in his hand, as if checking the makeup on his face. Behind them dashed an urchin, doing his best to keep up. In these crowded streets it was feasible. He rapped the roof to get the driver's attention and handed him paper money. "Stop here. I need you to wander off to one of these stores and purchase something. Take your time."

"Yessir." The driver's large sideburns rippled in the wind as he leapt out and strode past them.

"What on earth is this about?" Gordon

"Observation, Mr. Doyle. There is an urchin following us, and that very same creature was outside the Colonial Museum when we last left it. Is it coincidence that the very same urchin following us now, and that the previous time I saw him, seemed to have one of these punch cards on his person?"

"I would think not," muttered Gordon.

"Me neither."

Gordon looked around. "This is not a part of New Amsterdam for strangers to tarry in. Particularly ones in colorful capes such as yourself."

"Exactly the reason I chose it," Ixtli said, scanning the crowds pushing against street vendors, people dodging carriages. A tram thundered by, ringing its bell furiously. He pointed a young man out to Gordon. "Call that one over. The one selling those rotten-looking apples."

"Boy!"

The boy in question jogged over with the box of apples in front of his stomach, suspicion embedded in his glare. "What you want?"

Gordon showed his badge and grabbed the boy before he could turn and run.

Ixtli handed the boy a thick wad of paper money. "We have a job for you. That's half what you'll get if you succeed."

"It'd beat selling dodgy apples, you'll make a couple of weeks' worth from us," Gordon said, catching on. "And you don't want me asking where you got them from, now do you?"

The struggling ceased. "What you wanting then?"

"There's a mangy sort following this vehicle, no don't look, and we want you to follow him in turn. No doubt he'll spring off to inform someone of where we are when we reach our hotel. Follow him, but don't let him see you. Find us back at the Waldorf Hotel. Ask for Doyle."

The boy tugged on his cap. "Yessir."

"And here is our driver," Ixtli said. "Take the apples so the urchin suspects nothing."

Gordon did, and the driver, taking it all in his stride, just asked, "Shall I restart the cab, sirs?"

"Yes, let's move on."

The driver disappeared behind them. The cab shook as he climbed into his perch looking over the cab, and then the hansom jerked into motion. Ixtli settled back in.

"Clever," said Gordon.

"If it works." Ixtli looked down at the rotten apples. He was going to gibe Gordon about the hungry on the streets of New Amsterdam, and then decided to leave the man alone.

"So now we retire to the hotel and wait."

"You told me this was a pursuit for the moderate and patient."

Gordon sighed.

Their urchin showed up outside the hotel as they were just setting in to dine. Ixtli spotted the hotel staff confronting the young boy as he maintained his need to see them right away.

Ixtli and Gordon walked out to the street. "What do you have for us?"

"I know where the boy went." The boy was still out of breath from his run.

"Take us there!"

"What about my money?"

Ixtli felt around in his cape, pulled out enough for the cab fare, and looked at Gordon, who patted his pockets. "I left what I had on the table for the meal."

"We'll get to a bank, but after you show us where the boy went."

"Dammit, I knew you was going to gyp me."

"Look at us, do we look like the sort to play games like that?" Gordon yelled.

The boy looked him up and down. "I guess not," he conceded. "But I'm going to get my money." On that he was dead certain.

They hailed a hansom. "East River Waterfront," the boy said. They piled in, squeezing the boy between them. He reeked of sweat and body odor, and he grumbled about their lack of payment all the way.

As the great East River Bridge loomed and they slowed, the boy crawled up to poke his head around to the back and guide the cabbie toward a set of large brick warehouses.

HOLLERITH WAREHOUSING.

"Hah," Gordon said. "Nothing to fear from physiognomy indeed."

"Finesson could be innocent and unaware." Ixtli jumped out of the hansom and paid the cabbie.

Gordon agreed, and handed the driver a card he'd scribbled something on. "The constabulary will triple your usual if you hang around at the ready."

The driver nodded and accepted the promise of payment.

"Look," the boy said. "Be careful. The boys I followed was Constitutionalists. You don't want to tangle with that lot."

"Thank you," Ixtli patted him on the shoulder. "If we're not back in fifteen minutes, call the police."

"Like hell," the boy said.

"They'll pay you," Gordon said.

"I'll consider it."

And then he was gone, watching them from the shadows. No doubt ready to rabbit off at a moment's notice, but held there by the desire for his money to come back.

* * *

"So what are we looking for?" Gordon asked as they circled the building.

"An easy opening," Ixtli replied. There was a rumbling that seemed to permeate through the ground all around.

"We don't have a writ to enter."

"But I have diplomatic immunity." Ixtli found a window that was loose, and with some persuading, forced it open. "Care to accompany me lest my life be threatened and an incident between our respective countries occurs?"

Gordon licked his lips. "Damned if I do..."

Ixtli waited for the second part of the sentence. None came, so he pulled himself up and over into the warehouse.

Gordon scrabbled up and in after him. The warehouse was dark, shadows of pallets and crates loomed all around them. Gordon took out an electric torch and clicked it on.

The entire warehouse lit up, gas lamps all throughout springing up to full flame. A crowd of very serious-looking childlike faces stared at them, and at their head, a giant of a man, a dockworker, held a long coil of loop in his large hands.

"Welcome to the United Peoples," he growled. Ixtli stared at the long tattoo of a chopped-up snake on his left forearm. Don't tread on me, it said.

Ixtli doubted anyone would be able to, not with all that muscle.

Three more dockworkers stepped forward, surrounding them.

In short order both men were tied up, Gordon handcuffed with his own cuffs despite both giving a brief struggle.

"May I ask why we're being detained?" Gordon asked. He had a purple bruise over his left eye, and Ixtli admired his cool under the situation. Ixtli himself considered a prayer to the gods.

"You damn well know you was trespassing," the giant of a man growled. "Don't play coy, eh?"

"Okay. So what are we waiting for?"

"Who."

The three men melted aside, giving way to a man in a stovepipe hat and long tails. A craggy face regarded them both. This was interesting. They weren't dead yet.

"Mr. Hollerith?" Ixtli asked.

The man removed his hat and handed it over to an urchin. A stool was presented for him to sit on. "Justin Hollerith. Are you here to assassinate me?"

"Here to find the killer of that boy at the Colonial Museum," Gordon said.

"Well huzzah," Hollerith said. "You have found the killer."

Gordon tensed in his chair. "You?"

Hollerith shook his head. He snapped his fingers and the mass of urchins shifted. A massive curtain slowly rolled aside to reveal a machine that made the one at Hollerith's offices look like a toy.

The entire warehouse was filled with rotating shafts that went on and on, and thousands of gears. Young boys ran from station to station with armloads of punch cards.

That explained the vibrating floors and roads outside. Ixtli glanced around, wondering how it would be explained to his family that he had died, strapped to a chair in some dirty city up north.

No honor in this, he thought. None at all.

"Here is your killer," Hollerith said. "How do you plan on bringing it to justice?"

Gordon shook his head. "I don't understand."

Hollerith spread his arms wide to indicate the sheer presence of the machine. "You, Aztec, should know what we are going through right now."

"Indeed?" Ixtli perked up. The man was still talking, waiting for something, eager to prove... something. If they could keep him talking, then maybe there would be time for the boy outside to go for the police.

If he did ever go. That was a gamble.

"The tyrants and occupiers of our lands." Hollerith got up and Ixtli tensed. "The colonies tried to rise once, to be crushed on their boots."

"You're a dissident," Gordon hissed.

"Revolutionaries! Visionaries!" Hollerith stood up. "Gentleman, what you see before you is the engine of a new future. The British boot will be forced back. This machine is the constitution of the new United States of America."

"The what?" Ixtli remembered that the boy had called these people constitutionalists.

Now Hollerith paced in front of them. "A set of rules for governing us—fair, impartial, and written by the people. The tyrants refused to let man rule himself, and so we've had to go underground. Slowly, building our ranks. We have citizens all throughout the thirteen colonies, waiting for their moment to rise up."

One of the dockworkers took out a punch card from the end of a station. "Mister Hollerith." He handed it over.

Hollerith glanced at the card. He blinked. "I hold here your future, gentlemen."

Ixtli looked at the complex pattern of holes. "Really? The machine dictates your actions?"

"What is government but a set of programmed instructions we all agree upon? And in a democracy, it is blind, and her instructions carried out by men. This is no different.

"The things that happen to us, we feed them into the computer, and it sorts its responses and hands them back to us on our cards, telling us how to serve it best. Judgments, foreign policies, and now… war. It is our destiny, it always has been, to spill out throughout this country and claim it for ourselves. To spread from sea to sea. Already telegraph operators string throughout the thirteen, even through the Indian lands between us and the west coast, passing on and coordinating instructions with other constitutional machines running in parallel all throughout the land. The US will rise again."

"Manifest destiny, embodied within the unflinching intelligence of a computing machine," Ixtli said.

"You've heard of the theory? The machine decided that a diplomatic incident would be what we needed. It said to look out for anything resembling one, so that we could use that to gain recruits, and worry people about the threat of foreign murderers here in our city."

"The theory is that your race is somehow owed it all: the lands of the Mexica, the Indians, and what the British rule already. Yes, I've heard this before. In Texcaco, yes, in the Mexica–Americas war. Many of your border men, out of the reach of the British, were prodded on by the Louisiana French by having that belief dangled before them. An ugly scene."

"This will be different." Hollerith looked at the punch card. "I'm sorry, but as enemies of the state, you will not have a trial. You will be executed as spies. So says the Constitution."

"So says the Constitution," murmured the hundreds in the warehouse.

"You'll be taken to a room, where ten blindfolded men with rifles will fire. The Constitution will randomly load a pair of guns. Take them away."

Gordon struggled again, but Ixtli remained calm. "Now you are killing harmless public servants in the name of your cause, just like any other group of dissidents."

Hollerith refused the bait. "I have sworn to protect the Constitution, gentlemen, from all its enemies. Your rhetoric will have little impact on me."

The three dockworkers moved in, and Ixtli walked with them through the rows of furiously spinning clockwork and blank government officials' faces.

They were forced into a tiny closet, and the door was barred shut.

"Thanks for delaying them," Gordon said, leaning against the wall.

"I did what I could." Ixtli moved around in the dark, trying to find out if there was anything useful, but it had been emptied.

"When they find us dead, I imagine my heart will be cut out," Gordon said. "And you will be dead nearby of a gunshot, maybe?"

"It will stir up enmity, feed unity and a sense that they need to cohere against an outside force."

It wasn't just his death, but the betrayal of his country. Ixtli kicked at the door in frustration.

"Hey," a familiar voice hissed. The door cracked open and in slipped the boy. He left the door ajar, the welcome light bringing their temporary cell out of the deep dark and into murkiness. "I knew you'd get yourselves in it deep and end up losing me my money."

"Did you call the police?" Gordon asked.

"Police? No damn police. Just Slim Tim."

"Who's Slim Tim?" Ixtli moved closer to the boy.

"Who's Slim Tim? he asks. Slim Tim is me!" Slim Tim slit the ropes off.

"And no one noticed you?" Gordon asked.

Slim Tim shrugged. "They was busy with the lights." He smiled, and then counted off his fingers. On the last one something boomed loudly and Slim Tim chuckled. Light flashed and danced brightly.

Gordon pulled the last of his rope free. "Let's make a break for it."

They glanced out of the closet. Nothing but people tending the machine.

"Run," Ixtli said.

They skirted the dark walls, ducking and weaving around the dangerous moving parts of the living machine. The escape almost worked, but near the doors a man throwing switches paused, frowned, and shouted at them.

The cry went up all throughout the warehouse, and the ten men with rifles ran through an aisle of machinery, blindfolds loose around their necks. "Stop."

"Only two of the guns will kill us," Ixtli said. "Run for it, and whoever survives, get out to call the officials."

"Scatter," Gordon said, and they did. All ten rifles fired, and Ixtli felt relief. Nothing had hit him, no bullets pinged, they were all blanks. He turned the corner with the other three before the second round of fire, this one not loaded with blanks, could be fired.

They burst out of the main doors, ran down the corners out to where the hansom waited, and all three piled in shouting, "Go, go, go."

"You pay me now," Slim Tim said. "Very next thing."

Ixtli grabbed Slim Tim's shoulders. "You're damn right we pay you next." He shook the boy. "You will make a small fortune tonight, Mr. Tim, a small fortune."

Gordon met Ixtli the next morning at the airfield before he left and stuck his hand out. "Mr. Ixtli, my thanks."

Ixtli regarded the offered hand. A strange custom. He took it carefully and finished the American ritual, a sign of respect for what they had both been through. "Did you get Hollerith?"

Gordon shook his head. "They smashed the machine, and took their punch cards with them. We reduced their abilities significantly though, thanks to you."

"Thanks to you. I imagine my superiors would find this a fascinating tale. I have to wonder what they will do with the information. Computer-run governments and humans no better than automatons, run by small dots on a piece of paper."

"What a barbarous idea, letting machines rule you."

Ixtli looked around. "What is a government but rules and ideas that are set down on paper, and then interpreted and run by individual human machines? Is it really that far fetched?"

"But cogs and wheels? We will find these people and their cards and burn them out."

Ixtli nodded, relieved. The Constitutionalists had taken all their punch cards with them. Good. "Of course, that is the typical response of a nation. But Gordon remember this: all ten of those weapons fired were blank, we were never hit."

"What do you mean?"

"A government is the will of its people, and the will of Hollerith is twisted. He and his people want land, and revolution, and blood. Revenge against the British. Manifest destiny above all else.

"But if the pure ideals of an idea were really input into a machine, maybe it fought back, Mr. Doyle. Maybe it told all those soldiers to load blanks. And Hollerith indicated that maybe the machine hadn't ordered that man's death at the museum, but merely suggested they look for such an incident."

"Maybe," Gordon said. "Maybe."

"Consider it, that the ideas are what are important. If you ever come to Tenochtitlan, make sure to visit," Ixtli smiled. "Where the pursuit of truth reigns free, and all manner of theories live side by side, jostling each other."

They shook hands again, and then Gordon grabbed Ixtli's shoulder.

"I have a favor to ask, now that we have solved this crime and my men are looking for Hollerith, might I get your permission to send my notes and files to my brother? He fancies himself something of a writer and follows such things. Intrigue, and the sort."

"Of course," Ixtli said. "What is your brother's name?"

"Arthur."

"Just make sure my name is changed," Ixtli laughed. And with that last bit of business, the two men separated. Ixtli boarded the airship.

* * *

Somewhere past French Louisiana and over tribal lands, Ixtli reached under his coat and pulled out a stack of punch cards. An insurrection, guided by machine, could be imminently useful.

The basis of the computing machine's rules could be corrupted, maybe even by telegraph commands, or a hidden series of codes activated by punch cards slipped in by an agent. An agent who had been called north by a special signal, thanks to a series of preprogrammed instructions.

Ixtli's world faced threats. Spanish to the south, English colonies and French to the north, and the intermediate and forever fickle tribal societies in the midlands. Tenochtitlan was always aware of the need to keep the Europeans on their toes. Keeping the Europeans divided and fighting among themselves kept them from focusing their eyes on new land.

So now Ixtli held up the punch cards he had taken, the ones he'd replaced were now with the dissidents, and they were none the wiser.

He leaned out over the window, and dropped the cards to flutter in the wind.

Where they would land, he had no idea. It was not his place to know, or ask. He was just another agent in the vast machine that was his government.

Death on the *Crosstime Express*

Chris Roberson

A great deal of Chris Roberson's fiction output, of both novel and short story length, concerns the affairs of an extended family of adventurers known as the Bonaventure-Carmody clan. Like Michael Moorcock's famous Beck/Begg dynasty and Philip José Farmer's Wold-Newton stories before him, Roberson's multiverse (in his case called "the Myriad") is peopled with this reoccurring cast of characters, who manage to inveigle themselves into all the excitement to be found anywhere from zombie-filled Polynesian Islands to Counter Earths, from here to eternity. As he told the Web site Yatterings in an interview conducted July 2007, "I've got a real weakness for stories that mix genres, or at least blend different sub-genres, and I've always been a sucker for heroes." The Bonaventure-Carmody clan can be found in his novels Here, There & Everywhere, Paragaea: A Planetary Romance, Set the Seas on Fire, *and the forthcoming* End of the Century.

Chris is also the author of a series of alternate history tales about a space-faring Chinese Empire. To date, these include, The Voyage of Night Shining White, The Dragon's Nine Sons, Iron Jaw & Hummingbird, *and* Three Unbroken. *Chris is a three-time World Fantasy Award finalist, a two-time John W. Campbell Award for Best New Writer finalist, and both a finalist and a winner of the*

Sidewise Award for Alternate History. It is up to the careful reader to decide where in his Myriad the following story fits.

The airship which hung between the docking pylons, tethered fore and aft, was painted a dark shade of blue and trimmed with gold, the colors of the Crosstime Line. But even if one didn't recognize the coloration, the sheer size of the craft alone would have been enough to signal its importance. It dwarfed the other airships drifting at anchor in the Texican National Airfields on the outskirts of Waterloo. The smallest of the other craft, neither equipped with translocation engines nor rated for underspace passage if they had been, were locals, carrying passengers and freight to the Anglo-American Confederation, or across the seas to the French Workers Concordat or the Russian Czardom or Chinese Collective. Slightly larger were the intercontinua airships, which traveled to and from neighboring alternatives, spending hours, days, or weeks journeying through underspace to translocate into other worlds. But largest of all was the blue and gold immensity of the *Crosstime Express*, the pride of the line, which weekly made the journey from here to Helium and back again.

Vivian Starkweather checked the time. Slipping her watch back into its vest pocket, she held a lit match to the cigarillo clenched between her teeth.

"Don't worry, darlins," she said to the young women standing beside her at the base of the gangplank, jeweled bindis twinkling brightly in the morning sun against the dark skin of their foreheads. Starkweather expelled a stream of smoke from the corner of her mouth, and hooked her thumbs through her beltloops. "I expect we'll be boarding directly."

The Indian princesses didn't seem much to mind the delay, though, hardly noticing Starkweather's assurances, too busy making eyes at the younger members of the crew in their crisp white jackets and peaked caps, and especially at the ship's young steward, supervising the loading of comestible provisions onto the blue and gold craft.

Aside from being the site for the Crosstime Line's terminus, the only other item of interest about the alternative was that it was home to the Pinkertons, the private security firm routinely contracted by intercontinua businesses and governments alike. Many a smuggler, freebooter, or suspect fleeing prosecution had come to dread the baleful open eye which was the symbol of the men and women who lived up to their motto, "We Never Sleep."

Most of the intercontinua craft anchored around the airfield had come here for the same reason, ferrying passengers from neighboring alternatives, who now stood ready to mount the gangplank to the blue and gold airship. Travelers had made the journey here to catch the *Crosstime Express*, which would continue on to Helium, seat of the League of Worlds and hub of all intercontinua commerce in this region of the Myriad. A journey of less than three days, which shorter range vessels might take weeks or even longer to complete.

If the two young Indian women in their silk saris and silver bangles weren't bothered, though, there were others less sanguine about the delay. A pair of Russian monks in heavy cassocks shifted uneasily, their gaze darting back and forth nervously as they held their hands against their round bellies. And the mandarin whose ruby button atop his hat indicated the highest level of service to the emperor, in some distant alternative dominated by the Chinese throne, seemed ill-at-ease, as though uncertain about the correct protocol in such situations. But the most distressed by the inability of the passengers to board the ship were the trio of white-skinned men in their wool suits and bowler hats.

"This is intolerable, I say," blustered the man with the bushy mustache and red cheeks, who was evidently the leader of the three. "The agreement drawn up with the Crosstime Line clearly states that we are to have ample time to examine the security arrangements before departure."

Behind him stood a short, round man with a sheaf of papers in hand, and a slender man with a long nose and piercing blue eyes.

"I assure you, Mister Engel," said Captain N'Diklam, soothingly, "it will be only a momentary delay. We have had to take on relief crewmen, and it is simply taking longer to get them squared away than anticipated." The captain smiled, teeth white and even against his dark brown skin, and turned to confer with the bosun who had just ambled down the gangplank.

The three men were clearly not satisfied, but evidently saw little to be gained from pressing the issue at this point, and turned to walk away. They moved in concert, with almost military precision, the mustachioed Engel in the lead and the other two following at his flanks like a vanguard of birds in flight.

In the end, it was less than a quarter of an hour later before the gangplank was opened and the passengers allowed to board the *Crosstime Express.* Vivian Starkweather was one of the first onboard, to the consternation of the trio in their bowler hats, who were evidently some sort of security detachment that had booked passage to make preparations for another who would be joining them at a later stop on the journey. Starkweather, for her part, pretended not to notice the three men who glared daggers at her back, but had let her hand rest casually on the hilt of the Bowie knife hanging from her belt, as though to show that she was not without resources of her own. Rumored to be in the employ of one of the wealthier Texican gas-mining concerns, Starkweather was said to be journeying to Helium to negotiate an extremely lucrative trade agreement, but no one knew for certain.

In her mid-thirties, Starkweather was, if not classically beautiful, then at least ruggedly handsome. A few inches shy of six feet in height, with a mass of brown hair worn up in a bun at the back of her head, she had striking green eyes, a long nose, and strong jaw-line. She seemed to favor riding costume, trousers and matching jackets, with dinosaur-hide boots on her feet, a luxury item from an alternative far off in the Myriad where the terrible lizards never died out, a popular destination for wealthy hunters.

The other passengers who mounted the gangplank, after Starkweather and the bowler-hatted trio had boarded, included an Ambassador from the Reformed Dynast of Heliopolis and his slaves, from an alternative where the pyramid-builders still held sway; a group of Berber scholars from an Andalusia on an alternative dominated by a Mohammedan caliphate; the pair of Indian princesses in their finery, their luggage carried on the back of a miniature automaton elephant, steam hissing from its joints with each cumbersome step; a group of Maori from an alternative in which Polynesian princes ruled both hemispheres, though with their fearsome moko tattoos it was impossible to say whether they were diplomats or warriors; the ill-at-ease mandarin; an Aztec warlord in linen suit and tastefully garish waistcoat, with jade plugs in his lobes and a labret through his lower lip, traveling with a silent, unsmiling woman whose hair was cut in a bob and dyed purple, her hands and feet hennaed in sinewy patterns; and finally the pair of Russian monks in their heavy cassocks, whose nervousness seemed to vanish as they stepped onto the gangplank.

Starkweather, Engel and his security detachment, and the two Russians were the only passengers of European extraction in the first-class berths, with the rest riding in economy or steerage. Fair and even slightly tanned skin was something of a rarity onboard altogether, in fact, with only a bare handful of Europeans at all, and most of those either servants to other passengers or low-ranking members of the crew, like the sandy-haired steward who had so captured the attention of the Indian princesses.

The captain, Mba N'Diklam, was a follower of Sunni Islam, and a subject of a Jolof Empire whose reach extended far beyond the shores of western Africa. He smiled often, teeth straight and white against skin so dark it was almost black, and peppered his speech with words and phrases from his native Wolof. The rest of the crew in their crisp white jackets and peaked caps, on their lapels the blue-and-gold rosette of the Crosstime Line, were a mix of Malay, Tamil, Dayak, Athabascan, and European.

After the passengers had all boarded, and the luggage had been stowed, chimes sounded throughout the ship, signaling their impending departure. At the captain's invitation, the first-class passengers gathered in the drawing room to watch the launch through the heavily shielded portholes.

From takeoff through to the next scheduled landing, the *Crosstime Express* would remain sealed and pressurized, against the airless vacuum of underspace. The sound of the hatches being closed rang through the ship with an air of finality, and a few of those gathered in the drawing room seemed unsettled by the sound. Or perhaps merely unsettled by the thought of leaving the sane world of three dimensions behind when the translocation engine was engaged, and moving into the less sensible realm of underspace. The security detachment, in particular, appeared novices when it came to intercontinua travel, hailing from an alternative which had only recently learned of the Myriad and of the countless alternate worlds stretching out to infinity. But the two young Hindu women, as well, seemed somewhat unsettled, and huddled near one another on a low divan, talking in voices so low they could scarcely be heard.

Elsewhere, deep in the heart of the airship, the navigator cleared her thoughts, and set her mind on their destination. A seer, one of those rare souls able to peer beyond the fabric of the world, into and through underspace into the worlds beyond, the navigator was arguably the most essential member of the crew, as without her to guide them, once the translocation engine was engaged the ship could easily be lost forever, adrift and directionless in underspace. Almost equally invaluable, though, were the ship's defenders, senders able to broadcast their own thoughts into the ether; there were creatures who made underspace their home, monsters of pure appetite and sense-defying shape who swam in that strange region like sharks prowling the seas, and since conventional weapons were of little use against the creatures' diamond-hard skins, the only way to repel their voracious attacks was at the level of thought.

With a seer to guide them and a sender manning the defense, the ship required only an engineer to man the translocation engine, a pilot to man the helm, and a captain to command them.

When the *Crosstime Express* slipped its moorings, the captain ordered her elevated some three-quarters of a mile into the air. It was safest, when moving from world to world, to translocate from high up, to account for variances in elevation and geography from one alternative to the next. Translocation displaced the matter occupying the volume of space a vessel enters, and if the matter is merely empty air, the result will be little more than a brief flash and an audible bang, as the molecules of the atmosphere are excited, forced out of the way of the incoming vessel, nothing more dramatic than a bolt of midday lightning and a peal of distant thunder. If the vessel were to translocate into any material denser than water, though, the mass at the target couldn't be displaced quickly enough to accommodate the incoming vessel, and the craft would be compacted on arrival. An only relatively dense material like sand would likely only damage a vessel, not destroy it, but with a sufficiently dense material like rock or metal, an entire vessel could be compacted to only a fraction of its original size, with disastrous results for anyone onboard, and for any living things in the nearby space.

Naturally, most intercontinua craft were airworthy, as a result, and it was only the most reckless of souls who translocated while anywhere near ground level.

As the ground fell away beyond the portholes, Starkweather chatted amiably in Spanish with the Berber scholars over cups of strong Turkish coffee, spicing her own liberally with a splash of Tennessee whiskey from a flask she pulled from a hip pocket. A few moments later the ship's physician joined them, an older woman named Ortiz who was a Guanche native who spoke Castilian Spanish with the slight accent of the Canary Islands, her coffee so flavored with milk that it almost matched her tawny skin.

The Berbers, like Starkweather and all the other passengers onboard, were bound for the seat of the League of Worlds and hub of intercontinua trade, Helium. Knowledge, like wealth and natural resources, was something which the Heliumites had in abundance. And while the streets of Helium were not paved in gold, they may as well have been, as the alternative was rich in the lighter-than-air gas that gave the city-state its name. The gas helium was found in most all alternatives, but only a scant few, like Helium herself or Vivian Starkweather's native Texico, had the resources necessary to extract and refine it. And though only the most trusted diplomats could penetrate to the heart of the League of Worlds headquarters itself, all were welcome in the public areas of Helium, and so it was not uncommon to find natives of all imaginable histories jostling cheek by jowl in the markets and thoroughfares of Helium, including elfish or brutish men from alternatives where different strains of humanity came to dominate, or even some who, while they walked and talked like humans, were derived from other animals altogether, lagomorphs and lizardmen and talking apes from alternatives where species other than man rose to sentience and dominance.

The ship's steward entered the drawing room, a young man of European extraction who was no more than twenty years old and spoke with a faint Eton accent. He introduced himself merely as Patrick, and said that he'd been sent to see to the passengers' needs, and that the captain would be joining them shortly.

When the airship had reached a suitable altitude, the chimes again rang throughout the ship, this time signaling that the translocation engine would momentarily be engaged. A short while later a brief, high-pitched whine sounded in the drawing room, followed by an almost imperceptible juddering, and then faded almost, but not entirely, away, the whine persisting just at the edge of hearing, the vibration only barely perceptible in the faint ripples in the coffee within their cups, or the gentle shake of the feathers the purple-haired Aztec woman wore through her headband.

Once the ship was underway, propelled by jets of air from nozzles mounted on the outer hull, the propellers useless in the airless vacuum of underspace, the captain joined the first-class passengers in the drawing room.

Before Captain N'Diklam had made it two steps into the cabin, though, the three men of the security detachment, bowler hats now clutched in their hands, put themselves in his path.

"Captain, we need to discuss the security precautions you've taken for our empress's impending arrival." Engels blinked his eyes rapidly, punctuating his words with little stabs of his free hand, the fingers of the other wrapped tightly around the brim of his hat.

"And so you shall, gentlemen," N'Diklam said with an easy smile. "We won't be stopping at your alternative until late afternoon, the day after tomorrow, and I assure you that we will have everything settled to your satisfaction well before that time."

Behind Engel, the little round man and the other with the piercing blue eyes exchanged glances.

The tall African looked down at the smaller white man still blocking his way. "But in the near term, I would very much like a cup of coffee and a chance to speak to the other passengers," N'Diklam said, gently but with steel beneath his words. "If you wouldn't mind...?" He made a short motion with his hand, as if miming opening a door, and raised an eyebrow, waiting a response.

Engel, flustered, clenched the brim of his hat tighter, but with a final harrumph turned to the left and moved out of the way, his two companions following precisely at his flanks, as in a carefully practiced maneuver.

As the captain moved to mingle with the rest of the passengers, introducing himself and giving the assurances of himself and the whole Crosstime Line that their journeys would be pleasant ones, the three men of the security detachment drifted to the nearest porthole and, peering out with open-mouthed expressions of wonder, gawped like rustics at the unsettlingly shifting colors and strange geometries of underspace beyond.

That evening, after dinner, Captain N'Diklam, Starkweather, and a few of the other passengers gathered at the card table in the smoking room, while in the salon the ship's steward played a seemingly endless series of romantic airs on the aluminum grand piano for the entertainment of the Hindu princesses.

The Russians, with small glasses of vodka at their elbows, urged for a few rounds of durak, but the notion of a game with no winners, only a single loser for each round, soon wore on the other players, and another game was called for. N'Diklam exercised a bit of command authority and led the way with a hand of primero, which proved too complex for simple enjoyment but with stakes too low to be of much interest. When Starkweather instructed the others in the basics of Texican hold 'em, though, the group seemed to have found its proper tempo, and a number of hands followed.

Starkweather had the button, and was sitting on a pair of queens in the hole, when the bosun burst in, eyes wide and white in his dark face.

"It's the navigator!" he blurted out, rushing to the captain's side. "She's been *murdered!*"

And that signaled the end of the evening's entertainments.

It was long past the hour when the passengers might have been expected to retire for the evening, but most of them lingered in the salon, waiting to hear word about the poor navigator. The Aztec woman, her purple bob somewhat ruffled, was uncharacteristically chatty, and reported passing the crewmen carrying the body through the companionway to the medical bay, the blood seeping through the linen sheet which swathed her lifeless form. Her companion, in only his waistcoat and shirtsleeves, tapped one of his jade earplugs and scowled, muttering something beneath his breath about the unseemly waste of so much blood.

There was some concern over what would become of the ship, without the navigator to guide her through underspace. Would the *Crosstime Express* drift helplessly in that strange realm, never to return to the sane security of space-time, much less her intended destination? Those fears were quickly put to rest, however, when more seasoned intercontinua travelers among them explained about the standard practice of employing second navigators in the event of emergency. All agreed that brutal murder was likely not one of the anticipated emergencies, but were nevertheless relieved the protocol was in place.

A few of the crew mingled with the passengers, as the captain had evicted all but Doctor Ortiz, himself, and the bosun from the medical bay for the duration of the autopsy, and the crewmen were just as unsettled by the unexpected and brutal slaying as the passengers. The steward made a desultory attempt to lighten the mood by playing music hall tunes on the aluminum grand piano, but abandoned the attempt in moments, after catching a sharp glance from Starkweather.

Finally, the captain returned and gave a full accounting of the situation to the others. It appeared, he said, that the navigator had been assaulted at her post by an unknown assailant, and stabbed repeatedly with a slim blade. Nothing further was known about the incident, but the captain assured the passengers that the crew would be conducting a thorough investigation, and that on their arrival in Helium the matter would be remanded to the Crosstime Line and the authorities to investigate fully. In the meantime, however, the passengers should sleep soundly in the knowledge that he had increased the ship's onboard security, posting armed crewmen in all of the companionways and public areas day and night, and that he would allow nothing to threaten the safety of the passengers.

At the captain's side was a man of middle age with a double chin and tufts of hair sticking from his ears, who had the sigil of a seer emblazoned on the blue-and-gold rosette pinned to his lapel.

"Ladies and gentlemen, allow me to introduce Mr. Tanacre, our ship's second navigator," the captain said. "You have my complete assurances that Tanacre will be able to guide our course successfully through the remainder of our voyage."

Some of the passengers evidently harbored concerns about the man's qualifications, but it was Engel who stepped forward to give those concerns voice.

"How do *we* know that this tub of guts has the stuff to get the job done?"

The second navigator seemed flustered by the brusque and outright rude manner of the man, but with a glance to the captain he calmly explained. "Well," he began, his voice quavering slightly, "while my own mastery of the talent of seeing is not nearly so powerful or refined as that of the late navigator, still I am confident in my ability to fulfill my duties."

Engel narrowed his eyes. "Just what do you mean, 'not nearly so powerful?'"

"Well," the navigator explained, with mounting confidence, "the late navigator was so powerful a seer that she might even have been able to read another's thoughts if she so chose, and at the very least could have detected any extremes of emotion or distress onboard the *Express*." He paused, then humbly added, "I, on the other hand, am able merely to peer through underspace into other worlds, helping chart the *Express*'s course through this tumultuous region."

"Thank you, Tanacre," the captain interrupted. "And thank you," he said to the passengers, "for your patience and understanding in these unfortunate circumstances. Now, the second navigator is needed at his post if we are to reach our off-route stop tomorrow."

Captain and navigator excused themselves, and then singly or in pairs the passengers drifted away from the salon and back to their individual cabins for the night.

The following day passed quickly, with most of the passengers seeming to prefer the solitude of their cabins to the exposure of the public spaces, and so it was not until the evening meal that most of them were gathered together again. At the captain's insistence, the first-class passengers had joined him at the captain's table, which had been expanded by additional leaves for the occasion.

Whether by happenstance or design, the three men of the security detachment had been seated as far from the captain as possible. And when Engel began to belabor the captain about the failure of the crew to locate the killer, it wasn't hard to imagine that the placement had been by design.

Starkweather found herself seated next to the two Indian princesses. Chatting amiably over appetizers and aperitifs, the young ladies with the former and Starkweather with the latter, it eventuated that the two Hindus were wealthy heiresses from an alternative dominated by South Asia, and were on one last grand voyage together before one of them went off to university and the other got married. They hadn't traveled far at all from home before, and were almost as wide-eyed at the wonders of the Myriad as the backwater security detachment, though the young ladies handled it with considerably more grace.

Still, there were some realities of intercontinua travel that came as a surprise to them. For example, one of the two mentioned having been accosted back in Starkweather's Texico by a young man who insisted that he knew her, when the young lady knew for a fact that they'd never met. The young man had pressed the issue, referring to some intimate history that they'd supposedly shared, and it was only with the assistance of a passing Texican Ranger that the young lady had been able to extricate herself from the man's grip.

Starkweather, taking pains to reassure the young women about the safety of the streets of her native Waterloo, explained how worlds which were nearest one another in the Myriad, whose histories diverged in the relatively recent past, could produce nearly identical duplicates of the same person, one in each alternative. But while the two duplicates might resemble one another physically, sharing a common point of origin, their own personal histories would diverge as much and as quickly as did the histories of their world. Such misunderstandings and misidentifications as the young women had encountered were actually quite common in intercontinua travel. With a sly smile, Starkweather confided that she'd pretended to be her own duplicate, on several different occasions, just to avoid uncomfortable reunions with her own past associates.

Later, after the first course arrived, conversation around the table turned, as it often did, to politics. There was some dissension around the table about the League of Worlds, and particularly its noninterference accords. The League, to which the native alternatives of most of the passengers and crew belonged, worked to prevent the disruption of developing worlds, in the hopes that worlds unaware of the existence of the Myriad might not be exploited by their more technologically advanced neighbors. However, as others around the table were quick to point out, the noninterference accords were only enforceable among member alternatives. Others, and in particular the Tenth Imperium, an intercontinua power which dominated nearly as many alternatives as belonged to the League of Worlds, in particular had a long history of interference. And, in fact, it was a customary tactic of the Imperium to offer intercontinua technology to worlds that had not yet discovered the principle of translocation or yet developed the Talents, in exchange for their allegiance to the Tenth Imperium.

The Ambassador from the Reformed Dynast of Heliopolis, who had remained silent through most of the discussion, raised a grim specter when he suggested the possibility that the differing philosophies of the League and the Tenth Imperium might one day lead to armed conflict between the two bodies. It would be regrettable, the Ambassador insisted, but seemed to him to be inevitable. Something of a pall fell over the table, as the Ambassador's dire assessment settled in.

It was at this point, rushing to fill the silence, that Engel switched from opprobrium, directed at the captain and crew, to self-aggrandizement, directed at himself and his people. He boasted about how scientists of his own nation-state had independently discovered translocation the year before, and made contact with other worlds in short order. And that his own island nation boasted a disproportionately high number of Talents, or so he believed, including a member of his own detachment. He indicated the man with the piercing blue eyes, and explained that he had been found to have some ability to send, though understandably undeveloped and untrained.

Starkweather couldn't resist deflating the man, as puffed up as he was. She pointed out, casually, that in her own alternative it had been less than a decade and a half since William James pioneered the development of psychic abilities, fortuitously just in time for Nikola Tesla to complete the translocation engine. And yet with only a few years' head start, her own alternative was rapidly becoming a key player in intercontinua commerce, while his home was still barely dipping their toes into the shallow end of underspace.

Engel blustered, cheeks puffed and red, but failed to mount any effective retort, and when the next course arrived on the table, the conversation drifted on.

* * *

After dinner, Captain N'Diklam was joined by the bosun and the cook's mate in an impromptu recital. All three men hailed from the western shores of Africa in their respective alternatives, and had brought onboard sabar drums crafted from the wood of the baobab tree; though they came from widely divergent histories, the rhythm of the drums seemed to cut across the Myriad. While he was the commanding officer of the ship, in their informal ensembles N'Diklam played the Lambe, the squat barrel-shaped bass drum, letting the cook's mate set the tempo with the tall, slender Sabar N'Der, leaving the bosun to play the tenor Talmbat.

The rhythm of the sabar drums reverberated through the ship, and for a short while, at least, the tense atmosphere of the past day seemed to lighten, if only a little.

On the way back to her cabin, Vivian Starkweather nearly collided with Doctor Ortiz, who was visibly upset. With the promise of a nightcap of Tennessee whiskey and a fine Virginian cigarillo, Starkweather lured the woman to her cabin, and there got from her the reasons for her distress.

The doctor's report about the late navigator, it appeared, had differed in significant detail from that relayed by the captain to the passengers. Rather than being stabbed to death, the doctor explained, the amount of blood found on the navigator's body suggested that the woman's heart had stopped pumping long before she had died. In other words, the navigator had been dead before the knife had ever been plunged into her body.

"A sender," Starkweather said, nodding.

"It isn't unheard of," the doctor answered, plainly distressed. "A powerful enough suggestion could convince the mind to stop the heart's beating."

Starkweather took a long drag of her cigarillo, thoughtfully.

"What I don't understand is," the doctor went on, both hands wrapped tightly around her mug of whiskey, "if the killer was a sender, why stab a body that's already dead?"

Starkweather threw back the rest of her own whiskey in a single shot, then wiped her mouth on the back of her hand. "Darlin', that's a fine question."

* * *

Klaxons sounding in the middle of the night disturbed the slumber of the crew, and even woke most of the passengers in their sound-proofed cabins. It was a familiar sound in intercontinua travel, and hardly a cause for serious alarm, but even the seasoned travelers like Starkweather found it difficult to go back to sleep while the ship was under attack.

Beyond the pressurized hull of the *Crosstime Express*, the strange denizens of underspace swarmed, intent on consuming the ship and all within her. From time to time one ventured near enough that their diamond-hard hide brushed against the outer hull, sending vibrations rattling through the ship, setting teeth and nerves on edge.

Though virtually indestructible, the monstrous creatures of underspace were thinking beings, even if those thoughts were concerned only with their endless appetites and boundless rages. And since they thought, the creatures were susceptible to the talents of a sender. Like all the ships of the Crosstime Line, the *Express* numbered a sender among its crew as defender, on hand to project negative thoughts into the alien minds of the underspace dwellers, driving them away.

A quarter of an hour after the attack began the klaxons sounded the all clear, and the passengers and crew returned to their beds.

The next morning at breakfast, Starkweather overheard the ship's steward chatting with the pair of Hindu princesses at the next table over. The steward related that he had heard the ship's defender say that, while she was in the process of repelling the attack, she had sensed someone else assisting in the defense. At that hour, though, the second defender, who was her normal backup in such circumstances, was below decks and insensate with drink, and in no position to conjure thoughts within his own mind, much less project them into someone else's.

As he passed by her table, Starkweather asked the steward to fetch her a fresh cup of coffee, complaining that the one from which she'd been drinking had gone cold. And if the steward noticed the tightly folded piece of paper which Starkweather had tucked between the cup and saucer she handed him, he gave no indication.

* * *

Under normal circumstances, the *Crosstime Express* made no stops between the terminus on the one end and Helium on the other. On this journey, though, an off-route stop had been announced in advance, to retrieve the security detachment's sovereign. It seemed that, having only recently made contact with other worlds, having just mastered the principle of translocation and the rudiments of the talents, this new alternative's application for admittance to the League of Worlds had been accepted, and the sovereign would now be journeying to the headquarters of the League to sign the charter. It was something of a signal honor, since only delegates from member worlds and their personal security retinues were allowed within the walls of League headquarters itself.

The stop was scheduled for later in the afternoon on the second day of the voyage. At midmorning, the passengers lingered over coffee at table while breakfast was cleared away. The only first-class passenger not present was the member of the security detachment with the piercing blue eyes, who appeared to have slept late, and joined his two companions at the table looking bleary-eyed and squinting. A few moments after the blue-eyed man sat down, the ship's steward Patrick entered the room, and then in full view of the passengers collapsed to the deck with a pained expression.

While Patrick was being helped to the medical bay for examination and treatment by the Berber scholars, a klaxon began to sound on the ship, which most of the passengers mistakenly took to signal another incursion by underspace denizens. Starkweather and a few of the others quickly pointed out that the sequence of notes was all wrong, and that it signaled another danger instead. *Fire.*

There was, in the end, only one fatality, though several more of the crew were injured in the blaze. The fire had broken out in the cargo hold, and since the hatches had all been closed and secured, only a single compartment was affected. A crewman had been caught in the blaze, and not discovered until after the fire had been completely extinguished. And while he was badly burned, all of his clothing and body hair scorched off, he was quickly identified as one of the relief crew who had boarded at the terminus, shortly before the passengers. He had been a solitary figure, with a bushy beard, who kept to himself with his eyes down and his mouth shut. None in the crew could remember exchanging more than a dozen words with him, and those only related to his work.

The fire appeared to have been the result of a dropped match, a careless mistake that had set alight a bolt of inflammable material, part of a shipment of dry goods bound for Helium. What the crewman had been doing in the cargo hold was unclear, but it was assumed that he had sneaked off from his supervisors to smoke some illicit substance or other, the use of intoxicants being not unknown among ship's crew, though most such substances were contraband throughout League worlds.

A second death, following so closely on the heels of the navigator's murder, was unsettling to some onboard, but it wasn't until the dead man's effects were examined that any connection between the two was suspected. However, when a thin-bladed knife, still darkened with the navigator's blood, was found in the dead man's trunk, along with a handwritten letter apparently in the navigator's own hand, rebuffing the crewman's crude and unwanted advances, an apparent narrative began to emerge.

The crewman, it would seem, had been a spurned lover, who in a fit of jealous rage had stabbed the navigator to death, when she refused to return his affections. When he had in short order been caught in an unexpected conflagration, it has been simply a matter of just desserts.

The captain considered it a fait accompli, and the case closed, as he explained once he'd gathered all of the passengers into the drawing room.

But not everyone was convinced.

"I'm sorry, captain," Vivian Starkweather said, setting her reticule down on a chair and stepping forward, "but the second death does not solve the mystery of the first. It only compounds it."

The captain cocked an eyebrow, intrigued, but Engel, under some stress over the impending arrival of his sovereign, was somewhat more agitated.

"And just who, madam, do you think you are?" he asked, red-faced.

With a smile, Starkweather reached into the pocket of her jacket, and produced a badge on which was embossed a stylized human eye and the motto "We Never Sleep."

Engel looked at the badge uncomprehendingly, but the other passengers whispered to one another in hushed tones, muttering the word "Pinkerton."

Starkweather flipped the leather wallet shut over the badge and slipped it back into her pocket. "What I am, as of now, is the law around these parts."

"What business has a Pinkerton on my boat?" Captain N'Diklam asked, unsmiling.

"My outfit has been contracted by the Crosstime Line to ferret out a smuggling ring that seems to be using the *Express* as one of its principal conduits." She paused and then almost distractedly added, "You might want to find a third for your little drum group, captain. You should likely go ahead and take the bosun into custody, along with those two." She pointed at the pair of Russian monks. "The three of them are the main players in the smuggling ring, though there may be one or two others onboard that we haven't identified yet."

The captain didn't bother to question her, but snapped his fingers and ordered two of his crewmen to take the Russians into custody, and ordered them to locate the bosun and take him in hand, as well. The Russians, objecting loudly if unconvincingly, were dragged from the room.

"And you say that this smuggling ring is responsible for killing my navigator and crewman?" N'Diklam asked, puzzled.

"Nope." Starkweather shook her head, then stuck a cigarillo between her teeth and struck a match on the edge of a table. "The smuggling ring's a coincidence, I figure. The killings are unconnected." She held the lit match before her face, her long nose and strong jaw in stark relief in the flickering light, giving her otherwise ruggedly handsome features a somewhat demonic aspect. "But we'll get to your killer soon enough. The way I figure it, the killer is one of the people in this room."

"This is outrageous!" shouted Engel.

"You reckon?" Starkweather smiled, and leaned over to pick up her handbag from the chair beside her, the cigarillo still clenched between her teeth. "Think maybe it's you?"

Engel opened his mouth to object, then slammed his teeth shut again, eyes wide and bulging. "I won't stand for this!" He motioned for his two companions to follow, and then turned to the left to leave. Before he'd gone two steps, though, he collided with the man with the piercing blue eyes, who had turned right instead of left and blundered right into him.

"There it is," Starkweather said with a smile. Snapping her reticule open, she reached in and pulled out a heavy Colt Navy revolver, which she cocked and pointed at the head of the man with the piercing blue eyes. "I'd ask you not to make a move, friend, not so much as a twitch, or I'm liable to pull this here trigger."

Engel turned to look at his companion, evidently expecting to see the same outrage and annoyance he himself felt at this poor treatment, but was surprised instead to find the man staring calmly at Starkweather, piercing blue eyes narrowed and lip curled in a sneer. "Barclay, what's this all about?"

The man ignored the other, but continued to stare at Starkweather. "If you know what I am, you know I could drop you before you even noticed a twinge."

"That's as maybe," Starkweather said with a shrug, "but you can only think so many thoughts at once. Drop me and my partner'll finish you off before you take another breath."

From the door to the drawing room came the sound of a revolver being cocked, and the passengers as one turned to see the ship's steward in the open doorway, a Webley revolver in hand, pointed at the man's head.

"Patrick Lightfoot Carmody," the steward said, flashing a badge like the one Starkweather had produced. "Pinkerton."

The blue-eyed man sneered, but remained motionless. After a long silence, he said, in an unfamiliar accent, "How did you know?"

"Wrong place, wrong time, friend." Starkweather slid onto the chair, crossing her legs but keeping her pistol aimed at his head. "We were after other fish entirely and you just fell into our lap. And if not for the knife, we might not have guessed a thing." She paused, thoughtfully. "What was it? Were you worried that a stopped heart might not be assumed to be natural causes, but that someone might suspect there was a sending assassin onboard? So you make it look like a mundane murder, instead, which has benefits of its own."

"So *he* killed the navigator?" the captain said, jerking a thumb at the man. "But why?"

"The navigator was incidental," Starkweather explained. "He planned to kill someone else, and the navigator being such a strong seer meant that she had a good chance of picking up on the crime. So she was eliminated to clear the way for another murder."

"The crewman," the captain said, nodding.

"But why would Barclay want to kill your crewman?" Engel demanded to know.

"No reason at all," Starkweather said. "The question to ask, rather, is why would that crewman want to kill *your* man?"

Engel looked at her, confusion evident, while the blue-eyed man beside him stiffened.

"See, that *isn't* Barclay," Starkweather went on. "Or at least, not the one you know. I think you'll find, if you were to quiz him, that he won't be quite so up on trivia about your home alternative as the man you knew."

Engel turned from her to the man beside him, and edged away, cautiously. "B-Barclay?" he said, disbelievingly. "Is... it is true?"

The blue-eyed man didn't bother answering Engel, but continued to glare at Starkweather.

"Thing is," she went on, "your Barclay wasn't really the point of all this, either, but just another incidental means to an end. See, once your sovereign comes onboard, the next stop is Helium, and the headquarters of the League of Worlds. And nobody, but nobody, can get into the headquarters itself unless they're a representative of a member world. *Unless...*" She paused, significantly.

"Unless they're part of the diplomat's security retinue," the captain finished.

"Got it in one," Starkweather answered. "So the point of all of this was just to get someone in a position to walk through those golden doors uncontested, right into the midst of the League's ruling council. And if that someone had the ability to plant powerful suggestions in the minds of others, powerful enough even to help ward off underspace monsters when he thought his ship might get eaten en route, then I imagine implanting enough suggestions to stop the hearts of the entire ruling council wouldn't be beyond his abilities, and that he could do a considerable amount of damage before anyone managed to stop them."

"So who *is* this?" the captain asked, narrowing his gaze at the blue-eyed man.

"I imagine he answers to the name Barclay, just like Engel's late friend did," she said. "They're dead ringers and are both senders, after all. But I wouldn't be surprised if this version knew the Tenth Imperium national anthem back to front, and was no fan of the League of Worlds' notion of noninterference."

The blue-eyed man drew his lips into a tight line. "I admit to nothing."

"Figured you wouldn't. But I reckon the League has a seer somewhere that can get past those shields of yours."

"Shields?" N'Diklam repeated.

"I can explain that," said the ship's former steward, the young man who'd identified himself as Patrick Lightfoot Carmody. "I'm something of a seer myself, though I can't manage much more than a surface scan of someone's thoughts. This morning Viv slipped me a note, telling me about her encounter with Doctor Ortiz and asking me to scan the crew and passengers. I waited until everybody had sat down to breakfast, but as soon as I tried to see, I ran smack into someone's mental defenses. You don't get that kind of mental discipline just by accident. I knew then that the killer had to be someone in that room."

"When the supposed crewman was found dead, we were able to work out the motive, and narrow the suspects down to Mr. Engel and his friends. But we couldn't be sure which of the three it was." Starkweather took a final drag of her cigarillo and then ground it out under the heel of her dinosaur-skin boot. "We just had to keep an eye out, and wait for one of you to trip up." She smiled, and then to the blue-eyed man said, "Literally, in your case."

The *Express* was anchored at Engel's backwater alternative, which had only just discovered the secret of translocation. The suspected murderer had been rendered unconscious by a serum provided by Doctor Ortiz, and strapped securely to a gurney for good measure, and would be handed over to the authorities when the ship reached Helium the next morning. At the moment, though, the ship hung like a balloon over a muddy field, while a small brass band played a fanfare for an old woman dressed in lace-trimmed black.

Intercontinua craft always reentered space-time at the same coordinates that they left, so having entered underspace from one Texico, they had translocated to another. This one was part of a larger Louisiana, and subject to a British Crown that ruled more than half of the Earth. This Louisiana, though, was as much a backwater to this Britannic Empire as the alternative itself was to the Myriad, it seemed, if the expressions of the sovereign and her retinue were any indication of their feelings for finding themselves here in the muck and the mud, so far from Buckingham Palace.

Carmody and Starkweather stood at the landing, watching the old woman mounting the gangplank. She was evidently used to more pomp than the *Crosstime Express* offered, and was clearly displeased to be treated so much like a regular passenger.

"I feel almost like I should bow," Patrick said, smiling around his Turkish cigarette. The young man was clearly relieved to be a passenger himself for a change, and not a member of the crew, but Starkweather had merely said that the experience had likely done him some good, forcing him to actually *work* for a change. And besides, as a steward he'd had an easier time pitching woo at the Indian princesses who had caught his fancy, as he seemed to have lost something of his allure now that they didn't see him as a mere menial.

"Why the devil would you do a thing like that?" Starkweather said, and took a sip of whiskey from her flask.

"Well," Carmody answered, looking somewhat sheepish, "this alternative is more like my home than most, and when last I saw *my* England there was a duplicate of her on the throne there, as well."

"I don't know, Pat, I just don't much get on with kings and queens. In *my* alternative, we Texicans never had 'em, and the Brits got rid of them back in the days of Cartwright and Paine, back even before the Anglo-American Confederation got started."

Carmody nodded. "Well, people back home had all sorts of strange notions. They figured that white skin was better than dark, that Britain was where the best white skin could be found, and that Queen Victoria was the best of the whole lot."

"Victoria?" Starkweather said, and cast an appraising eye at the woman. At that moment, the woman slipped at the foot of the gangplank, and fell sprawling into the mud. "I don't know, Pat, doesn't look much like victory to me."

About the Editor

The version of Lou Anders who resides on Earth Prime has been nominated for the Hugo Award, the World Fantasy Award, and the Chesley Award, all for work done in his capacity as the editorial director of Prometheus Books' science fiction and fantasy imprint Pyr (*www.pyrsf.com*). He is also the editor of several critically acclaimed anthologies—*Outside the Box* (Wildside Press, 2001), *Live without a Net* (Roc, 2003), *Projections: Science Fiction in Literature & Film* (MonkeyBrain, 2004), *FutureShocks* (Roc, 2006), *Fast Forward 1* (Pyr, 2007), and the forthcoming *Fast Forward 2* (Pyr, 2008). In 2000, he served as the Executive Editor of *Bookface.com*, and before that he worked as the Los Angeles Liaison for Titan Publishing Group. He is the author of *The Making of Star Trek: First Contact* (Titan Books, 1996), and has published over 500 articles in such magazines as *The Believer, Publishers Weekly, Dreamwatch, Star Trek Monthly, Star Wars Monthly, Babylon 5 Magazine, Sci Fi Universe, Doctor Who Magazine,* and *Manga Max*. His articles and stories have been translated into Danish, Greek, German, Italian, and French, and have appeared online at *SFSite.com, RevolutionSF.com* and *InfinityPlus.co.uk*. Visit him online at *www.louanders.com*

Get more of your science fiction fix at SF Signal!

News / Reviews / Interviews / Points of View

All-original stories from some of the world's best loved SF writers

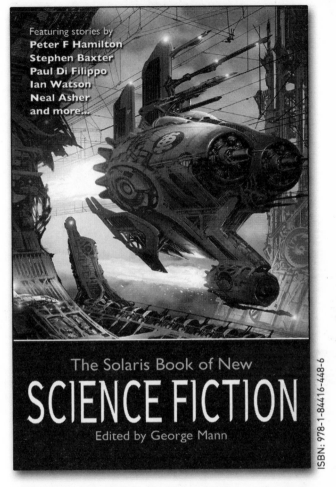

Featuring stories by
Peter F Hamilton
Stephen Baxter
Paul Di Filippo
Ian Watson
Neal Asher
and more...

The Solaris Book of New
SCIENCE FICTION
Edited by George Mann

ISBN: 978-1-84416-448-6

The Solaris Book of New Science Fiction is a short story anthology of the highest order, showcasing the talents of some of the world's greatest science fiction writers. The eclectic stories in this collection range from futuristic murder mysteries, to widescreen space opera, to tales of contact with alien beings.

www.solarisbooks.com

SOLARIS SCIENCE FICTION

More original stories from some of the world's best loved SF writers

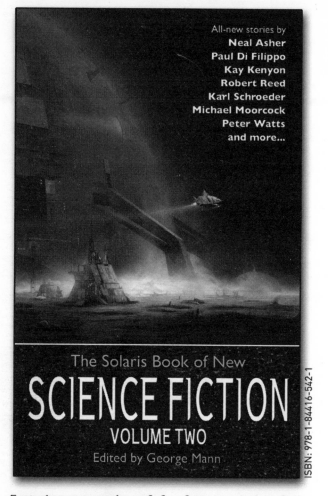

All-new stories by
Neal Asher
Paul Di Filippo
Kay Kenyon
Robert Reed
Karl Schroeder
Michael Moorcock
Peter Watts
and more...

The Solaris Book of New
SCIENCE FICTION
VOLUME TWO
Edited by George Mann

ISBN: 978-1-84416-542-1

Featuring new tales of far future murder, first contact, love and war from such well regarded and award-winning authors as Michael Moorcock, Robert Reed, Karl Schroeder, Kay Kenyon, Neil Asher and Eric Brown, this collection is sure to delight all fans of quality science fiction.

www.solarisbooks.com

SOLARIS SCIENCE FICTION